Amanda Stevens is an ⟨...⟩
novels, including the m⟨...⟩
Queen. Her books ha⟨...⟩
atmospheric, and 'a new take on the classic ghost story.'
Born and raised in the rural South, she now resides in
Houston, Texas, where she enjoys binge-watching, bike
riding and the occasional margarita.

USA TODAY bestselling and *RITA*® Award–winning
author **Marie Ferrarella** has written more than 250
books for Mills & Boon, some under the name Marie
Nicole. Her romances are beloved by fans worldwide.
Visit her website, marieferrarella.com

Also by Amanda Stevens

Little Girl Gone
Without a Trace
A Desperate Search
Someone Is Watching
Criminal Behaviour
Incriminating Evidence
Killer Investigation
Pine Lake
Whispering Springs
Bishop's Rock (ebook novella)

Also by Marie Ferrarella

Colton 911: The Secret Network
Colton 911: Secret Defender
Exposing Colton Secrets
Colton Baby Conspiracy
A Widow's Guilty Secret
Cavanaugh's Surrender
Cavanaugh Rules
Cavanaugh's Bodyguard
Cavanaugh Fortune
How to Seduce a Cavanaugh

Discover more at millsandboon.co.uk

JOHN DOE
COLD CASE

AMANDA STEVENS

COLTON'S PURSUIT
OF JUSTICE

MARIE FERRARELLA

MILLS & BOON

First Published in Great Britain 2022
by Mills & Boon, an imprint of HarperCollins*Publishers* Ltd
1 London Bridge Street, London, SE1 9GF

www.harpercollins.co.uk

HarperCollins*Publishers*
1st Floor, Watermarque Building,
Ringsend Road, Dublin 4, Ireland

John Doe Cold Case © 2022 Marilyn Medlock Amann
Colton's Pursuit of Justice © 2022 Harlequin Books S.A.

Special thanks and acknowledgement are given to Marie Ferrarella for her contribution to the *The Coltons of Colorado* series.

ISBN: 978-0-263-30327-8

0122

MIX
Paper from
responsible sources
FSC® C007454

This book is produced from independently certified FSC™ paper to ensure responsible forest management.

For more information visit: www.harpercollins.co.uk/green

Printed and Bound in Spain using 100% Renewable electricity at CPI Black Print, Barcelona

JOHN DOE
COLD CASE

AMANDA STEVENS

Chapter One

Deep inside a cave near Black Creek, Florida, the skeletal remains of a John Doe had remained hidden for nearly three decades. The forensic anthropologist called in by the local police chief estimated the deceased's age at time of death to be late twenties. He'd been tall, thin and right-handed. Good teeth, strong bones. And he'd been brutally murdered. Bashed in the back of the head and stabbed multiple times in the chest.

Overkill, Detective Eve Jareau thought with an inward grimace as she stood gazing down at the skeleton carefully arranged in the supine position on a metal table. The crawling flesh at the back of her neck surprised her. She wasn't a stranger to death. In the six years she'd been with the Black Creek Police Department, she'd witnessed the gamut from shootings to car wrecks to natural causes. Why these unidentified skeletal remains should have such a visceral effect was inexplicable.

Maybe it was her surroundings, she decided. The building that housed the forensic anthropology lab was old and creaky with too many lurking shadows. Despite the overhead lights, a perpetual gloom seemed to linger over the tables of weathered bones and shelves of forensic artifacts. The downpour pelting against the long windows did nothing to lighten her mood. Eve suppressed another shiver as she glanced at her boss, police chief Nash Bowden, who stood on the opposite side of the table. Whether aware of her scrutiny or not, he didn't glance up.

His disconnect was par for the course these days. He'd avoided eye contact and all but cursory conversation for the entire forty-five-minute drive from Black Creek to Tallahassee. Eve told herself she shouldn't take it personally. He'd always kept to himself. However, ever since his exwife had been arrested for the kidnapping of a four-year-old child, he'd retreated deeper behind his impenetrable walls. Thankfully, the little girl had been rescued and returned to her mother unharmed, but the whole town still reeled from the revelation. Eve could only imagine the blow it must have been to Chief Bowden—Nash.

Once upon a time, there'd been a spark between Eve and Nash. A fleeting moment of possibility that had fizzled in the face of his difficult divorce and the complicated reality of a workplace relationship. Still, something lingered in spite of the obstacles. Eve had to squelch the desire to reassure him that the kidnapping wasn't his fault. No one could have seen that coming. Instead, she'd wisely held her silence even when he'd called her into his office to offer her lead on the John Doe case.

The assignment was hardly a testament to her skills. No one else wanted the case. The seasoned investigators didn't have the patience or the inclination to put in the hours of tedious research and legwork that a cold case generally required, and the younger, more ambitious detectives were eager to nab the hot cases. Eve marched to a different drummer. Neither jaded nor single-minded, she enjoyed the challenge of a decades-old puzzle. She preferred working quietly and alone.

Forcing her attention back to the matter at hand, she watched in fascination as Dr. Allison Forester rotated the disarticulated skull to highlight the spiderweb pattern at the base.

"I suppose there's no way of knowing whether the blunt force trauma occurred before or after the stabbing," Nash said.

"Unfortunately, no." Dr. Forester ran a gloved finger over the deep indentation. "But a blow this traumatic would have incapacitated, if not killed him outright. Likewise, some of the stab wounds were deep and forceful enough to almost sever his ribs."

Nash nodded his understanding. "You're saying the victim suffered multiple mortal wounds. If he was already dead or dying from the head trauma, why stab him so viciously?"

"Rage," Eve muttered.

His gaze met hers briefly before he glanced away.

"Maybe he was trying to get away," Dr. Forester suggested. "The blow from behind was meant to finish him off."

A terrible vision swirled in Eve's head. The victim bleeding and near death, but still trying to crawl away from his attacker. He would never have seen the death blow coming.

Dr. Forester repositioned the skull and then moved to the side of the table to stand next to Nash. She was a striking woman with ash-blond hair and gray-green eyes. Every now and then, Eve caught her watching Nash through her thick lashes. Now she moved in close enough so that her arm brushed against his. He didn't retreat, Eve noted. In fact, if anything, he seemed to lean into her.

The subtle intimacy distracted her for a moment until she sternly reminded herself to stay focused. *This is none of your business.* But she couldn't help noting how Nash's dark eyes and hair complemented the woman's cool blondness.

A clap of thunder rattled the windows and Eve ran a hand up and down her arm where goose bumps rose among the freckles. *Who are you?* she wondered as she dropped her gaze to the skeleton. *And what were you doing down in that cave?*

The rolling thunder seemed ominous, like the harbinger of something dark and chaotic. When the lights flickered, Eve could have sworn an icy finger touched the back of her hand. She actually checked to make sure the skeleton hadn't moved. Then she chided herself for letting a storm and some old bones unsettle her.

"You okay?"

She glanced up at Nash's query. "What?"

His gaze seemed unusually intense. "You seem jumpy."

Her heart thudded despite her resolve as she glanced around the lab. "This place is a little too atmospheric for my taste."

"You get used to it." Dr. Forester's lowered voice sent another ripple across Eve's nerve endings. "After a while, you don't even notice the strange noises and electrical fluctuations."

"What kind of strange noises?"

The woman merely smiled. "At least we don't have to worry about working in the dark. We have a backup generator."

"That's good to know," Eve murmured.

"If it still works, that is. We may need a volunteer to go down in the basement and check the controls."

"This building has a basement? Doesn't it flood?" Eve asked.

"She's putting you on," Nash said.

"Oh."

Dr. Forester's eyes gleamed. "Only about the basement. I'm dead serious about the odd anomalies. If you spend enough time in this building, you're bound to experience something you can't explain."

Like the brush of a skeletal hand?

Eve couldn't tell if the woman was being serious or not. She decided to shrug off the nebulous warning. "Maybe we should finish up before the lights really do go out."

"Yes, that's probably a good idea." Dr. Forester exchanged an amused glance with Nash before she bent back to her work. She pointed out two places in the right radius and carpus before moving down the torso to the right tibia and the lower portion of the left fibula. "At some point in his life, our John Doe sustained multiple fractures to his right arm and leg and his left ankle, possibly from an automobile accident. He received medical treatment. The breaks fused cleanly."

"If he was treated locally, hospital records could help with the identification," Nash said. "Once we go public with the discovery, a relative or acquaintance may come forward."

"John Doe was down in that cave for decades," Eve said. "It's possible his family moved away from the area years ago."

"All speculation at this point." Nash turned back to Dr. Forester. "Anything else? What about clothing or jewelry recovered from the excavation site?"

"Bits and pieces of fabric and leather. No wallet. Nothing with an inscription. We did find something interesting, however." She pulled a small evidence bag from a drawer in the table. Dumping the contents into her palm, she picked up a small silver coin and held it between her thumb and forefinger.

Nash lifted a brow. "A dime?"

Dr. Forester swiveled the coin so that the tarnished silver caught a bit of light. "A Mercury dime with a small perforation at the top. The deceased probably wore it on a string around his neck or ankle for good luck. It's an old Southern superstition that dates back before the Civil War."

"I've never heard of that particular superstition," Nash said.

Dr. Forester gave him a knowing look. "I'm not surprised. You've never struck me as the mystical sort. Detective Jareau, on the other hand…"

Eve remained silent, her heart thudding in trepidation. *No, it can't be true. It's simply not possible.*

"You know anything about Mercury dimes?" Nash's voice tunneled through the cloud of dread that had descended.

"Only that they're collectible, depending on the condition," she mumbled with a shrug, but already an old memory had seeped out of her subconscious. She was in her childhood bedroom staring up at the glow-in-the-dark stars on her ceiling when her father called softly from the doorway, "Boo? You awake?"

She'd turned toward his voice. "Yes, Daddy."

"Shush. Let's not wake your mama." He came in and sat down on the edge of her bed, keeping his tone hushed. "I'm going away for a while, Boo. I didn't want to leave without saying goodbye."

Eve felt a stab of panic as she pushed herself up against the pillows. "Where are you going?"

"Back to Louisiana, where I grew up. One of my cousins has offered me a job down in New Orleans. I'll likely be gone for a good long while."

"Can't Mama and me come with you?"

"Not this time. You need to stay here and look after each other. Can you do that, Boo?"

"Yes, Daddy."

"That's my good girl." He smiled down at her as he

brushed an unruly lock of dark hair from his forehead. "I've got something for you. Kind of like a going-away present." He reached in his pocket and brought out a dime threaded on a piece of twine.

The coin shone in the moonlight as he dangled the string.

Eve let out an awed breath. "Your good-luck charm!"

"No, *your* good-luck charm. I still have mine. See?" He pulled the silver coin from his collar. "My daddy found it for me when I was your age and now I've found one for you. Mercury dimes in general are hard to come by, but one with a hole is even more special. Do you know why?"

She shook her head.

"Most people don't know about the power of certain coins. But someone a hundred years ago figured out this particular dime held a lot of good juju. They punched a hole in the top so they could wear it close to their heart for luck and protection." He put the coin in Eve's hand and closed her fingers around it. "It's our secret, okay? No need to tell Mama. She'll think it's just a silly superstition."

"I won't tell."

"Each night before you go to bed, stand at the window with that lucky dime. Look up at the moon and think about me. I'll be gazing up at the same moon and thinking about you. That way, we'll always be together no matter where we are."

He tucked her in and left the room, but Eve couldn't sleep. Her daddy was going away and she had a terrible feeling he was never coming back.

She threw off the covers and stole over to the window to stare out. A car was parked at the curb. She watched in fascination as her father ran down the front steps carrying a small suitcase in one hand and a paper bag in the other. He hurried down the sidewalk to the car, then opened the trunk and stored everything inside. He went around and got in on the passenger side. When the interior light came on, Eve saw a woman with short platinum hair behind the wheel and the silhouette of a man in the back seat.

A split second before the door closed and the light went out, the man turned to stare back at the house, searching through the shadows until his gaze met hers. He put a finger to his lips and then drew that same finger across his throat. Eve hadn't known then what the gesture meant, but the look on his face had terrified her. She'd wanted nothing so much as to climb out the window and run after her daddy, but instead she shrank back in the shadows and waited until the taillights of the strange car had disappeared down the street before crawling back into bed and pulling the covers over her head.

"Detective Jareau? Your thoughts?"

Nash's voice once again cut into her reverie, dragging her back into the spooky lab.

She lifted her gaze. "About the dime, you mean?"

"About the injuries, the dime, everything we've learned today." His eyes narrowed as if he'd read her mind.

Eve shrugged off the memory and stared back at him. "You're right about the injuries. That many old breaks could be key to identifying the victim. I'll enter all the information in the database as soon as we get back to the station."

Nash's enigmatic focus lingered before he said to Dr. Forester, "You'll let us know if you find anything else?"

"Of course." Her hand fluttered to his sleeve. "A word before you go?"

He hesitated almost infinitesimally, then tossed his key fob to Eve. "I'll meet you outside."

At any other time, she might have bristled at the dismissal, but now she welcomed the opportunity to escape.

She gave a curt nod and turned toward the exit without a backward glance at the bones.

Out in the hallway, she made sure she was alone before leaning against the wall and closing her eyes as she fingered the Mercury dime beneath her T-shirt. It had to be a coincidence. Her father had sent money to her mother and postcards to Eve after he'd left town. If he'd come back to Black Creek for whatever reason, surely he would have let them know. Surely he would have wanted to see his only child. The same little girl who had once thought the sun rose and set on her capricious father.

It's not him.

Eve's mother had always believed her husband had run off with another woman. Eve knew this because she'd once overheard Jackie Jareau confide in a friend that her husband had had a wandering eye ever since she'd known him. No doubt he was living a new life somewhere with a second family, her mother had lamented. He probably never gave a passing thought to the wife and child he'd left behind in Black Creek.

Despite that overheard conversation, Eve had never wanted to believe the reality of her father's abandonment. She'd desperately clung to the hope that he was out there somewhere, thinking about her every time he looked up at the moon.

Nearly three decades later, she still wanted to believe. Gabriel Jareau hadn't been savagely murdered and buried beneath a pile of rubble in some godforsaken cave. The Mercury dime was just a coincidence.

The lights in the hallway sputtered as if to disparage her fantasy. Unnerved, Eve glanced up at the flickering bulbs as she pressed herself against the wall. She didn't hear or see anything out of the ordinary, but an unnatural chill from the rain seemed to ooze in through the windows and doors. She had to fight the urge to flee back into the lab.

Hurrying down the hallway instead, she pushed open the glass double doors and then paused once more beneath the covered entrance, wishing she'd brought an umbrella. The rain was really coming down now as thunder rumbled overhead. It wasn't yet six in the evening—normally still daylight in the summertime—but the sky had already deepened.

The parking lot was nearly empty. No one was about on the walkways, either. Eve glanced back through the glass doors, hoping to see Nash striding toward the entrance. Nothing but shadows lurked in the corridor.

Why was she so nervous all of a sudden? What was she really afraid of? She was armed, trained and prepared to take care of herself when and if the situation warranted. No reason for her jitters. But she was also Gabriel Jareau's daughter, superstitious and eccentric to a fault. Like her father, Eve believed in signs and portents and she knew without knowing how she knew that something was about to go terribly wrong in her world.

Leaving the shelter of the overhang, she dashed across the drenched parking lot. As she sprinted around to the passenger side of Nash's SUV, she noticed that the interior light was on in a car a few spaces over. Something about the man's profile reminded her of the silhouette in the back seat the night her father had left home. Impossible, of course. Even if she'd seen the stranger clearly that night, she'd only been five years old and he would have changed beyond recognition in the nearly three decades that had passed. Still…there was something about *this* man…

As if drawn by Eve's scrutiny, he glanced up, and she could have sworn he put a finger to his lips a split second before the interior light went out.

It's nothing, she told herself. Just a man waiting for someone who worked in the building.

Then why had he turned off the light when he saw her? Why had he gestured her to silence? Or had he? Maybe the storm and her old memories were playing tricks.

A hand fell on her shoulder and she jumped.

"What are you doing standing out here in the rain?" Nash asked. "Didn't I give you the key?"

"You did. I was just…" She shook her head. "Nothing. It doesn't matter."

He cast an uneasy glance at the sky. "I don't think this storm is going to let up anytime soon. We should probably hit the road before it gets worse."

"Chief…"

Raindrops glistened on his lashes as he gazed down at her. "What is it?"

She wanted to tell him about her childhood memory and about the dime she wore around her neck. She wanted to mention the man in the car and explain the uncanny certainty that something dark was headed her way. But she wasn't yet ready to accept the possibility of John Doe's identity. She needed to talk to her mother first.

"You're right," she said on a breath. "We should get going before things get worse."

NASH CHECKED THE rearview as he exited the freeway onto the two-lane blacktop that would take them straight into Black Creek. The rain had momentarily slackened, but lightning flickered from a new bank of clouds that gathered on the horizon.

Traffic was light on the highway. If he wasn't careful, he could too easily fall into one of his dark moods, lulled by the rhythmic swish of the wiper blades. He lifted a hand and rubbed the back of his neck. He hadn't been sleeping well lately. Ever since his ex-wife had been apprehended for the kidnapping of little Kylie Buchanan, the old nightmares had returned—the same bad dreams that had followed him home from Afghanistan nearly twelve years ago and still squatted in the blackest corners of his subconscious.

Kylie was now safely home with her mother, and Grace had been transferred from county lockup to a mental health facility in Tallahassee for psychiatric evaluation. Nash hadn't been to see her yet, nor did he want to. The separation and divorce had dragged on for far too long—Grace had seen to that—and left him bitter. He bit back a lingering resentment for all those wasted years and reminded himself that his former wife was a troubled woman.

No matter how hard he tried, though, he couldn't rustle up much sympathy. What she'd put that little girl and her family through was unforgivable. Still, she'd saved Nash's life once and he didn't take that lightly.

Beside him, Eve stirred restlessly. She'd been quiet ever since they left the lab, but then he wasn't making conversation easy for her. He felt a pang of regret that he quickly crushed. Keeping Eve Jareau at arm's length had always been for the best. He had too much baggage going back even before Grace. Now more than ever he needed to keep that space between them, for her sake as well as his own.

"It wasn't your fault, you know."

The softness of Eve's tone drilled deep into his defenses. Her head was turned toward the window. He wondered for a moment if he might have imagined her comment. "I'm sorry. Did you say something?"

"What she did is no reflection on you."

He drew a sharp breath, caught off guard yet again by the power of her voice. "I doubt many people would agree with you about that."

"You're wrong. No one blames you. No one that matters."

She turned just as he shot her a glance. Their gazes met, held and then each looked away quickly, but not before her blue eyes revealed a naked longing that clawed right through Nash's resolve.

His hands tightened on the wheel. "I should have known."

"How could you?" Eve demanded. "You're not clairvoyant."

"If I'd paid more attention to the clues, I would have seen it coming. I would have figured out what she was up to."

Eve seemed to consider and discard the possibility. "I don't think you're giving Grace enough credit. It was very clever of her to emulate an old kidnapping in order to make it look as though the two crimes were connected. She forced us to consider the possibility that the same kidnapper who took little Maya Lamb twenty-eight years ago came back to take Kylie Buchanan. Not to mention all the evidence she planted that threw everyone off her trail, including the FBI. She fooled a lot of people. She had us chasing shadows for days. What happened wasn't your fault."

He drew a hand across his eyes. "I appreciate what you're trying to do, but I'd rather not talk about Grace, if you don't mind." *Not with you. Not with anyone.*

"Of course. I understand…"

He lifted a brow. "But?"

"You need to talk to someone. Keeping everything bottled up inside isn't healthy."

"Speaking from experience?"

"Speaking as a friend."

Why did her voice get to him so? It was soft, yes, but there was grit around the edges. He admired her toughness and determination. He admired a great many things about Eve Jareau, not the least of which were more shallow observations. The soft curves beneath the jeans and T-shirt. The scent of rosemary and mint that seemed to envelop him. The large SUV afforded plenty of space between them. No way he could smell her soap and shampoo from across the console, but somehow the clean scent of her hair and skin lingered in his memory.

He scowled at the road. "You didn't say much back at the lab. I'm surprised you didn't have more questions for Dr. Forester."

"Oh, I have plenty of questions."

He gave her a sidelong glance. Something about the shift in her tone triggered a faint concern. "Anything I should know about?"

She hesitated. "For starters, what was the victim doing down in that cave? He must have been lured there somehow. The cavern where the remains were found is hard to get to. The body wasn't just dumped there."

Nash nodded. "I've been through those tunnels. It's tough going under any circumstances, but it would be next to impossible to drag the body of a grown man through all those belly-crawls. Someone lured him back into that cavern and ambushed him. It's up to you to find out who and why."

She gave a sharp nod. "And I will."

Nash wondered if she felt as confident as she sounded. Maybe it was his imagination, but she seemed moody and pensive. On edge. What was going on with her anyway?

"Once we have Dr. Forester's full report, we'll release the findings to the press," he said. "Hopefully, someone will come forward. Even after all these years, I wouldn't discount the possibility that someone saw something."

She brushed a twig of hair behind her ears as she nodded. "That would certainly make my job easier. As for why I didn't have more questions for Dr. Forester, she was very thorough in her explanation."

"She knows her stuff," Nash agreed.

"You've worked with her before?"

The question was innocent enough, but Nash sensed something deeper than curiosity in the query. "A few times when I was with the Tallahassee PD." He wouldn't get into the coffee dates he'd shared with Allison Forester during his separation or the casual hookups since his divorce. Neither of them wanted a serious relationship, and Allie's go-with-the-flow attitude was just what he'd needed. His disastrous marriage had left him gun-shy, which was only one of many reasons he needed to keep Eve Jareau at arm's length and then some.

"I see," she murmured.

He gave her another side glance before returning his attention to the road. The rain was starting to come down again and he needed to stay focused. The pavement could get deceptively slippery in places. "How far are you in the missing-persons files?"

"It's a slog," she said. "The physical files are in bad shape. I may need to recruit some help."

"Resources are tight. We can only allocate so much to a case this old."

She turned with a frown. "Are you saying I'm on my own?"

"I'll give you as much help as I can, but we have to be realistic."

Not the answer she wanted, obviously, but he had a tight budget and a frugal mayor to appease.

"I'd like to go down in the cave," she said. "That won't cost anything but my time."

Her response surprised him. "What do you hope to

find? We went all through those tunnels after Kylie Buchanan disappeared, and Forensics combed through the cavern after the remains were excavated. I doubt you'll find anything useful."

"I'd still like to see that cavern for myself."

He nodded. "Fair enough. I'll contact the property owner as soon as we get back to the station and make the arrangements. He's planning on sealing the entrances permanently since the body was recovered, but I'm sure he can adjust the schedule to accommodate our investigation. I'll let you know what he says, but we'll need to wait for the weather to clear regardless."

"We?"

He could feel her curious gaze on him. "I'll run point. I'm not trying to micromanage your case," he hurriedly added before she could protest. "Like I said, I've recently been through all those tunnels. It's easy to get turned around if you're unfamiliar with the layout. As soon as we get the go-ahead, we'll need to arrange for proper equipment and backup. After everything that's happened, I don't want to allow even the smallest margin for error. Last thing we need is for something to go wrong down in that cave."

She nodded. "I never thanked you for giving me this case. I suspect it was more or less by default, but I appreciate the opportunity just the same."

"There was no default. I made you lead because you're a smart, diligent investigator. You're also tireless and you work well alone. But a case this old will require a lot of patience," he warned. "Besides the limited resources, you'll be following a trail that went cold years ago. Any leads you manage to turn up will need to be tracked down between your other cases. John Doe just isn't a priority."

"He is to me."

Nash shot her another glance, but the telltale bump and thud of a flat tire quelled his response. The vehicle careened toward the right and he swore under his breath as he gripped the wheel. "Great. Just what we need on a night like this."

"There was a lot of construction back at the lab. We probably ran over a nail." He saw her glance back at the road and he could have sworn she suppressed a shiver. "Do we have a spare?"

"Yeah. Let's hope it has air." He gently pumped the brakes and guided the vehicle off the road onto the narrow shoulder. He turned on his emergency flashers as he glanced in the rearview mirror. "Luckily there's not much traffic, but I can see the glow of headlights on the horizon. Put out the reflectors while I grab the spare."

They both climbed out and met at the rear of the vehicle. While Eve placed the triangular reflectors several yards from the SUV in both directions, Nash lifted the spare from the rack and got to work. Positioning his flashlight on the soggy shoulder, he used a tire iron to loosen the lug nuts.

Once the reflectors were set, Eve shouted over the rain, "Anything else I can do?"

"Keep an eye out for that oncoming vehicle." He glanced her way as he finished loosening the lug nuts. She'd walked some distance from the SUV and stood on the shoulder waving her flashlight beam back and forth on the ground to alert the approaching vehicle. The car was still some distance away, but she wasn't taking any chances. Nash liked that about her. Cautious and meticulous were good qualities in a detective, though he knew firsthand she had a reckless streak she kept well hidden. He'd glimpsed it once when she kissed him unexpectedly.

They'd blamed the incident on adrenaline and had never spoken of it again. But he'd thought about it over the years. Sometimes he thought about that kiss a lot.

Once he had the spare on, he hand-tightened the lug nuts, lowered the jack and used the tire tool to secure the bolts. By this time, the glare from the headlights reflecting off raindrops was blinding. Was it his imagination or had the car picked up speed?

He shouted a warning to Eve. She glanced back at him a split second before the car swerved toward the shoulder. She went down so quickly Nash was momentarily stunned. Then he leaped to his feet and rushed toward the spot where he'd last seen her.

The vehicle didn't stop or even slow. Instead, the driver gunned the engine and the car skidded violently toward Nash so that he had to dive out of the way. The car smashed into the nearest reflectors and sideswiped the SUV as the rear end fishtailed on the wet pavement. The sound of metal grinding against metal sent a chill up Nash's spine. He witnessed the collision in his periphery as he stumbled to his feet and sprinted through the torrent.

"Detective Jareau! Eve!"

He didn't see her at first. Had she been thrown down the embankment?

He swept his flashlight all along the shoulder and then down the rugged incline. She lay facedown at the bottom.

He took a quick survey over his shoulder. The car sped down the highway, the taillights already a blur in the rain.

Half running, half sliding, Nash descended the embankment and knelt beside Eve. She wasn't moving. "Can you hear me?" He heard a low groan over the downpour and his pounding heart. "Eve!"

She rolled onto her back and stared up at him. Raindrops splashed against her face. He tried to shelter her as best he could with his body. "Were you hit?"

"No, I slipped. I'm okay, I think. Just stunned."

"Don't try to move until we know for sure."

But she was already struggling to sit up. "The car didn't touch me. My feet slid out from under me when I jumped back. Next thing I knew I was rolling down the embankment." She put a hand to a scrape on her cheek. "Ouch."

"Are you sure the car didn't hit you?"

"Yes, but not for lack of trying. Did you see the way he swerved toward the shoulder? I didn't imagine that, did I?"

"No, I had to jump out the way, too. He hit my vehicle and kept going. It's possible the flashlight and reflectors disoriented him." Nash had seen it before. Sometimes in panic, people drove straight toward the object they were trying to avoid. He grasped her elbow and helped her to her feet.

"I couldn't get the plate number. Everything happened too fast, and the rain and headlights blinded me." She wiped her hands on the seat of her jeans. "What about you?"

"Just the first two letters. The vehicle looked to be a dark late-model sedan, which doesn't help much. Like you said, it happened too quickly and visibility was severely limited by the rain and glare of headlights." He checked her out in the flashlight beam. "Are you sure you're okay? That's a nasty scrape on your cheek."

She put her hand up to the tender spot and flinched. "I've had worse. Do you think your vehicle is drivable?"

"We'll soon find out. In any case, we should probably get everything off the road. I'll grab the tire and jack while you pick up the reflectors."

"Nash?"

He noticed she didn't call him chief. "Yes?"

She fingered a tiny silver chain at her throat. "I guess it's a good thing I wore my good-luck charm today."

Chapter Two

Nash was still in his office when Eve left the station later that evening. She glimpsed him at his desk through the glass partition that separated his office from the squad room. His head was bowed to his work and he seemed utterly absorbed in whatever he was doing. He didn't glance up when she paused outside his door. She wanted to ask if he'd had a chance to contact Mr. McNally about a cave excursion, but instead, she moved on without knocking. Best not to disturb him. Besides, she had other things on her mind at the moment.

Earlier, when they'd finally arrived back in town, she'd managed to convince him she really was okay. No cuts, no breaks. No need to go to the ER. Just the scrape on her cheek, which she'd cleaned and disinfected in the bathroom. Then, after changing out of her wet clothes into the spare set she kept in her locker, she'd settled in at her desk to update the database with Dr. Forester's findings and then to pore through the boxes of physical missing-persons files she'd brought up from the archives.

The task had proved frustrating in more ways than one. The folders were fragile and smelled of mildew from a flood ten years ago. The ink was so badly smeared on some of the reports as to render them illegible. Pages were stuck together or missing altogether. Labels had come unglued and fallen to the bottom of the file boxes. Before Eve knew it, two hours had rolled by and she'd barely made a dent in her search. She considered working another hour or two, but her muscles were already aching, so she decided to call it a night and start fresh in the morning.

Leaving the station, she cut across the parking lot to her car, glancing around for any vehicles that didn't belong and for any tinted windows that might hide watchful eyes. She hated feeling so paranoid. Nash was probably right about the panicked driver on the highway. The flashing lights and reflectors had disoriented him. And the guy in the parking lot at the lab was just a guy in a parking lot. Both cars had been dark-colored sedans, but so what? Plenty of vehicles on the road matching that description. She wouldn't have given either incident a passing consideration if not for the holed coin that had been found with the remains and the disturbing memory that had come creeping out of her subconscious.

The discovery of the skeleton wasn't yet public knowledge, but word had a way of traveling fast through a small town. What if the killer knew his victim had been dug up? Was he even now watching Eve's every move?

Chiding herself for her overactive imagination, she scrubbed a hand across her eyes. She was tired, verging on punch-drunk. The whole department had been running on nothing but adrenaline since little Kylie Buchanan's abduction. Now that the child had been found safe and sound, it was time to take a breath.

Eve drove through the wet streets with music streaming softly from the sound system. Darkness seemed to close in on her. Every shadow, every drooping tree branch caught her attention as the hair rose on the back of her neck. Overreaction or not, she couldn't shake the dark foreboding that had dogged her since leaving the lab.

It wasn't just the niggling worry of bad things to come, though. She felt restive, empty and a bit gloomy. Much of her off-duty time was spent alone, but she rarely felt lonely. She always had friends and family nearby when she needed them. Tonight, however, she experienced a strange hollowness in her chest that she couldn't explain and a creeping uneasiness that kept her glancing in the rearview mirror.

John Doe's possible identity wore heavily on her. She didn't like keeping secrets from Nash, but honestly, what did she really know at this point? If she confided her suspicion, he might feel obligated to remove her from the case, and that was the last thing she wanted. No one else would devote the time and energy necessary to solve an old homicide. And solve it she would, no matter what she had to do to get at the truth.

After pulling into her garage, she sat until her favorite song ended before lowering the overhead door. Then she exited through the side entrance into the backyard. It was a warm, humid evening. The rain had stopped, and a few stars twinkled. The air hung heavy with the scent of jasmine and honeysuckle, and the dull ache in her chest deepened. She paused once more, lifting her face to the shrouded moon as she fingered the dime beneath her shirt.

Daddy, are you there?

The breeze picked up, drifting through the leaves overhead and resurrecting an unnerving sense of being watched. Eve scoured the backyard, probing the bushes and shadowy corners, but no one lurked, living or dead. No one that she could see anyway.

She shivered, stroking a hand down her arm where goose bumps had once again popped. The sensation wasn't unfamiliar. For most of her life, she'd sensed a mysterious presence. On occasion, she would sometimes wake up in the middle of the night with a cold, dreaded certainty that someone watched her from the dark. When she was little, she would huddle under the covers till daybreak, but as she grew older, she'd sometimes get up and pad to the window to boldly search the shadows. Once, she'd seen someone staring back at her. She'd never told her mother about the interloper and to this day, she couldn't explain why. For one thing, she hadn't wanted to cause undue fear or worry, but something else, an indefinable need for secrecy, had kept her silent.

Don't tell your mama. She wouldn't understand.

Shrugging off the melancholy and her father's phantom caution, Eve hurried up the steps and unlocked the back door, casting a final glance over her shoulder before scurrying inside. Piling her belongings on the kitchen island, she considered having a drink to settle her nerves, but she hadn't eaten since lunch. Alcohol on an empty stomach was never a good idea. Besides, she still had business to attend to that evening. After fixing a hasty sandwich, she showered, dressed and headed out again, this time on foot.

Her mother lived two blocks over in the same house where Eve had grown up. The windows in the seventies ranch-style house were dark. Her mother must still be at work, she decided. Jackie Jareau's boss was a clinical psychologist who conducted group therapy sessions two evenings a week. Jackie stayed after-hours on those days so that Dr. Gail Mercer wouldn't be alone in the office with her patients.

Eve glanced at her phone. Just after nine. Surely her mother would be home soon. She sent a text just in case.

Hey, where are you?

Her mother responded immediately. Just leaving the office. What's up?

I'm at your place. I was hoping we could talk tonight if you're not too tired.

Never too tired for you. Everything okay?

Yes, I just want to see you.

Use the spare key. I'll be home in a few.

Eve went around to the back and collected the key from the hiding spot above the door. She let herself in and walked through the darkened house and down the narrow hallway to her old bedroom. Turning on a lamp, she glanced around. The bare bones of the room had changed little since she'd left home. The posters were gone, along with the garish lime-green wall color she'd once favored. Her mother had painted everything over in crisp white and replaced the bed linens with something more neutral and grown-up. But the furniture was the same and Jackie had sentimentally left all the stars on the ceiling. If Eve lay on the bed, she could still watch them twinkle as moonlight reflected off the foil.

Opening a dresser drawer, she rifled through the contents until she found the photograph of her father that had once rested on her nightstand. She carried the frame over to the bed and sat on the edge as she studied the photograph.

Twenty-eight years had passed since she'd last seen him. Almost a lifetime for Eve. A daddy's girl to her very core, she'd barely been five when he left. She'd adored him so, clinging to his hand when they went out, wrapping her arms around his legs when he returned home from one of his trips. Even after all these years, Eve remembered vividly Gabriel Jareau's snapping eyes and unruly hair. His mischievous smile and teasing manner. If she concentrated hard enough, she could still hear traces of his Cajun roots in his rich baritone.

She drew a thumb across the glass that protected his image. Her father had been a charming, handsome man. Tall, thin, right-handed. Good bones, good teeth.

Eve let out a slow breath as she fell back against the mattress and stared up at the peeling stars. She must have dozed off because she heard her father say clearly, "Boo? You awake?"

Bolting upright, she glanced around. The voice had been a dream, but the creaking floorboards somewhere in the house were real.

NASH DROVE STRAIGHT home after he left the station. He'd thought about stopping somewhere for takeout—Mexican or Cuban always hit the spot—but he experienced a strange sense of urgency that propelled him through the darkened streets, intensifying into a prickle at the back of his neck as he turned into the narrow driveway at his house. He cut the lights and sat for a moment scouring the property.

He didn't know why he felt so on edge. Eve's close call out on the highway had scared the hell out of him, but she was okay. Just banged up a little. This was something different. A gnawing foreboding that the other shoe was about to drop.

Could be nothing more than his imagination, he decided. An amplified dread brought on by the lingering strain of Grace's arrest and the icy realization of just how devious and cruel his ex-wife could truly be.

She'd planned the kidnapping meticulously, taking the little girl through the same bedroom window from which another child had vanished twenty-eight years ago. Then she'd stashed four-year-old Kylie in a remote cabin while

finalizing her plans to leave the country. Despite everything Grace had done to Nash over the years, the untold
grief she'd brought into his life, he would never have
thought her capable of something so dark.

Though, to be honest, he'd seen signs of her malice long
before the divorce. She'd tried any number of ploys during
their separation to lure him back into her web. He'd succumbed too many times to her deceitful machinations out
of guilt, weakness and the fear that he'd somehow been
responsible for pushing her to the brink. No more. Now
was not the time to backslide into his own dark place. He'd
come too far and he had too many responsibilities. He had
a town to protect and an old homicide to solve.

He'd assigned the case to Eve because he trusted her to
do everything in her power to solve it. But already Nash
had insinuated himself into the investigation, arranging
the consultation earlier with Allison Forester and then suggesting that he and Eve drive over to Tallahassee together.
She hadn't objected, but he wondered if she could see
through his motives. Despite his resolve to keep his distance, he was doing everything in his power to draw her
back into his orbit.

Not smart. She was too good a woman to get involved
with a man whose night terrors still woke him up in a
cold sweat, whose baggage was sometimes like a dead
weight resting on his shoulders. A man who every now
and then seemed one drink away from ending up facedown in a gutter.

He shook off his gloom and let himself into the house.
Flipping on the light, he tossed his keys in the wooden
bowl he kept on a small table near the door. Then glancing out the window, he hung up his holster and took care
of his weapon. Despite the fact that he lived alone, habit

dictated that he lock his gun in the safe and slide the key back into its hiding place.

There'd been a time not so long ago when he couldn't trust a bolted door to keep Grace from entering his home in the middle of the night and stealing through the darkened rooms. He'd once awakened to find her at the foot of his bed with a 9 mm aimed at his heart. After that, he'd made sure to secure both the weapons he owned before he went to sleep at night, and he'd had the locks changed on every door in the house. Even so, Grace had her ways. Sometimes when he came home from work, he could still sense her presence.

She couldn't get to him now. She couldn't hurt herself or anyone he loved, but Nash knew he wouldn't rest until he searched the house. Old habits really did die hard.

He started in the living area and made his way down the hallway, peering into the bedrooms and bathrooms until he reached the last door. The moment he entered the small room he'd converted into a home office, he knew something was wrong.

A warm breeze drifted through the open slider. He hadn't left it unlocked. He would never be that careless. It was possible the cleaning service he used might have neglected to close the door, but he'd never had any problem with them before.

He took in the room at a glance and then eased to his desk, removing the backup firearm he kept locked in the top drawer. Then he slipped through the door onto the concrete patio, his gaze scouring the bushes and all along the wooden fence.

Keeping to the shadows, he tuned his senses to the night. A dog barked down the street. A car horn sounded in the distance. He listened for the longest moment before he walked the yard, looking for evidence of an intruder. Then he backtracked to the office and examined the lock. No sign of a break-in. No footprints beneath the windows. Nothing. And yet he knew someone had been inside his house.

He went back into the office and turned on the overhead light. He'd left a few files stacked neatly on his desk. One of the folders contained his notes and copies of the photographs taken deep inside the cave where the bones had been discovered. Nash had kept hard copies for himself when he handed the electronic file over to Eve, though he wasn't sure why. He trusted her skill and instincts, but something about this particular John Doe bothered him.

The tingle at the back of his neck deepened. Someone had definitely been through those files. He was particular about the way he left things on his desk. The folders and photographs had been disturbed.

Retrieving a fingerprint kit from the SUV, Nash carefully dusted the folders, the slider and all the other flat surfaces in his office. He doubted the prints he lifted would be useful. Anyone with the skill and smarts to enter his house without breaking the locks wouldn't then become so careless as to leave his or her prints all over everything.

Why *had* someone entered his home? What were they looking for? Nothing obvious was missing. Not that he had a houseful of valuables, but why break in and leave the TV, his laptop and the little cash he kept in one of the desk drawers?

He went back to the folders and the cave photographs. His mind flashed to the bones on the metal table and then to Eve's jittery silence after they'd left the lab. He thought about the car that had swerved toward them on the side of the road. He couldn't help wondering if that near miss was somehow connected to the break-in at his house. To the human remains that had been hidden deep inside a cave for decades.

THE CREAKING FLOORBOARDS catapulted Eve upright on the bed. She thought at first her mother must have come home, but Jackie always wore heels to work and they made a distinct clicking sound on the old parquet floors. The footsteps Eve heard now were stealthy, as if someone in soft-soled shoes prowled through the darkened rooms.

She rose quietly and glanced around for a weapon. Her gun was locked up at home in its usual place beside her bed. Grabbing a snow globe from the nightstand, she turned off the lamp and eased across the room to peer out. A man stood at the end of the narrow hallway, silhouetted by the light filtering in from the street through the double windows in the den.

He called out, "Hello? Is someone there? Jackie, is that you?"

Recognizing her ex-stepfather's voice, Eve let out a relieved breath. "Wayne?"

"Evie?"

She dropped the snow globe to her side and scowled. She hated when anyone but her mother called her Evie. "Yes, it's me."

He gave a low chuckle. "Damn, girl. You scared me half to death."

"I could say the same about you." She came out of the bedroom to confront him. "What are you doing here anyway? You're lucky I didn't bean you with this snow globe."

"I was afraid someone broke in." He walked back a few steps and turned on the hall light. Eve blinked in the sudden brilliance. He gave her a sheepish grin as he held up a pipe wrench. "Looks like we had the same idea."

She reached inside the bedroom doorway and placed

the snow globe on the corner of the dresser. Then she turned back expectantly. Wayne Brody and her mother had been divorced for over two decades, having decided after barely a year and a half of marriage that they made better friends than spouses. Eve had nothing against the man. Not anymore. But if she were honest, she'd have to admit she'd never really warmed up to him, maybe because for years she'd harbored the secret hope that her real dad would come back home.

She was a grown woman now and had accepted the reality that Wayne had never been a threat except in her mind. Still, she wasn't particularly comfortable with him coming and going at all hours when her mother wasn't home.

She tried to keep her tone neutral. "You never said what you're doing here."

He toed a metal toolbox on the floor before bending to toss the pipe wrench inside. "Your mom asked me to come over and fix a leaky faucet in the hall bathroom. When I got here, the door was open, but her car wasn't in the driveway. Then I saw a light on at the back of the house and I was afraid someone was inside trying to pick her clean while she was gone." He bent to retrieve the toolbox and place it inside the bathroom door. "What about you?"

Eve bristled at the question despite herself. Why should she have to explain herself to her mother's ex-husband?

She scrutinized him as he busied himself at the faucet. He was in his early fifties, a man of average height, average build, average looks. His hair was light brown, his eyes a nondescript shade of blue. Nothing about Wayne Brody stood out in any way, unlike Eve's father, who had been tall, dark and movie-star handsome. But Gabriel Jareau had left Eve and her mother without a backward glance while Wayne Brody, for all his faults, had stuck around through thick and thin.

"I came by to see Mom," Eve said. "She texted a few minutes ago that she was on her way home. Could we back up for a minute? You said the door was open when you got here. You mean unlocked, don't you?"

He turned in surprise. "No, the kitchen door was wide open like I said."

"But I know I closed it when I came in," Eve insisted.

Wayne thought about it for a moment and then shrugged. "The wind must have blown it open. The latch sometimes won't catch unless you slam the door just right. I've been meaning to fix that, too."

This is not your house. It's not your place to fix my mom's back door. Or her leaky faucet, for that matter. But Eve kept that opinion to herself. Maybe she wasn't as grown-up as she liked to think.

Headlights arced in the driveway and shone through the frosted bathroom window. "That's probably Jackie now." Wayne came out of the bathroom and turned down the hallway toward the kitchen. "You coming?"

"In a minute. I want to have a look around first."

Wayne stopped dead in his tracks and spun. "You still think somebody came in through the back door? You think they could still be in the house?" He sounded a little excited.

"Not really, but I'll feel better if I make certain," Eve said.

"Maybe I should tag along just in case."

"Thanks, Wayne. I've got it covered."

He hesitated for a split second then nodded. "Still hard for me to wrap my head around you being a cop. Seems like yesterday your mom and I were teaching you how to ride a bike."

"Time flies," Eve murmured.

She waited until he'd retreated down the hallway and

then went about her search. She didn't expect to find anything. Wayne was probably right about the faulty latch. But the incident on the highway had left her shaken and wary. She wasn't about to take any chances, especially when it came to her mother's safety.

Jackie was just coming through the back door when Eve returned to the kitchen. Despite the bad weather, her mother looked attractively pulled together in slim black slacks and a green silk blouse that complemented her auburn hair. She wore pearls around her throat and gold hoops in her lobes, all thrifted or bought at the local discount store. Jackie Jareau had a flair for making her bargain-basement wardrobe look like a million dollars, a trait that had not been passed down to her daughter.

Balancing an umbrella in one hand and a grocery bag in the other, she seemed oblivious to the pair in the kitchen.

"Wayne, you here?" she called out as she placed the bag on the mudroom bench and folded the umbrella. Then she kicked off her damp shoes and slid her feet into her favorite fuzzy slippers. "I saw your truck out front. I ordered a pizza on my way home. How's that sound?"

"I'm right here," he said. "Pizza sounds great."

His proximity startled her. She jumped and whirled, glancing from Wayne to Eve and then back again. Her gaze narrowed as she draped her handbag over the back of a bar stool and placed the grocery bag on the counter. "What's going on here? Why are you two staring at me like that?"

Eve moved up to the bar. "Nothing's going on. We were just waiting for you. You didn't tell me Wayne would be here."

"Didn't I? Must have slipped my mind." She removed the items from the grocery bag and began storing them in the pantry.

Wayne leaned a shoulder against the doorway and

folded his arms as he watched his ex-wife move about the kitchen. His blue gaze seemed to take in her every move. "You missed all the excitement. Your daughter nearly knocked me in the head with one of your snow globes."

Eve tamped down her annoyance at his dramatics. "And you armed yourself with a pipe wrench. We both thought someone had broken in," she explained to her mother.

Jackie glanced over her shoulder, puzzled. "Why on earth would you think that? I've never had any concern here."

"Don't be lulled into a false sense of security," Eve said. "Crime is on the rise all over town."

Jackie sighed. "My daughter, the police detective."

"She's right," Wayne said. "You can't be too careful these days."

"I appreciate your concern, both of you, but I'm not about to live my life in fear."

"No one said anything about living in fear, Mom. Just be careful, okay? Especially when you get home this late."

Jackie turned from the pantry with a worried frown. "This is a very puzzling conversation. Why do I get the feeling you're not telling me everything? Has something happened that I should know about?"

An icy breeze blew down Eve's neck. All the doors and windows were closed so she wanted to assume the air conditioner had kicked on.

"Well?" Jackie pressed.

"Nothing's happened. I'm just asking you to be careful, that's all." Eve could feel Wayne's gaze on her now. Why did the man's presence irritate her so much? No reason to begrudge their friendship. He was a good guy who would do anything for her mother. A dutiful daughter should be grateful for that.

Jackie gave her a long look. Then she came over and tipped Eve's face toward the light. "How did that happen?"

Eve's fingers went to the tenderness on her cheek. "I slipped and fell. It's nothing. Just a scrape."

Jackie's gaze darkened. "How did you fall?"

"It's nothing," Eve insisted.

"Did you put something on it?"

"Yes, ma'am. Just the way you taught me."

Her mother was far from appeased. "I know there's more to the story. I can see it in your eyes."

Eve sighed. "Chief Bowden and I had a flat tire on our way back from Tallahassee. I slipped on the wet shoulder and tumbled down an embankment. That's the truth." *More or less.*

"What were you doing in Tallahassee?" Wayne asked.

He remained in the doorway with his shoulder against the frame, but the subtle tension in his voice belied his casual stance. His eyes seemed a little too piercing, his whole countenance frozen and unnatural.

That strange breeze whispered against Eve's neck like a ghostly caress.

Watch your back, Boo.

Chapter Three

Jackie didn't seem to notice the sudden crackle of electricity in the air. She grabbed a bottle of wine from the rack on the counter and then rummaged in a drawer for a corkscrew. "I don't know about you two, but I could use a drink. All this scare talk has put me on edge. Let's have a nice glass of wine and try to relax before dinner gets here."

Wayne straightened from the doorway. "None for me. I'd better get to that leaky faucet or I'll be here all night."

Jackie gave him an appreciative smile. "Thanks, Wayne. You're a lifesaver."

"I'm always happy to help. You know that."

"I do know." They exchanged an intimate glance.

Wayne disappeared back into the house and Eve stared after him as she plopped down at the bar. "Do you think it's a good idea to have him over here so often to fix things?"

Jackie leaned against the bar, cupping her wineglass in one hand. "You heard him. He's happy to help out."

"I'm sure he is, but maybe you should call a plumber or professional handyman now and then. Or even let me have a go at it."

"Why would I spend good money on a plumber when Wayne is just down the street?"

Eve sighed and shook her head helplessly. "Come on,

Mom. You'd have to be blind not to notice the way he looks at you."

Jackie seemed genuinely taken aback. "What on earth are you talking about?"

"The man still has feelings for you. Don't tell me you haven't figured that out yet." Eve reached for the wine bottle.

"Oh, good grief, Wayne doesn't have *romantic* feelings for me." Jackie gave a little bark of laughter. "That's crazy. We've been divorced for over twenty years."

"Yet he still lives right down the street from you. He comes running whenever you call." Eve poured herself a glass of wine. "There's no time limit on how long someone can carry a torch."

"You should know," Jackie muttered.

"What?"

"Nothing." Her mother was silent for a moment as she searched Eve's face. "Where is this coming from?"

Eve shrugged. "It's something I've thought for a while."

"Then why wait until now to bring it up?"

"Because I do realize it's none of my business," Eve said with a wry smile.

"No, it isn't," her mother agreed bluntly. "But let me clarify something for you anyway. Wayne and I go back a long way. We were friends before we got married and we've remained friends since the divorce. That's not going to change. We like and respect one another. We enjoy each other's company. There's nothing more to our relationship than that."

"Maybe not for you," Eve muttered.

Jackie's mouth tightened. "All right, that's enough. I know how you feel about Wayne. You've never even bothered to pretend. It was understandable when you were a child, but you're an adult now. It's time you start tending to your own life."

Eve grew defensive. "I do tend to my own life."

"Not that I can see. When was the last time you had a real date? Let me tell you something, Evie. Time flies by faster than you think."

"I know that."

Jackie gave her a sage look. "I hope you do. But something tells me you didn't come over to talk about either of our love lives. You certainly didn't come here to talk about my ex-husband."

"I didn't come to talk about Wayne, no. I want to ask you about Daddy."

Something flickered in Jackie's eyes before she glanced away. "What about him?"

"He sent money to you after he left, didn't he? How long did that go on?"

A bitter edge crept into her mother's voice. "Not long enough, but it hardly matters now, does it?"

Eve shrugged. "It matters to me. How long? A few weeks…a few months?"

"I don't know. I can't remember things that happened last week, let alone three decades ago."

"Try, Mom."

She sighed. "At first, he sent money home almost every week. Then it dwindled to once a month and then to nothing at all. That went on for a couple of months, the best I remember."

"Cash, checks, money orders?"

"Always cash. I thought he was crazy for trusting the post office, but Gabriel never did have a lick of common sense when it came to money."

"Did he include a letter or note?"

"Sometimes."

"What did he say?"

"I don't remember every word."

"Just the gist," Eve coaxed.

Jackie closed her eyes on another deep sigh. "Let me think. He talked about work sometimes and about where he was headed next. Mostly he talked about you."

Eve felt a strange flutter in the pit of her stomach. "What about me?"

"How much he loved and missed you. How sorry he was that he couldn't be with you. That sort of thing."

And yet he'd apparently abandoned her without a backward glance. "Do you still have those letters?"

"Why would I keep them?" Jackie topped off her wineglass. Was that a slight tremor in her hand or merely Eve's imagination? "I got rid of all that stuff years ago."

"What about the postcards he sent to me?"

Her mother's shrug seemed nonchalant, but Eve noticed how carefully she still avoided eye contact. "You used to have them pinned to the bulletin board in your room. I haven't seen them in a long time, so I figured you'd either thrown them out when you left for college or took them with you."

"Did Daddy ever mention coming back home?" Eve tried to keep the wistful tone from her voice, but Jackie heard something that caused her frown to deepen.

"He made it pretty clear the night he left that he wasn't coming back."

"Did the two of you argue?"

"We always argued."

"Strange," Eve murmured. "I didn't hear you that night. Sometimes I would."

"We should never have let that happen. Not that this excuses anything, but we were so young and both of us had quick tempers." Her mother's eyes glittered. "No one has ever been able to push my buttons the way Gabriel Jareau did."

"Do you think it's possible he came back to Black Creek without you knowing?"

"I guess it's possible, but he would have tried to see you if he'd come back. Whatever our problems, he loved you, Evie." Jackie's expression softened. "You should never doubt that."

"And yet he left me."

"He left both of us."

At the back of Eve's mind, she could see her father climbing into that unfamiliar car with the platinum blonde behind the wheel and the mysterious man looking out the window in the back seat.

"Mom?"

Jackie seemed to rouse from a deep reverie. "Hmm?"

"I overheard you tell someone once that he left you for another woman. Do you know who she was?"

Her mother's hand crept to her throat. "You heard that? Oh, honey, I'm sorry. I never meant for you to know."

"No need to be sorry. Like you said, it was a long time ago."

Jackie shook her head in regret. "You overheard that conversation and all this time, you never said a word."

"I didn't want to believe it."

"Of course not. You always adored your daddy. You thought the sun rose and set on that man. And he, you."

Eve swallowed. "So did you ever try to find out who she was?"

"No, I never did." Her mother glanced up. "This may sound harsh, but after a while, I really didn't care who she was or where they'd gone off to. I didn't have time to care. I had a child to raise, a mortgage and bills to pay. So many more important things to worry about than the identity of my husband's girlfriend."

But even after all these years, she couldn't quite keep the edge of resentment from her voice. She couldn't quite stifle the faraway look in her eyes when she mentioned her first husband's name.

Eve nodded. "I understand. Do you think she was someone from Black Creek? I mean, you must have heard talk, right? No one can keep a secret in this town." Yet John Doe's bones had remained hidden for decades.

Jackie picked up a towel and idly wiped a ring from the counter. "Why all these questions? He left so long ago. What difference does any of this make now?"

"Surely you can understand why I'm curious," Eve said. "He was my father and I remember so little about him. It's not the first time I've asked about him."

"No, but you haven't brought him up in a long time. I'd hoped you'd moved on as I have."

Have you, though? If you're so indifferent, why do you avoid talking about him? Why did you throw all of his things away when you knew I might someday want them?

"Just one more question," Eve said. "Was he ever involved in a car accident?"

Jackie had been lifting her drink, but now she paused with the glass in midair. "He had a motorcycle wreck the year you were born. I'm sure I've mentioned it before."

"I don't think so. If you did, I've forgotten. How severe were his injuries?"

"He was in pretty bad shape. Why?"

"Did he break his right arm? His right leg? His left ankle?"

The wineglass exploded in Jackie's hand and her face went deathly white. Red wine spilled over her fingers, mixing with the blood that gushed from a cut in her palm as the crystal crashed against the tile floor.

Eve jumped up and hurried around the bar. "Mom, you're bleeding. Here, let me see." She pulled her mother toward the sink.

Jackie seemed stunned. "I don't know what happened," she mumbled. "The glass just shattered in my hand."

Wayne appeared in the doorway. "I heard glass breaking. Everything okay in here?"

Eve glanced over her shoulder. How had he appeared in the doorway so quickly? Had he been eavesdropping on their conversation?

"Mom cut her hand."

"What? How?"

"A glass broke."

He avoided the shards on the floor as he rushed to the sink. "How bad is it?"

"It's nothing," Jackie insisted. But sweat beaded at her temples as she slumped against the sink, looking as if she might pass out at any second.

"Mom, you okay? Do you need to sit down?"

Wayne gently took her hand. "Let me have a look first." Eve put her arm around her mother's waist for support while he washed the cut under running water. The blood kept oozing. He wrapped her hand in a clean dish towel. "We'd better get you to the ER. Looks like you need stitches."

Jackie started to protest, but Eve quickly agreed. "He's right. It's deep and you may have glass slivers inside the cut that could cause infection."

"I'm parked right out front." Wayne ushered Jackie toward the door before Eve could protest. She tried not to resent his tendency to take over. Her petty grievances couldn't matter less now. The faster her mother got to the ER, the better. And Wayne's vehicle happened to be handy.

He glanced back. "Can you take care of things here?"

"Yes, of course. Just keep me posted."

She watched from the window until Wayne's truck pulled away from the curb and then she cleaned up the mess on the floor and carried the glass fragments out to the trash. After that, she killed a bit of time checking her messages and email before heading back down the hallway to her old bedroom. She sat down at her desk and removed the top drawer so that she could retrieve the envelope she'd long ago taped to the back. Surprisingly, her mother had never found her hiding place. Or if she had, she'd never said anything.

Peeling off the tape, Eve opened the envelope and dumped her father's postcards on top of the desk. There were only three—two from New Orleans and one from San Antonio. Those postcards and the dime she wore around her neck were all she had left of him.

Eve arranged the cards in chronological order according to the postmarks. The messages were brief and she knew them all by heart. *Miss you, Boo. Wish you were here, Boo. Be a good girl for your mama, Boo.*

Maybe it was Eve's imagination, but she noticed something now that had escaped her as a child. The handwriting on the San Antonio postcard looked subtly different from the two New Orleans postcards. She dug around in the drawer for a magnifying glass but couldn't find one.

Tension knotted her shoulders. She returned the postcards to the envelope and carried it with her into the kitchen. Perching at the bar, she massaged her sore muscles while she waited to hear from her mother.

NASH WAS STILL seated behind his desk when his cell phone rang. He automatically checked the screen before he answered. *Unknown Caller.*

His first thought was that Grace had somehow finagled the use of a phone, and he was in no mood to deal with his ex-wife tonight. He didn't want to listen to her excuses, or worse, her accusations. Nash never wanted to hear from her again, but that wasn't a realistic desire considering her nature and the fact that her trial would be starting soon.

Best-case scenario for him, her attorney would request a change of venue and then his department wouldn't be charged with escorting her to and from county lockup every day. He'd still see her in court, though. No getting around that.

The phone buzzed persistently. His gut instinct was to let the call go to voice mail, but as chief of police, he was never really off duty. He hit the accept button with a grimace and lifted the phone to his ear.

"Nash Bowden."

The caller remained silent, but Nash could hear music and laughter in the background.

"Hello? Anyone there?"

"You need to leave them bones alone," a gruff voice informed him.

"What?"

"You heard me," the woman said in a hushed tone. "Leave 'em be if you know what's good for you."

Not Grace, obviously. Nash tried to place the caller. She sounded older, at least fifty, with the grit of smoke and hard living around the edges.

He was instantly on alert and intrigued. "Who is this?"

"My name's not important. You don't know me. And don't bother trying to track me down. I'm throwing this phone away as soon as we're done."

So she was using a burner, which implied a certain amount of technical sophistication. Disposable phones could be traced, but not easily and not with the limited resources available to Nash's department.

"Your name matters a great deal if you're trying to interfere in an official police investigation," he informed her. "I need to know who you are and the reason you're making this call."

A slight hesitation. "You don't think what happened out on the highway tonight is reason enough for me to call you?"

He put the phone on speaker and placed it on his desk, then reached for pen and paper to take notes. "What happened on the highway tonight?"

"You should know. You were there."

An icy finger traced along his spine. "Were you driving the car that sideswiped my vehicle?"

"No, sir, I was not."

"Were you a passenger?"

Another pause. "That's not important, either."

"Are you saying what happened tonight wasn't an accident?" Nash pressed.

"I'm saying next time there won't be a close call."

"Is that a threat?"

"Call it a warning."

Nash scowled down at the paper. "What do you know about the remains that were found in McNally's Cave?"

"I know it's best to let the dead rest in peace."

"Do you know the deceased's name and how he came to be down in that cave? Do you know who killed him?"

He heard the sharp intake of her breath. "Lord, mister. Did you hear what I said? Leave 'em be. You have no idea what you're dealing with. *Who* you're dealing with."

"Then why don't you tell me?"

"I've said too much already."

"You haven't told me anything. Wait—"

The connection dropped, leaving Nash with nothing but a blank piece of paper and a dozen questions swirling in his head. He swore aloud, the four-letter expletive echoing unpleasantly in the silent room.

According to the female caller, the incident on the highway had been deliberate. The driver had purposefully swerved toward them, but why? If Eve hadn't lost her footing at that precise moment, the evening might have gone very differently. He didn't want to think about how close he'd come to losing her forever, but now he could think of nothing else.

Outside, the wind had picked up. Nash could hear the faint squeak of the garden gate as it swung back and forth in the breeze. Odd because he never left that gate unlatched. He'd checked it earlier, hadn't he? Or had he overlooked it in his haste to search the garden?

For the second time that evening, he removed his weapon from the desk drawer and went back out into the night. The ruffling leaves sounded like rain, and he could hear the tinkle of wind chimes in his neighbor's backyard. The moon cast a soft glow over the brick pathway he followed across the yard to the gate.

The wrought iron clanged rhythmically in the breeze. Keeping to the shadows, Nash peered through the metal rods into the side yard and out to the street. Oily puddles glistened beneath the streetlights. The night had deepened since his earlier search and an eerie hush seemed to fall over the landscape.

He opened the gate and stepped through. Pressing a shoulder against the side of the house, he eased through the darkness to the front yard. He didn't think he could be seen from the street, but someone must have been watching for him. Two houses down, headlights came on, the dual beams sweeping over him as an old pickup truck sputtered to life, and the driver U-turned and sped away.

Nash bolted across the yard and down the sidewalk, but the truck easily outpaced him. The driver turned on squealing tires at the next intersection and the vehicle was soon out of sight.

Nash stared down the street in frustration. It was useless to pursue on foot, and by the time he sprinted back home for the SUV or even called for a patrol car, the truck would be long gone.

Searching the night for a moment longer, he turned and strode back to his house. As he headed up the walkway, his phone rang again. *Unknown Caller* flashed on his screen.

He accepted the call and lifted the phone to his ear as he stepped back through the gate.

"You've been warned," the same gruff voice informed him. She sounded out of breath this time, as if she'd just run back to her truck. "Don't say you weren't."

Chapter Four

Despite her late night, Eve clocked in an hour early the next morning. She'd waited anxiously to hear from her mother before heading home the evening before. Jackie had called from the emergency room around eleven, insisting that, except for a few stitches, she was none the worse for wear. As soon as she got home, she took a pain pill and went straight to bed. Wayne had offered to stay over in case she needed anything, but Jackie had sent him on his way, insisting she'd had enough of his hovering for one night. Nor was she in the mood for any more of Eve's questions. Fair enough. She'd been through a lot and for now Eve decided it was best not to press her mother on the issue.

She'd walked home in the dark with her father's postcards safely tucked inside her bag, still pondering her mother's accident. How could a wineglass shatter in one's hand like that? It was almost as if her mother had unwittingly applied undue pressure to the fragile sides in distress, but why would Eve's questions prompt such a strong reaction? Why *now*?

Back at home, she'd stayed up until well past midnight studying the handwriting on the postcards. Her vision blurring from exhaustion and intense concentration, she'd finally convinced herself she had imagined the discrepancies. Did she really think someone had forged her father's handwriting in order to convince his estranged wife and five-year-old daughter that he was still alive?

Daylight had brought a clearer head and a mile-long list of things she needed to accomplish. She was deep into the musty-smelling missing-persons files when Nash stopped by her desk. She saw him approach out of the corner of her eye, but she pretended not to notice until he spoke.

"Good morning, Detective Jareau."

"Morning, Chief. You're here bright and early."

"So are you. No ill effects from that tumble you took last night?"

"I'm fine," she assured him.

He examined the scrape on her cheek and nodded. "Good. We've got a lot of ground to cover today."

Outwardly, Eve remained calm and collected, but as always in his presence, she felt an unsettling stir of butterflies in her stomach. After six years, her feelings for Nash Bowden should have long since withered and died, but somehow her attraction had only grown stronger.

When she'd first joined the Black Creek Police Department fresh out of the Florida Law Enforcement Academy, she'd heard the gossip about his troubled marriage and subsequent separation. Those rumors and the haunted look in his eyes—not to mention her rookie status—had convinced her the police chief was off-limits, especially to her.

But every once in a while she would catch him looking at her when no one else was around and the *way* he looked at her… She was only human. She'd slipped once and made the first move after a particularly harrowing arrest. They were alone after the danger had passed and she'd let adrenaline and her emotions get the best of her. Nash had kissed her back, not politely or tentatively, but with the pent-up passion of a drowning man.

The intensity of that kiss had persuaded Eve more than

anything else that the Black Creek chief of police was a dangerous man for a woman like her. She wasn't naive. A man who kissed the way he did might require far more from a partner than Eve was willing to give.

Not that any of that mattered these days. Nash had kept his distance after that kiss and she'd kept hers.

But now here he was, seeking her out yet again. His expression seemed all business so she tried not to wonder if his feelings had secretly lingered the way hers had. She tried not to think about what might have happened if she'd kissed him again that night. Kissed him the way he needed to be kissed.

She gave him a brief perusal, allowing her gaze to explore for only a split second before returning her attention to the file. He wore his typical uniform of jeans, casual shirt and boots. Eve was dressed much the same, having retired her uniform (except on formal or ceremonial occasions) when she made detective three years ago on her thirtieth birthday. She'd celebrated with a few friends and colleagues at a local bar, keeping one eye on the door in case Nash decided to join them. He hadn't. She'd gone home that night both intensely relieved and bitterly disappointed.

A few months later, news had spread through the grapevine that his divorce had been finalized. By then, Eve had been involved with a man she'd known from high school. Nice guy. Funny. Kind. Easy on the eyes. They should have made a good match, but her reticence to commit had eventually doomed the relationship.

So here *she* was, still nursing unrequited feelings for her superior. Funny how things worked out. Now that she and Nash were finally free to be together, they'd never been further apart.

She closed the file and folded her hands on the desk, allowing a hint of excitement to creep into her voice. "Does this mean we're a go?"

He looked momentarily startled, as if his thoughts had uncomfortably meshed with hers. "I'm sorry?"

"You said we had a lot of ground to cover today. I assumed that meant you'd contacted Mr. McNally about going down in the cave." Eve waited a beat. "The equipment and backup have all been arranged. I just need to know the day and time."

Something seemed to click at the back of his mind and he nodded absently. "The cave. Right. We'll get to that. Probably a good idea to wait a day or two in case any of the passageways flooded during the storm."

A day or two? Eve needed answers now. "I'd like to go down today if at all possible."

He perched a hip on the edge of her desk and gave her one of those hooded looks, the kind that made her momentarily forget their surroundings and circumstances. "What's the hurry? The remains were buried in that cavern for decades and they aren't going anywhere. Another day or two won't matter."

It matters to me.

"Besides, the delay will give Dr. Forester enough time to complete her analysis," he added.

"Okay."

He cocked his head at her obvious disappointment. "I know you're anxious to get down in that cave, but as I said yesterday, those tunnels are dangerous in the best times. We're not going to take any chances."

She nodded. "It's your call."

"Anyway, we have a more pressing issue this morning," he informed her. "It may be connected to the same case."

That got her attention. "What are you talking about?"

"We've got a lead on the vehicle that sideswiped us last night."

She sat up straighter, her heart thudding in trepidation. "How is that connected to the John Doe case?"

He stood. "Come on. I'll explain everything on the way."

Eve rose, too. "Where are we going? Wait," she said impatiently when he moved away from her desk. "How were you able to get a lead on that vehicle with just the first two letters of the license plate number?"

He turned back. "There's only one registration in our area that matches those two numbers and the vehicle description. The sedan belongs to a man named Ron Naples. Do you know him?"

Eve rolled the name around in her memory banks and then shook her head. "The name doesn't ring any bells. Should I know him?"

"No, but I thought I'd ask since you've lived here all your life. He's seventy-eight years old, lives out near Myrtle Cove. You and I are going to drive out there this morning and have a chat with him."

Eve bit her lip in contemplation as she came around her desk. "His age could explain the erratic driving. Like you said, he may have been distracted or disoriented by the flashing lights. Or there could be a medical problem." She paused. "But none of that explains why you think he's connected to John Doe."

"It involves an anonymous phone call I received last night. The sooner we get on the road, the sooner I can explain everything. You coming?" He didn't wait for her answer, but instead turned and strode down the corridor to the back entrance.

Wild horses couldn't keep me away, Eve thought as she hurried to catch up. She tried to ignore the knot in her chest and the warning shiver up her backbone. *This is just a case like any other.* But she knew better. Fingering the dime beneath her shirt, she followed Nash outside.

The day was already hot and steamy. She paused for a split second to scan the sky. Not a storm cloud in sight. Not the kind she could see anyway.

Her gaze rested on the damaged side of Nash's SUV. The ugly scrapes and dents reminded her all too vividly of that split second of panic when the car's headlights had blinded her, freezing her to the spot like a trapped deer.

She went around to the other side and climbed in. "So don't keep me in suspense," she prompted as Nash started the engine. "Tell me about this anonymous phone call."

He nodded as he slipped on his sunglasses. She could no longer read his eyes, but his mouth was set in a thin line. "Someone using a burner phone called my cell last night. The caller was female. Raspy voice, country accent. Older, I'm guessing, but not elderly. She refused to give me her name."

"How do you think she got your number?"

"I'm still trying to figure that out. The dispatchers don't give out my cell number and I can't imagine Tess ever letting it slip."

No, his administrative assistant was as loyal and discreet as they came. "What did the caller want?" Eve asked.

"She said we should leave the bones alone."

"You think she was referring to John Doe?"

"We haven't recovered any other bones that I'm aware of." He paused briefly to look both ways before pulling out of the gated parking lot onto the street.

Eve wiped her palms on the tops of her thighs. Was it possible the anonymous caller was the platinum blonde she'd seen in the car the night her father went away? His companion would certainly be older, at least in her late forties or early fifties, but it seemed a stretch to think it could be the same woman after all these years. However, if Gabriel Jareau had been murdered, the other two people in the car that night might know something. Who were they and where had they been living since that fateful night?

For years, Eve had sought to understand her father's abandonment. How could a man she'd loved and adored walk away from his wife and child without a backward glance? Now that those answers might be coming to the surface, Eve wanted nothing so much as to turn back the clock to the day before those unidentified remains had been found in McNally's Cave. Before her mother had broken that glass in distress. Before old doubts had once again started to niggle.

"You okay?"

She roused from her reverie with a slight jerk. "What? Yes, I'm fine. Why?"

Nash turned his head to study her for a moment. "You seemed a million miles away. You've been distracted ever since we left the lab yesterday. What's going on, Eve?"

The butterflies stirred again at the way he said her name. Softly. Intimately. Or was that merely wishful thinking?

She stared straight ahead and tried to sound normal. "It's this case. I know you said John Doe isn't a priority, but I can't stop thinking about it. And now that I know about the anonymous phone call, I'm more determined than ever to find out what happened down in that cave."

His voice lowered. "Are you sure that's all it is?"

"Of course. What else would it be?"

He seemed on the verge of saying something else, then turned back to the road. "Maybe I'm a little oversensitive these days. I'm well aware of all the stares and whispers.

People I've known for years have been avoiding me like the plague ever since Grace's arrest."

Eve felt outraged on his behalf, but she merely shrugged. "Ignore them. People in this town like to talk. They'll move on to something else in a few days."

"You don't ever wonder?"

"Wonder what?" she asked carefully.

"If I knew and covered for her."

Eve answered without hesitation. "Not for one second. You would never do that, especially when a child was involved. Besides, you were there when she was apprehended. If you'd wanted to warn her away or help her escape, you could have easily done so."

He said nothing to that even though Eve had the strangest feeling he wanted to open up. *Confession is good for the soul*, she started to remind him, but that would be extremely hypocritical considering the secret she now kept from him.

"What else did the caller say to you?" she asked.

"She implied the hit-and-run wasn't an accident. That the car deliberately swerved toward us last night."

Eve's fingers curled around the edge of the seat. "She admitted that? She actually tried to run us down."

"She claimed she wasn't the driver. She wouldn't admit to being a passenger, either, but she knew all about the incident. If she's right, I can only assume we were followed from the lab. Sure makes the timing of that flat tire suspect."

"Doesn't it, though?" Eve hesitated, her gaze fiercely focused on the road. Time for a small confession of her own. "I saw someone in the parking lot when I came out of the lab last night. The dome light was on in his car. He turned it off when he saw me. I could have sworn—" She broke off.

Nash shot her a glance. "What?"

She shook her head. "It just seemed strange that he turned the light off as soon as he saw me."

"Do you think he was waiting for us?"

"Maybe. He was sitting alone in a dark sedan when I noticed him."

Nash's voice sharpened. "Why didn't you mention this last night?"

"I didn't think much of it at the time. I figured he was waiting to pick someone up from work. Then everything happened so fast on the highway…" She shook her head, as if trying to clear away cobwebs from her memory. "Even now, I can't swear it was the same car. There are hundreds of vehicles on the road matching that description. But now that I know about the phone call, I'm finding it a little hard to chalk up the two incidents to coincidence."

"That phone call changes everything," Nash agreed. "Our cold case has suddenly become red-hot."

EVE STUDIED THE passing scenery in quiet contemplation. The buildings grew sparse as they approached the edge of town. Nothing out that way but a few scattered convenience stores with gas pumps, an automotive garage and an old church on one corner, the weathered spires rising up through a canopy of pecan trees.

Her mother had taken her to that church on Easter Sunday once. Eve could still remember the way Jackie's pretty floral dress had swirled around her slender legs, giving the dreamy illusion that she could float. Eve had hunted Easter eggs with dozens of other children that day, and afterward, they'd met her father for lunch at the diner. Eve had sat on his knee and helped herself to his root beer float. They'd seemed like a normal, happy family, but when she looked back, she had vague recollections of something she didn't understand simmering beneath the surface.

She tucked her hair behind her ears as she glanced at Nash. "Anything else I should know about that phone call?" she asked in dread.

"The woman said we'd been warned."

"Warned," Eve repeated numbly. Her thoughts raced as images flashed in her head. The strange car at the curb. The platinum blonde behind the wheel and the sinister man in the back seat. Her father's last goodbye.

What had that trio been up to the night Gabriel Jareau left town?

The lucky dime suddenly felt cold and ominous against her skin.

"There's something else you should know," Nash said. "Someone was in my house while I was gone. The slider in my office was open when I got home, but I couldn't find any sign of a break-in. No tool marks or broken glass. Nothing. I don't know how they got in."

"What was taken?"

He shrugged. "That's just it. Nothing seems to be missing. There was cash in a drawer and they left it. Didn't touch the laptop or TV. But I'm pretty sure they went through the folders on my desk."

"What do you think they were looking for?"

"I can only guess. I kept a physical copy of the John Doe file at home. The photographs from the excavation site were out of order. I know because I tend to keep things a certain way."

Why did he have a copy of the John Doe file at home? Eve wondered. Did he not trust her to work the case?

"I know what you're thinking," he said.

"I'm not thinking anything, just listening."

"You're probably wondering if I intend to meddle in

your investigation every step of the way, but that's not it. You're right. There's something about this case that grabs you and won't let go. I have a bad feeling there's more to it than an old homicide. I keep returning to that file and studying those images because something is nagging at me, like I'm missing something important." He paused on a grimace. "Does that sound as ridiculous as I think it does?"

"No, because I have the same feeling."

He frowned at the road. "I'm thinking we should work together on this one. Hear me out," he said before she could protest. "You'll still take lead, but I'd like to be involved in the investigation if that's okay with you."

Eve could hardly argue. "You're the boss."

"I'm not trying to pull rank, but this one has become a little personal for me. Right after I received the anonymous phone call, I saw an old pickup truck parked down the street from my place. As soon as I noticed the vehicle, the driver U-turned and sped away. That's when the woman called a second time to tell me I'd been warned."

"You think she was in the truck?"

"That's the impression I got."

"So she's watching your house."

"Apparently she was last night."

Why Nash's house and not hers? Eve thought. Did he have a connection to the case she didn't know about? Or was guilt and paranoia making her suspicious of his motives?

"Here's another question," she said. "Assuming your tire was sabotaged and we were followed from the lab, how did that person know we'd be in Tallahassee in the first place? I didn't mention our trip to anyone, did you?"

"Tess keeps my schedule and she always knows how to reach me, but she also knows to be discreet. If someone had called asking questions about my whereabouts, she would have been alarmed enough to try to get a name and number, and then she would have notified me immediately."

"So maybe our suspect followed us *to* the lab and waited in the parking lot for us to leave. Maybe someone has been keeping tabs on our movements ever since the remains were dug up."

He nodded. "Your mysterious man in the dark sedan."

"Or your anonymous female caller. Or both."

"We've got ourselves a real puzzle, don't we?" She heard her own excitement mirrored in his voice as he flashed her a grin, momentarily lightening the mood. She shrugged and answered with a reluctant smile, keeping things casual. But her pulse thudded as their gazes lingered for a split second. He turned back to the road and she turned back to the passing scenery.

They fell silent again, each lost in thought. Something had occurred to Eve as she stared out the window, but she was hesitant to bring up the subject of Nash's ex-wife. Grace Bowden was a tricky subject for more reasons than one.

"What is it?" he asked.

She turned. "What do you mean?"

"You're thinking hard about something. I can almost hear the gears turning. What's going on inside that head of yours?"

Eve averted her gaze, refocusing her attention on a tiny chip in the windshield. "Actually, I was thinking about Grace."

"What about her?" His tone hardened almost infinitesimally.

Eve braced herself. "Would you mind if I go see her?"

The silence seemed charged all of a sudden, like summer air before a lightning storm. "Why do you want to see her? I don't see the point."

"At the time of her arrest, she said she'd known about the grave in the cavern since she was a little girl. She thought Maya Lamb was buried there." Maya had been the first child to go missing, twenty-eight years before Kylie Buchanan.

Nash lifted a hand from the steering wheel and rubbed the back of his neck, a habit when he was either tired or stressed, or both. "Grace said a lot of things at the time of her arrest. She's not the most reliable narrator of her own story."

"You don't believe she knew about that grave?"

He dropped his hand back to the steering wheel. "Whether she knew or not, she was just a little girl when all that went down. She couldn't have had anything to do with John Doe's murder."

"Of course not. But maybe she wasn't the only one who visited that grave. She said as a child she spent a lot of time exploring McNally's Cave. Maybe she encountered someone else down there at some point."

"The killer returning to the scene of the crime?"

"It does happen," Eve insisted. "I know it's a long shot, but I'd still like to talk to her. Assuming she would agree to see me." Eve paused, trying to analyze his reaction from her periphery. "I'll be respectful. And I'll do my best not to say or do anything that will upset her."

"I'm not concerned about that. It's you I'm worried about."

"Me?" she said in surprise. "I'll be fine."

"You might not sound so confident if you knew her the way I do." He glanced in the rearview mirror as if fearful his ex-wife might have slipped up behind them. "She can come across shy and reserved with strangers, but underneath she's clever and manipulative. The most unrepentant person I've ever known, and that's saying something in our line of work. She isn't at all sorry she took that child. She's only sorry she didn't get away with it."

And yet you married her. Eve bit her lip and nodded. "I'll be careful."

He turned to scrutinize her. "Doesn't matter how careful you are. She'll still find a way to get under your skin and you won't even see it coming."

"If you're that concerned, come with me."

His mouth tightened and she could see the throb of a muscle in his jaw. "I'd rather not."

Was he worried Grace might still be able to get under *his* skin? Was it possible, after everything that had happened, he still had feelings for his ex-wife?

"I understand," Eve said. "Maybe it's for the best that I go alone anyway. She might feel more comfortable opening up to a stranger. If and when she agrees to see me, I'll let you know."

"This is a bad idea," he warned.

She drew a breath, determined to stick to her guns. "Maybe. But if you're really serious about letting me take lead on this case, then I need to do things my way. Grace may know something and not even realize it."

"I won't try to stop you," he said. "But when you're with her, you need to watch what you say and how you say it. Don't let her get inside your head. Don't let things get personal. And whatever you do, don't turn your back on that woman."

Chapter Five

They traveled the rest of the way in awkward silence. As they neared their destination, Eve finally turned away from the side window to study Nash's profile. At the mention of his ex-wife, he'd fallen into a deep funk. She didn't blame him. She could only imagine what must have gone through his head the moment he realized the woman he'd once loved was the suspect for whom he and the FBI had been searching for days.

She strove to relieve the tension by circling back to the subject of Ron Naples. "Can you tell me anything else about him? Do you know if he has family in the area?"

"I haven't had time to run a full background check," Nash said in a clipped, cool tone. "You know as much as I do."

"Do you at least know if he lives alone? We should be prepared for what we may walk into."

"We'll find out soon enough. You've got your sidearm?"

She tapped her holster. "Of course."

"Just keep your eyes and ears open. I'm not expecting trouble, but you never know. I wasn't expecting trouble last night and look what happened." He stopped for an on-coming vehicle and then made a left turn off the highway, heading deeper into the countryside.

"Could have been worse," Eve said.

He nodded, his expression grim. "Now that the adrenaline has faded and you've had time to think back through everything, have you remembered anything else about the vehicle you saw in the parking lot? Partial plate number, any dents or scratches that you noticed?"

"It was dark and raining. If the interior light hadn't been on, I would never have noticed it at all."

"What about the man inside? Can you describe him?"

She thought back, but all she saw in her mind's eye was the nebulous silhouette of the man in the back seat.

"He appeared to be alone. That's the only thing that comes to mind."

"Old, young, thin, heavyset?" Nash prompted.

"I didn't get a good look. I was distracted and the light was only on for a moment after I first saw him." She closed her eyes, focusing her mind on the interior of the car before the light had gone out. "Okay, maybe I do remember something. It's nothing concrete, but I have the impression he was middle-aged or a little older. Fifties, maybe. Average build."

Nash nodded. "That's good. What about hair color?"

"Brown, I think."

"See? We always remember more than we think we do. Just relax and let it all come back to you. What else?"

He put a finger to his lips to silence me. Had he, though? Or had that been a projection brought on by a twenty-eight-year-old memory?

Like Grace Bowden, Eve was an unreliable narrator of her story. So many years had passed since that final night with her father, and yet her memory of his departure was as clear as though it had happened yesterday. But that in itself was suspect. She'd only been five years old when he left. How could she have such a vivid memory of that night? Had she really witnessed him get into a car with two strangers or had everything been a dream brought on by the trauma of his departure?

The woods crowded in on them as they headed north toward the river. Spanish moss hung in thick sheets from the live oaks, and kudzu crept like a dark green shadow up dead tree trunks and over the rooftops of abandoned houses. The landscape was primal and menacing, the air heavy with the dank smell of the swamp.

All along the river, new homes had cropped up alongside prewar bungalows perched on stilts. Ron Naples's home was one of the latter, though the house and yard looked immaculate. A screen porch wrapped around the entire structure, allowing unobstructed views of the water, the woods and the road. No one was about. No vehicles in the driveway. No twitching curtains or barking dogs. The silence seemed eerie and oppressive. Eve suppressed a shiver as she got out of the vehicle and circled around to Nash's side.

"I haven't been out this way in a long time," she said. "It's like being miles from anywhere."

"If you ignore all the new houses," Nash said dryly.

"Yes, there is that. I'd forgotten how the river smells. It's a scent like no other." Her father used to bring her to a spot not far from there to fish. Mostly she'd picked blackberries while he kept an eye on their poles. Or had she imagined that, too?

Eve brushed a mosquito from her eyelashes. "We'll be eaten alive out here."

Nash opened his door and dug around for a can of insect repellant. They both sprayed themselves down.

"Place looks deserted," Eve said as they started across the yard. "Should I go around back while you take the front?"

"Let's see if anyone answers the door first."

Eve nodded and walked up the steps, holding the screen door open for Nash to enter behind her. The shady porch was filled with potted plants and wicker furniture. A good spot to have coffee and watch the sunrise, Eve thought. But despite the pleasant decor, there was something ominous about that space. She felt an inexplicable chill as she glanced through the screen out across the front yard.

"What is it?" Nash asked.

"Nothing. Just being cautious."

Turning, she moved up to the front door and rapped on the glass. When no one answered, Nash called out. "Mr. Naples, this is Chief Nash Bowden with the Black Creek Police Department. Can you please open the door?"

Eve listened for a moment. "I hear voices. Sounds like the TV."

Nash peered through the glass. "No sign of life that I can see. Go on around back, but keep your eyes peeled. Holler if you see anything."

Eve nodded and exited the porch. Already the adrenaline had started to pump, though she couldn't say why. Nothing seemed particularly out of place. The area was quiet and peaceful and yet she felt the same knotted tension in her stomach that she'd experienced yesterday at the lab. The same dreaded certainty that something dark had entered her life.

The foreboding deepened as she rounded the corner of the house. Sweat trickled down her back and dampened her T-shirt. She was glad for the weight of the Glock at her hip. She'd never had to draw her weapon in the line of duty, and she hoped today would be no exception. But someone had deliberately tried to run them down on the side of the highway. Nash's tire had been sabotaged and his house searched. What was going on here? Why had the anonymous caller warned him away from the bones?

Eve's mind raced as she moved into the backyard. The man she'd seen in the parking lot had been no older than midfifties so he couldn't have been Ron Naples. How was Naples connected to that mysterious man and to the anonymous woman on the phone? How were any of them connected to John Doe?

Pausing at the top of the back porch steps, Eve quickly surveyed her surroundings. A dozen or more flies clung to the porch screen, their greenish blue iridescence shimmering in the dappled sunlight. Overhead, a pair of buzzards circled. The still air smelled fusty, an earthy aroma of mud, moss and something Eve didn't want to name. Her heart thudded erratically, and she felt lightheaded as she turned in a slow circle, her gaze spanning the shade trees and the expanse of yard that sloped steeply down to the water's edge. A fishing boat bobbed at the end of the dock.

Something else bobbed just beneath the surface.

Eve froze in horror. Then, with a sharp intake of breath, she bolted down the steps and dashed across the yard.

NASH WADED INTO the shallow water to give Eve a hand as she tried to drag the body ashore. He'd heard her frantic yell all the way around the house to the front porch and his heart had pounded in dread as he raced toward the sound of her voice. She was still calling out to him when he half ran, half skidded down the slanted lawn. By the time he got to the bank, she'd already plunged into the river to grab the corpse.

"He's dead," she said over her shoulder when he called her name.

"I can see that." Nash grabbed the man's arms.

"I didn't know he was dead," she said in a rush. "When I first saw him beneath the water, I thought there was a slim chance he could still be alive. My only thought was to get him out of the water."

"You did the right thing." Nash kept his tone low and even. Her adrenaline was in overdrive. "Just relax. I've got him." He pulled the man out of the water and went through the routine of checking for a heartbeat and pulse even though it was obvious he had been dead for at least several hours, if not a day or more.

The deceased looked to be in his late seventies, fully dressed in khaki Bermuda shorts, a cotton button-up shirt and boat shoes. No sign of a violent attack that Nash could see, but he wouldn't touch the body again until someone from the medical examiner's office arrived. The ME or his investigator would take control of the corpse, running a series of preliminary tests at the scene and then overseeing transport to the morgue.

Rising, Nash cast a glance around their surroundings as he made the necessary calls. The day seemed unnaturally quiet except for the buzz of the blowflies and the soft click of Eve's camera phone.

"We'll need to set a perimeter while we wait," he told her. "There's tape in the SUV. You know the drill. Seal all the doors and the side gate. No one but authorized personnel gets through."

"Are we looking at Ron Naples?" Eve asked as she lingered for a moment longer, her gaze riveted on the dead man.

"Given the description and location, I think that's a pretty safe bet. We'll get verification soon enough. The most important thing right now is to protect the body and preserve the scene."

Eve still couldn't seem to tear her gaze from the corpse. "What's going on, Nash? Ron Naples's car nearly runs us down on the highway last night and now we find him lying facedown in the river. That can't be a coincidence." She glanced up, her blue eyes shadowed. "Everything that's happened seems to be connected to the discovery of John Doe's remains, but how?"

"We don't know anything at this point. Could be nothing more than an accidental drowning." Although an accident seemed doubtful. Like Eve, Nash didn't believe a coincidence likely, but it was best not to draw conclusions until the body had been properly examined and autopsied.

He moved back from the bank, where more blowflies had vectored in on the corpse. Left undisturbed, they'd lay their eggs in all the bodily orifices and first-stage maggots would appear within twenty-four hours. Nash appreciated the value of forensic entomology as much as the next law enforcement officer, but the carrion feeders always gave him the creeps.

Eve, on the other hand, seemed mostly undisturbed by the insect activity. She didn't shy away from the body or the blowflies, merely waved one away from her face as she continued to study the deceased.

"You really think this was an accident?" she asked.

"I think it's possible." Nash rubbed the back of his neck vigorously, where the flesh had started to crawl. "No visible wounds on the body. No sign of a struggle in the immediate vicinity."

Eve wasn't buying it. "It would certainly be a convenient accident if Ron Naples knew who murdered our John Doe."

Nash tried to rein her in. Tunnel vision was the enemy of every good investigator. "Let's not get too far ahead of ourselves. At this point, it's all guesswork."

She nodded and rose. "I'll set the perimeter."

"After you're finished, wait out front and try to keep the gawkers at bay until we can get some uniforms out here."

She nodded again and took off. He watched until she'd

disappeared around the corner of the house and then he turned back to the water and the corpse. What *was* going on here? And why did he have the nagging suspicion that Eve was keeping something from him? She'd been acting strange ever since they'd left the lab yesterday afternoon.

He told himself he was overreacting to her reticence. He tried to put his doubts aside and concentrate on the more immediate mission of protecting the scene, but every few minutes his mind would wander back to the lab, back to the expression on her face when Allison Forester had held up the Mercury dime.

She knows something.

Let's not get ahead of ourselves.

The first squad car arrived in less than ten minutes, followed by the department's crime-scene tech and finally the medical examiner, a heavyset man dressed in an ill-fitting suit. His name was Dan Wexler. Nash had worked with Dr. Wexler for years and found him to be both cooperative and intuitive. Despite his rumpled appearance and lackadaisical demeanor, he could be a real bulldog when all the pieces of a puzzle didn't fit neatly together, a trait Nash greatly appreciated.

By the time Dr. Wexler scrambled down the slope to the bank, he was sweating profusely. He shrugged out of his suit coat, then hung it from a nearby tree branch and mopped his face with a white handkerchief.

"What have we got?" he asked Nash as he wheezed into the handkerchief.

"Looks like a drowning. No sign of a struggle in the immediate vicinity. No visible marks on the body except for a few superficial scrapes on his face."

Wexler eyed him sagely. "I sense reservation. You have reason to suspect foul play?"

"Nothing concrete, but we need to keep an open mind

on this one." Nash glanced over his shoulder. "House belongs to one Ron Naples, seventy-eight-year-old white male."

"Description matches the victim." Wexler set his case on the ground and wiped his face. His complexion had turned an alarming mottled red in the heat. From the man's coloring and labored breathing, Nash was a little concerned he might soon have two corpses on his hands.

"You okay?"

"You mean other than being old, overweight and out of shape?" Wexler stuffed the handkerchief in his pocket. "Yeah, I'm good. You check for identification?"

"No. Except for pulling him from the water, he hasn't been touched."

"We'll run his prints regardless of what we find in his pockets. Neighbors could probably help out with next of kin, but I don't imagine you want any of them traipsing down here just yet."

"We're trying to keep everything buttoned up until CSU has a chance to walk the scene," Nash said.

Wexler glanced out over the river as he rolled up his sleeves. "Feel that? There's a slight breeze coming off the water. That always helps with the smell. Better to find them outside than inside, I always say. Nothing like that stench trapped inside four walls in the middle of summer to turn a strong stomach, and I reckon mine is about as strong as they come." He knelt with some difficulty beside the deceased, opened his case and got down to business. Nash watched from a distance as the ME began his preliminary tests and examination.

"No maggots yet that I can see." He waved aside a fly. "Was the body submerged or floating?"

"Submerged, although he'd already been moved by the time I arrived on the scene. Detective Jareau found the body. She went in after him because she thought he might still be alive."

"I'll need to speak with her. Position of the body can give us an idea of how long he's been in the water. When gases build up and release, a body tends to float to the top."

"So taking that into consideration, what do you think?"

"It's still too early to say with any certainty, but given the position and condition of the body, I'd estimate less than twenty-four hours. If you were to twist my arm, I'd say eight to ten hours. Don't take any of that to the bank. Time of death is hard to pinpoint under these circumstances because the body temperature and rate of decomposition are skewed by the water." Wexler moved around to the other side of the body. "I see some predation around the eyes, so the scavengers had time to find him. Those cutaneous abrasions on his face are probably from scraping against the sandy river bottom." He checked the dead man's hands for wrinkling and *cutis anserine*—goose bumps.

"Anything strike you as out of the ordinary?" Nash asked.

"Hard to say until we get him undressed, washed and on the table."

Now that the uniforms were stationed out front, Eve had returned to await Wexler's preliminary analysis. Nash tracked her from his periphery as she walked to the end of the dock and peered into a small fishing boat. Then she conferred briefly with one of the crime-scene techs. The young officer came over and plucked something from the bottom of the boat, bagging and tagging the item to add to the growing pile.

After a few moments, Eve left the dock and joined Nash on the bank.

He stood. "What did you find?"

She shaded her eyes and nodded toward the end of the

dock. "I spotted an empty whiskey bottle rolling around in the boat, which means you could be right about a drowning accident. I still find the timing suspect, but it's possible Mr. Naples had too much to drink and fell in the water. That could also explain his erratic driving, but only if you ignore the anonymous call you received afterward." She looked as if she wanted to comment further on the caller, but instead changed the subject as she inspected the corpse with a frown. "Does he look familiar to you?"

Nash studied her expression. "No, why? Have you seen him before?"

"I don't think so."

"But?" he pressed.

She shrugged. "I keep trying to put him in that car last night. I'm certain he's not the man I saw in the parking lot. He's too old. As to the car on the highway... I'm hoping something else will come back to me."

"I was there, too," Nash said. "The glare of headlights on rain was blinding."

"I know, but that car came so close to me. I should have seen something."

"That car came way too close," he reminded her. "There wasn't time to think about anything except getting out of the way."

Dr. Wexler rose and motioned to Nash. He joined the man at the water's edge.

"What can you tell us?" Nash asked.

"It's still mostly guesswork, but I don't see anything that challenges my original assessment. The body was likely in the water for at least eight to ten hours."

"That would put time of death around midnight last night," Nash said. Well after he'd received the anonymous phone call.

"As to cause of death, I won't know for certain until I

check his lungs. Even then, a drowning diagnosis is more about circumstances than tests, most of which are unreliable," Wexler explained. "If there are no obvious external injuries, we'll look at the organs and the victim's medical records to determine a natural cause—heart attack, stroke, a seizure of some kind. Any event that could have precipitated the deceased's fall into the water. The lab will run a full toxicology screen to check for drugs and blood alcohol content."

"How soon can we expect the autopsy?" Nash asked.

"We'll need to do it as quickly as possible. Now that he's out of the water, decomposition will accelerate." Wexler removed his gloves and wiped his hands on the white handkerchief. "Meanwhile, I'm done here. We'll bag him up and get him to the morgue. I'll let you know as soon as he's on the schedule."

"You said you wanted to speak to the detective who found him," Nash reminded him.

Wexler glanced up the bank to where Eve stood. "That her?"

"Yes. Detective Eve Jareau."

"Pretty girl, but don't tell her I said so. I don't mean any disrespect. It's just in my line of work, you tend to observe and enjoy beauty whenever and wherever you can."

Nash rolled his eyes. "She's a good investigator. That's all you need to observe."

"Didn't mean to offend." Wexler tucked the handkerchief back in his pocket. "I'll need some of your boys to lend a hand with the body."

Nash motioned to a couple of the uniformed officers and told them what was needed. Two of them went to fetch the gurney from Wexler's vehicle while another two helped bag the body.

Eve moved up beside him, her gaze scanning the scenery. "This place is neat as a pin. Grass freshly cut, trees and bushes meticulously trimmed."

"Not what you'd expect from a heavy drinker," Nash said.

"My thoughts exactly. Maybe that whiskey bottle was planted in the boat to make us think his death was an accident. Maybe Ron Naples wasn't the one driving his car last evening when we were almost run down."

"That's a lot of maybes, Detective."

"Do you disagree?"

"Let's wait and see what the autopsy turns up. Go check inside the house and see what you can find. I'll take the garage."

"The garage is empty," Eve informed him. "I already looked for a dark sedan."

That gave Nash pause. "Maybe he left his car somewhere last night. Maybe he panicked and ditched it after he sideswiped us."

"That's a whole lot of maybes, Chief. I'm thinking it was stolen. That would explain a lot."

Nash had been thinking the same thing. "We need to find that car."

She nodded, but still didn't move away from the bank.

"What is it?" he asked.

She hesitated. "I know you said we shouldn't get ahead of ourselves, but what does your gut tell you about everything that's happened in the past twenty-four hours?"

"That's a tricky question. Yesterday, I would have considered a drowning accident a strong possibility. No reason to believe otherwise. Today…" His gaze drifted back to the bank. "Let's just say, we need to process the scene as if we already know what happened. We'll only get one shot at recovering uncontaminated evidence."

"Yes, sir."

He frowned at her formality.

Oblivious to his disapproval, she lifted a hand to shade her eyes as she scanned the opposite bank where a few rooftops peeked out of the trees. "By midnight last night the rain had stopped and the moon was up. Anyone sitting out on one of those docks might have seen something."

"Once we finish here, we'll start canvassing," he said. "Find out if there's a Mrs. Naples in the picture or anyone else living here. And look for a photo of Mr. Naples inside."

She nodded and without another word walked away. Nash watched her climb the porch steps and pause at the top to twist her hair into a bun at her nape. Then, pulling on a pair of latex gloves, she disappeared inside the house.

He turned back to the river. Now that the body had been moved, the area once again seemed peaceful. The breeze was cool and refreshing, the lapping water against the dock almost hypnotic. But something dark lingered. Not a scent or any piece of evidence, but a feeling deep in his gut that the final shoe had yet to drop.

Lifting his gaze, he scanned the trees, where the ruffling leaves sounded like whispers. What were they trying to tell him? What secrets did this place hold?

Sunlight danced on the surface of the water, drawing his gaze once more to the river. He tried to picture the scene. Had Ron Naples come down to the dock after the rain last night? Facing the water, he might not have noticed a silhouette creeping down from the bank until it was too late. But why ambush a seventy-eight-year-old retiree? Merely to steal his car? Or had Ron Naples known something that got him killed?

Nash knew he should take his own advice and wait for the autopsy, but he had a very bad feeling about Naples's death. A seventy-eight-year-old man sideswipes a police vehicle, almost taking out the detective working a cold case, and less than twenty-four hours later, he turns up dead from an apparent drowning accident.

Was Eve right? Had someone else been driving that dark sedan last night?

And what did any of this have to do with the skeletal remains recovered in a cave at the edge of town, much less with his ex-wife's kidnapping of a four-year-old child?

Too many loose ends. Too many seemingly random events in a short amount of time. So much for living in a sleepy small town.

He turned as one of his forensics techs came down the bank toward him. He was young and ambitious and would likely be snapped up by a larger department with a bigger budget just when Nash was coming to rely on his proficiency. "Find anything?"

"The usual assortment of prints and fibers inside the house. No sign of a break-in or struggle. I'll take what we've collected up to Tallahassee and see what the lab can piece together for us. Anything in particular I should tell them to look for?"

"Anything out of the ordinary. Anything that sets off alarm bells."

"That doesn't exactly set parameters, Chief."

Nash gave the man a curt nod. "Just keep looking and let me know what you find."

The tech went about his business while Nash headed around the house to the detached garage. He peered through a window into the empty bay and then tried the side door. It opened with a squeak. He entered cautiously and felt along the wall for a light switch.

The garage, like the rest of the property, was neat and orderly with shelving along one wall to hold an assortment of paint cans, hand tools and jars of nails and screws. Lawn equipment was tucked neatly underneath the shelves, leaving enough floor space for one midsize sedan.

Nash walked around the area slowly, letting his gaze linger here and there before landing on a corkboard mounted above a worktable. Several notes and to-do lists had been pinned to the board, along with a photograph of a gray-haired man and a young woman. Nash detected a resemblance. The man was Ron Naples, and he assumed the female was a close relative, possibly a daughter. He removed the pin and pocketed the photograph.

Then he backtracked to the center of the garage, where a dark stain marred the concrete floor. He knelt and ran his finger along the edge of the spot. An oil leak. Seemed odd that a man who maintained his property so meticulously would neglect a potentially costly problem with his vehicle. The oil seemed relatively fresh. Maybe Mr. Naples hadn't yet noticed.

Nash finished inspecting the garage and then went back around to the front of the house, where a few neighbors and onlookers had gathered at the edge of the road. Some had walked over from their homes while others had left their vehicles along the curb. They had congregated in a tight little group, their gazes riveted on Nash as they spoke in low tones to one another. He went over to them. A few shuffled their feet and looked uncomfortable, not sure what to say or how to feel in the face of someone else's tragedy.

A man stepped forward, separating himself from the others. "What's going on?" he demanded. "We saw all the police cars parked out front. Did something happen to Ron?"

"How well did you know Mr. Naples?" Nash asked.

The man looked alarmed. "How well *did* I know him? Are you saying he's dead?"

"Of course he's dead," someone behind him piped up. "We saw them load up the body."

The first speaker turned back to Nash. "What happened? We're all Ron's friends and neighbors. I've lived across the road from the man for nearly fifteen years. Seems to me we have a right to know."

"Were you close?" Nash asked.

The man considered the question. "I guess I'm as close a friend as he has around here. Ron's a bit of a loner. Not easy to get to know until he's been around you for a while. He moved down here from Tallahassee when he retired. Wanted a quieter life, he said. His daughter still lives in the city. He drives over to visit her every other week or so. Drove." He corrected himself with a grimace. "Damn."

"Let's speak in private," Nash suggested. The man looked around at the group, then shrugged and followed Nash away from the curious onlookers.

"What's your name?" Nash asked.

"Walt Pearlman. Like I said, I live just across the road."

Nash gave the man a quick assessment. Pearlman looked to be in his late sixties, tall and trim with silver hair and a thick salt-and-pepper mustache. He was dressed like most of his neighbors in cargo shorts, a T-shirt and flip-flops.

"When was the last time you saw Mr. Naples?"

His brow furrowed as he thought back. "A couple of days ago, if memory serves. We both walked out to check our mailboxes at the same time."

"Did you notice anything unusual about his demeanor?"

"Not that I recall. We only spoke for a moment or two. He collected his mail and went back into the house."

"Did he seem distracted or upset?"

"No, but like I said, Ron was a loner. He didn't always stop to shoot the breeze like the rest of us do."

"Can you see Mr. Naples's property from your house?"

"Only if I'm sitting on the front porch or looking out the kitchen window. Look here, Detective—"

"Chief Nash Bowden."

He acknowledged the correction with a brief nod. "What happened to Ron? Heart attack?"

"Why do you think it was a heart attack? Did he have any health problems that you know of?"

"No. As a matter of fact, he seemed healthy as a horse, but the man was pushing eighty. Things start to go south for all of us after a certain age no matter how well we take care of ourselves." He paused. "So what happened to him, Chief Bowden?"

"I'm not at liberty to divulge the details of his death until we've notified next of kin."

The man's expression sobered as he nodded his understanding. "That would be his daughter, Lacy. She's his only family. Ron and his wife split up years ago."

"Is this her?" Nash took out the photograph he'd found in the garage.

"Yeah, although that picture must have been taken a few years back."

"You said Mr. Naples drove to Tallahassee regularly to see her. Do you know if he made that trip yesterday?"

"I doubt it unless she had some sort of emergency. He was there just last weekend."

"Would you happen to have her name and phone number?"

"I can get it for you, no problem. Ron gave me her contact information in case anything ever happened to him. You reach a certain age and you start to think about things like that. About dying alone and no one finding your body until days or weeks later."

"Did you see Mr. Naples's vehicle leave or return late yesterday afternoon?"

"No, but if I had the TV on, I probably wouldn't have heard his car."

"What about during the night?"

"Ron wouldn't have gone out at night, regardless. His eyesight was starting to fail him."

"Was he known to drink alone?"

"Ron? Never saw him drink anything stronger than black coffee." Pearlman shook his head. "Poor Lacy. Ron always spoke about her with so much pride. They were really close. His death will hit her hard."

Nash gently steered him back. "Did you notice if he had any visitors during the past few days? Any strange cars in the neighborhood? Anything at all out of the ordinary that you can think of?"

Walt Pearlman was silent for a moment as he digested that particular line of questioning. "You're not saying... What are you saying, Chief? That Ron was *murdered*?"

"These are just routine questions," Nash explained. "Please don't jump to any conclusions."

"It's hard not to when you won't say what happened to him."

"We're waiting for the autopsy," Nash said. "Until then I'd appreciate your discretion. I'd hate for anything to get back to Mr. Naples's daughter before I have a chance to speak with her."

Pearlman nodded. "Yeah, sure. I won't say anything, but people are going to talk. It's human nature, especially in a place like this. Lots of retirees out here on the river. Lots of people with time on their hands."

Nash glanced back at the group of neighbors. They were all watching avidly from a distance.

"If you wouldn't mind getting me the daughter's contact information, I'd appreciate it," he said.

Walt Pearlman started back toward the crowd, then

turned suddenly and came back over to Nash. "You asked about visitors. This is probably not what you had in mind, but there was a car with a cleaning company logo parked in Ron's driveway day before yesterday. That would have been Wednesday."

"Cleaning company? You mean like a biweekly house-cleaning service?"

"His regular cleaning lady retired a few months back and moved to Orlando to be with her family. I didn't think much of it when I saw the car in his driveway. I figured Ron had hired the service to take Maria's place. He was a bit of a neat freak. He liked things done a certain way, but he was getting too old to do everything himself."

"Do you remember the name of the cleaning service?" Nash asked.

"It's the one with the crown on the mop. You see their vehicles all over town."

"King's Maid Services."

"That's the one."

The same company Nash used. Another coincidence?

He was beginning to think nothing that had happened since John Doe's remains had been removed from that cave was by chance.

"Thank you for your cooperation, Mr. Pearlman."

"I'm glad I could help. I'll just head over to my place and get Lacy's number for you. If you need anything else, let me know."

Nash turned back to the house, where Eve stood staring at him from the front steps. He crossed the yard to join her.

"Anything?"

She shook her head. "The inside is as neat as the out-side. Everything cleaned, dusted and freshly vacuumed. I don't know if that means anything."

"The neighbor noticed a vehicle here on Wednesday

from a cleaning company. King's Maid Services. It's the same outfit I've been using for the past few months."

She lifted a brow. "Do they have a key to your house?"

"Yes."

"We can assume they also had a key to Mr. Naples's house. What do you make of that?"

"It's a long shot, but it could explain how someone was able to enter my place without breaking in," Nash said. "We should find out if the same person cleaned both homes. That could be our common denominator."

Eve nodded. "I'm on it."

"I know where their office and warehouse are located downtown. We can stop by on our way back to the station."

She hesitated with a slight frown then acquiesced. "Sounds good. I have a couple of other leads I want to chase down this afternoon."

Nash was immediately on alert. "Anything you care to share?"

"Let me see if anything pans out first. I'll keep you posted."

What the hell are you keeping from me? Nash wondered again as she came down the steps and brushed past him.

Maybe she was just being territorial. That would explain her reluctance to share leads. But Eve had never struck him as the type to allow ego to interfere in an investigation. He searched for another benign reason for her reticence. She liked to work alone, so maybe she felt awkward or even resentful of his intrusion into the case. On reflection, neither excuse held much water for Nash. Eve was a professional.

Whatever she was keeping from him regarding the John Doe case, Nash would uncover her secrets one way or another.

Chapter Six

King's Maid Services was located in a nondescript industrial park on the outskirts of downtown Black Creek. Loaded semitrucks lumbered down the narrow streets, slowing normal traffic to a crawl. Nash finally maneuvered around one of the vehicles, only to be stopped by flashing lights and descending crossbars at the railroad tracks bisecting the park. He drummed his fingers impatiently on the steering wheel while Eve stared out the side window.

"Bad timing," he muttered.

She turned with a frown. "What do you mean?"

He nodded toward the tracks. "I'm talking about the train. What did you think I meant?"

"Nothing. I was lost in thought, I guess." She looked momentarily disconcerted. "I keep thinking about Ron Naples and wondering if he knew something about the John Doe case that got him killed."

"*If* he was murdered," Nash stressed. "Hopefully the autopsy will provide a few clues if not a definitive cause of death."

"Yes, let's hope." She turned back to the window and fell silent. Nash didn't try to pursue further conversation, but instead used the opportunity to check his messages and then fiddle with the rearview mirror and the AC while they waited for the train to pass. It wasn't like him to be so restless. There was a time when he could spend hours on a stakeout without getting antsy, but the quieter and more introspective Eve became, the more impatient he found himself. Maybe it was for the best they go their separate ways that afternoon. He needed to do some hard thinking on this case. Needed to sit in a quiet place and try to connect some dots.

Finally the crossing bar lifted and he drove across the tracks, checking addresses before he turned down one of the rows of warehouses. He located the crown-and-mop logo painted on the plateglass window and pulled into a spot in the common parking area. A few people were coming and going from the stone-countertop company at the end, but the spaces on either side of King's Maid Services looked to be empty, attesting to the hard times that had fallen on area businesses.

Eve opened the door and paused on the threshold to survey the interior. Then she held the door open for Nash. He took off his sunglasses and stuck them in his shirt pocket as he glanced around the sparsely furnished office. A few minutes ticked by before a woman wearing jeans and a T-shirt with the same logo came in from the back. She looked to be around forty, a petite brunette with hazel eyes that opened wide in shock when she took in their guns and badges.

"What's happened?" Her hand flew to her heart. "Is it my son—"

"We're here about one of your clients," Nash quickly explained.

She closed her eyes on a relieved breath. "Thank goodness. My boy is stationed overseas. He's been away for nearly a year, but I still have a tendency to fear the worst."

Nash gave her a sympathetic nod. "We didn't mean to

alarm you. I'm Nash Bowden with the Black Creek Police Department and this is Detective Eve Jareau."

She glanced from one to the other as she sat down on the edge of the desk. "How can I help you? You say you're here about one of our clients?"

"Are you the owner of the business?" Eve asked.

"Yes, sorry. I'm still a bit rattled. It's not every day the police come walking through my door. Anyway, I'm Delia Middleton. My maiden name was King." She tapped the logo on her shirt. "I took over the business after my dad died last year."

"We're here about Ron Naples," Eve told her. "His house is on River Road near Myrtle Cove. One of your vehicles was seen in his driveway day before yesterday. We'd like you to check your records and tell us who you sent out there to clean his house that day."

Delia Middleton looked uneasy. "May I ask why you need that information? Has he filed a claim against one of my cmployees?"

Eve pounced. "Were you expecting him to?"

"No, of course not. It's just… I can't think of any other reason the police would be here asking me to pull my records."

"Mr. Naples is dead," Nash said. "We're trying to piece together what happened. Talking to the people who last saw him alive is routine."

"He's dead?" She looked shocked. "What happened to him?"

"As I said, we're still trying to piece it together. Can you tell us who cleaned his house the day before yesterday?"

She rose. "Yes, of course. It'll take me a minute to pull up his file. I think I already know but let me make certain." She went around the desk and sat down at the computer. "Normally, we work in teams of two," she explained. "That makes moving furniture easier. Except for office buildings, of course. Depending on the size, we may send as many as four if we can spare the personnel."

"We're only interested in Mr. Naples." While he conversed with Delia Middleton, Eve had positioned herself at the window so that she could peek at the computer screen.

"I'm getting to Mr. Naples," Delia said. "He was an exception to our two-member crew. He was very uncomfortable around strangers. He would allow only one person in his home at a time. Despite that restriction, he was particular about how he wanted things done. His usual house cleaner has been with us for years. Mary is very good with people and she and Mr. Naples got on well. She's been servicing his home for the past month and he seemed satisfied with her performance. But she called in sick this week and we had to send someone else out to his house."

"Who took her place?" Nash asked.

The woman glanced up with a frown. "One of our new employees. Nadine Crosby."

"How new?"

"She started on Monday. Walked in cold asking for a job. I don't normally hire without a trial run, but we were shorthanded and Nadine had references and could start immediately."

"If Mr. Naples was as picky as you say, wasn't it risky sending someone unproven out to his house alone?" Nash asked.

"I explained about Mary's illness and asked if he'd like to reschedule, but he insisted we keep to our regular routine. I had no one else available in his time slot so I decided to take a chance on Nadine."

"Can you tell us where we can find her?"

Delia bit her lip. "I wish I could. I'm afraid she didn't come to work today."

"Did she call in sick?"

"No. She just didn't show up."

"Did you try calling her?"

"No answer." Delia turned from the computer screen and folded her hands on the desk as she glanced up at Nash. "Do you know that feeling you get when your instincts warn you not to do something, but you go against your better judgment and do it anyway? I knew Nadine would be a headache from the moment she walked through the door. I could just tell. I'm not one to judge on appearances, but she had a look about her."

"What do you mean by that?" Nash asked.

She took a moment to answer. "You've heard the old saying, 'rode hard and put away wet?' That's Nadine Crosby. I know that sounds harsh, but it's an apt description. Every mistake that poor woman ever made seems carved on her face. Plus, she's a smoker, and that can also take a toll. Not that she ever lit up around me," she hastily added. "We have a strict nonsmoking policy on the job, but I could smell it on her clothes every morning when she clocked in."

Nash thought about the raspy voice on the phone. *You need to leave them bones alone.*

"Is Nadine from around here?" Eve asked.

Delia rotated her chair to stare up at her. "Born and raised in Black Creek, but from what I understand, she left town years ago. She's only recently moved back."

"Did she say why she came back?"

"Her brother still lives here. I guess she wanted to be close to her remaining family."

"Have you ever met him?"

"The brother? Once when he came to pick up Nadine." Delia suppressed a shudder. "Talk about bad news."

"Why do you say that?"

"He had this look about him. It's hard to explain, but the way his gaze kept darting around the warehouse made me think he was scoping out anything valuable enough to steal. Put it this way. I would never want to meet him alone in a dark alley."

"Can you describe him?" Eve asked.

"Midfifties, maybe. Five nine—five ten, stocky build. Brown hair going gray. Dark eyes, same as Nadine. Piercing. Like he could see right through you."

"That's very precise," Eve said.

Delia grimaced. "He made an impression."

"Do you know his name?"

"Nadine called him Denton. I don't know if that's his first or last name. I guess it would be odd if she called her own brother by his last name, though."

Eve's line of questioning intrigued Nash. Was she trying to place the brother in Ron Naples's stolen sedan? Was he the mysterious man she'd seen in the lab parking lot?

Eve flashed him a glance as if she'd somehow sensed his curiosity. Her gaze said, *Trust me. I know what I'm doing.* He gave her a vague nod.

She turned her attention back to Delia with an answering nod. "Is Nadine younger or older than the brother?"

"A little younger, I'm guessing. She put down her age as fifty on her employment application."

"Do you have a photograph of her?"

"No, it's not a requirement for our records."

"Can you describe her?"

Delia paused. "Scrawny but tough. Rough around the edges, but a real hard worker when she bothers to show up."

"I'd like to take a look at her employment application," Eve said. Her tone remained polite, but she didn't make it sound like a request.

Delia balked, glancing from Eve to Nash as if hoping he would intervene. "I'm trying to be as cooperative as I can, but our employee records are confidential."

"We can get a warrant," Eve said. "But it'll be easier on all of us if we don't have to go that route."

Something flickered in the woman's eyes, a combination of anger, defiance and panic. Nash exchanged another glance with Eve. She knew as well as he they didn't have grounds for a warrant, not even close, but her hollow threat worked on Delia. She printed off a copy of the application and handed it to Eve without a word. She perused the single page with a furrowed brow and then passed the form to Nash.

He skimmed the information and glanced up. "This is her current address?"

"It's the only one I have on file." Delia's phone rang just then. She took it out of her pocket and glanced at the screen. "I'm sorry. I have to take this. It's one of our suppliers. I'll only be a moment." She got up and walked into the back room.

Eve had turned back to the window. "What do you think?" Nash asked as he rounded the desk and glanced at the computer screen.

"She seems a little cagey but that may just be nerves. Some people get jittery around the police."

Nash moved up beside her at the window. "Why all those questions about Nadine Crosby's brother? Do you know something I don't?"

Eve frowned. "No, of course not. It just seemed a viable angle after Delia mentioned him." She paused. "Doesn't it strike you as curious, or even opportune, that Nadine Crosby had only been on the job since Monday? She was sent alone to Ron Naples's house on Wednesday and two days later he's found dead, his car is missing and Nadine doesn't show up for work this morning."

Nash leaned a shoulder against the window frame as he studied her expression. "You'd tell me if you learned something I needed to know about this case, right?"

"Like what?" She met his gaze without flinching, but there was a defensive quality to her voice and demeanor that made him wonder again about what she might be hiding.

"You've been acting strange ever since we left the lab yesterday." He tried not to sound accusing, but it came out that way despite his best effort.

She picked up on his tone and gave him a cool look. "Define strange."

"Quiet. Secretive."

"A lot has happened since we left the lab yesterday. What may seem secretive to you is contemplative to me. I told you. I can't stop thinking about this case."

"You said earlier you have a couple of leads you want to pursue on your own. Why?"

"It's nothing concrete—just a hunch. I don't want to waste your time if it doesn't pan out." She folded her arms. "Is this going to be a problem for you? You gave me a case that no one else wanted and told me I could run with it. Either I'm lead detective or I'm not. Either you trust me or you don't."

He was pushing things too far, Nash realized. His experiences with his ex-wife had made him too suspicious. Eve didn't deserve that. She was a good detective, perfectly capable of running her case as she saw fit and chasing down leads without his interference.

"You're right. I apologize. This case has gotten under my skin, too. It's been a stressful twenty-four hours."

She seemed to want to press the issue further, but then

thought better of it. "I'll go check around back and see if I can sniff out anything. It's stuffy in here anyway. I could use the fresh air."

"Wait a minute." He stopped her as she moved by him toward the door. "Are we good?"

She took a moment, then nodded. "Yeah, we're good."

"Eve…"

He wasn't sure what he meant to say to her. Maybe he just wanted to utter her name so that he had an excuse to study her upturned face, to let his gaze linger over the curve of her lips and the tiny errant strand of auburn hair that brushed against her cheek. He resisted the urge to tuck it back. Now was not the time or place. He doubted there would ever be a time and place for them. That ship had sailed years ago when he'd allowed Grace to dictate the terms of his freedom. Before that even, when he'd returned from Afghanistan with a bullet wound in his shoulder and a slew of nightmares that only grew more disturbing with the passage of time.

She cocked her head slightly. "Is there something else?"

He wondered if she'd noticed his hesitation. Wondered if she sensed the darkness that lay deep inside him. A darkness that his ex-wife had fed on, gathered strength from, but Eve was different. She could either be his salvation or his ruin and Nash wasn't about to take that gamble. "Just be careful."

His caution seemed to take her aback. Or was it something she'd read in his eyes? "Of course. I always am."

"I'm serious," he said. "It seems we kicked a hornet's nest when we recovered those bones in that cave. You may not have secrets, but John Doe sure does."

He could have sworn he saw a shiver go through her. "Do you ever wonder if some secrets are best left buried?"

"That's an odd sentiment for a police detective."

A shadow darkened her expression as she wound a finger around the silver chain at her throat. Her eyes seemed liquid and fathomless. *An enigma wrapped in a riddle.* They'd worked together for the past six years and had shared the intimacy of a kiss, but at that moment, Nash had the feeling he didn't really know Eve Jareau at all.

She seemed to shake herself then and gave a nervous little laugh. "Maybe I'm more exhausted than I realized. I didn't sleep well last night."

"That makes two of us. Go around back and check things out," he said. "I'll finish in here."

After she left, he remained at the window, staring out. The sun beat down relentlessly on the parking lot. He scoured the line of vehicles, looking for a black sedan or the pickup truck he'd spotted the night before racing away from his house. For a moment, he considered the possibility that Delia Middleton could be his anonymous caller, but she didn't have the rasp or the deep country accent of the woman on the phone. Nadine Crosby seemed a more likely candidate.

Delia returned a moment later and said briskly, "You got what you came for. I've given you everything I have on Nadine Crosby. Good luck tracking her down."

He handed her a card. "Call me at this number if she gets in touch."

Delia wiped her hands nervously on the sides of her jeans. "Could I ask you a question before you leave?"

Nash nodded. "Go ahead."

"You think Nadine had something to do with Mr. Naples's death, don't you? She and her brother? That's why you're here asking all these questions about them."

"Neither is considered a suspect at the moment. As I mentioned earlier, we're looking to speak with anyone who may have last seen Mr. Naples alive." Nash walked to the door and then paused to glance back. "By the way, can you tell me who cleaned my house this week?"

The question seemed to take her by surprise. "Your house?"

"Your company sends a team to my place every Thursday," he said. "When I got home last night, someone had left an outside door open to my office."

She grew wary and defensive. "Are you blaming my people?"

"Not necessarily, but it would be helpful to know who was in my house yesterday."

She went back around to the computer and sat down, but she didn't tap any keys, merely stared straight ahead at the blank screen.

"Is something wrong?" Nash asked.

"I can't help wondering what my dad would have to say about all this." She seemed to be talking to herself. "He was such a good judge of character. Never in a million years would he have hired someone off the street the way I did. He was always so careful about vetting and references. You have to be when you're sending employees into private homes. The legal ramifications are enormous. I knew it was a mistake to hire her, but she caught me at a bad time. I was desperate for help, and to be honest, I felt sorry for her. It was obvious to me she'd had a rough life and I figured she needed the money. So I decided to give her a chance."

"Is that your way of telling me you sent Nadine Crosby to my house yesterday?"

Delia closed her eyes on a deep sigh. "Yes. She was a substitute for a member of your usual team." She cringed as if waiting for Nash to berate her.

"Where do you keep your clients' house keys?" he asked.

She blinked, as if the question had caught her off guard.

"In a safe. I hand them out each morning as needed and the teams return them when they come in to clock out."

"Has anyone ever kept a key overnight?"

"Absolutely not. They'd be fired on the spot if they ever tried such a thing. I may be a pushover in certain areas, but I'm a stickler when it comes to my clients' house keys."

"Who has access to the safe?"

"Only me."

Nash slipped the folded employment application in his pocket. "Thanks for your help. We'll be in touch."

Outside, he put his sunglasses back on as he searched for Eve in the bright heat. He almost ran headlong into her coming around the building. He resisted the urge to put his hands on her shoulders to steady her. Or maybe to steady himself. Spending so much time with her was doing things to him. Making him think thoughts he had no right to.

"Sorry," she said. "I have a bad habit of rounding corners without looking."

"Did you find anything?"

"The back door was open. I took a peek inside. Nothing struck me as unusual. Just a bunch of cleaning equipment and supplies. How about you? Did you learn anything more about Nadine Crosby?"

"Only that she was a member of the team sent to clean my house yesterday."

Eve's eyes widened. "So we have that common denominator after all. But why would she leave the outside door of your office open when she could have easily glanced through the files on your desk while she was there?"

"Maybe she was afraid of getting caught. Or maybe someone else wanted a look at those files."

"Like her brother?"

Nash stared down into her upturned face, noting the vivid blue of her eyes and the way the sunlight caught the auburn highlights in her hair. He quickly glanced away. "Let's go find Nadine Crosby and ask her."

THE ADDRESS ON Nadine's employment application led them to a trailer park on the outskirts of Black Creek. The mobile homes were old, the paint faded and chipped, but the grounds were shady and pleasant. Nash located Nadine's place and pulled into the narrow driveway.

Ever since Delia Middleton had mentioned Nadine's brother, Eve couldn't help wondering if they were the pair she'd glimpsed waiting for her father the night he left home. Had he unwittingly gotten into a car with his killers that night? Had he suspected what might happen when he came into her bedroom to say goodbye?

Eve's mind rolled back until she was once again at the window staring out into the darkness. She could see her father under the streetlight as he stored his belongings in the trunk and then climbed into the car beside the blonde without ever once turning to look back in regret. But the man in the back seat had glanced back. He'd met Eve's gaze and warned her to silence.

"The place looks deserted to me," Nash said. "You think she's already cut and run?"

"It's possible. Or maybe she just hasn't had a chance to settle in yet." But Nash was right. Like Ron Naples's house, the mobile home wore an air of abandonment. Save for Nash's vehicle, the driveway was empty, the blinds drawn at every window.

They climbed the wooden steps to the small porch and Nash knocked on the door. It opened silently and Eve peered around him to glance inside. She could make out the shapes of furniture in the dimly lit room, but little else. She sniffed the air. Nothing but the faint scent of marijuana drifting out from the shadows.

Nash pushed the door wider, letting in a shaft of sunlight. "Police! Anyone home?"

"Y'all looking for Nadine?"

Eve turned at the timid inquiry. An elderly woman with a walker observed them curiously from the back deck of the neighboring mobile home. She looked to be well into her seventies if not eighties, white-haired and stooped, but her gaze was razor sharp.

"Have you seen her today?" Eve asked.

"Not today, hon. She moved out. Packed everything up and took off in the middle of the night."

"When was this?"

"Last night around midnight or a little after."

Right around the time Ron Naples had drowned.

"I'm guessing she skipped out on her rent," the woman added. "They don't give you much leeway here. You fail to pay on time, they'll dump all your belongings on the curb."

"Did she say where she was going?" Eve asked.

"I didn't talk to her. The commotion she made loading up her truck woke me up. I looked out my bedroom window and saw her make three or four trips back and forth to her trailer. Then she drove off and hasn't been back since."

Eve walked to the edge of the porch and tried to assume a friendly demeanor. "Do you know if she has friends or family in the area that she might be staying with? Her brother, maybe?"

"I didn't even know she had a brother, but come to think of it, there's been a man coming around once or twice." A breeze ruffled the woman's cotton-fluff hair as she gazed off in the distance, her eyes narrowing as she thought back. "Husky fellow. About yay high." She measured the air several inches above her head. "None of my business who he was or why he was here, but I didn't like the looks of him. I could tell he was trouble from a mile away. Now that you mention a brother, though, he and Nadine did bicker like siblings. I could hear them through my window."

"What did they argue about?"

"I couldn't hear them that well. Just a word or two here and there. But in my experience, a guy like that almost always comes around when he needs money."

"Do you know his name?" Nash asked.

"Only thing I ever heard Nadine call him was bastard."

"Can you describe him?" Eve asked.

"Not tall, not short. Stout but not fat. Brownish hair, best I recall." She shrugged. "I never looked too close. I figured it best to keep my distance."

"What about Nadine? Can you describe her?"

"Skinny as a fence rail, that one. Meth head, most likely. You see that wasted look a lot around here." She glanced across the space between them. "Sometimes I'd see her sitting out there on the steps after dark drinking beer and smoking one cigarette after another. I tried to strike up a conversation a few times, but she made it clear she didn't want to be bothered by the neighbors."

"What about eye and hair color?" Eve asked.

"Her eyes reminded me of the muscadine grapes that grew wild in the woods where I grew up. Dark with almost a purplish hue. And intense. Like she was thinking bad thoughts when she looked at you. Her hair's white like mine, only from a bottle, I think." She shrugged. "That's about all I can tell you."

"Was she close with any of the other residents?" Nash asked.

"Like I said, she kept to herself. Never saw her so much as nod in anyone else's direction."

"You said she drives a truck?"

"An old pickup. Don't know the make or model, but it made a God-awful racket when she took off last night."

"What about the man she argued with? What kind of vehicle did he drive?"

"Couldn't tell you that. I never saw him drive up. He either walked here or left his car in the public parking area out front." She shifted her weight against the walker, her gaze darting from Nash to Eve and then back. "Now I got a question for the two of you. What did she do?"

"Nothing that we know of," Nash said.

"She must have done something or you wouldn't be here. Is she dead?"

Eve gave her a puzzled look. "Why would you ask that?"

"I've been around for a long time. In my experience, things don't end well for people like Nadine."

"She's very much alive as far as we know," Eve assured her.

"Well, then, somebody else must have died. Either way, Nadine Crosby is long gone from this place."

Chapter Seven

A search of the mobile home yielded little more than a trash can full of beer bottles and a pair of overflowing ashtrays. The cheap furniture had been left behind, but the beds had been stripped and the cupboards emptied. Whether she'd been involved in Ron Naples's death or not, Nadine Crosby obviously didn't plan on returning to the trailer.

Back at the station, Eve and Nash parted ways. He disappeared into his office while she climbed into her own vehicle and headed out. She parked down the street from her mother's house and reconnoitered for several minutes even though she told herself she was being paranoid. Despite her mother's accident the night before, she'd gone into work that morning and wouldn't be home until after five.

But Eve was more worried about running into Wayne Brody. She wanted to make sure he wasn't hanging around on the pretext of fixing leaky faucets or sticking doors or whatever. He had a full-time job so hopefully he'd be occupied until Eve was long gone.

The aging neighborhood languished in the midafternoon heat. Eve rolled down her window, letting the nostalgic sounds of lawn mowers and yard sprinklers lull her for a moment while her mind drifted back to her childhood.

Despite the lingering trauma from her father's abandonment, she'd been a happy kid, or at least a contented one after Wayne moved out. She and her mother had always been close. They'd done everything together—shopping, movies, trips to the water park in the summer. Eve had missed her dad—would always miss that twinkle in his eyes and the bedtime stories he'd concocted from his own experiences—but the tension in the house had faded with his leaving. Jackie had seemed more relaxed and easygoing. Or so it had seemed at first. So she had tried to pretend.

Looking back, Eve realized she'd always sensed something bubbling beneath the surface that she hadn't understood. Her mother's blue eyes had been shadowed with something indefinable even when she'd laughed at her child's silly jokes.

Then Wayne had come along and there'd been a different kind of tension in the house. He and Jackie never argued, never so much as disagreed on what to have for dinner, but neither had there been much laughter or open affection. They'd seemed more like amiable roommates than husband and wife. Eve hadn't been old enough to analyze their short-lived marriage, but in retrospect she could only describe it as passionless, though they had shared a bedroom and almost certainly a bed.

She didn't want to think about that. Even now as an adult, the thought of any intimacy between her mother and Wayne Brody made her queasy.

Taking another look around the neighborhood, she closed the car window and got out. Senses on alert, she kept a sharp eye out for any unfamiliar vehicles in the neighborhood in case she'd been followed from the station. Was someone watching her at that very moment?

She cast a wary glance over her shoulder as she crossed the street and turned up her mother's driveway. Making sure she was hidden from any prying eyes on the street, she retrieved the spare key from over the door and let herself into the mudroom.

She'd grown up in that house, was as familiar or more so with the layout and furnishings as she was with her own home. But stepping through the doorway into the kitchen felt as if she'd entered a stranger's abode. She didn't understand her apprehension. She didn't understand why she was looking back now and questioning that shadow in her mother's eyes and the way Jackie would sometimes jump when Eve walked into the room, as if she'd been a million miles away.

She called out softly, "Mom, you home?"

No one answered. No sound at all in the house except for the sudden pounding of her heartbeat in her ears.

What was going on here? Why was she suddenly on edge in her childhood home? Why was she suddenly so uncomfortable with her memories?

"Mom?"

She walked through the kitchen and down the hallway to her old bedroom, pausing to peek inside before she continued into her mother's room. She stood on the threshold and glanced around. She'd always been fascinated by Jackie's space. Everything so pristine and orderly. Bed neatly made. Not so much as a speck of dust on the dresser or chest, no stray clothing dropped on the floor or tossed onto the overstuffed armchair by the window.

Eve had always thought the room pleasant, but it hit her suddenly that her mother's private space was almost antiseptic with the soft gray walls and monochromatic linens. The room said nothing about Jackie's personality or her past.

When Eve left for college, Jackie had stressed that this would always be her home. She never needed permission to come over. But using the spare key to let herself into the house was one thing; searching her mother's bedroom another situation entirely. Eve would hate it if someone came into her home and went through her things. Bottom line, though, she was a cop, so she tamped down her misgivings and crossed the room to her mother's closet.

Eve had long ago discovered the boxes of mementos her mother kept shoved in a corner. She'd gone through them once looking for photographs of her father. Now she dug down through the keepsakes to uncover the school yearbooks at the bottom. Arranging them chronologically, she sat cross-legged on the floor and pored through the pages, running her finger down the list of names until she found the person she was looking for among the sophomores—a girl named Nadine Crosby.

Eve expelled a sharp breath, as if she'd taken a hard punch in the gut. She hadn't seen the blonde's face that night, had never known her name until now. *Nadine Crosby.*

Her hair was long in the photograph, but the same white-blond from Eve's memory. Her gaze was slightly hooded, her smile edging from shy to coy. She was attractive, but more striking than beautiful with her dark eyes contrasting so vividly against her platinum tresses.

So you're her. My dad's other woman.

After all these years, the blonde behind the wheel had a name and a face.

Eve thumbed back a page and located her mother's smiling image. She and Nadine Crosby had gone to school together, had likely been in some of the same classes. How well had Jackie known her? Had her mother suspected the icy blonde was the reason her husband had left her? Or was she as oblivious to the other woman's identity as she claimed?

After the initial shock, Eve went back to the beginning of the yearbook and traced the names in her father's senior class until she stopped once more on the name Crosby. Denton Crosby. *I could tell he was trouble from a mile away.*

Yes, Eve thought. He'd had that look even in high school. Dark, intense eyes. A sneer instead of a smile. Tough guy. Bad news all around.

Eve had met guys like Denton Crosby both in her line of work and as a child when her father's friends had come around. Despite Gabriel Jareau's charm and easygoing demeanor, he'd been drawn to people like Nadine and Denton Crosby, people who flaunted laws and social mores. People her mother would never allow into the house when they showed up on their motorcycles or in their souped-up cars with loud mufflers.

In Eve's mind, she could see Denton Crosby looking out the car window, zeroing in on her bedroom window as if he'd somehow known she was watching them.

Of course, she could be wrong about the brother and sister. She had no real proof they were the pair who'd waited in the car for her father that night. She hadn't been able to see either of them clearly. There came a point, though, when a string of events could no longer be considered coincidental.

After returning everything to the box except for the one yearbook, she shoved her mother's keepsakes back into the corner of the closet. She moved into the bedroom and was just heading out into the hallway when a sound stopped her cold. Someone had come in through the back door.

She thought at first her mother had come home from work early. Eve tried to come up with an appropriate excuse for being in Jackie's house in the middle of the day. She waited for the familiar click of her mother's heels on the parquet floor, but nothing came to her except a tense, waiting silence.

Inching her way along the wall, she peered through the small dining room into the kitchen. A man stood at the open refrigerator taking stock of the contents. Then, grabbing a beer from the door, he turned and fumbled through the nearest drawer for an opener.

Wayne Brody tossed the lid in the garbage, then took a long swallow from the bottle as he moseyed from the kitchen through the dining room and into the den. He walked around the room, touching this, touching that, before pausing in front of the window to stare out at the street.

Eve didn't know what to make of his behavior, nor could she figure out why she didn't confront him. *Wayne, what the hell do you think you're doing?* His conduct seemed odd and overly familiar even for Wayne. So instead she hung back in the hallway, pressing her back against the wall as she watched him.

After a moment, he returned to the kitchen and polished off the beer while retrieving his toolbox from the mudroom. Disposing of the empty, he grabbed another bottle from the fridge and ambled back into the dining room, but this time he headed for the hallway instead of the den.

He was coming straight toward her. Still unsure of why she felt the need to hide from her mother's ex-husband, she scurried back to Jackie's bedroom and tracked Wayne through a crack in the door. She told herself he could have a perfectly innocent reason for his visit. Maybe he'd come back to finish the leaky faucet task he'd abandoned the evening before when Jackie cut her hand. Maybe Eve felt the need to conceal her presence because Wayne Brody wasn't the only one violating her mother's privacy.

He paused at the bathroom and bent to set the toolbox

on the floor. Then he slowly straightened, his gaze riveted on Jackie's bedroom door. Eve shrank back, wondering if he'd spotted her through the crack. She heard the soft thud of his boots as he came toward her. She retreated to the closet, leaving the door ajar so she could track him if he came into her mother's room.

The footsteps stopped. A second later, he toed the door open, then stood on the threshold, one arm propped on the door frame as he surveyed his ex-wife's private domain. He took a long swig from the bottle, his gaze seemingly fixated on the bed. Then he meandered around the room much as he'd done in the den, drawing his hand along the top of the dresser, down one of the bedposts and across the linen duvet cover.

Returning to the dresser, he opened the top drawer and removed what looked to be one of Jackie's nightgowns. Holding the silky fabric against his face, he breathed in deeply before moving back to the bed.

Eve's skin crawled as she watched him. She wanted nothing so much as to kick open the closet door and scream at him to keep his hands off her mother's things, to get the hell out of her house and never come back. But she held back now because she needed to know what he was up to. How often did he come into her mother's home when she was gone and touch her things?

Setting his beer on one of the nightstands, he stretched out on top of the bed and propped his head on the pillows. Wrapping the nightgown around both hands, he snapped the fabric taut, as if testing the strength. Eve shivered as her hand crept to the dime beneath her shirt.

Taking out her phone, she snapped a photograph through the crack in the door. The click of the shutter sounded as loud as a rifle shot to Eve. She wasn't even sure she had him in focus, but she didn't want to risk giving herself away by taking another. Holding her breath, she waited for him to react to the sound. Engrossed in his own creepy thoughts, he remained seemingly oblivious to her presence.

Finally, he rose from the bed, fluffed the pillows and smoothed the impression of his body from the duvet cover. He picked up the beer bottle and wiped away the moisture from the nightstand with his sleeve. Then he returned the nightgown to the dresser drawer and left the room.

Eve trailed after him, watching from behind the bedroom door as he picked up the toolbox and disappeared down the hallway. He obviously hadn't come here to repair the leaky faucet or anything else. He'd brought his toolbox in case Jackie came home unexpectedly and caught him.

His behavior was beyond unsettling. Eve was shocked but not surprised. Not really. Maybe there was a reason she'd never warmed to Wayne Brody. Kids had good instincts about certain people. Maybe deep down she'd sensed something dark and disturbing behind his good-guy demeanor.

She'd have to tell her mother, of course. The sooner Jackie rid herself of Wayne Brody's presence in her life the better. But it might be a bitter pill for her to swallow. Jackie's first husband had left her for another woman. She'd always comforted herself with the knowledge that even though her marriage to Wayne hadn't worked out, she was capable of attracting someone loyal and decent. Someone who loved and adored her and wanted nothing more in the world than to care for her and her child.

Eve would have to find a way to break it to her gently, but break it to her she would. Her mother needed to know what kind of man Wayne Brody really was.

Of course, that would mean admitting to Jackie that Eve had also entered her house and gone through her things. That would mean she'd have to come clean about her suspicions regarding the identity of the skeletal remains. Jackie would be angry and hurt that Eve hadn't told her earlier, but she'd get over it. Their disagreements never lasted long.

Nash was a different story. He'd have every justification for taking the case away from her just when she was finally getting the answers she'd so desperately needed for years.

Checking both ways down the street for Wayne's truck, she returned to her car and lowered the window to allow heat to escape while she phoned her mother at work. Jackie answered on the first ring.

"Dr. Mercer's office."

"It's me, Mom."

"Evie? Why are you calling me on the office phone? You know I don't like to tie up the line with personal calls."

"I know, Mom, but I was afraid you wouldn't answer your cell."

Jackie was instantly alarmed. "What's wrong? Are you okay?"

Her anxious tone reminded Eve of Delia Middleton's earlier concern about her son. "Yes, I'm fine. I just wanted to check and see how you're feeling today. How's the hand?"

"It hurts, but I'll live."

"I'm not surprised. That cut is deep. I thought I might come over later and do some chores for you. Whatever needs to be done, just name it. Maybe afterward we could talk."

Her mother hesitated. "That's sweet of you, Evie, and in a day or two I'll take you up on the offer. Today I just want to go home, take one of my pills and crawl into bed. It's been a long day. I'm exhausted and my head is throbbing."

"But you have to eat. I could bring dinner," Eve suggested.

"Wayne already offered, but I told him not to bother. If I get hungry I'll make some scrambled eggs and toast."

"Speaking of Wayne—"

"Don't start," her mother warned. "I'm not in the mood."

"But there's something you need to know."

Jackie held firm. "There is nothing I need to know that can't wait. I'm asking you to respect my wishes. Give me some space. Is that too much to ask?"

"No…"

"I'll call you tomorrow. We'll have dinner together soon, I promise. Right now I need to get back to work."

She hung up before Eve could utter another word, much less a proper goodbye. That wasn't like Jackie, but then, her mother's brush-off only added to Eve's growing list of strange behaviors in the people around her.

Someone rapped on the passenger-side window. Eve glanced around to find Wayne Brody peering in through the glass. How long had he been standing there and how much had he overheard?

Reluctantly, she lowered the window. He propped his forearms on the door and ducked his head to give her a curious stare. "I thought that was you. What are you doing parked all the way down here?"

"I pulled over to make a call," Eve lied. "Safety first."

His gaze dropped briefly to her holstered weapon. "Still on the job or are you headed home?"

Eve shrugged and forced a nonchalant tone. "Still on the job. I happened to be in the area, so I thought I'd drive by Mom's and see if she's home."

He looked skeptical. "It's the middle of the afternoon. You know she never leaves the office before five."

"I was hoping she'd knocked off early today."

"Why didn't you just call her to see if she's home?"

His interrogation irritated Eve. She was tempted to confront him with what she'd seen inside her mother's bedroom, but she wanted to talk to Jackie first. Why give

Wayne the chance to come up with a plausible excuse, one that might leave Eve looking paranoid and vindictive in her mother's eyes? Jackie had always been strangely defensive when it came to Wayne Brody.

Eve scowled across the seat at him. "Not that I should have to explain myself to you, Wayne, but I already told you—I was in the area anyway. Now it's your turn. What are you doing here?"

His gaze was very direct, almost too intense. Did he know she'd been watching him? "I live in the neighborhood, remember?"

She nodded through the windshield. "Your house is down that way."

"I ran home for a late lunch and thought I'd fix that leaky faucet while I'm here. One less thing for Jackie to worry about."

"Did you check with her first?"

"Why would I do that? I know where she keeps the spare key. She told me a long time ago I could come and go as I needed to."

Eve's gaze narrowed. "How often is that?"

He cocked his head. "Can I ask you something? I'd like an honest answer. What's your problem with me?"

"Who said I had a problem?"

He grinned. "You've never made any bones about it. When Jackie and me got married, you were just a little kid. I could understand your bratty behavior back then. You didn't like the idea of someone taking your daddy's place, let alone sharing your mama. But you're a grown woman now, Evie."

"Don't call me that."

"Maybe you should get your own life, *Eve*, and quit sticking your nose in your mama's personal business."

"Maybe you should take your own advice," Eve shot

back. "Stop hanging around my mother and hoping for something that's never going to happen."

His tone remained amiable, but his gaze hardened. "You don't know anything about me. Or Jackie, either, for that matter. You think you know her, but you don't. Not like I do."

"What's that supposed to mean?" Eve demanded.

"Jackie and I share a bond that even you can't break, though God knows you've tried. We have history."

"Yes, and there's a divorce in that history, in case you forgot."

He gave her a knowing look. "It kills you that we're still friends, doesn't it? More than friends. I would do anything for her and she knows it. Unlike Gabriel Jareau."

Eve gripped the edge of the car seat. "Leave him out of this."

"Why? Because you still want to believe he was someone special? I get that," Wayne said. "Your daddy had a way about him. Everybody liked him. But when you got past his smile and all that smooth talk, he was just a petty criminal like all his buddies. You ever ask yourself what kind of man turns his back on his own child?"

Yes, Eve thought. *Every day since I was five years old.*

"You ever ask yourself why he up and left the way he did? What he might have been running from?"

Eve's voice rose sharply. "What are you talking about?"

Wayne hesitated, as if on the verge of revealing some deep, dark secret about her father. Then he said with an enigmatic smile, "You really have no idea what he was capable of, do you?"

Chapter Eight

Eve couldn't stop thinking about the confrontation with Wayne Brody and the implication that her dad had been mixed up in something illegal. That should have come as no surprise. She'd always suspected he and his companions had been up to no good that night. As much as she hated to admit it, Wayne was right about one thing. There must have been a reason her father had left town the way he had.

Wayne was certainly no innocent, either. His creepy little visit to her mother's bedroom was beyond disturbing. Eve had never considered him dangerous and even now, she was hard pressed to imagine him a physical threat to Jackie. But she couldn't know that for certain. She had to find a way to warn her mother without putting her on the defensive. She had to get to Jackie before Wayne could somehow spin the situation in his favor. Eve had learned years ago never to underestimate her ex-stepfather and the inexplicable connection he shared with her mother.

As she settled in at her desk, she tried to put Wayne Brody out of her head and immerse herself in the John Doe case. It was a relief when Nash called her into his office late that afternoon to go over their notes. Even then, her mind kept wandering until Nash finally tossed his pen onto the desk and closed his notebook.

"What's up?"

Eve answered absently. "What?"

"You're distracted. You've barely said two words since we started."

"I'm sorry." Eve tried to shake off her mood. "I'm worried about my mom. She cut her hand last night, and I'm afraid the injury may be more serious than we first thought. I talked to her a little while ago and she seems to be in quite a bit of pain."

"I'm sorry to hear that," Nash said. "Has she seen a doctor?"

"Yes. Her ex-husband drove her to the ER last night."

Nash lifted a brow. "Her ex-husband?"

Eve made a face. "Wayne Brody. They've remained close since the divorce."

"And you don't approve?"

"Wayne is…" She struggled for the right word to convey her concern and disgust. "No. I don't approve."

Nash settled back in his chair, willing to listen. "How long ago did they split up?"

"Over twenty years ago."

He looked amazed. "And they've managed to remain friends all that time?"

"Unfortunately, yes."

He tilted his head as he took in her expression. "Why don't you like him?"

Eve wanted to tell him what she'd witnessed earlier at her mother's home, but bringing personal problems into the workplace was never a good idea, so she tried to sum up her concern as succinctly as possible. "I don't trust him. I don't believe he's the kind of man he pretends to be. I think he's carried a torch for my mother all these years and he'll do anything to ingratiate himself with her." She stopped short and took a breath. "But that's more information than you ever needed to know about Wayne Brody.

Let's get back to our notes. I promise you'll have my un-divided attention from now on."

"I think we've pretty much covered everything. Unless you have something you want to add."

"No, I'm good."

He straightened and shuffled some papers on his desk. "Then take off. Go see your mother."

"I appreciate the offer, but she won't be home from work yet. Besides, I've still got reports to file."

"The reports will keep until morning. Go home, Eve. Come back in the morning with a fresh prospective."

She was tempted to do just that, but once she got back to her desk and saw the stack of reports waiting to be com-pleted and filed, she decided to dig in for a bit. As usual, she lost track of time. When her stomach grumbled, she finally pushed away from the desk, stretched and collected her things from her locker before heading out.

Once at home she went through her regular routine of sorting through the mail and searching through the fridge for something to eat. Then she took a long shower, put on some comfortable shorts and her favorite T-shirt and went out to the backyard to relax.

The freshly mown grass tickled her bare feet as she walked across the lawn to the old swing suspended from a tree branch with chains. Settling herself on the cush-ions, she folded one leg beneath her while gently toeing the swing back and forth. She sat for the longest time watching the light fade as twilight crept in. Her garden grew shadowy and redolent. She thought about calling her mother, but Jackie had made it clear she wanted the eve-ning to herself. Fair enough. She'd been through a lot, but Eve couldn't help wondering if her mother's insistence on being alone was a pretext to avoid more questions about Eve's dad.

The scent of the angel's trumpet against the fence hung heavy on the evening air, triggering a powerful melancholy. Eve found herself thinking again of the night her dad left as she drew the coin from her neckline and caressed the cool metal between her fingers.

Someone's coming, Boo.

Which had come first? she later wondered. Her father's phantom warning or the telltale squeak of her garden gate?

She tensed, her head whipping toward the sound as a figure materialized in the dusk. Instantly, she thought of the Glock in her nightstand drawer. Then she flashed to Wayne Brody pawing through her mother's private things and his subtle taunt that she knew nothing of the bond they shared, nothing of the crimes her father had committed before he left town.

"Who's there?" she called out.

"It's me."

Her heart tripped at the sound of Nash's voice even as she experienced a sharp sense of relief that her ex-stepfather hadn't come calling.

Nash had never been to her house before. How did he even know where she lived?

And how disconcerting to see him striding so surely across her shadowy backyard as if he'd been there many times before.

All this went through her mind in the blink of an eye as he approached. He still wore the clothes he'd had on earlier, so Eve figured he'd come straight from the station.

"Don't get up," he said when she started to rise. "I hope it's all right that I stopped by without calling first. I rang the doorbell, but I guess you didn't hear it."

She dropped back down on the cushions. "How did you know to look for me out here?"

"I heard you mention once that you spend most of your

evenings in the garden." He glanced around at the lush vegetation. "I can see why. This must take an awful lot of work."

Eve tucked the dime back into her neckline. "Most of it was planted before I moved in, but I like to putter around out here and pretend I know what I'm doing. I actually enjoy pulling weeds. It's mindless but productive." *You're rambling, Eve. Just shut up.* She paused to stare up at him. "Why are you here?"

"I thought we should talk."

That either sounded ominous or promising, but Eve allowed nothing more than mild curiosity to seep into her voice. "About the John Doe case?"

His slight hesitation sent a shiver up her spine. "Yes."

"Would you rather talk inside?" Would that be more or less nerve-racking? she wondered. "It's still pretty warm out here and the mosquitos will be bad now that it's getting on dark."

"No, I like the fresh air. I've been cooped up in the office for hours." He canted his head and drew a long breath. "What's that scent?"

"Angel's trumpet. It blooms all summer long. Sometimes the fragrance can be a bit overpowering in the heat." There she was, rambling again. Small talk had never been her strong suit, especially when caught off guard. Even less so when it came to Nash Bowden. Why was he really here?

"Angel's trumpet," he murmured. "Is that the one with the big bell-shaped flowers? My grandmother grew it in her garden. She had a little place in Franklin County near the Gulf. I spent every summer there until I joined the army." His tone subtly altered. "Seems like a lifetime ago now."

Nash had never been one to share his personal life with his colleagues. This glimpse into his past mesmerized Eve.

She drew up her legs and wrapped her arms around her knees. "Are you and your grandmother still close?"

"She passed away while I was stationed overseas."

"I'm sorry."

He shrugged. "No need to be sorry. She lived a long, happy life and then went peacefully in her sleep. That scent took me back to her for a moment."

"Do you want to sit?" She unfolded her legs and scooted over to make room for him on the swing. He sat down beside her, brushing up against her bare thigh. Another thrill shot through her. She tugged on the cuff of her shorts and told herself to relax. She'd been in Nash's company all day long. This was no different. But somehow being here with him in her fragrant garden seemed too familiar, almost unbearably intimate.

Could he tell she was nervous? Could he sense the flutter in her stomach and the sudden rush of adrenaline through her veins? Her face felt flushed. Could he see that, too? She'd tried so hard to keep her emotions in check ever since that ill-conceived kiss, but they were sitting so close and tonight he seemed so vulnerable and approachable. She wondered what had brought on his reflective mood.

"The autopsy is scheduled for seven in the morning," he said, dousing the heat of her attraction with a splash of cold reality.

"Oh. Okay. That's pretty early."

"There's really no need in both of us attending," he said.

She gave him a pointed glance. "Are you volunteering?"

"If you've no objection."

"You don't need my permission, obviously, but that's fine by me. I've never gotten used to autopsies."

"No one does. I'll let you know if anything interesting turns up." He curled his fingers around the chain and used his feet to rock them to and fro. They swung in amiable silence for a moment, their faces tipped to the breeze. The perfume from the flowers deepened, lingering in the senses like a memory. In such a dreamy setting, it seemed almost obscene to discuss murder, but they were both cops and there was an old homicide and possibly a fresh one still to solve.

"Any news on the Nadine Crosby front?" she asked.

"Not yet. Have you heard anything?"

She tucked back a loose strand of hair. "I plan to talk to Delia Middleton again tomorrow. She may have remembered something now that the initial shock of finding us in her office has worn off. I'd also like to speak with some of the other employees. Maybe one of them knows something about Nadine's whereabouts."

"Let me know what you find out."

She nodded, staring straight ahead, but she could see him from her periphery, knew that his eyes were on her, too. *This is so strange*, she thought. Disconcerting and titillating all at the same time.

"How's your mom?" he asked. "You seemed really worried about her this afternoon."

"I'm still worried. I haven't seen her today, but when I called earlier, she said she wanted to take a pain pill and go to bed. I'm trying to respect her wishes, but it's hard because I need to talk to her about something important and it could drive a wedge between us if I'm not careful."

"That's a tough one," he said. "Does it have something to do with the ex-husband you mentioned earlier?"

Eve nodded. "I found out something upsetting about Wayne, but she always gets defensive when I bring him up. It's like he has some kind of weird hold on her."

"Are you sure it's something she needs to know?"

Eve turned and met his gaze in the twilight. "I caught him in her house earlier going through some of her personal things. It makes me wonder how often he's done that in the twenty years since they split. Then he laid on her bed and garroted the air with her nightgown."

"He what?"

She simulated Wayne's disturbing action. "I've never thought of him as dangerous, but his behavior is troublesome, to say the least."

"That is troublesome," Nash agreed. "Sometimes it only takes the smallest trigger to set someone off."

Was he thinking about his own situation with Grace? What had prompted her to abduct little Kylie Buchanan? Had she been trying to fill a void or to get Nash's attention?

"Then you think I should tell her?" Eve asked.

"I think you have to."

It was such a relief to confide in someone, but she had no right dropping that burden on Nash. Grace's court date was coming up soon. He had more than enough on his plate without taking on Eve's problems. "I'm sorry. I didn't mean to get into all that again. You didn't come over here to listen to my problems."

"I wouldn't have asked if I didn't care." He stretched his arm along the back of the swing. "Tell me more about this guy. You said he and your mom have been divorced for over twenty years. He never remarried?"

"I doubt he even dates," Eve said. "He bought a house down the street from my mom's so he can be at her beck and call night and day. That's not normal, right? It's not just me."

"It sounds a little codependent," Nash said.

"Yes, and my mom only encourages him by using him as her private handyman. The least little thing goes wrong and she calls Wayne to come over and fix it."

"Maybe she still has feelings for him, too," Nash suggested.

Eve winced. "Bite your tongue. To be honest, I don't

think she ever got over my dad. If I were to ask her, she'd deny any lingering feelings, but she gets this faraway look in her eyes whenever he's mentioned. He was her first love. They were high school sweethearts although they didn't marry until my mom turned twenty-one."

"Is your dad still in the picture?"

Eve tensed. *Yes, I think he might be.*

Now would be the perfect time to come clean about her suspicions regarding John Doe's identity. Confess everything and let the chips fall where they may. Maybe Nash would surprise her and allow her to remain on the case. But he had protocol to follow and Eve wasn't willing to take the chance he'd make an exception. Not when she'd just learned the identity of her father's companions, possibly his killers. Assuming, of course, the skeletal remains were his.

"He left when I was five," Eve said. "He took off one night and never came back."

"You never heard from him again?"

"He sent a few postcards to me and some money to my mom, but he never called or tried to see me. Mom always believed he left us for someone else. Another woman. I guess his new love was the only family he wanted or needed."

"That must have been hard on you, losing your dad like that."

"I adored him. For him to just up and leave us… It was devastating." Nash's arm was still draped along the back of the swing. Eve resisted the urge to lay her head against him. "That was the same summer Maya Lamb went missing. She was only a little bit younger than me and she didn't have a father to protect her, either. For the longest time, I was terrified that her kidnapper would come in through my bedroom window one night and take me, too."

"You weren't the only one with that fear," Nash said. "I talked to a lot of people about Maya's abduction after Kylie Buchanan went missing, when we still thought there might be a link. My impression is that the town never got over Maya's kidnapping. Twenty-eight years after Maya disappeared, a shadow still hovers over Black Creek. Maybe that's why Grace was able to convince even law enforcement that the same person who abducted Maya also took Kylie. We were predisposed to look for that connection."

His eyes gleamed darkly in the moonlight. Eve could sense his warmth, could almost hear his heartbeat. He'd never talked to her so openly about his ex-wife's heinous crime and Eve had never felt so close to him as she did at that moment.

"Grace knew intimate details of Maya's kidnapping because, like me, she's lived in Black Creek for most of her life," Eve said. "As a child, she even became friends with Maya's twin sister, Thea. That surely made an impact on her. Years later, she used everything she'd learned from Thea, everything she'd taken from their home when she decided to abduct Kylie Buchanan. I'll say it again, Nash. She was very clever. No one could have seen that coming."

He was silent for a moment. "You're right. She is very clever. Which is why I think it's a mistake for you to talk to her."

"I know you do, but she may not agree to see me anyway. The subject could be moot."

"She'll see you."

Eve could hear the tension in his voice. "How do you know?"

"Because I know her. The chance to garner empathy from someone who works closely with me would be irresistible to her."

"I don't empathize with her."

"Not yet."

Eve's hackles rose in defense. "Give me a little credit. I know how to handle myself."

He looked as if he wanted to argue that point, but then he conceded. "Sorry. I have a tendency to overreact when it comes to Grace. I know you can handle yourself. I wouldn't be here otherwise."

"What do you mean?"

He stopped the swing with his foot. Everything suddenly seemed a little too quiet in the garden. "A forensic psychiatrist named Linda Anderson called the station earlier to set up a time for your visit."

Eve turned in surprise, searching his profile in the dusk. "Why contact you? I'm the one who made the request."

"She needed to confirm you'd gone through the proper channels. It's complicated with Grace's hearing coming up. Her attorneys also had to sign off on the visit. They've limited your time and the scope of the interview. You won't be allowed to ask questions about Kylie Buchanan's kidnapping."

"I understand."

"The meeting will be video recorded so you'll need to keep the focus on the John Doe case. It's imperative you not give Grace anything that she and her attorneys can use in court."

"When can I see her?" Eve was suddenly nervous about the prospect.

"Tomorrow morning, nine o'clock sharp. Dr. Anderson will make all the necessary arrangements. An escort will meet you at the metal detectors and take you back."

"That soon?" Eve had thought she might have a day or two to prepare.

"I suspect Grace had a hand in the timing. Her immediate need for attention undoubtedly overcame her desire to have me stew for several days about what she might be up to."

"I'm sorry this is so hard for you," Eve said. "If there was any other way—"

"Don't worry about me. I'm fine." He didn't sound so fine.

"You don't need to worry about me, either. I'll make sure I'm at the hospital on time and I'll be careful what I say to her. I'm guessing that's why you're here, isn't it? You could have told me about the autopsy over the phone. You were hoping you could talk me out of going to see her."

"Yes," he replied candidly. "I didn't think it would work, but I had to try."

"You're really that concerned?"

"She'll have an agenda," he warned. "She always does."

"And yet you married her." The comment slipped out before she could stop herself, but she really didn't regret her bluntness. She'd wondered for years how such an ill-fated match had come about. *But look at Mom and Wayne Brody.* People married for all kinds of reasons. She still didn't understand why or how her mother could have succumbed to Wayne's charmless courtship. Had she been that lonely after Eve's dad split?

"I married her because she saved my life," Nash said. "But that's a long story and I think Grace has occupied too much of our time as it is."

Was he talking about tonight or the past six years? Eve ran a hand up her bare arm, where goose bumps had risen despite the steamy heat. Had his fingers brushed against her hair or was that merely her imagination?

He glanced out over the garden toward the house. "I've always wondered about where you live," he said unexpectedly.

She swallowed. "You have?"

"Sometimes I've tried to picture you out here in your garden."

Eve had no idea what to say to that. The low rumble of his baritone voice in the dark made all those goose bumps tingle with awareness. "My childhood home is a few blocks from here. My mother still lives in the same house where I grew up."

"It's a nice neighborhood. I like all the trees." Was that a note of disappointment in his voice? Had he wanted the conversation to go in a different direction? It would be up to him to steer her back, Eve decided. She'd made the first move once and the humiliation still lingered, despite the intensity of his response.

"It's been just my mom and me for most of my life," she said. "When I left for college, it was the first time we'd spent more than a night apart."

"Is that why you came back to Black Creek? To be near her?"

"I lived in Tallahassee for a while after I graduated. It never felt like home."

"I get it," he said. "Roots are important. Or so I'm told."

She turned at that strange edge in his voice. "What about you? Where did you grow up?"

"My dad was in the military so we lived all over the place. Spending summers with my grandmother was the closest thing I had to roots."

How crazy that Eve had worked with him all these years, had dreamed about him more often than she would ever admit, and she was just now coming to know him. She wasn't sure what to make of his visit, much less his openness. If he was about to make his move, why now when she was keeping a secret from him?

As if sensing her hesitancy he said, "I should go. I've

interrupted your evening for far too long." He rose. "I'll see you tomorrow."

She untucked her legs and stood. "I'll let you know when I get back from Tallahassee."

He stared down at her in the darkness. "You know what I'm thinking so I'm not going to say it."

Eve tipped her head so that she could meet his gaze. "You don't need to worry about me. I'll be careful."

"That wasn't what I was thinking."

He reached out, cupping the back of her neck to pull her to him. Eve tried to brace herself, tried to summon the willpower and common sense to send him away. She said breathlessly, "Nash, what are you doing?"

"What I've wanted to do all day. What I've wanted to do for years. I can't stop thinking about you, Eve."

As much as she wanted to melt into him, she couldn't. Not yet. Not until there was complete honesty between them. Not when he needed to protect himself. "We can't do this. Once Grace's psychiatric evaluations are completed, a date will be set for the competency hearing. You have to be careful about appearances."

"Grace and I are divorced. I don't owe her anything."

"I know, but her attorneys will be looking for any angle to present her as a sympathetic victim. You're the ex-husband. They'll try every trick in the book to turn you into the villain, to make it seem as though you're the one who pushed her over the edge. You have to do everything you can to protect yourself."

"By protecting myself, I'm allowing her to manipulate me."

"It's not the same thing," Eve insisted. "You've warned me over and over to be careful with Grace. Now I'm asking you to do the same."

He pulled her to him anyway, but instead of kissing her,

he rested his forehead against hers. It was a tender moment. A vulnerable gesture that further eroded Eve's defenses.

She closed her eyes, drawing in the scent of him and the radiating warmth of his nearness. She still wanted him, but now she also wanted to know him, to protect him. To give him strength in the stressful days that lay ahead of him. In the space of one evening, her feelings for Nash Bowden had deepened profoundly.

Finally he pulled away and took her hand. She walked him to the back gate, where they said good-night and parted. She stood listening for his ignition and only when the sound of his engine faded into the night did she close the gate and go inside.

EVE HAD THE strangest dream that night. She was back at her bedroom window staring down at her father as he climbed into the front seat beside Nadine Crosby. But when the figure in the back seat glanced up at her, Denton Crosby's nebulous features morphed into Wayne Brody's. He grinned, lifting a finger to his lips and then across his throat.

She awakened in a cold sweat, unsure of whether a noise or the dream had roused her. Staring up at the ceiling, she willed herself back to a calmer place before another sound catapulted her upright in bed. She reached for her weapon as she rose, then padded to the window to glance out at the garden.

Searching through the shadows, she let her gaze rest for a moment on the back-and-forth movement of the swing. Had the rattle of the chains awakened her? There was only a mild breeze, not enough to set the swing in motion. Someone was out there. She knew it with a certainty that bordered on premonition.

Be careful, Boo.

She glanced over her shoulder, almost expecting to find a silhouette lurking in a corner of her bedroom. She swept the room and then turned back to the window. She could see someone in the shadows just beyond the swing. The same interloper she'd spied outside her bedroom window all those years ago? Or was she imagining an intruder?

Hiding behind the linen curtains, she watched the shadow for another moment and then slipped across the room and out into the hallway. She didn't turn on the light. Moonlight shimmering in through the windows guided her through the silent house. She paused at the back door to peer through the glass panel. Then she let herself out, closing the door behind her with a soft click. She hid among the trees and bushes, maneuvering soundlessly through the vegetation so that she could come up behind the swing. If someone was there, she hoped to catch him unawares.

The breeze lifted her hair and teased through the thin cotton of her pajamas. Eve pressed the Glock against her thigh, trying to convince herself she'd overreacted to a shadow even as her instincts warned of danger. A cloud passed over the moon, throwing the yard into pitch-blackness. Somewhere behind her, she heard the telltale snap of a twig. She whirled, shifting her weight automatically as she lifted her weapon. "Who's there?"

"Evie?"

She drew a sharp breath. For one paralyzing moment, she could have sworn Gabriel Jareau had returned from the dead—or from wherever he'd been the past twenty-eight years. In the next instant, the visitor laughed, a low, menacing sound that prickled the hair at the back of her neck.

"Who are you?" The laugh had come from her left. She turned toward the sound. "Come out where I can see you."

"I can't do that, Evie."

She used both hands to steady her weapon. "Show yourself."

"It's been a long time. You wouldn't recognize me, kiddo. But I'd know you anywhere."

"You're not my dad."

"Never said I was."

She braced her stance. "I know who you are. Your name is Denton Crosby. You were with my dad the night he left town. You and your sister, Nadine." Eve spotted a dark silhouette hovering under the oak tree. But when he spoke again, the voice came from another area of the yard. How could he creep so seamlessly through her garden? Was he, too, a ghost or did he have a companion? His sister, perhaps?

Eve thought about all those times as a child when she'd awakened in the middle of the night with the spine-tingling certainty of being watched. She'd wanted to believe her father had come back to keep her safe from Maya Lamb's kidnapper, but she'd never been able to justify the feeling of malignancy that had radiated from the unknown watcher. It was the same malice that enveloped her now as she searched the shadows.

"So you know who I am." He spoke with a note of regret. "I really wish you'd left well enough alone, Evie. Your knowing my name complicates things."

"Murder is always complicated." She tracked the sound of his voice, turning her head slowly as her gaze raked the darkness. "Is that why you killed Ron Naples? Did he complicate things?"

"Who?"

"He was an old man. Surely not a threat to someone like you. What happened? Did he catch you stealing his car? Or was your sister the one who pushed him into the river?"

"You don't know what you're talking about. You have no idea about any of this."

"I know more than you think," she countered. "I saw you in the car waiting for my dad the night he left town. I can place you in his company. Only he didn't leave town, did he? You and Nadine killed him. When you heard about the discovery of the remains in the cave, you were afraid I'd remember. So you took Ron Naples's car and tried to run me down on the highway, hoping the police wouldn't be able to trace the incident back to you."

"You think you've got it all figured out, don't you? Gabriel always said you were too smart for your own good." The disembodied voice taunted her, though Eve liked to think there was worry in his tone.

She inched around a tree. "You killed my dad and buried him down in that cavern, hoping his body would never be found."

"Evie, Evie. If you only knew the can of worms you're about to open."

He was behind her now. Eve sensed his presence a split second too late. A hand clapped over her mouth, pulling her back against a muscular body as the barrel of a gun pressed against the base of her skull. "Drop your weapon." When Eve resisted, he pulled the hammer back on his revolver. "I said, drop it."

She let the Glock fall to the ground.

"Kick it behind you."

Again she did as she was told.

He booted the gun into the bushes before he removed his hand from her mouth. "Don't even think about screaming."

She said over her shoulder, "What do you want?"

His warm breath fanned against her neck as he brought his lips close to her ear. "Listen carefully. What happened down in that cave needs to stay buried."

"It's too late for that."

"No, it's not. A smart girl like you can still fix things. Drop the investigation and no one else has to get hurt."

She swallowed back her fear, certain now that Denton Crosby had entered Nash's home and looked through the John Doe files. How else would he know that she'd been assigned to the case? He'd been one step ahead of her ever since the remains had been recovered. "I don't have the authority to drop an investigation," she told him.

"That's not what I hear. You're in charge, aren't you? Leads dry up and evidence goes missing all the time. If you know what's good for you and yours, you'll find a way."

Eve half turned, trying to catch a glimpse of his features. "Is that a threat?"

"It's a fact." He poked her in the back with the gun barrel. "Now face straight ahead and don't try that again. I don't want to hurt you out of respect for my old friend, but I will if I have to."

"Don't want to hurt me," she repeated incredulously. "You tried to run me down with a stolen car."

"If I'd wanted you dead out on that highway, you'd be lying in a morgue right now. I only meant to prove what an easy target you are. I can get to you whenever I want. I always could. You'd best remember that. Now put your hands behind your back where I can see them."

She clasped her hands against the base of her spine. "Why don't you want me to see your face? I already know who you are."

"You don't know half as much as you think you do." He nudged her again with the revolver. "You need to understand something. This isn't just about Nadine and me."

"Who else is involved?"

"Oh, I can give you an earful if you're willing to listen. How about we start with that sweet mama of yours?"

An icy chill swept down Eve's backbone. "Leave her out of this."

"I can't do that, Evie. You want the truth, don't you? Well, here's a hard one for you, kiddo. I've known Jackie since high school. That girl was always a looker. A real heartbreaker. Had a little crush on her myself back in the day. But she was never as high and mighty as she pretended to be. You think she didn't know what Gabriel was up to all those nights he didn't come home? You think she didn't suspect what he had planned *that* night?"

Eve's heart thudded. "What are you talking about?"

"She knew all along the kind of man she married. A lot of women are attracted to danger, but some just don't want to admit it."

"Stop talking about my mother as if you know her," Eve snapped. "You don't know anything about her."

"I know plenty. More than you could ever imagine. Gabriel Jareau was my best friend. The two of us were like brothers. He told me things about his wife he never told another living soul."

Eve wasn't about to let the likes of Denton Crosby speak ill of her mother. But even as her defenses hardened, she wondered if a small part of her was afraid to hear any more of his accusations. "As if I would believe anything coming out of your mouth. If you're planning on killing me tonight, why don't you just get on with it? Your blathering on this way is starting to wear on my last nerve."

He laughed. "You know what? You sounded an awful lot like your old man just then." His humor faded and his voice deepened. "Gabriel always did have a tendency to pop off when he should have kept his trap shut and listened. Maybe he'd still be alive."

Eve's nails dug into her palms. "Is that a confession?"

"I said *listen*. You know what Jackie told Gabriel before

he left her? She said she'd kill him if he ever tried to come back. Shoot him straight through the heart if he ever tried to call or see you again."

"That's a lie," Eve said even as her mind raced back to those postcards and the discrepancy she'd noted in the handwriting. She didn't believe for a moment that her mother had forged her father's handwriting to prove he was still alive, but someone had. She was more convinced than ever that Gabriel Jareau had been long dead when the last postcard had been sent.

"You expect me to take your word for any of this?" she demanded. "You know what I think? You're trying to deflect guilt onto my mother when you're the one who killed my dad. You lured him down into that cave and ambushed him. What I don't understand is why. You said he was your friend."

"I said he was like a brother to me. Why would I want to hurt him?"

"Then why do you care about the John Doe investigation? Unless…my father wasn't the one buried in that grave. Unless you're trying to protect someone else."

"*Listen* to me. I'm only going to say this one more time. I could have silenced you a long time ago if I'd been of the mind to. I could have shot you in the back tonight and saved myself a lot of grief, but I decided to try to talk some sense into you instead. I don't want to hurt you, but you can't be running around all over town yapping about what you think you know. You keep going down the path you're on and it won't only be me that ends up in prison. How long do you think your mama would last in a place like Lowell? That hellhole just about killed my sister and she's as tough as they come. What do you think it would do to a woman like Jackie?"

"Nadine was in prison?"

He ignored the question. "Ask her about the last time she saw your daddy alive. Ask her why she wouldn't let him come inside the house to see you the night he snuck back into town."

Eve half turned. "He came back?"

"Of course he came back. He thought the sun rose and set on you. Maybe that was the last straw for Jackie after he up and left the way he did. Maybe she made good on her threat and somehow got him to meet her down in the cave."

"That doesn't make any sense. Why on earth would she lure him to the cave? The tunnels are difficult to navigate even if you know what you're doing."

"Oh, she knew what she was doing, all right. Jackie knew that cave like the back of her hand. We all did. That was our place back in the day, but I'm guessing she never told you any of that. I'm guessing she's gotten real good at keeping secrets. You might want to ask yourself what else she's been hiding before you keep trying to dig up the past."

Chapter Nine

The next morning, Eve made a quick detour to Dr. Forester's lab before heading over to the hospital for her interview with Grace Bowden. The forensic anthropologist was curious about the anonymous DNA swab Eve dropped off, but she agreed to run the test discreetly and let Eve know as soon as the results came back.

She pulled the dime from her collar and caressed the metal between her thumb and forefinger before getting out of the car at the hospital. *I'm getting close to the truth, Daddy.*

Careful what you wish for, Boo.

Shivering despite the heat, she let her gaze roam over the austere brick-and-glass facade as she thought back over the events of the past two days. She hadn't known it at the time, but her life had changed the moment those bones had been discovered. When Nash had offered her lead on the investigation, she'd naively been excited and intrigued by the prospect of working a cold case on her own terms. But that was before she'd learned of the holed coin that had been found at the burial site. That was before her mother had reacted so strongly to Eve's questions about her dad, before Denton Crosby had made his wild accusations in her garden. *I'm guessing she's gotten real good at keeping secrets. You might want to ask yourself what else she's been hiding before you keep trying to dig up the past.*

Eve closed her eyes and took a calming breath. Whatever else she uncovered in the course of her investigation, she'd soon know the truth about John Doe's identity. If the DNA tests turned up a familial match, she'd have to reveal the results to Nash, and then he'd have no choice but to remove her from the case. She'd already forced his hand by going behind his back.

No matter his decision, though, she couldn't just walk away. She couldn't allow Denton Crosby's accusations about her mother to dangle forever at the back of her mind. She had to find out what happened down in that cave all those years ago even if it cost her a job she loved and the trust of a man she admired. Even if it led her down a path she might end up regretting forever.

Shaking herself out of a dark reverie, she let the dime drop back into her collar as she steadied her pulse and refocused. Time enough to worry about the consequences of her actions later. Right now she had to prepare for the interview with Grace. If Nash's ex-wife was half as cunning and clever as he made her out to be, Eve couldn't afford to let her guard down even for a second.

Upon entering the psychiatric wing, she signed in and surrendered her weapon before going through the metal detector. Then she was led down a hallway to a small windowless space that reminded her of the interrogation room at the station. The attendant ushered her in and left. She noted the cameras mounted in two corners before seating herself at the table facing the only entrance. A few minutes later, the same attendant opened the door and stood aside for Grace Bowden to enter. He nodded to Eve and told her if she needed anything he'd be right outside.

Grace stood for a moment, taking in the room before

she crossed to the table and sat down opposite Eve. They'd briefly met once when Grace had come into the station and a second time when Eve had stopped in at Grace's antique doll store looking for a gift. That was before she and Nash had had their moment, although he and Grace had been long separated by that time. Eve couldn't remember now what she and Grace had talked about. The dolls had been out of her price range so she'd browsed for only a few minutes and then left.

She tried to keep her expression courteous but guarded as she took in Grace's appearance. She was dressed in jeans, sneakers and a light blue cardigan that she tugged around her body as she settled in at the table. The street attire surprised Eve. *What were you expecting? A straitjacket?*

Grace's dark blond hair was pulled back and braided, her eyes slightly dilated, making Eve wonder if she'd been sedated. Eve tried to picture Nash and Grace together, but she couldn't make herself go there.

As if to mock her denial, the gold wedding band on Grace's left ring finger gleamed in the overhead lighting as she folded her hands on the table. "So you're Eve Jareau. You're older than I thought you'd be."

Eve decided not to take the observation as a slight seeing as how she and Grace were close to the same age. "We've met before," she said. "Do you remember?"

Grace took a moment to think back then shook her head. "No, I'm sorry. I can't seem to place you. But I grew up in Black Creek so it's likely our paths have crossed more than once. We may even have gone to the same school."

"Very likely," Eve agreed.

"They said you're a homicide detective with the Black Creek Police Department. That means you work with my husband."

Had she stressed the last word or had Eve imagined the emphasis? "I'm with the criminal investigations unit so I work on all kinds of major crimes. Cold cases are of particular interest to me."

Grace sat forward, her previously hooded eyes now curious and alert. "Really? Because I'm fascinated by old crimes, too. Take the Maya Lamb kidnapping case. She was taken right here in Black Creek, right in my own backyard, so to speak. That alone would have captured my interest, but there were so many holes in her mother's story, so many loose ends that never got tied up. Nash says that's one case that may never be solved."

How casually and intimately she spoke of her ex-husband, as if they'd had a conversation about Maya Lamb over dinner the evening before. Eve wanted to explore Grace's fascination with the Lamb case and ask about the details from that crime that she'd incorporated into the kidnapping of Kylie Buchanan. But she had a feeling that was exactly Grace's intent, to steer her into the forbidden territory of Kylie's abduction.

She said carefully, "He could be right, but I hope not. Maya's family deserves to know what happened to her."

"Oh, yes, her family," Grace said dismissively. She gave Eve an unabashed appraisal. "Nash always speaks so highly of his detectives. I'm surprised he never mentioned you."

Was that meant as another slight? Had Grace somehow intuited Eve's feelings for Nash and was trying to get in a few digs? The notion made Eve distinctly uncomfortable. "I'm sure he has more important things on his mind." She summoned a professional briskness to her tone. "Anyway, thank you for agreeing to see me. I'm here because I thought you might be of help on one of my cases."

Grace nodded. "Another cold case, I'm told."

"Yes, a homicide. I'd like to talk to you about the skeletal remains that were discovered in McNally's Cave a few days ago. We've yet to identify the victim, but we do know he was murdered."

"He?"

"The victim was a tall white male, probably in his late twenties."

One brow lifted in puzzlement. "And you think I know something about his murder?"

"Not the murder, per se," Eve explained. "You said in your statement that you'd known about the burial site in the cavern since you were a child. You used to visit the grave because you thought Maya Lamb was buried there."

"It always comes back to Maya, doesn't it?" Grace's voice turned plaintive, her eyes dreamy and sad. "That kidnapping changed us all. People our age grew up knowing what happened to her could happen to any of us. That gnawing fear tainted our childhoods in ways we may never understand."

Eve felt a prickle of apprehension at the base of her spine. Was Grace trying to establish a sympathetic rapport by playing on their common history? That Eve had had a similar conversation the evening before with Nash only deepened her trepidation. No way Grace could have known about his visit, let alone their discussion concerning Maya Lamb's kidnapping, but she'd obviously tapped into an emotional tell that Eve had failed to suppress. The woman's insight and instincts bordered on the uncanny. Eve was beginning to understand Nash's dire warnings.

"Let's get back to that grave," she suggested. "Why did you think Maya was buried there?"

Grace shrugged. "As I said, Maya's kidnapping made a huge impact on me. She was the only one I knew of in town who'd gone missing, so it seemed a logical assumption at the time."

"Yet you never told anyone about your find. Not the authorities. Not even Maya's mother or sister." Eve tried not to sound judgmental, but a faint note of censure crept into her tone despite her best efforts.

Grace tugged the sweater around her slim body as if she could somehow ward off Eve's disapproval. "I was just a little kid. Besides, everybody in town knew what kind of mother Reggie Lamb was. She left her children alone at night while she partied with her degenerate friends. She let lowlifes stay in the same house where those little girls slept. God only knows what went on once she passed out. If she'd been sober the night Maya got taken, she could have protected her daughter. That's the most important job a mother has—to keep her children safe. Don't you agree, Detective Jareau?"

"Yes, if she's able." Too late, Eve recognized the woman's trap. Grace now claimed she'd kidnapped Kylie Buchanan to remove her from an abusive situation with her father. Eve had unwittingly skirted a little too close to sanctioning her motive.

"Maybe I felt so much sympathy for those girls because I was neglected myself as a child," she continued in that wistful tone. "If my great-aunt hadn't taken me in when my parents abandoned me, I don't know what would have happened. Maybe I would have met the same fate as poor Maya. Maybe that's why—" She glanced down at her entwined hands.

Careful. She's weaving a story her attorneys may eventually present in court.

As if intuiting Eve's reservations, Grace drew a breath and lifted her gaze. Her eyes were wide and guileless. "I don't expect you to understand, but when I stumbled across what I thought was Maya's grave, I just wanted to protect her. She'd suffered so much. I didn't want anyone disturbing her rest, especially someone as unfit and undeserving as Reggie Lamb."

No, Eve thought. *You didn't tell anyone else about that grave because you liked keeping secrets. You liked the power they gave you.* Grace had admitted as much to the FBI agent she'd taken hostage before her arrest. Now that she'd had time to plot and plan, she'd tweaked her story to have a more sensitive slant.

Eve said, "Didn't you at least think Maya's twin sister deserved some closure? You were supposed to be her friend."

Grace seemed to visibly shrink in her chair until she seemed very small and frail. Misunderstood. "It's easy to think that way now, but until you've walked in my shoes, do you really think it's fair to judge me for something that happened when I was a lonely little girl?"

Eve felt properly chastised, but in the next instant, she realized that was exactly the reaction Grace wanted to invoke. "Maybe not, but it doesn't matter anyway, since Maya Lamb wasn't buried in that grave."

Grace studied her for a long moment as if gauging an opponent's mettle. Did she find her worthy or lacking? Eve wondered.

"Unfortunately, my time with you is limited today, Detective Jareau, so perhaps you should get to the point of your visit."

"Yes, that's a very good idea," Eve agreed. "You said you spent a lot of time exploring the cave as a child. Did you ever see anyone down there? Did you ever get the sense that someone else had visited the grave?"

"The killer, you mean?"

"Anyone," Eve stressed.

She canted her head in contemplation. Her complexion was lightly tanned, Eve noted, but her hands were pale and graceful, as if she took great care to protect them from the sun. She really was a lovely woman. There was something about her comportment and the tone and cadence of her voice that drew one in despite knowing what she'd done. Nash was right about his ex-wife. Grace Bowden was as disarming as she was cunning. The mark of a true sociopath.

"I did see someone in the cave once," she said thoughtfully. "I remember that I'd lit a candle so that I could read my book. It was always so peaceful and cool in Maya's chamber and I liked that we had our own secret place. No one ever came looking for me so I could stay as long as I wanted. That day, I'd only been down there for a little while when I heard someone in the tunnel. I was startled by the sound because the chamber was so well hidden. You wouldn't be able to locate the entrance unless you knew where to look."

"How did you happen to find it?"

"I don't even remember." Grace smiled her dreamy smile. "I like to think it was divine intervention."

Somehow I doubt that. "What did you do when you realized someone was in the tunnel?"

"I blew out the candle and hid in one of the recesses."

"Did you get a look at this person?"

"It was very dark once the candle went out." She closed her eyes on a shiver. "But there was a glow in the tunnel that grew brighter and brighter as he neared the chamber. I think he had on a headlamp. You know, the kind miners use?" Her hand fluttered to her forehead. The gesture and her tone seemed almost trancelike. "The beam caught me in the face when he stepped into the cavern. I was terrified he'd see me."

"Can you describe him?"

"No," she said in a small, breathless voice. "But his shadow on the wall looks like a monster."

Eve was taken aback by Grace's use of the present tense. She found herself leaning forward, hanging on the woman's every word. "What else do you see?" she gently prompted.

"I can't see anything. I'm pressed too far back into the wall. I don't dare peek into the chamber because if he finds me he'll bury me under the rocks with Maya. Do you think she's a skeleton by now? Have the rats picked her bones clean?"

Eve's scalp prickled. "Are you sure the person in the cavern is a man?"

That notion seemed to give Grace pause. She opened her eyes, straightened her head and said in her normal voice, "I always thought so. But now that you mention it, all I heard was a sort of whispery singsong. Could have been male or female, I suppose."

"Were you mimicking that voice just now?"

She seemed genuinely perplexed. "What do you mean?"

Eve shrugged. "Never mind. Whom was he talking to?"

"Whoever was in the grave. I thought at the time it was Maya."

"What did this person say?"

"I didn't hear anything specific. Just a bunch of mumbles. It sounded like a chant or a prayer or something. That's really all I remember. But he knew his way around the cavern and through the tunnel so he must have been down there many times before."

"You only saw this person once?"

"That I recall."

"You never saw anyone else?" Eve asked. "What about

outside the cave? Anyone wandering through the woods? Any vehicles parked along the road?"

Grace sighed. "It was all so very long ago."

"You said you closed your eyes when you saw the shadow, but maybe you noticed something a split second before and don't remember. Could I show you some photographs to see if one jars your memory?"

Grace glanced behind her toward the door. When she turned back around, she looked anxious. "Go ahead."

Eve pulled the yearbook from her bag and opened it to a marked page. She turned the book toward Grace and pointed to Gabriel Jareau's photograph. "Do you remember seeing him down in the cave?"

"I don't think so. He's very good-looking. Who is he?"

"It's better if we don't use names. It's important that I get your spontaneous response to the photographs." The image of her father was meant as a test to see if she could get an honest reaction from Grace. If Eve's suspicions were correct, Gabriel Jareau had been dead and buried years before Grace had started going down into the cave.

She tapped the page. "I think I would remember if I'd seen him before. He reminds me of Nash."

The offhand remark jolted Eve. She'd never noticed even the slightest resemblance, but Grace's observation unnerved her. Had she subconsciously made the same comparison when she first met Nash? Was that why she'd been so drawn to him? Why she couldn't get over him? Or was Grace messing with her again?

Eve flipped the page and pointed to Denton Crosby's senior photo. "How about him?"

She wrapped her arms around her middle and shivered. "I don't like that one."

Eve studied her expression. "Do you remember seeing him in the cave?"

"I think I've seen him somewhere. His eyes…" She turned away from the yearbook and said in her little girl voice, "I don't like the way he looks at me."

"In the cavern?"

Grace kept her gaze averted. "Please, please don't bury me alive."

A chill danced along Eve's spine. "Grace, where are you? What do you see?"

Her voice lowered to a forced rasp. "Keep your mouth shut, you hear me? You go blabbing to anyone about what you saw down here and I'll come through your bedroom window one night while you're fast asleep. You'll disappear just like the other kid did and no one will ever know what happened to you."

Eve sat stunned. "Grace?"

She glanced around the room in confusion. Then she met Eve's gaze and sighed. "I have to go back to my room now."

"Would it be all right if I come back another day and see you? You may remember something after our talk."

"I suppose that would be okay." Grace ducked her head as if suddenly shy. "Will you do something for me, Detective Jareau?"

Eve said noncommittally, "If I can."

She glanced up through her lashes and gave Eve a knowing smile. "Tell Nash I can't wait until we're together again. Tell him I'll be waiting…no matter how long it takes."

NASH GLANCED IN the rearview mirror, automatically noting the color of the vehicles behind him on the interstate. He was still a few miles out from Tallahassee, but his foreboding continued to deepen. He told himself his trip into the city had nothing to do with Eve's visit to the psychiatric ward. She was smart and capable and he trusted she could hold her own against his calculating ex-wife.

He'd been planning a follow-up visit with Allison Forester anyway, and after attending Ron Naples's autopsy earlier, he'd carved out a little spare time from the rest of his morning to make the trip. Any new developments in the John Doe case could have easily been discussed over the phone, but he needed to have a more personal conversation with the forensic anthropologist. A casual arrangement had suited them both since their first spontaneous coffee date. No strings attached. No questions asked. But now that he'd acted on his feelings for Eve, he felt he owed Allison a clean break. His experiences with Grace had left him with an intense aversion to lies and subterfuge.

He checked the rearview again as he exited the freeway. A dark sedan had been trailing him for miles. When the car failed to follow him down the off-ramp, he told himself he was being paranoid. *Relax. No one is following you. No one is lying in wait at every corner.*

No sniper firing from a distant window. No exploding IEDs in front of him. No body parts strewn along the roadside.

He swore under his breath. He'd gone nearly a week without a nightmare and now all of a sudden his mind had gone back to that dark place in the middle of a sunny morning. Maybe everything that had happened with Grace had triggered something in his subconscious. The memories tended to come back in times of stress. Or maybe the images in his head were a graphic reminder that Eve really didn't know what she was getting into.

He rubbed a hand across his eyes and made a right turn. The lab parking lot was half-empty. He found a space near the rear entrance and showed his credentials to the guard stationed in the lobby. Allison was in her office when he arrived. He made his way through the tables of bones to the glass enclosure at the back.

She looked up in surprise at his knock, then motioned him inside. He moved a stack of files from the only available chair in the room and sat down, his gaze taking in her workspace. The cluttered desk and overflowing filing cabinets were a stark contradiction to her unruffled demeanor.

"Did we have a meeting that I forgot? Not that I'm complaining," she added with a quick smile. "I'm always happy to see you."

He sounded abrupt and businesslike by comparison. "Anything new on our John Doe?"

"Nothing to report yet. I told you I'd call you if I found anything."

He nodded. "I know, but I had some time to kill this morning so I thought I'd drive over and talk to you in person."

She tossed her pen on the desk and assessed him for a long moment. "You okay?"

"I'm fine."

"You don't look fine. What's going on, Nash?"

He wouldn't insult her intelligence by pretending ignorance. "Am I that easy to read?"

"Far easier than you like to think." Her gaze remained steady. "Are the headaches back?"

"No worse than usual."

"Are you sleeping?"

"No more than usual."

She cocked her head. "Something's not right. Are you going to make me guess what it is?"

"No guessing. No games," he said. "I came here to tell you that I've met someone."

Other than a raised eyebrow, she seemed unfazed by

his blunt confession. Nash didn't know whether to be relieved or offended by her placid reaction. "Is it serious?"

"I don't know yet."

"I see." She sat back in her chair and folded her arms. "Well, since you haven't mentioned any names, you have to let me guess. You owe me that much." The corners of her mouth twitched as she held up a hand to silence his protest. "One guess, Nash. That's all I'll need. You've fallen for the earnest Detective Jareau, haven't you?"

"How did you know?" he asked in surprise.

She seemed pleased with herself. "You forget that I'm a detective, too. I'm accustomed to searching for subtleties and anomalies that no one else would notice, so I couldn't help observing the way you looked at her the other day. And the way she looked at you."

He frowned. "I didn't notice any looks."

"Then you were either blind or still in denial at the time. I might have chalked the whole thing up to my imagination if not for Detective Jareau's reaction to you. She isn't very subtle, is she? I suspect she's been pining after you for ages. And knowing you as I do…" She got up and came around the desk to perch on the edge. "You've been ducking and running as if your life depended on it. How on earth did she manage to catch you?"

"I don't think she's been pining." Nash felt oddly protective of Eve and her feelings for him. He'd been aware of her attraction ever since she'd impulsively kissed him, but she'd backed off as soon as he'd responded. For whatever reason, they'd both been ducking and running since.

Allison gave him a sage look. "Despite what you say, things must be serious if you're actually admitting you have feelings for her."

"Nothing's happened," he said. "Not yet. Maybe not ever. But I thought I should let you know where I stand.

I didn't want you thinking I'd gone behind your back with Eve."

"Stop right there, Nash. Don't you ever apologize or feel guilty for moving on with your life." Her quiet ferocity made him wonder if she spoke for herself or someone else. "You have a right to see whomever you want. You and I have never been exclusive. We both knew the score when we started seeing one another. If you've found something real with Detective Jareau then I'm happy for you both."

"Thanks."

"But…" Her expression sobered as she continued to regard him. "That doesn't mean I'll stop caring about you. We've been friends for a long time, and I feel that gives me the right to offer a piece of advice."

He waited without comment.

"Be careful, Nash. Slow things down until you get your footing. How well do you even know this woman?"

He had no doubt she meant well, but his defenses shot back up. "We've worked together for six years. I know her pretty well by now."

"Maybe you only think you do."

"What's that supposed to mean?"

She gave him a careful study. "You value honesty above all else. It's why you felt the need to come here today and clear your conscience. Are you sure Detective Jareau has been completely candid with you?"

His voice cooled. "What's your point?"

"She came by the lab this morning with an interesting request."

"Eve was here this morning?"

"She didn't tell you?"

"No, but she was coming to Tallahassee anyway. Since she was already in the city, she probably wanted to see if you had any additional information on John Doe."

"She wasn't following up on the case, Nash. She came here to drop off a DNA sample."

A DNA sample? *What the hell, Eve?*

Ever since they'd left the lab two days ago, Nash had had a bad feeling she was hiding something from him. He'd wanted to believe she was just being cautious, crossing t's and dotting i's as she chased down leads. But if she'd brought a DNA sample to the lab, then she must have a pretty good idea of John Doe's identity. Why keep something that important from him?

"Whose DNA?" he asked.

"I have no idea. It was an anonymous swab. She asked me to run a comparison with John Doe and to let her know as soon as I had the results. She also asked that I not say anything to you."

"She named me specifically?" Anger bristled, but his demeanor remained cool and steady. "Did she say why?"

"She was pretty closemouthed about the whole thing. She said she wanted to be discreet in case her hunch didn't pan out."

That seemed to be her go-to excuse when she didn't want to share information. Nash didn't like what he was hearing. He couldn't imagine Eve withholding evidence just to claim credit for closing a case, but any other explanation was even harder to stomach. "What else did she say?"

"That was about it. She was in and out in less than five minutes. She said she had somewhere else she needed to be."

"Have you run the test?"

"That'll take some time," Allison said. "DNA abstraction from skeletal remains is still a delicate process. Don't expect the results for at least a week."

"Can't you rush it? This is important, Allie. I wouldn't ask if it wasn't."

She shrugged. "No promises, but I'll see what I can do."

"Thanks. Call me as soon as you have the results. Me, and no one else."

"Understood." She followed him to the door. "I meant what I said earlier. If things are just getting started with Eve, maybe you should cool it for a while. After everything Grace put you through... I don't want to see you get hurt."

Nash was as irritated with Eve as he would be with any detective who'd compromised the integrity of an investigation, but he also felt the need to defend her. Not just from a personal perspective, but as one of his own. "Eve is a fine detective. She's always been diligent and by-the-book. Whatever lead she is pursuing, she must have a damn good reason."

Despite his lofty words, he left the lab feeling blindsided. He didn't like secrets. He'd had his fill of deception with Grace. He'd ignored his instincts when it came to Eve because he wanted to trust her. He still wanted to trust her. He still hoped she had a solid explanation for her silence, but the fact that she'd kept something as significant as a DNA sample to herself made him question her motives.

It made him wonder if she was trying to protect someone.

Chapter Ten

Eve kept a watchful eye as she exited the freeway onto the two-lane highway where she and Nash had been ambushed two nights ago. That experience alone would have made her cautious, but the interview with Grace had ratcheted up her apprehension. She'd been in the woman's company for all of thirty minutes and yet she had a feeling that Grace Bowden had somehow gleaned more information about her than the other way around.

Since her arrest, Grace hadn't shown any real remorse for the kidnapping of an innocent child. What might she do if she felt threatened by another woman?

You're not the other woman. Grace and Nash are divorced. Their marriage was over a long time ago.

A fact that seemed lost on Grace.

Whatever she knew or thought she knew about Eve, she wasn't in any position to exact revenge. No matter the outcome of her hearing, she wouldn't be free to cause harm for a very long time. Denton Crosby, on the other hand, could come and go as he pleased, and he'd taken great satisfaction in proving to Eve that he could get to her whenever he wanted. He'd entered her backyard last night with seemingly no trepidation whatsoever. If she hadn't awakened when she did, he might have found a way into her house.

She told herself his allegations against her mother were

ridiculous, the wild claims of a desperate man trying to deflect guilt and stall an investigation so that he could cover his tracks. But the image of the shattered wineglass in her mother's hand crept back in, making Eve wonder again why questions about her father had upset her mother so much. Had Jackie known he'd returned to Black Creek to see Eve? Had she really kept him from his daughter?

Fingering the Mercury dime beneath her shirt, Eve let her mind drift until the peal of her ringtone joggled her back to the present. She frowned as Nash's name flashed on the screen. He knew she'd be on her way back from Tallahassee by now. Was he that anxious to hear about her meeting with Grace?

She tapped her wireless earpiece to answer.

"Where are you?"

Nash's terse question took her by surprise. He sounded… suspicious, but of what?

She told herself a guilty conscience had conjured the wariness in his voice, but her immediate leap reinforced the need to come clean as soon as she had the DNA results.

Shaking off her disquiet, she gave him an approximate location.

"Are you coming straight back to the station?" he wanted to know.

"That's the plan. Why? Has something come up?"

"Yes, but we can talk about it when you get here."

"Something about the case?" Eve tried to keep her voice even. "Nash, what is it?"

"Nothing I want to get into over the phone," he said, still in that clipped tone. "How did the meeting with Grace go?"

Eve let out a relieved breath. No wonder he sounded stilted. He'd probably been brooding about her interview with Grace all morning. "It was…interesting."

"Did anything useful come of it?"

"I'm not sure yet. But you were right to warn me about her. Grace is a very complex woman."

"That's one way of putting it," he muttered.

"I don't know what to make of some of the things she said. It was almost as if…" Eve groped for an accurate description. "She almost seemed hypnotized, as if she were recounting her time in the cave in a trance."

"Are you sure she wasn't acting?"

"I'm not sure of anything when it comes to Grace. But I'll tell you more about our meeting when I see you. Traffic is light. I should be there in twenty."

"Anything else I should know?"

"About Grace?"

"About anything. You were chasing down mysterious leads yesterday. You never told me how they panned out."

She wanted to discount that note of suspicion in his voice as projection, but something had definitely changed since they'd last talked. "I don't have anything to report yet, but I'll keep you posted."

"You do that, Detective."

Okay, she hadn't imagined that.

Why the deliberate formality? she wondered. After their intimate conversation in the garden last evening, it seemed as though their relationship had taken a new turn. This time, Nash had made the first move. This time, he'd been the one willing to throw caution to the wind until Eve had reminded him of the need for discretion in light of the upcoming hearing. Now she didn't know what to make of his chilly reserve. What had happened in the ensuing hours to alter his attitude so drastically? Or was he merely keeping a wall between their personal and professional lives?

"Is everything okay? Between us, I mean." She asked the question he'd asked the day before. "Are we good?"

"No reason why we wouldn't be, is there?" He changed topics abruptly. "You haven't asked about the autopsy."

"How did it go?"

"Preliminary diagnosis is inconclusive even though the pathologist found froth and sediment in the lungs and airways. It looks like Ron Naples drowned, but we have no way of knowing whether it was accidental."

"His car was stolen and used in a hit-and-run," Eve said. "I have a hard time believing his death was accidental or coincidental."

"You still think Ron Naples is somehow connected to John Doe?"

She thought about Denton Crosby's warning the night before, could almost feel the hard nose of his revolver pressed against the back of her skull. "I'm certainly keeping an open mind, aren't you?"

"Yes, but a lot of things don't add up," Nash said.

"Maybe not yet. Cold cases are never easy or straightforward, especially when so much time has passed. But somebody always knows something," Eve said. "We just have to keep digging until we catch a break."

"You seem confident of a closure," Nash observed. "But if we're unable to identify John Doe, the odds are against us. Unless you have a lead I don't know about."

A long silence spooled out between them until Eve said with a sinking sensation, "You know, don't you?"

"Know what?"

She waited another moment. "You've talked to Dr. Forester. She told you I came by the lab this morning with a DNA sample."

More silence. Then, "Why didn't you tell me?"

She winced at his disappointed tone. "I was going to as soon as the results came back. At this point, it's nothing more than a hunch."

"You seem to have a lot of hunches lately, particularly when it comes to this case."

"I do have an explanation—"

His voice turned curt again. "Save it until you get back to the station. I expect a full accounting. No excuses, no more talk about hunches. I want specifics. Are we clear on that?"

"Yes, we're clear."

"In the meantime, you should know that Mr. McNally has halted demolition at the cave to give us a chance to explore. Unless you no longer feel the need."

Eve jumped at the chance. "No, I do! I still think it's important." Vital, in fact. She needed to examine the excavation site. Needed to *feel* the place where her father had drawn his last breath. Had he somehow left a clue for her? Something esoteric that had remained trapped belowground for decades? Not a ghost, but a lingering emotion. "I'm more compelled than ever," she said. *You have no idea.* "How soon can we go down?"

"I've freed up a block of time later this afternoon. See me in my office as soon as you get back. I'm serious about this, Eve. I can't have any of my detectives going maverick. We're a team here. No exceptions. You need to fill me in on everything you know about this case. I don't want to be blindsided again."

"Yes, sir," she agreed, wondering if they would ever get back to that dreamy, hopeful place they'd experienced in her garden the night before.

NASH'S DARK MOOD lingered after his conversation with Eve, but at least she'd finally admitted to keeping things from him. What those things were, he would soon find out. And if she remained evasive... Well, he'd cross that bridge when he came to it. No quarter could be given because of his feelings for her. The opposite, in fact.

His phone rang just as he pulled into the station. He parked in the gated lot and kept the AC running while he took the call. "Bowden."

"Nash?"

He tensed at the sound of his ex-wife's voice. "Why are you calling me, Grace? You know I can't talk to you."

"Don't be mad," she cajoled. "I just needed to hear your voice."

"Is Dr. Anderson aware of this call? Or your attorneys?"

"This doesn't concern them."

"Everything you do concerns them," he said in exasperation. "You're in serious trouble. You need to start acting like you understand the consequences of your actions."

"I wasn't in my right mind. You know that, Nash. You know I would never have hurt that little girl." Her voice grew small and tremulous. "I realize this doesn't excuse what I did, but I kept thinking about the child we lost. She would have been the same age as Kylie. When she came into my doll shop looking so sweet and innocent and shy... things got all confused in my head."

Nash braced himself against her manipulation. There was a time when she'd known exactly how to push his buttons, but he'd learned the hard way that his ex-wife was nothing if not a consummate actor. "You weren't the only one who lost a baby. The miscarriage affected me, too, but what happened to us five years ago doesn't justify taking someone else's child. What you put her mother through is inexcusable."

Her voice grew petulant. "I thought you, of all people, would understand. You know what's it like when things get all jumbled inside and you can't tell up from down or right from wrong. You were still a mess when we met, or have you forgotten the nightmares and flashbacks? The times I sat up with you all night when you couldn't sleep?"

He was quiet for a moment. "I haven't forgotten anything. I understand more than you think. No matter what you say now, we both know the real reason you took that little girl. You wanted my attention and you got it."

"Can you please come see me?" she pleaded.

He stared blindly out the window. "I can't help you this time, Grace. You need to start listening to your attorneys."

"Nash, please—"

"I'm hanging up now."

"No, wait!" she cried desperately. "That woman you sent to see me… Eve Jareau?"

His fingers tightened around the phone. "I didn't send her. She came of her own accord. But what about her?"

"Are you having an affair with her?"

The question was completely out of line and he was quick to call her on it. "Neither of us is married or in a committed relationship, so no, we're not having an affair."

"Are you seeing her romantically?"

He clung to his patience. "Grace, what is the point of this call? You and I have been divorced for a long time. We were separated for even longer. My private life is none of your business."

She reverted back to her trembling voice. "I'm just so afraid, Nash. I need you to tell me everything is going to be okay."

"I can't do that. You planned every part of Kylie Buchanan's abduction right down to the smallest detail, including planting evidence to make someone else look guilty. That's called premeditation. Everything is *not* going to be okay."

Her voice dropped to a hush. "I can't go to prison, Nash."

Even after all this time, even after everything she'd

done, she still thought she could claw her way through his resolve. "You should have thought of that sooner."

"Why do you have to be so mean to me?"

He mentally counted to ten. "I'm not being mean. I just don't buy your act, so I'm hanging up now."

"Wait! What if I can help you solve another case? Wouldn't that carry weight with the judge?"

Nash had every intention of severing the call but instead he found himself asking reluctantly, "Which case?" Then he immediately berated himself for falling for such an obvious ploy.

"The remains that were found down in McNally's Cave. Detective Jareau showed me some pictures in a yearbook. I recognized a face."

"If you're making this up—"

"I'm not! I swear to God I saw this person in the cave. That's important, right? That could help you solve the case."

Nash wasn't buying it. Not yet. "Did you tell Detective Jareau about this person?"

"I'd rather talk to you. Can you come see me?"

The wheedling again. The constant maneuvering and bartering to get what she wanted. Some things never changed. "No, but I can have Detective Jareau get in touch with you again."

"What if I refuse to talk to anyone but you?"

"Then there won't be any reason to put in a good word with the judge."

"Nash—"

"Goodbye, Grace."

EVE WOULD HAVE fretted all the way back to town about Nash's intentions if her phone hadn't intruded once more into her thoughts. She immediately worried that he was calling her back to fire her on the spot, but the screen informed her that the number of the caller was unavailable.

She tapped her earpiece to answer and then returned both hands to the steering wheel. "Detective Jareau."

"*Eve* Jareau?"

She frowned at the deep rasp. For a moment, she thought the caller might be trying to disguise her voice. Her mind immediately went back to Grace Bowden and the way her tone had altered between fearful and menacing when she recounted her time in the cave.

Eve said warily, "Who is this?"

"I hear you've been looking for me."

Eve drew a sharp breath. "Nadine Crosby?"

"Last time I checked."

Eve glanced in the rearview mirror. The coast was clear behind and in front of her. If someone had followed her from the freeway, they were hanging back so far she couldn't spot them. "How did you get my number?"

"You've been leaving your card all over town. Wasn't hard to track you down."

Eve figured the woman had been informed of her and Nash's queries either by her former boss or her former neighbor. Obviously, she hadn't disappeared without so much as a word as they'd both pretended, but Eve decided not to press the issue. "I'm glad you called, Ms. Crosby. It's important that we speak in person. Can we set up a time and place to meet?"

"You can call me Nadine. No need to be fancy. I knew your daddy a long time ago. He talked about you so much I kind of felt like I knew you."

At the mention of her dad, Eve swallowed back her emotions and said, "Can we meet… Nadine?"

"Why do you think I'm calling? I reckon you and me got a lot to talk about."

"Name the time and place," Eve said.

"There's a gravel turnoff just past the next mile marker on the right."

Eve flashed another glance in the rearview mirror. How did Nadine know her location?

"Are you following me?" she asked.

"I've been behind you for miles. You can't see me but I'm back here."

Eve gripped the wheel. "Should I expect another flat tire soon? Are you going to try to run me down like your brother did?"

"Denny didn't touch you, did he?"

"No, but I can't say the same for poor Ron Naples."

Silence stretched. "I had nothing to do with that."

"But your brother did, didn't he?"

"It was an accident," Nadine insisted. "Denny just wanted to borrow a car. No one was supposed to get hurt."

"And yet someone is dead. What happened?" Eve asked. "Did Mr. Naples catch your brother *borrowing* his car?"

"I wasn't there. I don't know what happened. Besides, I didn't call to talk about Denny."

"Ron Naples's death is only one of many things we need to discuss," Eve said. "You used your position with King's Maid Services to let your brother into people's homes. A man is dead as a result and that makes you an accomplice. It's in your best interests to tell me exactly what happened."

"I can't tell you what I don't know." The hoarse voice sounded strained, as if she were holding back a painful cough. "Denny said he wanted to scare you bad enough to get you to back off. He needed a car that couldn't be traced back to him. Nobody was supposed to get hurt," she repeated. "I'm willing to meet with you, but I have to protect myself. If you send cop cars my way once we hang up, I'll see them long before they see me."

"How?" She must have someone up ahead watching the road for her, Eve decided. Her brother?

"Never you mind how. If you want to meet as bad as you say you do, then watch for the mile marker. Make that turn and follow the road back into the woods for another mile or so until you come to a tree with a yellow ribbon tied around the trunk. There's a burned-out car back in the bushes. You can see it from the road if you're watching for it. Pull to the side and wait. I'll call you again."

"I'd prefer to meet someplace public."

"That's not going to happen. Like I said, I've got to protect myself. No one else is going to watch my back." She paused on a harsh cough. "We do this my way or we don't do it at all."

Eve told herself she would be stupid to even consider Nadine Crosby's terms, but instead of turning her down cold, she said, "I only have your word that you mean me no harm. What I've learned of your past doesn't exactly instill confidence. How do I know I'm not driving into an ambush?"

"You don't. You'll just have to trust me, I guess."

"Trust you?" Eve found that suggestion laughable. "That's not so easy considering the last time I saw my dad he was getting into a car with you and your brother."

"That's why you've been looking for me, isn't it? You want to hear about that night."

Eve's knuckles whitened where she gripped the wheel. "Do you know what happened to him?"

"I know some of it. I'll tell you as much as I can so long as you don't try anything funny. Come alone. That's the most important thing to get right. I get wind of the cops or anyone else tailing us, I'll disappear so fast you'll think I'm a ghost."

"Disappearing may not be as easy as you think," Eve warned.

"I still have a few friends in these parts and plenty of back roads to get me across the state line without being seen. I'll leave town with your daddy's secrets and you won't ever see me again."

"Nadine—"

"Make up your mind, girl. Come alone or don't come."

"Wait—"

Nothing but silence.

Eve knew better than to meet with Nadine Crosby in a remote location alone. She wasn't some wet-behind-the-ears rookie out to make a name for herself. She knew proper procedure. Call for backup and approach with caution. Do whatever needed to be done by the book in order to bring Nadine and Denton Crosby in for questioning.

But their arrest would mean opening Eve's mother up to a line of unsavory accusations. Not for a moment would Eve allow herself to believe that Jackie had been responsible for her father's death. For all she knew, Gabriel Jareau could be alive and well, living in another state with his second family.

But what if he wasn't?

What if he *had* returned to Black Creek to see her? What if someone had lured him down into that cave and murdered him in cold blood?

John Doe had been stabbed so violently his ribs had almost been severed. Then he'd been bashed in the back of the head with a blunt force instrument. Eve had said it herself—the sheer brutality of the kill suggested uncontrollable rage. No matter how hurt and angered Jackie had been by her husband's betrayal, she could never have attacked him so viciously.

You don't know her. Not really. Not like I do.

Eve shot another glance in the rearview. Was that a dark sedan behind her? An old pickup truck? The nearest vehicle was still too far away to identify, but Nadine Crosby was back there somewhere watching and waiting from a distance to see if flashing blue lights appeared on the horizon or if Eve instead made that turn.

Don't do it, Evie. You're smarter than that.

Was she? The temptation to find out what Nadine knew about her father was overwhelming. Eve checked her weapon and then her phone. Still plenty of battery left. Still time to call Nash and let him know what she was up to. At the very least she should alert someone of her whereabouts. She couldn't possibly be so foolhardy as to head off into the woods to meet a woman who may or may not have been a party to two violent deaths.

The turn was coming up quickly. Already Eve could see the numbers painted down the front of the mile marker post.

Don't do it.

She had every intention of speeding on by, but at the very last moment, she whipped the wheel to the right and her rear tires spun out on the gravel shoulder. For a moment, she thought she might roll the vehicle before she managed to regain control. Hitting the brakes, she rocked to a stop and took a moment to catch her breath.

She waited to see if someone came up behind her before easing across the railroad tracks. The unpaved road narrowed almost immediately. Fencerows of honeysuckle and palmettos crowded against the shoulders while hardwoods wove a thick canopy that obliterated the sunlight. As she bumped along the road, she kept a watchful eye for the burned-out vehicle and the tree with the yellow ribbon. She spotted the ribbon first and then the car. It had been rolled into a thicket of scrub brush so that it was almost invisible from the road unless one knew where to look. Eve stopped and stared out over the rugged terrain. She wondered if the sedan might be the same car that had almost run her down on the highway, but in the next instant, she realized the model was older, and judging by the kudzu already snaking through the broken windows, it had been abandoned years ago.

Lowering her window, Eve drew in the fresh scent of the woods as she watched the road. Five minutes went by and then ten. She got out of the vehicle so she had a better view of the area around her. The place felt lonely. Abandoned. Even the songbirds sounded forlorn.

She tried to stay focused, but her mind wandered back to the holed coin found with the bones. That couldn't be all that was left of her father. That couldn't be her only clue. Something remained down in that cave and if need be, she'd search every dank nook and crevice to find it.

I won't give up, Daddy.

Some things are best left buried, Boo.

When the faded pickup truck came into view, Eve's hand automatically went to her weapon but she didn't draw. Instead, she rested her fingers on the handle as the truck stopped a few feet away facing her.

Her phone rang and she lifted it to her ear.

"Leave your gun and phone in the car and lock the doors," Nadine instructed.

Eve kept her tone accommodating. "Why don't you get out of your vehicle and we'll talk here?"

"You have to the count of three and then I'm gone," Nadine advised.

"All right, you win." Eve unholstered her weapon and

placed it on the seat along with her phone. Then, lifting her shirt above her waistline, she turned slowly so that Nadine Crosby could see she was unarmed.

The truck eased up beside her. Nadine said through the open passenger-side window, "Get in."

"Where are we going?"

"Just down the road a piece. I know a place where we can talk without worrying about somebody coming upon us."

Eve glanced around. The chances of that seemed slim. They were off the beaten track and she hadn't reported in. Anything could happen on this isolated road and no one would be the wiser. She could end up disappearing just like her father had.

As if sensing her unease, Nadine said through the window, "I'm not going to hurt you."

Eve moved up to the truck. "How do I know that? How do I know you won't take me deeper into the woods and shoot me?"

Nadine shrugged. "If I wanted to kill you, I sure as heck wouldn't go about it this way. You're young and strong. You could overpower me if you had a mind to. If I was going to do you in I'd try to catch you by surprise."

She did appear frail, Eve thought. A faded gray tank top revealed her jutting collarbone and scrawny arms, and the once-platinum hair was now more gray than blond. She was Jackie's age or thereabouts, but she looked least ten years older.

So this was the woman Gabriel Jareau had left his family for. Eve couldn't help comparing Nadine Crosby to her still attractive and vibrant mother.

Why her, Daddy?

No answer came to Eve.

As if sensing her unkind assessment, Nadine said sharply, "Get in."

Eve climbed into the cab and slammed the door. The ragged interior smelled of motor oil and mosquito repellant. Nadine hung an elbow out the window as she waited for Eve to settle. She wore baggy shorts with the tank top, and Eve couldn't help noticing that her bony legs were covered with bruises. Nadine turned her head and coughed out the window. She really didn't seem well at all. Eve tried to harden her resolve, but an inexplicable emotion crept in and softened the edges. She turned to stare at the burned-out vehicle rather than at Nadine.

The tailpipe rumbled noisily as they bounced down the road. The sound should have grated, but Eve welcomed the intrusion because it broke the unnerving silence of the woods. She watched the scenery and tried to keep track of how far they'd driven. Not that it would matter if Nadine or her brother decided to put a bullet in her skull.

About a mile or so in, they came to an old farmhouse. The yard was so overgrown with brambles and weeds that only the top half of the clapboard structure was visible from the road. Vines had claimed the second story, winding in through broken windowpanes and twisting around the brick chimney. The place must once have been lovely with gnarled shade trees ringing the perimeter and clumps of orange and yellow daylilies popping up through the weeds. Now the derelict home looked a bit haunted.

Nadine turned the truck so they faced back out toward the road. Eve glanced over her shoulder, raking her gaze over the house and into the woods beyond. "What is this place?"

"Only place I ever truly felt safe." Nadine's breathing sounded ragged as if she couldn't pull in enough air. She turned off the engine and rested her head against the seat as her hands dropped to the worn upholstery, fingers curled upward like an anemic plant stretching toward sunlight.

Eve asked in alarm, "Are you okay?"

"Just need to catch my breath." She slowly seemed to regain her strength. She motioned out the window back toward the house. "My folks bought this property years ago when land was still dirt cheap around here. My daddy was a master carpenter," she said with pride. "He built that house with his bare hands. Me and my brother grew up here."

"Do your parents still live in the area? Is that why you came back to Black Creek?" Eve asked.

"They died when I was a kid. Hit head-on by an eighteen-wheeler as they pulled out on the highway."

"I'm sorry," Eve murmured. She didn't like this experience, this unwelcome pity for the woman who had all but destroyed hers and her mother's lives.

"We didn't have any other family and no one else wanted to take us in so we were shuffled from one foster home to another until Denny turned eighteen and got us out."

"That's a tough life," Eve said.

Nadine shrugged. "Some have it a lot worse. At least I had my brother. And later, Gabriel." She flashed Eve an uneasy look. "The three of us were family."

Eve's sympathy vanished. "He already had a family."

"He had us first," Nadine said with a hint of defiance. "We all went through high school together."

"So did he and my mother."

She nodded. "I know. I remember her."

Was that bitterness in her voice? Hatred, even? Eve hardened her gaze. "Then you must have known when my parents got married. You knew my dad had a wife and kid, yet you left town with him anyway."

"You know what they say. You can't help who you fall in love with."

"That's just a convenient excuse," Eve snapped, even as she reflected on her own feelings for Nash. It wasn't the same. He'd been separated for a long time when she finally acted on her attraction. Then she'd pretended the kiss hadn't meant anything, just an adrenaline rush that had gotten the better of her. After that she'd kept her feelings hidden until he'd come to her.

It's not the same.

Nadine's head was still reclined against the seat, her eyes closed. "He never stopped loving you. Not for a single second. He cared about your mama, too, but Gabriel was never meant to settle down. He had too much of a wild streak. He craved danger and adventure like a junkie craves a fix. We were alike in that way."

"Did you kill him?" Eve blurted.

Nadine turned her head, looking pained. "Why would I kill him? He was my heart."

"Then why does your brother want me to drop my investigation into the remains that were found in McNally's Cave? If you cared about my dad the way you say you did, why wouldn't you want to know what happened to him?"

Nadine's head lifted and her wary gaze suddenly turned piercing as she studied Eve's face. "You really don't know?"

Eve shook her head.

"You need to stop asking questions about them bones before people start putting two and two together."

"What are you talking about?" Eve demanded in frustration. "Putting what together?"

Nadine's voice lowered as if she were afraid of being overheard out in the middle of nowhere. "Sooner or later someone will figure out that we took her."

"What?" Everything inside Eve stilled. She had the awful feeling another bomb was about to explode.

"The little girl that went missing years back." Nadine's voice was a hoarse whisper. "We took her."

Eve's mind refused to go there for a moment. Then she said on a breath, "You and your brother kidnapped Maya Lamb?"

"Me, my brother...and Gabriel."

Chapter Eleven

Eve recoiled, pressing up against the door as if putting physical distance between her and Nadine could somehow lessen the impact of the woman's stunning confession. It couldn't be true. Gabriel Jareau had been a lot of things, but he was no kidnapper. Nadine was trying to save herself. *Don't believe a word she says.*

A wave of nausea rolled through Eve, and for a moment she thought she would lose her breakfast. Leaning out the open window, she drew in deep gulps of air and tried to calm her churning stomach. All the while, her mind continued to scream, *No, no, no—it can't be true!* She would never believe it to be true. Her beloved father had kidnapped Maya Lamb? *No!*

Nadine waited patiently beside her. "You okay?" she finally asked.

Eve wiped the cold sweat from her brow with the back of her hand. "I feel sick."

"I shouldn't have blurted it out the way I did. It must have been a shock. Just sit quietly and take a few more deep breaths. It'll pass in a minute."

But it wouldn't pass. The revulsion curling in Eve's stomach was just the beginning if there was even so much as a kernel of truth in Nadine's confession.

"I don't believe you," she said as much to herself as to her companion.

"I know," Nadine said in a pitying voice. She lifted her hand as if to pat Eve's shoulder, then seemed to think better of it. She draped her arms over the steering wheel and hunched forward. "I'm telling you the truth, though."

"Truth or not, why are you telling me any of this? What do you hope to accomplish?"

Nadine rested her head briefly on the steering wheel. "I guess I thought after all this time you deserved to know the truth about your daddy."

"What's in it for you?" Eve mustered up a cold stare. "You must be trying to get ahead of something. You think if you blame my dad for masterminding Maya Lamb's kidnapping, the law will go easy on you and your brother. That won't happen," she assured her.

"I never said Gabriel masterminded anything. None of us did. And there's nothing in it for me except maybe a little peace," Nadine said in resignation. "But I don't expect you to believe that, either."

"It doesn't add up," Eve countered. "I saw him get in the car with you the night he left town. Maya wasn't abducted until weeks later."

"That's the way we planned it. Gabriel told everyone we knew that his cousin down in New Orleans got him and Denny jobs on an offshore oil rig. They'd be out in the Gulf for weeks. We knew plenty of guys from Black Creek that worked on those platforms. No reason for anyone to doubt him."

"It was a lie?"

"We needed people to think we'd left town for good. We needed a good alibi for the night she disappeared."

Eve's mind raced as she tried to throw up roadblocks to Nadine's story. "How come there was never a ransom demand? That *is* why you kidnapped her, isn't it? To squeeze money out of June Chapman?"

"Who?"

"Maya's grandmother. You must have thought she'd pay up because the child's mother didn't have any money."

Nadine shrugged. "I don't know anything about that. All I know is that we got half the money up front, half on delivery. Denny said it was cleaner that way."

Eve stared at her in horror. "What do you mean, on delivery?"

"Somebody approached my brother a few days before we left town. They offered us a hundred thousand dollars each to nab those girls and take them to a drop point. Fifty thousand up front, the rest when we delivered them."

Eve frowned. "Girls as in plural?"

Nadine nodded. "That was the deal. We were supposed to take the pair in order to get all the money, but it didn't work out that way."

Eve thought about all the years that Thea Lamb had looked for her twin. All the guilt she must have suffered for being the one not taken. "Who paid you?"

"I don't know. Denny would never give us a name. I'm not sure he even knew. He said this person told him about a secret organization made up of cops, feds and even some social workers that arranged for children in jeopardy to get a second chance."

"By kidnapping them?" Eve asked in disbelief.

"The way he explained it, the organization had to disappear the kids in order to save them. When things went right, it was as if they'd vanished into thin air. They were hidden away in safe houses until they could be given new names and placed in decent homes with people who cared about them. After my time in foster care, it seemed like we'd be doing those little girls a kindness."

"What about their mother?" Eve demanded. "Did you have no regard for the agony you put her through?"

"I felt bad for Reggie. I did. But whenever she started to weigh on my mind, I'd tell myself that she brought it on herself by letting creeps like Derrick Sway come into her home. Everyone knew it was only a matter of time before some pervert took advantage of the situation." She glanced at Eve. "When I thought about things in that light, it was easy to convince myself we were doing the right thing by those little girls."

"The right thing?" Eve stared at her for a moment. "You never once considered the possibility that you could be handing them over to traffickers?"

Nadine winced. "We didn't know about that kind of thing back then. Not really. It wasn't all over the news like it is nowadays. Maybe we didn't want to know. Maybe we wanted to believe we were doing the right thing because a hundred thousand dollars apiece was enough for all of us to have a second chance."

Even if Eve could swallow a word of Nadine's story, she certainly didn't buy the justification. "How did that second chance work out for you?"

Nadine answered bluntly. "Not good. We only got half the amount for one kid and cash never goes as far as you think it will. Once Denny and me parted ways, I started cleaning houses just to get by."

"If the plan was to kidnap the twins, why did you only take Maya?" Eve asked.

"Gabriel didn't show. He'd gone off by himself earlier to try to get a glimpse of you playing in the yard or something. When we got the go signal, he was nowhere to be found. Denny couldn't take both kids by himself so he grabbed the one closest to the window and brought her back here where we were all supposed to meet up. Then we were to take them both to the drop. We waited for a bit, but when Gabriel didn't turn up with the other kid, Denny went out looking for him. He had to make sure Gabriel didn't get caught or something and that the police weren't already looking for us. He came back a couple hours later with blood all over his hands and clothes."

Dread seeped into Eve's voice. "My dad's blood?"

Nadine nodded, her eyes shadowed with old grief. "He said he found Gabriel down in the cave. Somebody had stabbed him in the heart and bashed him in the head with a rock. He was already cold, Denny said. Nothing he could do but pile stones on the body and hope no one would find him until we got away."

Eve wrapped her arms around her middle. "And you believed him?"

"He was my brother. He wouldn't lie about something like that."

Of course he would lie. People did a lot worse to save themselves. "What made him think to look in the cave?"

"It was only a couple of miles from Reggie's house. If anything went wrong, we were supposed to head there to hide out until we could figure a way to get out of town. We'd stashed a little cash and some fake IDs down there just in case."

"What did you do with Maya?"

"We took her to the drop. What else could we do?" she asked in a matter-of-fact voice. "We sure as heck couldn't take her back home. She'd already seen our faces. We had to go through with our plans despite losing Gabriel."

"What happened at the drop?"

"A car came and picked the kid up. We never saw her again."

Anger welled in Eve's chest. She gripped the edge of the seat as a terrible image formed in her head. "You sat there and watched a four-year-old child get into a car with strangers?"

"Yes," Nadine said quietly.

Eve had to take a moment. "You left town that same night? Where did you go?"

"Here and there."

"San Antonio?"

Nadine blinked. "Why does it matter where we went?"

"My father sent three postcards to me after he left town. Two from New Orleans and one from San Antonio."

"I know. I was there when he sent them," Nadine said.

"The postcard from San Antonio came after the kidnapping. Did you send it?"

"We needed people to believe he was alive and well and we were all still miles and miles from Black Creek. Last thing we wanted was for someone to start asking questions about Gabriel's whereabouts. So I copied his handwriting as best I could and hoped it would be good enough to fool his kid."

"Did it ever cross your mind that Denny could have killed my dad for his share of the money?"

"He wouldn't do that."

"Your brother seems to be capable of a lot more than you want to admit."

Nadine gave her a shrewd look. "People do sometimes fool you, don't they? Even your own kin. But if Denny had wanted to kill Gabriel for money, he would have made it quick. Whoever attacked your daddy must have had a powerful grudge to do what they did to him. They say you don't know what a person is capable of until they've been betrayed by the person they love most."

Eve understood the insinuation and turned the tables. "Are you speaking from experience? Did my dad betray you? Maybe he decided he wanted to be with his family more than he wanted to be with you."

Nadine shook her head slowly. "There was only one person besides Denny and me that even knew Gabriel was back in town that night."

Eve hardened her demeanor against the insinuation. "There's no reason in the world for me to believe you. If you are telling the truth about the kidnapping, there's absolutely no reason why I shouldn't arrest you on the spot."

"I'm telling the truth, all right, at least as much of it as I know. But if you take me in I'll deny every word of it until my dying breath."

"Why? If you really want peace, why not take responsibility for what you did and accept the consequences?"

"I can't go back to prison. Not at my age. I don't want to end my days in a cage."

"You may not have any say in the matter," Eve told her.

"No, I thought it through before I called you. Without evidence, it's your word against mine."

"There's evidence somewhere. If I have to search every inch of that cave, I'll do it. If it takes me the next decade, I'll find it," Eve promised.

"I can't stop you from trying, but it's been nearly thirty years and we made sure we covered our tracks."

"Criminals always think they've covered their tracks, but something gets forgotten or left behind. People talk."

"Maybe *you* need to think this through," Nadine said. "You keep pushing like you are and people may start to wonder if you're trying to put the blame on me and my brother to protect someone else. And for what? Take a good look at me. Do I look like I have enough time left to serve a long prison sentence? Chances are I'd be dead before they could ever bring a case to trial."

Eve gave her a long once-over. "What's wrong with you?"

"Stage four lung cancer. Nothing they can do about it. The doctors say I waited too long to come in and get checked out."

Eve stared at her for a moment longer, taking in her gaunt features and sallow complexion. "I'm sorry."

Nadine glanced away. "Don't be. Maybe I'm getting what I deserve. Even if Maya Lamb ended up with a better life, it wasn't our place to take her."

"Do you think she could still be alive?"

"I don't know. I hope so. I pray so."

Eve did, too, but they both knew the odds were not in Maya's favor.

"Why did you come back after all this time if not to turn yourself in?" Eve asked. "Surely it wasn't just to clear your conscience with me."

"I came back because Denny was here. And because I heard another little girl had gone missing."

Eve's voice sharpened. "You thought he had something to do with Kylie Buchanan's abduction?"

"Doesn't matter what I thought. You caught her kidnapper dead to rights, didn't you?"

"Yes."

"Well, then." She shrugged as if everything had worked out for the best. As if she hadn't just confessed to the crime of the century by Black Creek standards. As if she hadn't just shattered Eve's memory of her adored father.

"So what now?" she asked.

"I can't just let you walk away from this," Eve said.

Nadine's smile seemed more like a grimace. "That's what I figured you'd say. Which is why I took precautions before I came here."

"Meaning?"

"I called my brother and told him what I intended to do. He's on his way out here to try to stop me. He's probably getting close by now."

Eve glanced over her shoulder.

"You're right to be afraid of him," Nadine said with a nod. "Denny gets mean when he's cornered. But if we hurry, I can drop you back at your car and you can high-tail it to safety before he gets here. Or you can wait and try to take us both in at the same time."

"So you let her go?" Nash stared at Eve in disbelief.

She stared right back at him across his desk. "What would you have me do? I could hardly take on Nadine and her brother without a weapon."

"That's my point. What were you thinking, meeting this woman unarmed out in the middle of nowhere? To make matters worse, you left your phone behind so you couldn't call in for backup. Did I hear that right?"

She had the grace to look embarrassed. "I know it sounds bad."

"Damn right it sounds bad. You're a seasoned officer of the law, Eve. You had to know better."

"I knew it was a risk, but she offered information I couldn't get anywhere else. I weighed my options and decided to hear what she had to say. What would you have done in my place?" she asked in a reasonable tone.

"I would have called in my whereabouts and made sure backup was on the way." A pat answer, but he couldn't say with absolute certainty that he would have reacted any differently.

"I made a split-second decision to follow my instincts, and in light of what I learned from Nadine, I think the risk was well worth it."

Nash refused to give her a break. "And if she'd pulled a gun on you?"

"I would have handled the situation. Give me a little credit."

"I'd like to, but you're not making it easy." He leaned

back in his chair, still scrutinizing her disapprovingly. "This isn't like you—withholding information on a case, refusing to call in for backup. What's going on with you?"

"Does any of that really matter given what we now know about Maya Lamb's kidnapping?" Her voice remained calm but her knuckles whitened where she gripped the arms of the chair. Nash wanted to argue that of course it mattered. Safety and conduct always mattered. Going off half-cocked was never a good look for a detective. But he conceded her point for the moment.

"Why did she come to you with this information?"

"She said she heard I'd been looking for her."

Nash frowned. "We've both been looking for her. Why call you and not me?"

"Maybe because you're the chief of police. Your position would likely intimidate someone like Nadine." She tucked back her hair in frustration. "Again, I feel like you're missing the point."

"No, I'm just trying to get a clear picture of how this meeting went down." Because Nash still had the feeling Eve was holding out on him. "I'm trying to understand why Nadine Crosby remains a free woman."

"Even if I'd managed to bring her in, she said she would deny everything," Eve explained. "It would end up being my word against hers. You and I both know her confession would never hold up in court."

"Which is why you should have followed protocol," he couldn't help stressing.

She closed her eyes briefly. "I know. I'm sorry. But if I hadn't met with her, we wouldn't have as much information as we do." She loosened her grip on the armrests and got up to pace. "This is the first break in Maya Lamb's case in nearly three decades. At least now we know where to look for evidence and witnesses so that we can start piecing it all together. If there's even the slightest chance she's alive, her family deserves to know the truth. If she's not, they still deserve justice."

"They deserve not to have their hearts broken all over again," Nash cautioned. Eve had gone over to the window to stare out. He swiveled his chair to track her. "How do we know Nadine Crosby is telling the truth?"

"Why would she lie about something like that? She's a dying woman."

"According to her."

"I believe her. She looks deathly ill." Eve turned and leaned back against her hands. "I think she wanted to clear her conscience before she dies."

"Why did she feel the need to clear her conscience with you? That's the part I don't get. Tell me what I'm missing." Nash cocked his head as he continued to regard her. "What are you still not telling me?"

"I came straight here after my meeting with Nadine so that I could relate our conversation while it was still fresh in my head. Doesn't that count for anything?" Her gaze remained steadfast and steely, but he could detect a slight tremor at the corners of her mouth.

"What's going on with you, Eve?" When she didn't answer, he repeated the question in a softer voice. "What is it?"

She closed her eyes on a breath. "You're right. There is something else."

He waited patiently.

"Nadine told me a third person was involved in the kidnapping."

Nash stared at her in surprise. "Why didn't you mention this before? Did she give you a name?"

The silence dragged out between them.

"Eve?"

"Gabriel Jareau."

"Jareau. Is he—"

She nodded. "My father was the third kidnapper."

Nash rocked forward in his chair, stunned by the revelation. "Your father conspired with Nadine and Denton Crosby to kidnap Maya Lamb?"

Her gaze burned into his. "They were paid to abduct both girls that night. Only according to Nadine, my dad never showed up at Reggie's house."

"Paid by who?"

"Nadine doesn't know or wouldn't say. I believe my dad was double-crossed by one or both of his accomplices for his share of the money. Then he was buried beneath a pile of rocks in McNally's Cave in the hope that his body would never be found."

Chapter Twelve

Eve was quiet all the way out to the cave. For all that she had revealed to Nash, she was still holding back something important, something possibly devastating—the insinuation that her mother may have killed her father. She could barely stand to roll the possibility around in her own mind, let alone put it out in the universe for endless speculation. Before anyone else went to that dark place, she had to talk to Jackie. She had to find out if her father had really come to see her on the night of the kidnapping.

She could sense Nash's gaze on her from time to time. She hid behind her sunglasses and stared straight ahead.

He was the first to break the strained silence. "The DNA sample you dropped off at the lab was yours?"

"Yes."

"How long have you known about John Doe?"

"I still don't know for certain, but I've suspected his identity ever since that first day at the lab when Dr. Forester showed us the holed coin recovered from the grave." She pulled the Mercury dime from her collar and held it up for Nash to see. The silver seemed to shimmer with an uncanny glow, but Eve knew it was only sunlight and not magic. "My dad gave me this coin on the night he left town. He always wore one just like it. He said they would bring us luck, but I guess his ran out down in the cave."

"Why didn't you say anything?" Nash asked. "Why keep it to yourself when you knew it could change the course of our investigation?"

"I never intended to keep it from you for this long. I wanted to talk to my mom first, but then she was injured and I had to put it off. I kept telling myself I just needed a little more time, but the truth is, I didn't want to believe it was my dad down in that cave. Somehow speaking my fear aloud made it seem too real. Too final. I wasn't ready to say goodbye and, yes, I do realize how irrational that sounds."

"I get it," Nash said quietly.

The note of tenderness in his voice brought a wave of unexpected emotion. It made Eve think they might yet find their way back to the intimate place they'd tentatively explored in her garden last evening. "No matter how many years went by, I still believed he was out there somewhere, still alive and still thinking about me. It was a comfort, you know? Then to find out he'd been murdered…that someone had attacked him so viciously and buried his body down in that cave…" She trailed off. "It's hard enough to let go of a fantasy, much less to accept such a brutal truth."

He nodded, letting her ramble on for as long as she needed to.

She closed her eyes briefly. "Leaving us was one thing, but abducting a child? How am I supposed to wrap my head around that? How does one ever make peace with something like that?"

"What he did is no reflection on you," Nash said. "That's what you told me, remember? Besides, if Nadine's story is true, then your dad didn't kidnap anyone. It's even possible he changed his mind and tried to stop the abduction. Maybe that's what got him killed."

Eve wanted nothing so much as to cling to that small sliver of hope, but she couldn't dismiss or diminish the degree of her father's participation. "I appreciate what you're trying to do, but there's no way to whitewash his involvement. Even if he changed his mind, he was ready to take those girls from their home right up until the last minute. What does that say about his character?"

"*If* Nadine's story is true," Nash stressed. "We shouldn't accept her account at face value. Let's not forget that Ron Naples is dead and Nadine all but admitted that her brother killed him. At this point, they'll say anything to try to save their own hides. We need to bring them in and interrogate them separately. Make each of them worry that the other could turn."

"I agree, but they could be halfway to Georgia by now."

"We've got eyes in every corner of the county. We'll find them," Nash said with a confidence Eve was far from sharing.

She'd allowed Nadine Crosby to go free and now the weight of that decision bore down on her. What if the woman had been bluffing about her brother? If Eve had called her on it, Nadine could be sweating it out in an interrogation room at that very moment. But without her weapon, Eve had decided to play it safe and now Nadine could already be headed for the state line. Maybe she and Nash were wasting their time trawling for evidence in the cave when their efforts might be better targeted to the back roads.

"How much farther?" she asked.

"Five minutes."

He turned onto the gravel road that led back to the gated entrance. Deep tread marks from heavy equipment crisscrossed the soft earth on the other side of the fence, a grim reminder that the cave entrances were to be closed for the deadliest of reasons. Two teenagers had drowned and a man had been murdered down there. Never again,

Mr. McNally had vowed. The fence and locked gate hadn't been enough to keep thrill seekers and criminals out of the cave even after the first bodies had been recovered. Blowing up the rock with dynamite and shoving the piles of debris down into the holes with a bulldozer would seal the cave once and for all.

Two uniformed officers milled about the rocky mouth that dropped nearly straight down into the first cavern. Nash pulled up behind the squad car and they got out. Eve helped him retrieve their equipment from the back of the SUV and then they went through the gate, scrambling up a gentle incline to stand at the precipice, gazing down into the pitch-black abyss.

"You sure you want to do this?" Nash asked. "Some of the passageways can get pretty dicey, and the tunnel back to the cavern is a belly-crawl for most of the way."

Eve nodded. "I can handle it."

"Just stay calm and keep breathing," Nash advised. "And don't get separated."

"I'm not about to go off on my own if that's what you're worried about."

"All right, let's do this," he said.

They used a belay rope to lower themselves down to the cave floor, pausing at the bottom to unharness and fan their flashlight beams over the limestone walls. Then they turned off their flashlights and headlamps and allowed their eyes to adjust to the sensation of total darkness.

Being belowground was an unsettling experience for Eve. Far more unnerving than she could have imagined. Close places normally didn't bother her and she hadn't been afraid of the dark since she was a child. But this was different. The blackness seemed unnatural somehow, the cool air against her face like the caress of a ghostly hand.

Daddy? Are you still down here?

No answer.

She drew a calming breath, grateful for Nash's know-how and steady presence. Otherwise, she might have crawled right back up out of that cave. The unseen walls seemed to close in on her as the distant drip of water echoed through the series of tunnels and chambers.

After about five minutes, Nash turned on his headlamp and tucked his flashlight under his belt. Eve did the same, following him silently through the first narrow tunnel into a room larger than the first. She glanced around the lime-stone walls and tried to appreciate the surreal beauty of the underground terrain. *This isn't so bad.* The tunnel had been tight, but at no point had she felt trapped or panicky, and the room they stood in now was spacious and ethereal.

The entrance to the second tunnel was a bit closer, the third one even narrower. Nash again took the lead, and when he dropped to his hands and knees a few yards in, Eve felt her first prickle of fear.

She was certain she hadn't made a sound, but he must have sensed her unease. He turned, keeping his headlamp averted so as not to catch her in the face. "You okay?"

She nodded then said on a thin breath, "I'm fine."

"Sure you want to keep going?"

"Yes. Don't worry about me. I'm not claustrophobic," she assured him.

"We may run into water at some point. If the tunnel is flooded, we'll turn back."

Eve was a good swimmer and had never been afraid of water, but there was no room to maneuver in the tunnel. No place to surface if a passageway flooded. And if their lights went out, they'd be operating in complete darkness. But that was the worst-case scenario, and nothing like that would happen. *Everything will be fine.*

The limestone floor grew damp as the tunnel tightened.

Eve took deep breaths and tried to stay focused, keeping Nash in the beam of her headlamp. When he momentarily disappeared from her line of sight, her heart dropped before she realized he'd stepped from the tunnel into another room, this one the largest of four. The sound of water grew louder and as she emerged from the passageway, she could see the beam of his flashlight glistening on a dark surface.

"So this is the underground pool I've heard so much about," Eve said in awe. She balanced on the slippery ledge to get a better view. "This is where the FBI found Kylie's doll, trapped in a powerful whirlpool. An agent almost lost his life when Grace hit him from behind and knocked him into the water."

Eve wasn't sure why she felt the need to recount the details of Grace's crimes. Nash was undoubtedly more familiar with them than she. Maybe the kidnapping was still fresh on her mind since her meeting with Grace or maybe being down in the cave brought back the panic of those first few hours after Kylie had gone missing when the outcome of their search was still in doubt.

"The vortex could have pulled him to the bottom and no one would have ever known what happened to him," she muttered.

"I'm well aware of Special Agent Stillwell's close call," Nash said.

Eve turned. "Sorry. I wasn't trying to make a point. I guess I'm a little nervous about being down here after everything that's happened."

"No need to apologize. This place does have an effect." Nash moved up beside her and hunkered on the ledge, sweeping his flashlight beam over the water. "Grace would have known that once the doll was found we'd waste precious hours scouring every square inch of the cave."

"But how did she know the doll would be found? That's

what I don't understand." Eve trained her beam straight down into the water and shivered. The pool looked bottomless. "The doll wasn't found during the initial canvas. She must have come back later and planted it, but how could she have known Agent Stillwell would come down here and take another look?"

"It was a reasonable assumption that a more thorough search would be conducted at some point. Even if the doll had never been found, she planted other clues in less obscure locations to throw us off track. She thought through every scenario."

"Sometimes it almost seems as if her instincts are supernatural." The way their voices echoed across the water drew another shiver down Eve's spine. For a moment, she could almost imagine Grace peering up at her from down below.

Nash would have none of that illusion. "There's nothing supernatural about Grace. She thinks ahead and she knows how to read people. Like any good con artist," he added under his breath.

Their headlamps were off, but Eve could see his profile in the reflected glow of their flashlights. He looked dark and mysterious. A man haunted by his past—but weren't they all?

"I can't help wondering—" She stopped abruptly.

"What?" he pressed.

"Nothing. It's none of my business."

"You want to know how Grace and I got together."

"You don't owe me an explanation," Eve said. "Besides, this is hardly the time or place."

"Maybe it's the perfect place." Nash played the light around the walls. "I can see why she would be drawn to the cave as a kid. She would have liked the darkness and the echoes." He moved the beam slowly over the water. "All those secret places."

"You would never know to look at her. The way she dresses and wears her hair...her demeanor. She seems almost shy at times."

"When it suits her," Nash said. "Nothing Grace does is by accident."

"But surely she wasn't always that way." Eve was still trying to figure out how Nash had been taken in by someone as calculating as his ex-wife had seemed earlier.

"She may not have always been capable of kidnapping a four-year-old child, but the cunning was a constant in varying degrees. It just took me a while to figure her out. Neither of us was in a good place when we met, and I think we sensed a kinship in the other. Grace seemed lost, as if she couldn't find her place in the world, and I knew that feeling only too well." He shifted, balancing the flashlight on his knee. "That's something they don't tell you when you come back stateside after combat deployment. You don't feel like you belong here anymore. There are days when you actually miss being over there. It's worse when you've left friends behind. Survivor's guilt is a very real thing."

His hushed voice echoed through the chamber, like a soft breeze whispering across Eve's nerve endings. He'd never talked to her this way before. She doubted he'd talked to anyone like this, even Grace.

"We had that in common," Nash said. "That feeling of displacement. She was different from anyone I'd ever known, and I liked that about her at the time. She didn't ask a lot of questions and she didn't mind long silences. So many people feel the need to fill every hour of every day with some kind of noise, but Grace was content to sit quietly in the dark. No music, no TV, no phone calls. It was soothing at first, that silence. Healing. I think it might have saved me. But the harder I worked to find normal, the harder she fought to keep us trapped in a void." He paused, rolling the flashlight across his thigh. "I'm not explaining it very well. Maybe after all these years I still don't understand it myself."

"There are a lot of things I still don't understand about my past," Eve said. "I've never known why my parents split up. Why my father left the way he did, why my mother gets so flustered and uncomfortable when she hears his name. Nadine's story explains some things, but it also raises more questions."

"That's why we're down here," Nash reminded her as he rose. "We should probably get moving."

Eve nodded. "I'm glad you told me about Grace. In the six years we've worked together, I still sometimes feel I don't really know you at all despite…certain moments."

He turned at that, his eyes glinting down at her in the muted light. "You took me by surprise that day."

"I surprised myself," she admitted. "Or maybe *embarrassed* is a better word."

"Why were you embarrassed? It's what we both wanted."

He said it so pragmatically and yet Eve felt her every nerve ending react to his comment. "It was inappropriate. You were my superior and not yet divorced."

"Grace and I had been separated for years. We should have divorced a long time ago."

"I'm old-fashioned, I guess. I didn't want to do anything that would interfere with a reconciliation."

"There was never any chance of that," he assured her.

"I didn't know that, though. I backed off because it was the right thing to do and you never came near me again even after your divorce so I assumed…." She shrugged. "It really doesn't matter."

"It does to me," he said. "When this is over, I'd like the chance to show how much it matters."

Eve's heart thudded. *When this is over...*

"Let's just press on for now," she said, refusing to think farther ahead than the next tunnel. Refusing to commit when she still had her father's murder to solve. "The sooner we explore the cavern the sooner we can get out of here."

He said nothing to that, but turned to chase away shadows with his flashlight.

The interlude already seemed distant as Eve followed him off the ledge. Maybe it was her imagination, but the darkness seemed deeper now, the dank chill more pervasive as she tuned her senses to the subtle sounds of the cave. *Daddy, are you down here?*

Nothing came to her still but the faint, eerie whistle of air through one of the passageways.

GRACE HAD BEEN right about the entrance to the tunnel. The mouth was so well camouflaged that one would be hard-pressed to find the opening without prior knowledge or a guide. Eve scrambled over a pile of stones and then followed Nash into a recessed area of the limestone wall. Inside the hollow, he pointed to the black hole that would eventually lead them to the hidden chamber where the bones had been recovered.

He shined his light back into the opening. Nothing but limestone and darkness as far as Eve could see. He tucked the flashlight into his belt and turned on his headlamp before stooping to enter the tunnel. A few yards in, the walls narrowed and the ceiling dropped so that they had to maneuver the confined space bent double. Then on their hands and knees. Then flat on the floor, propelling themselves forward with knees and elbows. Another right turn and the channel tightened yet again. Eve took deep breaths, trying to control her racing pulse. She couldn't help thinking about her father's last journey through that same passageway. Had he still been alive or had someone dragged his body back to the hidden chamber for burial?

Nash said over his shoulder, "You doing okay?"

She voiced the fear that had been preying on her poise. "Are you sure we'll be able to get back out?"

"The worst is almost behind us. The tunnel should start to widen just ahead."

Eve lay flat on her stomach, arms stretched in front of her. "How do you suppose anyone found this passageway?"

"People are naturally curious about places like this. Nothing can stay hidden forever."

I'm counting on that, Eve thought.

"The walls in the chamber are covered with old graffiti," Nash said. "From what I understand, teenagers used to come back here to party until those two kids got caught in a flooded passageway and drowned. That's when the owner fenced the property and put a locked gate at the entrance. But people still climbed the fence and came down here, which is why he's now undertaking more drastic measures. But I'm not telling you anything you don't already know. You were born and raised here."

"That was before my time," Eve said. "My friends and I never paid much attention to this place."

"You were smart. It's easy to get turned around down here. Even without flooded passageways, caves are dangerous if you don't know what you're doing." Nash turned back to the task at hand, and as he'd predicted, the tunnel soon began to widen until they were able to crawl then stoop then stand as they approached the entrance to the chamber.

He hovered in the opening, splaying his light over the walls and into the deep recesses before he motioned to

Eve. She took out her flashlight and turned off the head-lamp as she stepped into the room. For a moment, she felt almost breathless as her scalp prickled a warning. *Daddy, you in here?*

The graffiti on the walls was faded and peeling from the moist environment. A dozen or more wine bottles with burned-out candles littered the floor, along with a few rusted beer cans.

"So kids really did come down here to party," she said in a hushed voice.

"Apparently so."

Nash remained stationary as Eve walked around the room, playing the flashlight beam over murals and dozens of personal messages proclaiming love and marking territory. Donna was here. Andy was here a year later. Carla loved Kenny nearly thirty years ago. Jackie loved Gabriel on New Year's Eve. And so on and so on…

Eve swept the beam over the messages, froze and slowly backtracked. *Jackie loves Gabriel.*

She thought at once of Denton Crosby's insistence that her mother was all too familiar with the cave. *Oh, she knew what she was doing, all right.*

Doesn't mean a thing, Eve told herself. So her mother and father had once partied in McNally's Cave. According to the messages, dozens of their contemporaries had come down here at one time or another. It meant nothing.

But what if it did? What if she not only learned that her father had been a conspirator in Maya Lamb's kidnapping, but that her mother had been responsible for his death? How would she handle such a terrible revelation? How did one overcome something that insidious? Eve didn't want to go there, but the insinuation had burrowed deep, which she assumed was exactly what Denton and Nadine Crosby had intended.

She glanced back at Nash, tracking the beam of his light as he crossed the chamber and knelt. He scooped up a handful of pebbles from the floor and sifted them through his fingers.

"This looks fresh," he said. "I think they must have already begun filling in the second entrance when I called. It was never large enough to accommodate even an average-sized adult, but I guess Mr. McNally doesn't want to take any chances." He rose and picked his way through an obstacle course of scattered stones and small boulders.

Eve watched for another moment and then turned back to the graffiti, tracing her finger slowly over the names. The message had been written on New Year's Eve in the same year her dad had graduated from high school with Denton Crosby. A couple of years later he and Jackie were married with a baby on the way. Had he already been seeing Nadine? Had he already felt trapped by the confines of marriage and parenthood? Had he considered Eve a burden from the moment she'd been conceived?

Beneath the love message, a crescent moon dangled from the word *eve* in New Year's Eve. *Each night before you go to bed, stand at the window with that lucky dime. Look up at the moon and think about me. I'll be gazing up at the same moon and thinking about you. That way, we'll always be together no matter where we are.*

The memory was almost a physical jolt. She clung to her lucky coin as she traced the outline of the moon with her finger. *I'm here, Daddy.*

I wish you hadn't come, Boo. I wish you never had to know.

She turned, almost expecting to find her father's ghost hovering behind her. Instead, she saw nothing but the scattered remnants of his secret grave. *Daddy?*

"Eve?"

She'd been so caught up in the moment that her name so softly spoken startled her yet again. She splayed her beam over the walls in a frantic search for the disembodied voice.

"Nash?" When he didn't answer, she called in a shaky voice, "Where are you?"

"I'm here."

She moved the beam toward the sound of his voice. "Where? I can't see you."

He stepped from a deep cavity in the wall. "I'm right here. I thought I'd found another tunnel, but it only goes back a few feet."

"Do you suppose that's where Grace hid when she heard someone in the tunnel?"

"If you believe her story."

"I'm inclined to," Eve said. "You didn't see her face this morning when she recounted the experience. I could have sworn she was a frightened little girl. And, no, I don't think she's that good of an actor."

"You don't know her," Nash said.

"You're right, I don't. But let's assume she did see someone down here. She may be the best chance we have of finding John Doe's killer."

"She'll only agree to cooperate if there's something in it for her," Nash warned.

"Maybe this time she'll do the right thing."

"Don't count on it. She called me after your meeting. She said she recognized someone from the photos you showed her."

"Yes, she had a strong reaction to Denton Crosby's image. But why call you when she'd already talked to me about it?"

"She thinks if she helps solve the case, it will sway the judge in her favor."

"Will it?"

"I don't know. After what she's done?" He had just stepped out of the recess and started toward Eve when she heard a low rumble from above. She lifted her gaze to a sliver of light in the ceiling.

"Did you hear something?"

He cocked his head, listening. "Sounds like an engine."

"That close to the opening? You said Mr. McNally shut down the operation, right?"

"Yes, everything's on hold until he hears back from me."

The sound of the engine grew steadily louder.

"Maybe they're moving some of the machinery to another job site," Nash suggested.

Before Eve could respond, a small explosion on the surface sent an avalanche of rocks and debris down through the cave opening, pelting her upturned face until she scrambled for cover. Pressing against the wall, she pulled her shirt up over her nose and mouth. The air was suddenly so thick she could scarcely draw a breath.

"Nash?" She choked on a mouthful of dust.

He responded at once. "Over here. You okay?"

"Yes. Where are you?"

"I'm still on the other side of the cavern. Stay put. I'll come to you."

But no sooner were the words out of his mouth than another explosion shook the cave ceiling, dislodging a chunk of limestone that came crashing to the floor behind her. She yelped and dived out of the way. A boulder that size could have crushed her skull.

Someone above was detonating charges all around the opening. Rather than sealing the entrance, the explosions were filling the chamber with a deadly combination of rock shards and fine dust. Was that the intent? Eve wondered. To obscure the chamber where her father had been buried?

"Nash?" When he didn't answer, she fought back a wave

of panic as she coughed harshly into her shirt. She eased away from the wall and peered up at the ceiling. The hole had doubled in size. Before she could duck out of the way, another avalanche rained down upon her.

She stumbled through the dust, calling for Nash. "Can you hear me?"

"Someone's using a bulldozer," he said. "This whole place is about to be filled in."

"Where are you?"

"Don't worry about me." His voice sounded muffled. "Head for the tunnel!"

Fear shot through her. "Are you hurt?"

"No, I'm okay. I'll meet you at the tunnel."

"I don't know where it is! I can't see anything through the dust."

"Keep your face covered. I'll come find you."

She tried to follow the sound of his voice, but the chaos had completely disoriented her. She'd taken only a few steps in what she thought was the right direction when something struck her on the head hard enough to knock her off her feet. Dazed, she tried to crawl to safety, but the avalanche came harder and faster, cutting off her air and obliterating her sense of direction. She couldn't breathe. Panic set in. She was about to be buried alive in the same place where her father's bones had remained hidden for nearly three decades.

Daddy?

I'm here, Boo. Just take my hand.

Chapter Thirteen

Eve had only a hazy recollection of the actual rescue. If pressed, she could call up a vague image of being lifted from the cavern through the hole in the ceiling and then gently placed on the ground by Nash and her fellow officers. By the time the EMTs arrived, she was lucid, sitting up and insisting that she was fine, though she had to admit her head hurt and her right arm just might be broken. She cradled it against her body while arguing with Nash that he needed to be out searching for Denton Crosby instead of fussing over her.

"That's being handled," Nash assured her as one of the techs checked her vitals.

"You've got a pretty big goose egg on the back of your head," the tech observed. "Could be a concussion, and that right arm is almost certainly fractured. We'll give you a ride to the ER so you can get patched up."

"I feel fine," Eve insisted. "I don't need to go to the hospital."

"Why do cops always make the worst patients?" he wanted to know.

"You're going to the ER," Nash informed her. "Head injuries are nothing to take lightly, and besides that, I'm not about to send you out in the field with a broken arm."

"It's probably just bruised or sprained."

"We'll soon find out."

Eve put up a good fight, but in the end, common sense and Nash's stubbornness won out. Three hours later, she was ensconced in a cubicle at the hospital having undergone a series of MRIs, X-rays and EEGs. Her mother arrived just as she was wheeled back into the room from having her arm casted. She hovered at Eve's bedside, smoothing the covers and berating her daughter for not having called her sooner.

"I'm fine, Mom," Eve said wearily. "I didn't see the need to worry you."

"Thank goodness Chief Bowden thought otherwise." Jackie plumped Eve's pillow. She was composed so long as there were tasks to be done, but when she stopped long enough to observe the superficial injuries on Eve's face and arms, her eyes filled with tears. "Oh, Evie! Just look at your poor face. You were only just starting to heal from your last injury. And that arm!"

Eve held up her cast. "We're a matching pair now."

Jackie scowled down at her. "This is not a laughing matter."

"Sorry. Must be the morphine," Eve murmured. "By the way, where is Chief Bowden?"

Her mother lifted a brow as if she'd picked up on something in Eve's tone. "He hurried out as I was coming in. Police business, I guess."

Eve sat up in bed. "Did he say what it was?"

"I didn't ask. I was too worried about you at the time." She put her hand on top of Eve's. "Why didn't you tell me about the remains that were found in the cave?"

Eve lay back against the pillows. "We were trying to keep it under wraps until we had a positive ID. But I should have known better. Word always gets around in this town."

"I thought something was up when you asked about Gabriel's broken bones. Is that how you knew it was him?"

"We still don't have a positive ID, but I suspected John Doe's identity because of this." Eve pulled the dime from her collar. "Daddy gave this to me on the night he left town. He always wore one just like it, remember?"

"Yes." Jackie sniffed. "For a grown man, he had a lot of silly superstitions."

What would you say if I told you Daddy helped me get out of that cave alive?

He hadn't, of course. His presence had been nothing more than Eve's imagination. Her subconscious conjuring a familiar voice to calm her fears. That was the logical explanation.

"A holed coin just like this was recovered from the cave along with the remains," she said.

Her mother couldn't take her eyes off the dime. "Gabriel's coin?"

"I think so." Eve let the dime drop to her chest, no longer bothering to hide it inside the neck of her hospital gown. "I need to ask you something, Mom."

"What is it?"

"Did Daddy come back to town? After he left us, I mean. Did he try to see me on the night Maya Lamb went missing?"

The color seemed to drain from Jackie's face as she stared down at Eve in distress. "How could you possibly know that? You were in your room when he came. I wouldn't let him come inside."

"Why?"

"*Why?* After everything he'd done I was supposed to welcome him home with open arms? He left me with a child to raise and a mortgage to pay and he thought he could drop back in to play daddy whenever the mood struck him. It wasn't going to work that way. He made his choice." The level of her bitterness shook Eve. After twenty-eight years, her mother was still that angry?

"You had every right to send him away," Eve said. "I'm not trying to second-guess your decision. I just want to know the truth."

Jackie's blue eyes glittered with unshed emotion. "Who told you he came back?"

"Nadine Crosby."

Her mother recoiled from the bed as if Eve had physically struck her. "When did you talk to that woman?"

"This morning. Mom…" Eve searched her mother's face. "Did you know what they were up to that night?"

"What are you talking about?"

"Nadine said they were paid to kidnap Maya Lamb. They were supposed to take both twins, only Daddy never showed up after he came to see me."

Her mother stared back at her in confusion, but there was an inexplicable darkness in her eyes, a strange note of dread in her voice. "You're not making any sense."

Maybe she wasn't, Eve thought. She was starting to mumble and slur her words. The medication was kicking in big-time. She leaned back against the pillows and closed her eyes. "Daddy left town with Nadine and Denton Crosby because they needed an alibi for the night the twins were to be taken. He wanted everyone, including you and me, to think he was miles away and that he was never coming back. But he did come back. What happened when he came to the house?"

"I already told you, I wouldn't let him inside. Not when he had the smell of that woman all over him. I would have sooner seen him dead."

Eve tried to muster up the energy to open her eyes, but she seemed to sink deeper into the pillows. She was so tired. She was physically exhausted and emotionally drained, but she needed to stay alert. Her mother had just told her something important, something she needed to remember…

She had the sense that Jackie was leaning over the bed, peering down at her. "Evie?"

"Hmm…"

"Go to sleep, sweetheart. You don't have to worry about your daddy ever again."

EVE SPENT THE night and most of the next day in the hospital, but as twilight hovered on the horizon, she got up, dressed and signed herself out. The on-call doctor had advised that she take it easy for the next several days, to which Eve had readily agreed. But she would have agreed to almost anything to get back home to her own bed. She would have called Jackie to come and pick her up, but Nash arrived just as she'd finished dressing and signing all the release forms. He'd volunteered to take her home, and once there, he insisted on staying while she settled in.

On the way home, he'd filled her in on the search for Nadine and Denton Crosby. The station had been bombarded with anonymous tips and sightings, but nothing had panned out so far.

Eve didn't want to think about them at the moment. She'd taken a painkiller as soon as she got home and now she languished in a hot bath, keeping her casted arm high and dry on the edge of the tub, while Nash puttered around in her kitchen, scrambling eggs and toasting bread. They ate on her back porch where they could watch the sunset. Afterward, they migrated out to the swing, gently swaying in companionable silence as the sky turned from golden pink to lavender and then inky blue. Stars began to twinkle through the clouds as a crescent moon rose over the treetops.

Eve thought about the crescent moon drawn on the wall of the cave. *I'll be staring up at the same moon, Boo...*

She shivered as a light breeze whispered through the magnolias, stirring a lusciously scented melancholy.

Nash draped his arm over the back of the swing, his fingertips lightly brushing her shoulder. Eve gave him a sidelong glance as she slid toward him. His arm came around her at once and he pulled her closer until their thighs touched and she could rest her head on his shoulder.

"Do you think we'll ever find them?" she asked.

"The Crosbys? We'll find them."

"How can you be so confident? Too much time has passed. They've left the state by now. They may even have left the country."

"I don't think so," Nash said. "I think they came back to Black Creek for a reason. They won't leave until they've tied up all the loose ends."

"Like me?"

"You can place the three of them together. That's not much, but it's something."

"Nadine claims my dad came to see me on the night of the kidnapping. She said Denton went out looking for him when he didn't show up. Do you think it's possible I saw them together that night and just forgot?"

He absently massaged her shoulder. "Have you asked your mom about that night?"

"She said he came by the house but she wouldn't let him in. Not after the way he left us."

"Can't blame her for that."

"No," Eve said, but she couldn't shake the disconcert-ing notion that there was more to the story than her mother had let on. She sighed heavily, her gaze fixated on the rising moon.

"Tired?" Nash asked.

"A little."

"Maybe it's bedtime."

The low rumble of his baritone stilled her heart. She lifted her head so that she could see his profile in the dark. "It is getting late," she whispered.

His hand came up to tangle in her hair as he brought his mouth down to hers. The kiss was neither languid nor fiery, but a slow burn that built and built until Eve broke away on a gasp. Then she cupped his face in both hands, searching his eyes before she stood and took his hand.

He followed her into the house, pausing in the kitchen to kiss her and then again in her bedroom doorway. By this time, Eve was floating as much from anticipation as the painkiller. She got into bed and waited. Nash sat on the edge and removed his boots, then lay back beside her on top of the covers. Eve snuggled up against him and his arm came around her again.

When she would have taken their caresses to a more intimate level, Nash held back. "We need to take things slow. I've got a lot of baggage going back a lot of years. You need to know what you're getting into."

"It's been six years," she said. "If that's not taking things slow, I don't know what is."

His eyes gleamed in the moonlight. "Exactly. It's been six years. What's another night until you have a chance to think a little more clearly? Morphine and adrenaline is a powerful combination."

"I left the morphine back at the hospital and the adrenaline wore off sometime last night. My head is clear and I'm not about to change my mind."

"I'm counting on that."

She lay back against his shoulder. "You're not the only one with baggage, you know."

"Then we both need the chance to think things through."

She slid her hand into his. "I'm glad you're here." He squeezed her fingers as she nestled against him. "I feel like I could stay like this forever."

He kissed her forehead. "Sleep. I'll be right here when you wake up."

BUT HE WASN'T there when she woke up. Eve picked up her phone from the nightstand and glanced at the time. It was after seven. She couldn't remember the last time she'd slept that late on a workday.

The scent of fresh coffee drew her out of bed and down the hallway, where Nash stood shirtless in her kitchen. For a moment, she indulged herself in a delicious fantasy before he turned and said briskly, "Coffee's ready." He poured her a mug and brought it to her.

"You're not going to have a cup?"

"I need to get to the station. You okay here alone or should I call your mom to come over?"

"She has work today. Besides, I don't need a babysitter," Eve told him. "What I need is to get back to work."

He nodded to her cast. "Not with that arm. Take some time to recuperate."

"How much time?" She followed him back into the bedroom while he dressed.

"As much time as the doctor says you need." He kissed her forehead as he buttoned up his shirt. "I'll call you later."

"Nash, wait." She trailed him back out of the bedroom and down the hallway to the front door. "Why are you in such a hurry? What's going on?"

"I'm running late. I'm always in the station by seven."

"If you don't tell me what's going on, I'll get dressed and come down to the station myself."

"You would, wouldn't you?" He tucked back a strand of her hair. "Nadine Crosby just turned herself in."

"What? When?"

"A few minutes ago. She says she'll only talk to the person in charge. Says she wants to cut a deal."

"She's turning on her brother?"

"Unless this is some kind of ploy the two of them have cooked up. We'll soon find out."

"You have to let me come with you," Eve said. "I'm the one she talked to before. Maybe she'll want to see me again."

"If I need you, I'll call you. Right now the best thing you can do is rest. I don't need to remind you that you'll have to qualify with that arm, so take care of it."

She relented but only because she wasn't yet dressed. She hurried back to the bedroom to throw on jeans, sneakers and a T-shirt before heading out. She was on the front porch struggling to lock the door with her left hand when a FaceTime call came in. Grace Bowden's image appeared on her screen.

Eve couldn't have been more shocked. "Grace? How did you get my number?"

"You left your card, remember?"

"Did I?" Eve didn't think she had, but she didn't press the issue. "Why are you calling?"

"I want to see those photographs again. The yearbook photographs? I've remembered something."

Eve glanced over her shoulder to scour the street. She didn't think that Denton Crosby would be so bold as to show up at her house in broad daylight, but after he'd tried to bury her alive in the cavern, he might be desperate enough to try anything.

"What's going on?" Grace wanted to know. "You seem flustered."

"I was just on my way out. Hold on a minute." Eve opened the door and walked back inside. Retrieving the yearbook from a bookshelf, she carried it over to the table and sat down to open the cover.

She positioned the phone so that Grace could see the page, then tapped the photograph of Denton Crosby. "You seemed to recognize this man yesterday You saw him down in the cave at some point, didn't you? He threatened you, told you if you said anything about what you'd witnessed, he'd come through your bedroom window and abduct you the way that Maya Lamb had been taken."

Grace nodded. "When I saw you yesterday, the memory was only a glimmer, but I remember more clearly now. He caught me spying on him in the cave. He grabbed my hair and hauled me out of the alcove. I thought he was going to kill me."

"How old were you then?"

"I don't remember exactly. Ten or thereabouts."

"Had you seen him down in the cave before?"

"Yes, several times, but he never saw me until that day."

"Are you sure it was this man?" She pointed again to Denton Crosby's image.

Grace squinted as if trying to get a better look through the camera. "No, not him. The photograph above him. *That* man. He's the one who attacked and threatened me."

Eve turned the yearbook around and ran her finger down the page, pausing on Denton Crosby's image. Then she lifted her gaze to the photograph above him. Her heart started to flail as she picked up the phone. "Grace, are you sure it was him?"

"Of course I'm sure. Is this going to help solve your John Doe case?"

Eve's heart was beating so hard by this time she could barely think. She felt a cold sweat break out at her temples. "I'm going to have to call you back, Grace."

"No, wait!"

"What is it? Did you remember something else?"

Grace paused. "No, it's just…" She seemed to peer over Eve's shoulder. "Who's that behind you?"

"What?" Eve glanced over her shoulder, scanning the room behind her and peering into the shadowy hallway.

"I saw someone behind you," Grace insisted. "Someone's in your house, Detective Jareau. I think he's the man in the photograph."

Chapter Fourteen

Eve tried to keep her tone neutral even as her pulse raced. "I have to go now, Grace." She severed the call and punched in Nash's number.

Before the call connected, a familiar voice said from the hallway, "Put the phone down, Evie."

She turned slowly, blood pounding at her temples. "I told you never to call me that."

Wayne Brody leaned a shoulder against the door frame and regarded her with a mixture of amusement and anger. "You have no idea how much you reminded me of Gabriel just now. He used to give me that same look of contempt. Even in high school, he always thought he was better than me, cooler than me, when he was never anything but a petty criminal."

"You showed him, didn't you?" Eve's gun was on the console table in the foyer. If she could maneuver around... "You killed him the night he came back to town. You saw him at the house, followed him down to the cave and murdered him in cold blood. Why?" The answer came to her in a flash. "You were in love with my mother."

"It was always Jackie," he said. "I've loved her for as long as I can remember. The three of us could have been a family. I would have taken care of you the way Gabriel never could. But you wouldn't give me a chance, would you? You thought you were better than me, cooler than me. No matter how hard I tried, you looked at me the way he always looked at me."

Eve took a tentative step toward the foyer. "I was just a little kid. You can't blame me for the failure of your marriage. My mother should never have married you. She never got over my dad."

"That's a lie!"

She lunged for the gun as he lunged for her, ruthlessly grabbing her casted arm. The plaster did little to protect the fracture as he wrenched her arm behind her. She fell backward in agony, banging her head on the sharp corner of the console table. Blood ran down into her eyes as she cradled her arm and suppressed a scream.

He grabbed her injured arm and yanked her to her feet. Eve's training kicked in then and she fought him, using momentum and surprise to slam him to the floor. She grabbed a porcelain vase and smashed it against his head. When she dived for the gun, he grabbed her by the ankle and pulled her back down to the floor. She was dizzy now from pain and blood loss. He took advantage of her weakness, grabbing her hair and hauling her into the bathroom. The window was open. He must have crawled through while she'd been outside.

"What are—"

"What I should have done years ago when you were a bratty kid." He gritted his teeth as he forced her to her knees beside the bathtub. "They'll think you took too many painkillers and fell asleep in the bath. You already look like hell, so a few more cuts and bruises won't be noticed." He put in the stopper and turned on the water full blast, pushing her head down into the tub as the water began to rise. "You may have gotten out of that cave in one piece, but today is the day your luck runs out, Evie. Just like it eventually ran out for Gabriel."

Eve struggled to get away, but he had the upper hand. He held her head under until her lungs screamed for air and her strength continued to wane.

Still she fought him, thrashing her head from side to side, flailing her hands wildly until his hold slipped and she came up gasping for breath even as she swung her casted arm for his head. She must have connected because the plaster shattered and Wayne fell backward on the tile floor, cracking his temple against the edge of the tub.

Protecting her arm against her body, she stumbled out of the bathroom and limped down the hallway to the foyer to throw open the front door. Jackie stood with her hand lifted as if getting ready to knock. She took one look at Eve and gasped.

"Evie! What happened?"

"Mom, we have to get out of here."

When she would have collapsed, Jackie put her arm around her waist for support. "We have to get you back to the hospital—"

"You're not going anywhere, either of you."

Jackie's gaze shot to the hallway, where Wayne stood with Eve's gun.

"Wayne? What on earth—"

"Get out of the way, Jackie. This has gone on long enough. Let me end it."

"What are you talking about? Wayne, put down that gun this instant!"

"I wish I could, but it's too late for that. I don't want to hurt you, Jackie. I never wanted to hurt anyone. I just needed you to realize that I was your soul mate. I'm the one you should have married, not him."

"Wayne—" Jackie looked helplessly from her ex-husband to Eve. Understanding dawned and her voice softened. "Put down the gun, Wayne. Please. Let Evie go. You and I can talk for as long as you like."

"It's too late for talk. Just let me finish this. There's no hope for us so long as she's around. Look at her. She's the spitting image of Gabriel."

"There's no hope for us if you hurt my daughter."

"Why couldn't you just love me?" he asked in tears. "Why did you have to make me prove myself to you?"

"How did you prove yourself?" Jackie asked gently.

"You know how. You've always known."

Jackie drew a breath. "You killed Gabriel."

"It's what you wanted. I heard you say so."

"I never meant—" She stopped and drew another breath. Eve realized too late that her mother had been slowly inching her body in front of hers. If Wayne fired, she intended to take the bullet.

From her periphery, she saw a shadow move on the front porch. She and Jackie were still standing in the doorway so that Wayne's view was blocked. He couldn't see Nash easing around the corner to put himself in position. Their gazes met and Nash nodded.

"Mom," Eve said under her breath. "Drop to your knees."

"Wh—"

Eve collapsed, taking her mom down with her. Before Wayne could get off a round, Nash stepped into the doorway and fired.

Chapter Fifteen

Two weeks later, Nadine Crosby was dead and her brother, Denton, remained a free man. She'd collapsed at the police station before making an official statement and confession and had been rushed to the hospital, never to awaken from a coma. Everything she'd told Eve that day in the woods remained inadmissible. With two of the three conspirators dead, the chances of convicting Denton for Maya Lamb's kidnapping remained slim, and without any physical evidence or eyewitnesses connecting him to Ron Naples's death, murder charges would not be forthcoming. Eve was beyond frustrated but no less determined to find justice for the victims' families.

As for Wayne Brody, he'd been transferred to the county lockup as soon as his injuries healed. Jackie refused to see him. She was a changed woman since the shooting. Moody and withdrawn. Eve told herself it was understandable. Finding out her ex-husband had killed her first husband because he'd been secretly in love with her since high school was a lot to process. Sometimes in the dead of night, something Wayne had said came back to haunt Eve. *You know how. You've always known.*

She thought about his insinuation now as she stared out the window, unable to sleep. Behind her Nash stirred in bed.

"What is it?" he asked drowsily.

"I can't sleep."

"I'm the one with insomnia, remember?" He threw off the covers and came to stand behind her at the window. Wrapping his arms around her, he pulled her back against him. "What's going on?"

"I thought the truth would feel different," she said.

"You thought it would bring closure." He rested his chin on the top of her head. "Doesn't always work out that way, does it?"

"How do you cope?" she asked. "With Grace. With what happened over there. With everything."

"Most of the time, not very well," he said candidly. "Lately, when things get bad, I think about you. I remind myself how lucky I am that I made it back home and that I get to spend my days with the woman I love. My nights, too, when I'm especially lucky."

She let her head fall back against his shoulder. "We are lucky." She touched the coin beneath her nightgown as her gaze lifted to the moon glimmering above the treetops.

Goodnight, Boo. Have a happy life.

Goodbye, Daddy.

* * * * *

COLTON'S PURSUIT
OF JUSTICE

MARIE FERRARELLA

To
Tiffany & Edy Melgar,
And
Their Fantastic Little Girls,
Elliana & Adelyn.
Rays of Sunshine Do Not Come Any Brighter.
Love,
G-Mama

Chapter One

Funny how thoughts can suddenly sneak up on a person out of the blue, Caleb Colton couldn't help thinking. One minute, he was letting himself into his riverfront penthouse condo, feeling far wearier than his thirty-nine years actually warranted. The next minute, it had suddenly hit him that a major anniversary was coming up soon.

Twenty years since his father, the former Judge Benjamin Colton, had died in a tragic car accident when his vehicle had fatally slid on a stretch of icy road.

Closing the door behind him, Caleb stood there in the dark penthouse, waiting for at least a shred of emotion to slam into him.

It didn't.

There was a time when he wouldn't have believed that he could be this removed from such a life-altering event. After all, his had always been such a close-knit family. But that was before his father, a much sought-after guest at the most exclusive social gatherings, had dragged the family name through the mud with his secret dealings.

And for what? For money.

The knowledge left him feeling hollow.

During his last decade on the bench, his father took kickbacks from private-prison owners and juvenile-detention-facility owners. In exchange for these secret payments, Ben Colton sentenced an increasing number of adults and teenagers to those selected facilities.

And for a while, Caleb recalled, no one seemed to be aware of what was actually happening. On the surface, everything seemed to be going well. As a result, there was money for everything: fine clothing, a lavish lifestyle, a huge house in an up-and-coming neighborhood in Blue Larkspur, Colorado.

In short, there was more than enough money for everything he and his eleven brothers and sisters could have ever wanted.

As far as he knew, the family all believed they were able to live this kind of life thanks to their father's inheritance—until it was brought to light by an enterprising investigative reporter that there *was* no such inheritance.

The source of the money—all of it—was from bribes he pocketed.

Caleb poured himself a glass of ginger ale. He

was far too exhausted to drink any alcoholic beverage at this hour. It would instantly knock him out on his feet.

Sitting down in the dimly lit living room, he raised his glass to his father's memory in a mock toast.

"Why did you do it, Dad? You were smart enough to know better. You certainly should have known it couldn't have lasted. You threw away our good name and your reputation for things that in the final analysis had no real intrinsic value. And worse than that," he added with a trace of restrained anger, "you broke Mom's heart.

"But she stood by you despite all that." Caleb laughed softly to himself as memories insisted on flooding his brain. "We all did. And then you died," he concluded, "leaving the rest of us to clean up your mess.

"It took us twenty years, Dad, but we did it. We are working on making restitution to all those people who were made to suffer thanks to you. Because of the Truth Foundation that Morgan and I, as attorneys, set up, we managed to exonerate each and every one of the people you wrongfully imprisoned or gave overly harsh sentences to so that your pals could keep them in their private institutions that much longer.

"Funny thing is," Caleb said as he took another

sip from his glass, "I know that in a very odd way, you did it all out of love.

"But the money never meant that much to any of us. Trust me, we would have all been a lot happier poorer—as long as the family's integrity remained intact."

Caleb sighed as he set the glass down on the coffee table. After a moment, he pulled himself up to his feet. He *really* needed to get to bed, he thought. He was putting in far too much time at his office and at the Foundation. His workaholic nature had wound up killing his marriage years ago, and if he wasn't careful, it would eventually wind up killing him, too.

"Too bad you never thought to ask any of us if we would have minded being poorer," Caleb murmured under his breath as he made his way up the stairs. A sad smile twisted his lips. "Especially Mom." Ever since his father had dropped that awful, soul-jarring bombshell that he was being arrested for being on the take, it had upended all of their lives. As the oldest—by ten minutes, thanks to being born ahead of his twin sister— Caleb had felt an overpowering need to be there for his mother and his siblings and to somehow right the wrong that had been done.

Even now, Caleb still felt that same sense of responsibility. That need to be there for everyone in every capacity was what had ultimately brought about the end of his marriage to his college sweetheart. For all intents and purposes, their union had suffered an untimely death before it was even five years old.

Over the years, two more long-term relationships he was in came to an end for the same reason. What he felt was his calling took precedence over any sort of romantic relationship. Because of that, at this point, Caleb had resigned himself to remaining single for the rest of his life.

Heaven knew he had enough things to fill up his world that required his attention, what with helping head up the law firm of Colton and Colton, and his family. And, if all that wasn't enough, there was the Truth Foundation. He and Morgan had put the organization together to try to atone for some of their father's transgressions by helping the wrongfully convicted overturn their sentences.

This morning, the first thing on his agenda before his day officially began was to swing by his mother's house. He wanted to make sure that she was doing all right.

To him, Isadora Colton was nothing short of completely incredible. When the truth about what Ben Colton was doing suddenly came to light and their whole well-ordered world just blew apart, his mother had never complained, not even once. Despite the glaring subterfuge and the humiliation it generated when the general population became aware of it, she never wavered, never stopped loving the man she had married, the father of her twelve children.

An ironic smile curved Caleb's lips. That old country-and-western classic about standing by her man could have been written about his mother, he thought. Considering what she had gone through, the woman looked amazingly youthful. Had to be good genes, he thought. There was no other explanation.

Caleb rang the doorbell to the house where they had all grown up before letting himself in. Absently, he pocketed his key.

"Are you up, Mom?" he called out, knowing full well that she was. She had always been an early riser. He couldn't remember a day when she had remained in bed past 7:00 a.m., even on weekends.

Usually, she was up before then.

"In the kitchen, dear," Isa called out. The youthful-looking blonde beamed at her oldest born as he walked into the kitchen. "To what do I owe this unexpected surprise?" she asked Caleb, then tilted her head in his direction, enabling her eldest to brush a kiss against her cheek.

"I just wanted to see how you were doing, Mom," he told her, doing his best to sound cheerful and nonchalant.

"I'm doing just fine, Caleb," his mother answered honestly. Turning from the stove and the breakfast she was preparing, the light suddenly dawned on her. Isa fixed her oldest son with a knowing look. "This is because of that awful anniversary that's coming up, isn't it?" she asked, knowing full well that that had to be why he was checking up on her.

In her opinion, Caleb's furrowed brow gave him away. Of all her children, she knew that her oldest son had taken his father's betrayal the hardest.

Caleb laughed softly to himself, shaking his head. "I could never put anything over on you, Mom."

"Why would you want to, dear?" Isa wanted to know. "It's always best to be honest," she told Caleb, repeating the sentiment that, for the last two decades, she had insisted govern all of their lives. "Remember," she underscored. "No secrets. *Ever.*"

"I'm a lawyer, Mom," he needlessly reminded her. "That could make things a wee bit rough when it comes to matters of attorney-client privilege."

Isa inclined her head. "Challenging, perhaps," she agreed. "But not impossible. Here, eat something," she said, placing the platter she had just finished preparing in front of where her son usually sat instead of her own place setting.

"Isn't that supposed to be your breakfast?" he protested.

Isa waved away her son's words. "No, it's yours," she informed him as if it was a foregone conclusion.

Caleb leveled a look at her as he attempted to push the plate back to its rightful place—in front of her chair. "You couldn't possibly have known I was coming over."

Isa's eyes narrowed ever so slightly as she gave him a penetrating look. "Couldn't have I?" she questioned in a manner that effectively contradicted his protest. "Don't argue with your mother, Caleb. I know everything." She moved the plate back in front of him. "Now, eat."

Experience told him that he would save himself a lot of time, not to mention effort, if he just went along with what his mother had just said. Besides, it wasn't as if there was only one serving of food available in the spacious house. Thanks to the inheritance that his maternal grandparents had left her and an inborn knack for frugality, it could be maintained that after everything was said and done, Isa Colton was doing quite well.

Isa flashed her son a warm, broad smile as Caleb finally took his seat at the spacious kitchen counter that had been part of the extensive renovations that her children had gifted her with for her sixtieth birthday.

Isa sat right next to him, nursing the cup of coffee that she had poured for herself earlier.

"This is nice," she commented about his taking his breakfast beside her. "Like the old days."

Isa refrained from saying anything further on

the subject, feeling that it might cause Caleb to reflect more deeply and that could only stir up unwanted memories.

"Can I get you some coffee?" she offered, beginning to rise again.

Caleb placed his hand over hers, stopping her before she was on her feet. "No thanks, Mom. I'll have enough coffee over the course of the day to sink a battleship. Maybe even two battleships." He nodded at the breakfast plate before him. "This is good."

"It's simple," Isa pointed out. She knew better than to pretend to be an excellent cook. Isa was aware of her limitations. She smiled at her son. "I could always do simple."

Caleb sighed as he shook his head. Some things never changed. In a way, he found that rather comforting. "You've got to learn how to take a compliment."

Isa pretended to look surprised. "I thought that was what I was doing," she said with a straight face.

Ingrained habit had him glancing at his watch. It was getting late, he realized. There were papers at the office he just remembered he needed to sign.

Finishing the rest of the reassigned eggs and toast quickly, Caleb wiped his mouth and then deposited his napkin on the plate. He began to take his plate to the sink, but this time it was his mother's turn to stop him.

"I'll take care of that," Isa told him.

Caleb relented, then asked her again, "You're sure you're all right?" He wanted to double-check that she actually was. His father's death was twenty years in the past, but it still had a way of burrowing in and upending their lives when they least expected it.

Isa patted her son's cheek. "I couldn't be better, darling," she assured him. "Really," she underscored. "Why wouldn't I be? My son just stopped by to have breakfast with me."

Caleb laughed, amused. "It doesn't take much to satisfy you, does it, Mom?"

Isa's eyes twinkled. "That's what I've been telling you all along, dear," she said. She rose from the counter at the same time that Caleb did.

"What are you doing?" he asked when his mother fell into step beside him.

"Why, I'm walking you to the front door," she replied matter-of-factly.

"I know where the front door is, Mom," Caleb said with a laugh. "I've used it often enough."

"I know," she replied. "But walking you to it gives me a few more moments to savor your presence. We mothers can be greedy that way," she informed him with a smile that was nothing short of charming.

As he stopped by the front door, Caleb took his mother's hands in his. She had made it sound as if this was a rare visit on his part instead of quite the opposite.

"I was just here a few days ago," he reminded her.

"I know," she answered. "But I don't take anything for granted anymore, you know that."

Despite the smile curving her lips, his mother was very serious. Caleb knew what she was referring to.

His father had done that to her, Caleb couldn't help thinking. Ben Colton's deceptions had done that to all of them, robbed each and every one of them of that all-important gift they had once been born with: trust.

Luckily, that hadn't affected the family dynamic.

But it very well could have, Caleb thought. It could have made them suspicious of everything someone else did from that long-ago day forward.

Caleb lingered for a moment, holding his mother's hands in his.

"Well, if anything changes, you know where to find me," he told her, giving her a quick kiss good-bye.

"Yes, I do, Caleb. And I know where to find you even if *nothing* changes," Isa assured her son with a chuckle.

About to leave, Caleb looked at his mother over his shoulder. Impulsively, he added, "I'll swing by tomorrow morning," and then he was gone.

Because of the unusual lack of traffic that morning, Caleb arrived at work quickly. Once upon a time, before his father had sold out his integrity—and *before* he was appointed judge—this had been his office.

Caleb could remember how impressed he had been when he'd first walked into it.

The space had seemed a great deal bigger to him back then, but he had been about five or six and easily impressed by everything—especially by his father, he recalled. The man had seemed like a giant to him, as if he was at least ten feet tall.

Too bad he'd had to learn otherwise, Caleb thought, parking his car in his usual space and getting out.

It appeared that Morgan was already there, he noted. Her car was parked right next to his.

Caleb walked inside, telling himself he needed to shake this oppressive feeling that had descended over him. He had work to get to and he couldn't waste time mentally floundering around in the past. Dwelling on it would change nothing. He and Morgan had spent almost the last decade trying very hard to make up for his father's terrible misdeeds and offenses, to restore the lives that had been so badly damaged by their father's actions.

"Hi," Caleb said by way of a greeting. "Did I miss anything?" he asked, referring to the fact that she had gotten to the office ahead of him and their assistants.

"Yes, Annie called," Morgan answered, stopping him dead in his tracks.

"Annie?" he repeated, surprised.

"Yes. Annie." Morgan glanced up for a second. "Your ex-wife."

"I know who Annie is," Caleb answered, slightly annoyed by his twin's attitude. Why was Annie calling him at the office? "Did she say what she wanted?"

"Yes," Morgan answered, obviously preoccupied. "For you to call her back."

Caleb pressed his lips together, trying to be patient. "You are a regular fount of information this morning."

"I do my best," Morgan answered cheerfully before looking back at the brief she was working on.

"Seriously, did she give any indication why she was calling me so early in the day?" *Or at all?* he added silently.

"Haven't a clue," Morgan replied, thumbing through the pages on her desk. And then she paused for a moment to look up from the brief she was reviewing. "Maybe she wanted to give the two of you another chance."

Yeah, right, he thought. That ship had sailed a long while ago.

"I don't think that would exactly sit too well with her husband and their three kids," Caleb quipped.

Morgan got back to work again. "You're probably right. I guess you're just going to have to call her and put that question to her yourself."

Caleb nodded, more to himself than to his twin. "I guess so," he murmured.

Morgan looked up just as he was leaving her office to go into his own. "I wrote the number down if you need it," she told him, holding up a Post-it note.

"I have it," he answered.

His ex-wife's situation had changed since they had been together but very little else had, including her phone number.

Caleb couldn't help wondering what was up. His and Annie's divorce had been amicable enough. He had even sent a wedding gift when she went on to marry Pete Jackson, a man who, unlike him, could give her the time she more than deserved.

But Caleb truthfully couldn't remember when she'd called him. Since the divorce, they didn't exactly get together all that much.

Any other woman might have held what had come to pass against him. Rather than put her or at least their marriage first, he had immersed himself in his family and in trying to right the wrongs his father had committed. Restoring family honor became all-important to him.

Sadly, Annie and their marriage had somehow gotten lost in the shuffle, falling by the wayside until he had a little free time to devote to her and to it.

For some reason, while he made all these excuses to himself about why he was too busy to come home, he'd felt that Annie would understand, that she was all right with this crusade he had undertaken, the crusade that had all but consumed his soul.

He should have known better.

Even a saint would have had trouble adjusting to the situation, and Annie was still a flesh-and-blood woman who had every right to expect her husband to be there for her rather than always rushing off like some self-appointed superhero.

He got out Annie's number and stared at it for a long moment.

He hadn't a clue what had prompted her to call him today, but he was determined not to let her down, no matter what she was going to ask him to do.

When Caleb heard the phone on the other end begin ringing, he braced himself.

Chapter Two

"Hello?"

The moment he heard Annie's voice against his ear, Caleb felt as if he had instantly been thrown back into another era.

It took him a second or two to get his bearings and remind himself that Annie was no longer his college sweetheart or his wife. She was now Pete Jackson's wife and the happy, fulfilled mother of Pete's children. Annie, he knew, made a wonderful mother.

Everything was as it should be—for her. That it wasn't for him, well, Caleb thought, he had no one to blame for that but himself.

"Annie, it's Caleb," he told her needlessly. "Morgan said that you called and wanted to speak to me."

"I did, and I do," she answered.

He could have sworn that Annie was stalling. He would even say that she sounded nervous. That was highly unusual for the normally self-assured woman. Whatever had prompted Annie to call had obviously undermined her confidence.

He immediately wondered what was wrong.

Since Annie didn't say anything further to cast light on the situation, Caleb decided to try to coax the information out of her.

"About?" he pressed.

He heard her take in a deep breath. "It's about my cousin," she finally said, the words coming out slowly.

He thought for a moment, but no image came to mind to correspond with the word *cousin*.

"I'm sorry, Annie," he apologized. "But I'm drawing a blank." Caleb moved the pile of papers on his desk closer to him. He needed to get started signing these things, he reminded himself.

"My cousin Nadine," Annie said, her tone indicating that she obviously expected him to remember the woman. "You met her at the big Christmas party my family threw that first year we were married." The long-ago memory appeared to stir something within her as Annie sighed. "That was a long time ago, and I guess I shouldn't really expect you to remember," she admitted. "But you *did* meet her."

He was still coming up empty. "I'll take your word for it," Caleb said. Just because he couldn't remember—another testament to the fact that he had never devoted enough time to Annie when they were married, he thought—didn't mean that it hadn't taken place. "Anyway, moving on. What about Nadine?" he asked, trying to prod the conversation along.

"I was talking to her last night and she needs help."

"Legal help?" Caleb guessed, thinking that had to be the reason why Annie had thought of him and not someone else.

"Among other things."

Caleb stopped signing papers and gave the phone conversation his full attention. "What other things?"

He heard Annie sigh again. "It's kind of complicated," she told him. "I should let Nadine tell you all this herself."

"Do I even get a hint?" he wanted to know.

He could tell Annie was wrestling with herself—and then she finally said, "Suffice to say that Nadine feels that someone is after her."

"Feelings of persecution?" he guessed.

"No, these aren't feelings of persecution," Annie insisted. "'Feelings' don't send warning emails or make threatening phone calls. If Nadine thinks that someone is actually following her—she mentioned a sedan—then I'd bet big money that she is right. And that it has something to do with her father, my uncle Al. As I recall, the oil company displayed interest in his fracking rights." Her tone changed to one of supplication as she qualified, "Would you look into it for her, Caleb? After work. For me?"

Back when they were married, there had been so many things, things he could have attended to but hadn't because something else had taken precedence.

How could he justify turning his back on her now?

"It would have to be after six," he told Annie. "Would your cousin be all right with that?"

"Absolutely. After six would be fine." Caleb could all but hear the smile in her voice. "Should Nadine come to your office, or—?"

He nodded, then realized that of course Annie couldn't see him. "The office would be great," he assured her. "Could you call her and give her the directions?"

"Sure. They're tattooed on my heart," she said dryly, adding, "I'm sorry, you're going out of your way to do me a favor and I'm being sarcastic."

Because she had apologized so quickly, Caleb gave her a pass. "It's not like I don't have it coming, Annie. If that's the worst thing you've got, I'd say I'm getting off pretty easy. So, is it settled? You'll call your cousin and ask her to meet me in my office so we can discuss whoever's after her and why."

She evidently caught the slight note of skepticism in Caleb's voice. "My cousin doesn't make things up, Caleb."

"I didn't say she did," he answered, closing the door to that subject. Switching gears, Caleb asked, "Is your cousin's last name the same as yours was?"

"Yes. Sutherland," she said for good measure. "Why? Is that a problem?" Annie queried.

He wanted to look into the woman, but he felt it wouldn't be tactful to say as much to his ex, at least for now. "No, I just want to keep everything organized for Rebekah."

"Rebekah?" Annie questioned, slightly confused.

"Rebekah Hanlan, the assistant that Morgan and I share," he told Annie. "Rebekah's a stickler when it comes to following rules. She's going to want to know what name to fill in on the schedule," he explained.

"Just so you know, the basis of the issue is that her dad, my uncle Al, who has the beginnings of dementia, signed over the fracking rights to his land to Rutledge Oil. Nadine thinks he was coerced and she's trying to prove it. The phone calls and other stuff started after that."

"Anything else?"

"No," Annie answered cheerfully. "I'm good."

"Yes, you are," Caleb freely admitted.

He owed her, Caleb thought. Big-time. The fact that she had turned her life around and was happy with the way it had had worked out didn't change any of that. If helping her cousin out helped to balance the scales between them a little, well, so much the better.

"Your cousin will come to the office at six?"

"Six-*ish*," Annie corrected.

"Six-ish?" Caleb repeated quizzically.

Annie laughed softly in acknowledgment. "Nadine has a habit of running late at times," she explained. "I just don't want you to think she's forgotten your meeting if she arrives at the office a few minutes after the appointed time. I know how much you appreciate punctuality."

"I'll cut her some slack if she gets here late—as long as it's not *too* late," he qualified.

"Duly noted," Annie told him. "And, Caleb?"

He was just about to terminate the call and stopped. "Yes?"

"Thank you."

Caleb smiled to himself. No doubt about it, he liked being on the same wavelength as Annie. There was a time—it seemed like eons ago now— that had been the norm.

"Don't mention it," he responded.

As he hung up, he tried to remember what this cousin-in-need looked like. Still failing, he decided to go another route and look the woman up on so-cial media.

He came across various references to Nadine participating in, and getting arrested at, protest demonstrations. The woman, he decided after scanning one story after another, turned out to be quite a crusader.

Caleb glanced at the pile of unsigned papers that were still on his desk. They were his priority.

But then his curiosity got the better of him.

How long could verifying information regarding Annie's cousin take him? Besides, he thought, he never liked coming into a meeting, *any* sort of a meeting, unprepared.

Maybe he would even be able to find enough to help him tactfully tell Annie that she should distance herself from this so-called activist before it wound up getting her into trouble as well.

At least it was worth a shot, he thought as he began his research into Nadine.

SHE HAD BEEN at it for over an hour.

Nadine Sutherland had given up trying to concentrate on fashioning the earrings she had set out to create for her client. The inspiration just wasn't coming.

She had learned a long time ago that in order to be successful, she had to be entirely focused on the job at hand, and right now, all she could think of was how angry she was with Rutledge Oil for taking advantage of her father.

She could feel a tightness forming in her chest whenever she thought about it.

Didn't the people there have *any* sort of a moral conscience at all?

Al Sutherland was a man who was getting on in years. Worse than that, he was verging on full-blown dementia. He couldn't have realized what he was doing when they talked him into signing over his property rights. Property rights that allowed the oil company to gain all the fracking rights over his land.

Another wave of anger washed over her.

How could anyone do such a thing? she silently demanded for what felt like the thousandth time. And, growing dementia or not, how could her father have agreed to doing something so life-altering without even *trying* to consult her?

Or at least someone in the family?

The answer was that he obviously hadn't known what he was doing. Although, heaven knew, her father was not about to admit to doing something so irresponsible and, let's face it, she thought, downright foolish. That would point to the fact that her father *hadn't* been in his right mind, at least not at the time when he had agreed to relinquish his rights.

And, despite an intense search on her part, Nadine was not able to find any sort of indication that any money had exchanged hands to solidify this deal. What that meant, as far as she could see, was that the oil company was actually guilty of stealing fracking rights to this land from her father.

Plain and simple, Rutledge Oil had duped him.

Not that her father would ever admit to anything like that happening.

It seemed like the less control he actually exhibited over his actions and thoughts, the more her father would lash out at her or at anyone else who might even remotely suggest that this land rights "transfer" had been done in an increasingly frequent moment of complete confusion.

Her father would rather die than admit to the steady encroachment of debilitating dementia.

Nadine sighed, frustrated. She pushed aside the incomplete earrings that refused to take shape despite her best intentions. She felt really worn out.

Of all the causes she had ever championed, all the reasons she had put herself out there, holding up signs and attempting to secure the public's attention for one purpose or another, this was by far the fight that was the most personal to her.

The one that counted above all the others.

And the one she felt doomed to lose if something didn't finally turn her way.

Which was why she had finally put aside her stubborn pride and turned to her cousin Annie for help. And it wasn't just because this was a family matter.

It was a fight that appeared as if it involved her very safety as well. She'd investigated to the point that she had obviously not just rattled someone's cage but had gotten that "someone"—apparently Rutledge Oil, or at least someone *in* there—very angry as well.

Apparently, that "someone" within the oil company was determined to turn the tables on her and exact revenge for her interference. Right now, she could only assume the kind of form that "revenge" might take.

But a sinking feeling in her stomach told her that she already knew. She had heard stories about the oil company intimidating people—or worse. There were several people who dared to challenge them and suddenly disappeared.

There were times when she really longed for the simple life when she didn't have to worry about what tomorrow might bring.

But then, Nadine reminded herself, a life like that would be extremely boring to someone of her nature and, more importantly, someone with her drive. Besides, people needed to have someone stand up for them, and she was willing to take on that position.

Still, Nadine mused, looking back at the earrings that refused to come to life, right about now, there was something to be said for "boring."

At that moment, as she lost herself in thought, the phone rang.

Chapter Three

Nadine could feel her heart pounding. Hard. It took a few moments for it to resume a normal beat. These days, what with the threatening emails, the nasty phone calls, not to mention the hang-ups and having to suddenly look over her shoulder, positive that there was someone following her, intent on harming her, Nadine's heart had hardly had a chance to resume a normal rhythm in weeks. She would have gone to the police, but she knew they would turn a deaf ear because she was an activist and thus a troublemaker in their book.

She almost didn't answer the phone. But, she reasoned, that would be cowardly. In essence, that would be letting the other side know that they had succeeded in intimidating her, and she absolutely refused to do that. Nadine was not about to quietly fade into the woodwork and let the bullies win. She could never live with herself. She spent her life protesting corporate bullies and promoting causes supporting the less fortunate, and she wasn't going to give in now.

Summoning her anger to her, Nadine cloaked herself in it and jerked up the receiver on her old landline.

"Hello?" she all but barked.

"Nadine? Is that you?" Annie questioned. Her cousin didn't usually sound this way, concern instantly evident. "Is everything all right?"

Hearing a familiar voice, Nadine exhaled, letting the breath out as quietly as she could. She waited for her heart to settle down. Again.

"Sorry, I didn't mean to shout, Annie. I wasn't expecting to hear your voice on the other end of the line."

Annie didn't need any further explanation. "They've been bothering you again, haven't they, Nadine?"

There was no need for Annie to elaborate any further. Both she and Nadine knew exactly who "they" were.

"Once or twice," Nadine replied elusively.

She wasn't about to go into any further details. She didn't want to worry her cousin any more than she already had when she asked Annie for her help in the first place.

"Well, I think you can stop worrying soon. I called up my ex, Caleb Colton, about your problem and he said that he can meet you at his office after work. That'll be around six, or a little later, if that's all right with you," Annie told her.

Nadine felt a sense of relief but thought that maybe she was being overoptimistic. She thought that she would be used to it by now. She had lost count of the number of times she had been disappointed when it came to things that she had championed. Organizations she wanted to make changes never kept their word. People or corporations with power should put others' needs ahead of their own, she felt, and she was sure Caleb would be no different.

Still, she appreciated her cousin's effort. And who knew, maybe Caleb could actually do a bit to improve her father's situation.

"That's perfect with me," Nadine quipped. "I can't seem to get any work done today, so anytime he can make it is fine." She debated saying the next thing, then decided that she could confide further in Annie. "Just between you and me, this thing with Rutledge trying to make me back off really has me rattled—not to mention hopping mad," she added.

"And you're sure the people who are following you are working for the oil company that forced Uncle Al to sign over the fracking rights?" Annie asked.

"Who else would it be?" Nadine wanted to know. "Dad's not exactly a lovable person, but

the oil company is the only one with something
to gain—and my digging into their actions is making them really uncomfortable—something else
that tells me I'm right to suspect there's something
shady going on."

"You know," Annie speculated, "I can't believe
that Uncle Al would sign over his fracking rights
voluntarily. He's such a stubborn man and no one
could ever talk him into doing anything he didn't
want to."

Nadine sighed before she caught herself. "You
remember him the way he was, Annie," she told
her cousin. "Dad's not quite like that anymore."
There was a trace of mournfulness in her voice,
a trace she would only allow to come through
around her family.

"How bad is he?" Sympathy echoed in every
one of Annie's words.

"Well, he's got more good days than bad," Nadine informed her, doing her best to hang on to
that thought for as long as she could. "But sometimes," she admitted, "when I look at him, I can
see that he's not really there at all. Oh, Annie, it's
such an awful, awful disease, robbing everyone,
not just the victim.

"Don't get me wrong," Nadine was quick to add.
"Most days, Dad is his usual feisty old self and you
couldn't tell that there was *anything* wrong—except for maybe his less-than-friendly disposition.

And pride won't let him have anyone living at the house to help, not since Mom died. But he's always been like that," she reminded Annie. "He can be like that for probably weeks at a time. And then, suddenly, for no apparent reason, he'll just disappear into himself."

Her mouth suddenly went dry as the words she uttered weighed heavily on her tongue.

Taking a breath, she continued before Annie could make a comment—or worse, pity her. "Luckily," Nadine said, "it doesn't last all that long. It's kind of like his mind is playing hide-and-seek with his brain. But it's really very scary while it's going on."

"Well, I can't help with any of that," Annie admitted regretfully. "But at least I can have Caleb work on getting that oil company to back off. If he's successful, he might be able to get the oil company to give back fracking rights that go with it it."

Hope reared its head once again. She could almost feel it coursing through her veins.

"Do you really think that's possible?" Nadine asked. "I mean, I'm sure they tricked Dad, but is there any way to even prove that?"

"If anyone can find a way, Caleb can," Annie assured her.

Nadine paused for a moment. Normally, she

wouldn't ask her cousin this sort of personal question, but these were not normal times.

"If he's really that good, that conscientious, what made the two of you break up? I don't even remember what it was five years ago," Nadine asked. "I know it's none of my business, but I have to confess you've made me curious."

"Let's just say that we were better at being friends than being a couple," Annie said. "The problem with Caleb is that he has a great deal of integrity. Much more than his share."

There was no bitterness in her voice. It was just the way things were, Annie thought.

"He was always rushing off to somewhere because he was trying to make up for everything his father had done or to work with the Truth Foundation, as you might recall. Caleb insisted on carrying the entire burden on his shoulders, trying to deal with the shame and humiliation his father had caused his mother and the rest of the family. Not to mention that Caleb put *all* of his energy into trying to make up for what his father did while a judge on the bench, sentencing so many people to years in jail when they could have been given lighter sentences—or set free altogether.

"Are you still there, Nadine?"

"I'm still here. That sounds just awful," Nadine couldn't help telling her cousin. She felt bad for Caleb, but at the same time, she admired the fact that he was trying to right wrongs that had been done—same as her.

"Oh, it was," Annie said. "And I'm just speaking from secondhand knowledge," she pointed out. "The amazing thing is that Caleb's mother never resented her husband for any of what it turned out he put her and the rest of the family through. She really stuck by the man.

"I have a feeling she would have stuck by him through his trial and any sentence that the judge gave him. Lucky for Ben Colton, though, he wound up not having to face any of it."

Nadine was familiar with the particulars of the tragedy. Everyone in the area was, even though it had taken place all those years ago. "I wouldn't exactly call dying in a freak auto accident 'lucky,'" she pointed out.

Annie disagreed. "Oh, I think that Caleb's father would have. He was a very proud man and, after all the heights he had risen to, plummeting down that far and then possibly being sent to the same prison he had sentenced others to might have actually amounted to absolute torture for him.

"This was actually the better way out—for Ben. And, eventually, for all of his victims. Caleb made sure that as many of the victims who were still alive all received restitution for what they had gone through. The money from his father's insurance policy was awarded to several victims' families."

"What about Caleb's mother?" Nadine asked. "Didn't she need the money?"

"The money was used with Isa Colton's blessing," Annie said. "Like I said, she is a very rare woman. Didn't I already tell you all this?"

"Some of it is beginning to come back to me," Nadine admitted. "But not the bulk of it. You know, Caleb's mother might have been a forgiving woman," she went on. "But me, I would have just wanted to go for the jugular over something like that. For instance, what that oil company executive—or henchman—did was absolutely awful, and as far as I'm concerned, the man—or woman—should be drawn and quartered for the way they took advantage of my father when his mind was so obviously on hiatus."

"Given Caleb's integrity, I'm sure he would agree with you. The first step, though," she reminded Nadine, "is proving it."

Nadine laughed softly as she thought that comment over. "That first step, though," she agreed, "is a real doozy."

"I don't doubt it, but trust me, if anyone can get to the bottom of all this and make the oil company back off, Caleb is your man. Just be honest with him and be sure to tell him everything," Annie counseled.

"I wasn't planning on doing anything else," Nadine told her. She was a great believer in honesty.

"Good. Let me know how it goes."

"I'll be sure to give you a firsthand report," she promised her cousin.

"I'll be waiting," Annie said. "Talk soon," she said just before she terminated the call.

Nadine hung up the receiver and then pushed the landline farther back on her makeshift desk. There was nothing she could do at the moment except wait.

And maybe cross her fingers, she thought.

She didn't do waiting very well. She was more of a take-charge type of woman when it came to getting justice. Was Caleb the same way?

Nadine's eyes strayed toward the unfinished earrings she had pushed aside earlier. Since she was supposed to be sitting and waiting, she told herself that she could at least be productive and earn some money while she was doing this sitting. Heaven knew that money would certainly come in handy right about now, she thought. She sincerely doubted that ex-in-law or no, Caleb Colton would not offer his services cheap.

With that in mind, Nadine forced herself to focus on creating the best pair of earrings that she was capable of creating. She had been a jewelry maker for a number of years now and liked the freedom of being her own boss.

Nadine sat down and went to work.

IT TOOK SOME DOING, but Caleb finally managed to get back to the office at ten minutes to six. It was who he was.

No matter what other people did, Caleb had always hated being late for anything—big or small. That was what had caused him to always be on time from an early age. He had practically made being on time—or more accurately, being early—into a religion.

As he entered the suite of offices, Caleb passed the assistant that he shared with his twin sister. As he walked by, he glanced in Morgan's direction.

When their eyes met, Rebekah Hanlan shook her head.

"She's not here yet," the older, tastefully dressed assistant informed him.

"Let me know the minute she gets in," Caleb told the woman.

Rebekah looked at him as if he had started babbling nonsense. She had known Caleb and his twin ever since they had to take over the law firm.

"I wasn't planning on holding her captive," she cracked.

It had been one of those long, endless days that just insisted on going go on and on, but somehow, the sarcastic remark did the trick. The comment managed to infuse enough of a spark within him to bring some life back into his veins.

"Good to know, Rebekah." He nodded down the hall. "I'll be in my office."

"And here I thought I'd have to send out a search party to find you," Rebekah quipped. "I'll send this Nadine person in when she arrives—provided she does arrive."

"According to my ex-wife, the woman is more than desperate. She'll arrive," Caleb assured her with confidence.

"Uh-huh," Rebekah murmured, sounding less than convinced regarding what he had just expressed.

Caleb didn't have time to debate Rebekah. He just wanted to meet with Nadine, get a few things squared away and, heaven willing, go home to get a little dinner and down a well-deserved nightcap.

He'd reached out to a PI he worked with and ordered a full background check run on her. The woman was definitely someone who couldn't be labeled *boring* in any sense of the word, Caleb thought. From the looks of things, when she took on a cause—and she had taken on more than her share—she didn't do so in half measures. Instead, Nadine apparently threw herself headlong into everything that she undertook.

Compared to Nadine, Caleb couldn't help thinking, Annie was laid-back. Nadine didn't seem to hold back at all.

Ever.

Well, he thought, it took all kinds. He just hoped that this crusader wouldn't bug him too much. They both seemed to seek out justice for others, but in different manners. From the bits and pieces he had put together, it seemed that Nadine Sutherland had a knack of rubbing people the wrong way. And although it was always for a good cause, he was in no mood for putting up with that, Caleb thought.

"Oh, the things we do for family," he muttered to himself.

The next moment, it struck him that, despite the fact that they were no longer married and that Annie had gone on to marry someone else and create a family with that man, he still thought of the Sutherlands as his kin. Maybe not first tier, the way he thought of his mother and his siblings, but Annie was most definitely family, he thought with an ironic smile.

Just then, Caleb heard the computer on his desk buzz, rousing him out of his thoughts. That was Rebekah's way of getting in contact with him from her desk.

"Yes, Rebekah?"

"She's here," Rebekah announced, not bothering to say the woman's name. "Do you want me to send her in?"

"Can't talk to her while she's out there and I'm

in here, now, can I?" he asked the assistant matter-of-factly.

"Just thought you'd want a couple of minutes to
pull your thoughts together," Rebekah informed
him crisply.

He knew the assistant was fishing for some sort
of a compliment or acknowledgment of her ef-
ficiency. There was nothing to be gained by not
doing so.

"That's very thoughtful of you, Rebekah, but
my thoughts are as pulled together as they're going
to be. You can send her in."

"Will do," Rebekah answered. Then Rebekah
brought Annie's cousin into his office.

Chapter Four

Because politeness had been instilled in him from a very young age, Caleb slowly rose in his chair when Nadine was brought into his office.

Even though he had seen a great many photos taken of her, he couldn't take his eyes off the woman in front of him.

Nadine Sutherland looked to be about five-seven, had a very slim, athletic build and dark brown, shoulder-length hair that was shot through with auburn highlights. She couldn't have been described as drop-dead gorgeous, but she had the kind of face that lingered on a man's mind long after the impression created by a stunner would have just faded away.

It was hard to reconcile that face with the woman who had a string of arrests attached to her, even if all those arrests were attributed to non-violent marches for a whole list of causes that she espoused and was devoted to.

Caleb put his hand out in greeting. "Nadine?" he asked by way of creating an actual connection between them.

"That's what my dad calls me," she answered, secretly wondering just how much longer that particular piece of information would continue to be true. Anticipating the day her father no longer recognized her filled her with sorrow.

The next moment, she found herself thinking that Annie's ex looked more like a handsome male model in a high-end fashion magazine than a lawyer.

"Why? Were you expecting someone else?" she suddenly asked, thinking that something might have come up since Annie had spoken to him earlier today and he was scheduled to meet another person at this time. "Because if you are, I can come back tomorrow morning—or wait, or—"

"No, no 'or,'" Caleb told the woman, stopping her from continuing and waving a hand at her protests. "Why don't you just take a seat and we'll talk about why you're here."

Rebekah, who had brought the woman in, did not appear to be leaving. "Thank you, Rebekah," he said formally. "You may go home now."

Rebekah's eyes swept over Nadine, then went back to Caleb. "Are you sure about that? Because I can stay if you need me."

"I won't be needing you," he informed her with

finality, then, glancing at Nadine, he promised, "This won't take long." His attention went back to Rebekah. "I'll see you tomorrow."

The assistant shrugged her shoulders. "Have it your way," she murmured, then walked out of the office.

When he looked back at Nadine, he saw Nadine staring at him. "Sounds like you've decided that this is over before it's even started."

"Not exactly," Caleb felt honor bound to state. It was, he immediately realized, an unfortunate choice of words on his part.

"Then, *what* 'exactly'?" Nadine wanted to know.

He had to tell her what was on his mind after having done his investigation into who this woman was. "I have to admit that I do have my doubts about whether someone is harassing you," Caleb admitted.

"Go on," Nadine told him.

There was an edge in her voice. The kind of edge that let Caleb know the woman he was talking to was preparing herself for a less-than-friendly confrontation.

Caleb pushed on. Saying anything less than the truth seemed disingenuous to him. He had always been a great believer in honesty.

"In an effort to make sure that I would render

you the best possible help that I could, I had a background check run on you today," he told her.

Nadine stared at him. Annie hadn't said her ex was such a stick-in-the-mud. His action only meant one thing to her—that he viewed her to be some sort of an emotional troublemaker.

She raised her chin. He wouldn't be the first, she thought in annoyance. There were members of her own family who thought of her that way. That had never stopped her from doing what she felt was right.

"You have a great many arrests on your record," Caleb continued.

She had told herself that since this was Annie's ex and he was supposedly doing her a favor, she would hear him out. But the moment he said anything about her arrests without even mentioning the causes she had undertaken instantly put her back up. Logically, she knew he wouldn't have been able to come to any other conclusion if he had run that background check on her, but she wasn't looking for logical. She was looking for empathy, for understanding—and he wasn't displaying any of that. But did he even know about her dad's condition and what had been done to him?

Nadine took the only option open to her. She went on the attack. "Yes, I *do* have a lot of arrests next to my name," she agreed, "but that doesn't give you a reason to feel so smug and superior about the situation. Have you ever felt as adamant about anything the way I feel about the causes that I've undertaken and continue to undertake? Even with your foundation?"

Caleb's eyes narrowed. He wasn't about to give her a summation of all the causes and people he'd helped. "Forget about it."

He was bluffing, she thought. In striking out, she had managed to hit a nerve. "Why? Did someone try to ace you out of a parking space you had your eye on?"

The woman did have a way about her that could rub a saint the wrong way, he thought. *Really* rub them the wrong way.

But even so, there was something in her voice that managed to connect with him as well as *to* him.

Caleb answered, "As a matter of fact, I *have* felt adamant about something. Really adamant," he underscored. "In his capacity as a judge, my father wrongfully sent a lot of people to privately run prisons. He did that in exchange for money and for kickbacks.

"My twin sister and I started the Truth Foundation as a way to try to pay those people—in some cases, their families—back. In essence to try to make up for the suffering they had gone through because of my father."

"I thought you were a lawyer," Nadine said,

thinking of the reason why she had agreed to have her cousin's ex-husband look into the matter for her. She needed a lawyer, not a saint trying to earn his halo.

"I *am* a lawyer," he answered. "But there's nothing in the rules that says I can't do good, too," Caleb pointed out. "The way I look at it, trying to make up for what my father did only helps me to increase the scope of my focus whenever I undertake any case."

Caleb had to admit that the list of Nadine's arrests had thrown him for a moment. Until she had gotten so defensive just now, he had forgotten the kind of feelings he had experienced trying to fix all those wrongs that his father had done.

There was no "good" reason for doing something so heinous just to be able to take care of his family.

He knew without asking that his mother and his siblings would have *all* been a great deal happier on far less if Ben Colton acted differently.

But there was no point in wishing for events of the past to be transformed. All he could do was move on and try to make amends as best he could.

That was all, he thought philosophically, that any of them could do.

"I'm not judging you," he told Nadine in an attempt to forestall any rift that might be in the making. He wanted her to understand that he was on her side. Admittedly, he had temporarily lost sight of that, but luckily, his "vision" had returned. "As a matter of fact, I applaud your dedication. Not everyone stands up for what they believe in or makes the kind of sacrifices that having a set of beliefs that aren't always popular requires."

She found herself waiting for the punch line, the words that would negate what he had just said. When it didn't come, she heard herself putting her skepticism into words.

"You're kidding, right?"

The woman was really defensive, Caleb thought. He found himself feeling sorry for her and whatever had made her react this way.

Thinking back to what Annie had said about her cousin and the things he had gleaned from what he had read, Caleb realized this was what happened when a person found themselves fighting battles all on their own. Caleb had no doubt that there were lots of "warriors" out there who had taken part in the protests. But in the end, Nadine evidently fought these battles by herself.

Thinking fast, Caleb decided that it was time for Nadine not to feel as if she was waging a war on her own.

"Has any fracking started on your father's property yet?" he inquired.

"No, but it's scheduled to start by the end of the

month," Nadine answered. The frown on her face seemed to travel clear down to the bone.

Caleb nodded. "Good."

"Good?" she questioned, stunned. "How could something like that be thought of as 'good'?"

"Because if it hasn't started yet, this is the best time to get a stay in place against the fracking that's *about* to begin on your dad's property."

"Really?" she questioned. "You can actually get a stay put in place?"

For the first time since she had found out about this awful development involving her father's so-called "deal" with the oil company, a deal he professed to have no memory of and refused to discuss, she felt real hope.

Maybe she was just being premature and fool-ishly optimistic, Nadine thought, but she clung to that hope, absorbing it and taking refuge in that positive feeling.

Caleb nodded his head to confirm what he had just told her. Embarrassingly, his stomach chose that exact moment to rumble and remind him that he had been so busy with one thing and another today, his last meal of memory had been breakfast.

His stomach rumbled again, a bit more insis-tently this time. "As you've probably guessed, I haven't had anything to eat since early this morn-ing."

Nadine felt her optimistic feeling fading away.

She knew this had been too good to be true, she thought. He was using his rumbling stomach as a way to retreat and get out of resolving her father's situation.

"I didn't mean to keep you from your dinner," Nadine began, resigning herself to giving the man a way out.

Caleb looked at Annie's cousin, his mind racing as he made a quick calculation. He really didn't just want to leave her up in the air about this situation.

"Listen, why don't you come with me to dinner?" Caleb suggested. "We can eat and discuss the possible next steps that are available to you and that you can take in order to fight whatever fracking claim Rutledge Oil thinks it can get away with. What do you say?"

Nadine paused and thought for a moment. Usually, when someone was trying to hit on her, all sorts of radar would go off in her head. Most men, she had come to realize, didn't see past her looks. Over time, it had made her more than a little suspicious.

But she had a feeling this wasn't about the attorney possibly hitting on her. Annie's ex was being sincere, not to mention genuine. Despite her initial wariness, Nadine had a feeling that Caleb meant what he said about not just wanting to help her but intended to come up with a way to put that "help" into real action.

Besides, he was talking about going out to eat. That meant out in public at a restaurant. It wasn't as if he was planning on whisking her off to his apartment or some hotel room.

And even if that *was* his intention, Nadine thought, she was a big girl. A big girl who knew how to take care of herself.

She needed to stop having her imagination run away with her.

"All right," Nadine agreed. And then she asked, "What restaurant are we going to?"

He saw that she had taken her cell phone out of her purse. Caleb raised a quizzical brow as he looked at her phone. "Atria. Why, are you going to call and make a reservation?" he wanted to know, somewhat amused. "If that's what you're thinking," he said, giving her a way out, "there's no need. I have a long-standing friendship with the owner."

"I'm calling Annie."

She had lost him again. He didn't understand. "Why?"

Nadine grasped at the first thought that occurred to her. "I told Annie I'd let her know how everything went."

"It hasn't 'went' yet," Caleb pointed out good-naturedly. "It's ongoing."

Even as Caleb said that, he couldn't help wondering if Nadine was calling her cousin because she wanted Annie to know where she was going to be.

But then, thinking back again on the background check, he supposed that he couldn't really blame her. All the people—and their families—that his father had duped when he had been on the bench must have felt the same thing about him.

"Tell Annie I said hi," he told Nadine as he rose from his chair and crossed over to where he had hung up his overcoat.

Their eyes met for a moment. He looked confident and completely unfazed that she was calling the person who had asked him for this favor.

This man, Nadine decided, was on the level. The last fragments of her distrust totally slipped away.

She closed her phone again.

"Can't get a signal?" Caleb guessed, putting on his overcoat.

He had brought hers over, as well, and now went to help her on with it. He was careful not to allow his hands to linger on her shoulders, although Caleb had to admit it was difficult not to. Despite his reservations, he was finding himself intrigued by Nadine Sutherland and her passionate nature, as well as attracted to her.

"I've decided to call her later, after we've had dinner and talked."

"Does that mean you've decided to trust me?" he asked, crossing to the office door and holding it open for her.

She started to protest that he didn't need to hold the door for her, then decided she was being too defensive. "I've decided to go with my gut instinct," she said to Caleb, walking out. "Besides, I've never been to Atria. Eating there might be fun."

"Well, it's definitely tasty," Caleb assured her.

"Why don't we go in my car?" he suggested once they were outside the building. "After we've had dinner, I'll drive you back here, but there's no reason for both of us to drive to the restaurant separately."

She supposed that did make sense, and now that she had relaxed a little, at least enough to trust the man, there was no point in both of them looking for parking spaces.

"Okay," Nadine agreed, surprising him as they approached his vehicle. "I agree."

Chapter Five

"So, is Atria the way you envisioned it would be?" Caleb asked Nadine after they had been shown to a table that was off to the side of the restaurant and the receptionist had handed them each their menus.

"I'm not sure what I was expecting," Nadine answered, looking around after Caleb had helped her with her chair. "But it's very homey." The restaurant's lighting struck her as just right. Not too bright and not too dim. "Is the food as good as they say?" she asked him.

"Better," he replied confidently. "Why don't you open your menu and see if there's anything that looks particularly good to you," Caleb suggested, "and you can find out for yourself."

Nadine left the menu closed in front of her. "To be honest, I lost my appetite the day I found out about what Rutledge Oil had done."

"Righteous anger is all well and good," Caleb told

her. "But we can't have you passing out from hunger at what could turn into an inopportune moment."

His wording amused her despite herself. "Is there an 'opportune' moment to pass out from hunger?" Nadine asked.

"When you're trying to rouse empathy or a sense of kinship from a third party," he said without any hesitation.

Nadine smiled at the attorney. He seemed to have a sense of humor, but he was also serious about taking on her fight, she thought. That made her feel hopeful.

"I'll keep that in mind," she said, referring to what he'd just said about arousing sympathy.

Caleb caught himself thinking that Nadine had a very captivating smile. It wasn't the kind of smile that caused all sorts of unbidden thoughts to suddenly rise up in a man's mind, crowding to the forefront. It was a genuine, compelling smile that instantly made someone want to befriend this woman.

In his opinion, it must be her best weapon when she marched for all those causes she espoused. As a matter of fact, in some cases, one look at that smile of hers could make someone instantly change sides, Caleb mused.

Unless, of course, the people in range of that smile were underhanded, soulless henchmen who were determined to steal what they couldn't buy outright.

He felt himself growing indignant and immediately put a lid on his reaction. This was about dinner, not the oil company, and he didn't want to jump to conclusions. He intended to look into the company and their dealings at length. But first things first.

"But for now," Nadine went on to say, "I think I'll go on remaining upright."

"Okay, then you'll eat," he concluded, his tone indicating that her choice at the moment was a simple cut-and-dried one.

Nadine wanted things between them to remain clear. "There's no need to buy me dinner," she told the attorney.

"No one said anything about 'need,'" Caleb stated matter-of-factly. "I just find it awkward to eat in front of someone who is stoically abstaining from having any food." He leaned in a little closer. "When did you last eat?" he asked unexpectedly.

She raised her eyes to his. "Do you want the truth or do you want me to make something up?"

This was an unusual conversation for her and she was trying to buy some time. Ordinarily, she would have just created a convenient fiction that suited her needs. But there was nothing ordinary about this conversation. Or, she was beginning to think, the man she was having it with.

"The truth," Caleb instantly responded. "Always the truth."

The way he had just said it, Nadine felt that he actually strongly believed in that credo. How about that! She had actually found an honest man, she thought.

"Sometime this morning," she admitted vaguely.

Since there had been nothing outstanding about the meal to set it apart from any other meal she'd had in recent memory, the event had just melded into all the other meals that she'd had of late, usually on the run.

"Then you'll have something to eat." Caleb said the words as if they were a foregone conclusion.

It wasn't that she didn't want to eat; it was just that she really didn't want to waste any time doing it. If the man was pressed for time, Nadine didn't want to waste any of that time eating. She wanted to spend it talking and planning.

But he was the one laying down the terms, she reminded herself. His beach, his ocean, so she might as well just agree and save them all a lot of time.

Flipping open the menu, she glanced down the columns and made her decision.

"I'll have the shrimp scampi," Nadine said, closing her menu and setting it down on the side of the table.

"And?" Caleb prodded, his eyes meeting hers.

Was he talking about something to drink, she wondered. Alcohol, taken in the proper amounts, didn't make her fuzzy, but she had taught herself to abstain from it unless she was in the company of someone she actually knew—*and* as long as it was a social occasion and not one that required any serious thought or discussion on her part. Consequently, she usually didn't partake these days. She wanted to remain sharp and understand everything that was said.

"Water," Nadine said, finally answering his question.

"Nothing else?" he asked as their server approached their table. "You're sure?"

"I'm sure," Nadine told him.

Nodding, he turned toward the server, gave the woman Nadine's order and then placed his own, which turned out to be down-to-earth. He ordered a medium-rare, bone-in steak with mashed potatoes and green beans. He also asked for a glass of red wine.

He closed the menu and looked at Nadine as he surrendered it to the server. "Last chance to change your mind."

Nadine shook her head. "I'm good," she assured the attorney.

His mouth quirked in a quick, fleeting smile as his eyes swept over the woman sitting opposite him.

"Obviously," he agreed.

Nadine felt her heart flutter a little and quickly

tamped down her reaction. The man was a little too attractive for his own good, she thought.

The server returned almost immediately with Caleb's glass of wine and Nadine's glass of bottled spring water. She also brought a basket of warm dinner rolls and set that on the table between them.

Flashing a smile at her customers, the young woman promised, "Your dinners will be ready soon," and then retreated.

"Would you like a roll?" Caleb asked, moving the basket toward Nadine.

She shook her head. "No, not right now, thank you."

"Well, as my stomach already embarrassingly informed you, I'm starving," Caleb told her. He took the top roll out of the basket. "Warm," he commented the moment he picked it up. "There's just nothing better than a warm dinner roll."

As if to prove it, Caleb took a bite out of the one in his hand.

He closed his eyes then, savoring that first bite as if he had just tasted something that was nothing short of heavenly.

"There's no doubt about it. Atria's got the best bread in the state. There's garlic in it, so it might put a cramp in a person's social life for the day, but I guarantee that it's well worth it—most definitely if you've got nothing planned for the rest of your evening," he added with a wink.

Nadine couldn't help wondering if he was pushing the rolls, or subtly telling her that she had nothing to worry about from him romantically or otherwise this evening.

Either way, he had managed to sell her on the rolls.

She eyed the near-full basket, finally breaking down. "Maybe I will give them a try."

The smile on his face rose all the way up into his eyes.

"You won't regret it," Caleb promised. Picking out a likely candidate for Nadine, he held the roll up to her lips, offering it to her. "Go ahead," he coaxed. "Take a bite. Nothing will ever seem the same again," he guaranteed with a grin.

She looked at him, thinking that sounded like overkill. She couldn't help wondering if there was some sort of additive included in the roll.

"It's just a roll, right?" she asked him cautiously.

"No," he said. "It's heaven in dough form."

Since he was still holding the roll for her to sample, she put her hands around his and brought the roll to her lips. Her eyes remained on his, and as she took that first bite, she could have sworn she felt a warm shiver dance up and down through her entire body.

Nadine wasn't all that sure if it was because of the roll, or the man who was holding it out to her.

All she knew was that she hadn't experienced this sort of an electric reaction in a long, long time.

"Good?" Caleb asked, watching her face.

"Good," she echoed with assertion. After a moment, she finished eating the piece in her mouth and took a deep breath. It was time to get back to the real reason she was here. "I don't want to be a killjoy, but—"

"You'd like to get back to talking about your father's case," Caleb guessed.

She nodded her head. "Exactly."

In all honesty, Nadine felt that she had just experienced an extremely strong connection between herself and Caleb and, if she didn't feel as if her back was up against the wall, maybe she would even be inclined to explore that further.

But she felt as if she was running out of time and she really didn't want to waste any of it, especially since it seemed like it was slipping away from her at an increasing speed. Especially when it came to her father.

The server arrived and brought their dinners. Setting them down unobtrusively, the server slipped away.

"Do you really feel that you can get some sort of an injunction?" she questioned, desperate for some actual reassurance.

Caleb wanted her to understand what his thoughts were based on. "Now that I think about it, I did meet your father back when I was first married to Annie. It was just the one time, but I remember that he made an impression on me. He was outspoken and grounded in his beliefs. He certainly wasn't the kind of person who was given to vacillating. And I seriously doubt that he could be talked into doing anything that he didn't wholeheartedly believe in."

Nadine wasn't sure that she followed what he was telling her. "So what are you saying? That you think my father actually did sign those papers willingly?"

Caleb set his knife and fork down for a moment. This was a lot more important than his steak and his pinched stomach. Al Sutherland could have sold the rights and his activist daughter could be lying, trying to revoke his actions, but somehow he didn't think so. Nadine's actions were too obvious to be covert.

"No, from what you've told me and what I witnessed, he would have hung on to anything he felt was his, which means that someone found a way to either hoodwink your father, or just out-and-out take advantage of him and get his signature on that document by subterfuge, especially if he has a reduced mental capacity.

"Either way, I think Rutledge Oil disingenuously obtained those fracking rights from your father. I'm going to investigate and find a way to prove what happened. I'll even do it pro bono."

Picking up the knife and fork, he resumed eating. The food here was just too good to ignore for long, Caleb thought, biting into another piece.

Nadine could have thrown her arms around the man's neck and kissed him, but that might have started something else entirely, something she wasn't prepared to follow through on. So for the time being, she just put her hand on top of his and squeezed it.

"If you could do that, I would be in your debt forever," she told him.

Caleb looked as if he was about to shrug off the declaration as if it was just something she had uttered in the heat of the moment.

Undeterred, Nadine wanted him to understand exactly what she was telling him. "I mean it. This is something I intend to pay you back for, no matter how long it takes." She was that grateful to him.

Caleb laughed, nodding at the plate that was sitting in front of her. "Well, for openers, you could eat your dinner before it gets cold."

Nadine smiled as she looked at him. "Shrimp scampi is good hot or cold."

"You just can't help arguing, can you?" he asked. But it wasn't meant as a critical comment.

And Nadine didn't take it as such. "I guess being stubborn is just in my blood," she said dryly.

Caleb finished his meal. He had to admit that being full felt a great deal better than running on empty.

"Well, if we wind up going to court over this, and I'm pretty sure that we will, you're going to have to work on controlling that penchant you have for arguing. Seriously," he emphasized.

Nadine was about to say something about what he had just said when the melodic chime of her cell phone interrupted their conversation.

She held up her hand, stopping Caleb from continuing. "Excuse me, it's probably my client, wondering if I made any progress on those earrings."

Caleb took a sip of his wine, nodding as he thought her words over. "Annie said something about that. That you like to design original pieces of jewelry."

Nadine shrugged as if it was no big deal. "It pays the bills," she replied.

Rummaging in her purse, she found her cell phone and took it out. Whoever was on the other end of the call hadn't hung up. She said, "This is Nadine Sutherland."

She fully expected to hear a woman's voice on the other end. Instead, what she heard was a metallic sound. The kind that was used when the person who was calling was attempting to disguise their voice.

This wasn't the first time she was hearing that, either.

The moment that eerie squawk came through the speaker, she stiffened and braced herself.

Sitting across from her, Caleb saw the change in Nadine's demeanor immediately. Her face had instantly paled, taking on the unnerving color of parchment.

Rather than say anything out loud, Caleb waved his hand in front of her to get Nadine's attention, then mouthed, "Who?"

She didn't respond. Instead, she had pressed her lips together, looking, he thought, not afraid but like someone who was bracing herself for something terrible to happen.

Whoever was on the other end of the call was definitely intimidating her. Caleb would bet money on it.

Chapter Six

Caleb quickly took out his cell phone and hit the first key. Someone responded on the other end immediately.

"Yes, boss?"

Caleb kept his voice low so that Nadine's caller couldn't overhear. "Jason, I want you to trace this call," he ordered, and then he gave the investigator Nadine's cell phone number.

Caleb looked in Nadine's direction, and using hand gestures, he indicated that she put her call on speaker and place the phone on the table between them. When she complied, he placed his own device close enough to be able to record.

Caleb couldn't help noticing that Nadine's hands were shaking, but he stifled the urge to take her hand in his in an effort to comfort her and show his support. Getting this recording was the important thing at the moment.

Fortunately, Caleb had several investigators

who did work, like Nadine's background check, for him, Morgan and the Truth Foundation. Discovery of his father's deception had taught him not to take anything at face value.

The moment he'd set down his phone near Nadine's, the eerie voice crackled as he issued a threat to her.

"You were warned to stop sticking your nose where it doesn't belong. Now you're going to have to face the consequences for doing that."

And then the line went dead.

Picking up his own phone, Caleb immediately asked his investigator, "Did you manage to get a location?"

"Just a general area," Jason responded. "Whoever it was wasn't on long enough for me to pinpoint the exact location that the call was coming from." He did not sound happy about what he had just said.

It wasn't what he wanted to hear, but he was prepared for it. "Do the best you can," Caleb told his investigator. "I'll be in touch."

Closing the cell phone, he tucked it back into his pocket as he looked at Nadine. Her face still looked extremely pale. "Are you all right?" he wanted to know.

Ordinarily, she would bluff her way through this, saying it would take more than a disembodied voice making threats to get to her. But the incident was still too fresh in her mind for her to shrug off. And besides, it was not the first time.

But the caller had threatened her with retaliation. That was a new development. Usually, he just ordered her to back off or she would regret it. He had gone past that now, telling her she was going to pay for what she had done. The implication made clear as to just how that payment was going to be extracted.

Caleb was still looking at her, waiting for an answer.

Nadine cleared her throat. "I've been better," she told him in a voice that was still somewhat shaky, even though she was desperately trying to hide that. Shifting the focus off herself, she asked, "Who did you call?"

"Jason D'Angelo, one of the investigators our law office has on retainer. I knew it was a long shot, but I was hoping he could trace the call."

"But he couldn't?" It was only half a question. The way things were going lately, this latest wrinkle didn't really surprise her.

"He's still working on it," Caleb answered, thinking that leaving his statement with a small opening for success allowed a drop of hope to dribble through for Nadine. He studied her face. "I take it this wasn't the first of those you've received."

"No." The way she said it left no room for any

doubt that the warnings had had a definite edge to them.

Again, he struggled with the urge to comfort her, but Caleb pushed on. "The next logical question would be how many of those calls have you received?"

Nadine didn't have to stop to think about her answer. Each call, including this one, was indelibly etched in her mind.

"Three," she told him. And each call had left her feeling more vulnerable. "Mr. Deep Voice has called me three times. But this is the first time he said I was going to have to pay for 'ruffling' the oil company's feathers. Chickens have feathers, right?" It was a rhetorical question. He noticed that her voice was growing stronger. Any lingering fear was beginning to abate. "Seems rather appropriate, if you ask me."

Studying her, he thought he knew where her head was at. "It's good that you're not shaking in your shoes, but there's such a thing as being too brave," Caleb pointed out.

She raised her chin. She didn't like being told how to act "I've been dealing with bullies for most of my life."

"I didn't say to let them scare you off. I just don't want you thumbing your nose at them, either." He thought back to the call she had just received. "If I don't miss my guess, it sounded like the person on the other end was a guy."

Her eyes narrowed as she grew more defensive. "So?"

"So," Caleb continued his thought, "I really doubt that the oil company picked him for his fetching demeanor."

"What's that supposed to mean?" she asked.

"It means," Caleb told her, "that he can probably hurt you."

"Well, I know a few things about taking care of myself—" she began to protest indignantly.

"I'm glad to hear that, but this isn't up for debate. You asked Annie and she asked me to help you. I intend to assist, which means that you're going to listen to what I have to say—and, like it or not, you're going to go along with it."

"Look—" Nadine began to protest. Taking on a fighting form had always helped her deal with any fear that might be building up within her. It made her feel more in control of the situation—and she needed that right now.

Caleb had raised his hand to get their server's attention. "We'd like the check, please," Caleb said to her once she approached.

Caleb waited until the young woman had left the immediate area before he said to Nadine, "I'm going to take you to your home."

Her brow furrowed. Had he forgotten? "But

I left my car at your office," Nadine politely reminded him. "You said you'd take me back there so I could pick it up, remember?"

"I remember," he assured her. "But that was before I saw you get that phone call and overheard that creep threatening you. Don't worry. I'll have one of my investigators drive your car over to your place. Right now, my first priority is making sure that you're safe."

"I can be safe driving myself home," Nadine protested.

She refused to be thought of as some damsel in distress who was in need of rescuing. If she began thinking of herself that way, everything would just wind up collapsing on her.

"I'm not doubting you," Caleb emphasized. "My concern is about the people you're dealing with. From what I picked up, they've just escalated the stakes in this little game they're bent on playing."

As he watched, Nadine straightened her shoulders. For all the world, she reminded him of someone who was bracing herself for a fight.

With him.

"But—" she began again, determined to state her protest to this man, in no uncertain terms this time.

But just then, the server returned, so Nadine held her piece. The young woman placed the check next to Caleb on the table.

He glanced at it, noting the amount as he opened up his wallet. Placing two fifties on the small tray, he added an extra twenty to cover a generous separate tip for the server.

Rising, he moved around behind Nadine and drew her chair out for her.

"Nadine, this matter is not up for discussion," he informed her in no uncertain terms, his voice polite but firm.

How did she get him to understand? She really didn't want to fight with someone who was supposed to be helping her.

"Look, you have impeccable manners, Caleb, but I wasn't discussing this with you, I was saying no," she informed him.

But Caleb shook his head. "Sorry, I'm afraid I can't hear you. It's just too noisy in here." With that, he escorted her out of the restaurant.

Forced to follow him to his car, Nadine got into his vehicle and buckled up. But he noticed her body language as he got in on the driver's side. Her arms were crossed defiantly in front of her chest.

"Is that your way of protesting my decision?" he wanted to know, starting up the vehicle.

"No," she said genially. "This is my way of not telling you my address so you're going to have to drive me back to your office and let me get my car."

"Sorry to disappoint you," Caleb told her, his

tone matching hers as he pulled out of the parking lot, "but I already know where you live." She looked at him, surprise and disappointment mingling in her features. "I did a background check on you today," he reminded her.

"You're a brave woman, Nadine. No one is questioning that. But bravery doesn't have to include being foolhardy. As a matter of fact, to my way of thinking, bravery would definitely *exclude* being foolhardy or reckless. Do you agree?" he asked.

Nadine frowned, but she knew she couldn't argue with him. Much as she hated to admit it, he was making sense.

"I agree," she said grudgingly.

Caleb nodded. "That's much better." He glanced at the silent radio. "Want to listen to something?" he offered, about to turn it on.

"I take it you're all talked out?" Nadine guessed.

Caleb laughed at the suggestion. "I'm an attorney. I'm never 'all talked out,'" he told her.

"Fair enough." She nodded. "But I'd rather talk than listen to anything on the radio."

When she said that, she felt that she'd given Caleb an opening and expected him to start talking. When he remained silent, she glanced at him quizzically. There was a very thoughtful expression on his face.

What was that all about?

"That was your cue to start telling me how you

think we can stop these people from doing what they appear to have their hearts set on doing." When Caleb still made no immediate acknowledgment, she shifted in her seat to look at him. "Caleb, did you hear what I just said?"

"I think you were right," he said thoughtfully, sounding preoccupied.

She had no idea what he was talking about or what he was referring to. "In English, please."

He glanced up into his rearview mirror again. A silver sedan he'd glimpsed a few minutes ago was still there, following them—not too close, not too far. He supposed that it could just be a coincidence.

There was only one way to test his theory, he decided.

Caleb turned right at the next corner.

The sedan turned right as well.

"You said you thought you were being followed," he told Nadine.

"I was," Nadine answered. "At least I thought I was," she amended.

It was easy with everything that was going on lately to allow her imagination to get carried away.

"You were right. You *were* being followed," Caleb added with finality, turning again at the very next intersection. This time he deliberately turned left.

The silver car turned left, as well, keeping up the same speed.

"You still might be," he underscored.

Nadine's breath caught in her throat as she twisted around in order to get a better look behind her. She had moved so fast, it felt as if the belt was cutting into her throat. Slipping her thumb beneath it, she moved it aside.

She didn't like what she saw. "It's the same car from yesterday."

There were a lot of silver sedans in the area, he thought. That was an exceedingly popular color for a car.

"Are you sure?"

Nadine had to remind herself to breathe. Somehow, this situation didn't feel as bad, because he was with her. Why, she didn't know.

"I'm sure. There's a slight crack in the front windshield on the right-hand side," she told Caleb with certainty.

He squinted as he looked up into the rearview mirror. She was right, he realized. "You can see that from here?" Caleb questioned. "You must have amazing vision."

"No," she denied. "Just a good memory. I threw a rock at the driver the first time I saw him following me. It was in an effort to make that Neanderthal realize that I wasn't going to be intimidated. I was also hoping that it would make him back off." She frowned to herself as the memory of the encounter came back to her. With a sigh, she told Caleb, "It didn't."

"You do realize that you can't keep taking those kinds of chances with these people, don't you?" he stated.

"Well, I wasn't about to lie down and play dead, either," Nadine said stubbornly.

"I'm more worried about one of the company's henchmen losing their temper and *making* you dead," Caleb informed her. From where he stood, that was entirely possible.

Nadine couldn't help laughing softly. It helped relieve some of the tension she was feeling right now. "You do know that's not grammatically correct, right?"

"I'm not interested in being grammatically correct," he said, stepping on the gas and putting distance between them and the driver who was following them. "I'm interested in keeping you alive."

He almost sounded as if he meant it, Nadine thought. "That's very nice, Caleb," she responded, "but—"

"There is no 'but' here," he informed her sharply. "There's only the bottom line, you remaining alive."

Caleb was searching his rearview mirror again, looking for any sign that the silver sedan was keeping up with them. He thought he caught a glimpse of the vehicle and sped up again. He continued making unexpected twists and turns down the various streets until he was finally satisfied that he had lost the vehicle.

Caleb slowed his car down and Nadine looked around the immediate area, attempting to orient herself. She had thought she was fairly familiar with where she lived, but she had to admit that, at least for the moment, she felt completely lost.

Chapter Seven

"Are we lost?" Nadine asked point-blank.

Despite the situation, Caleb had to admit that he liked the way Nadine had said "we" instead of "you" when she asked the question. Someone else would have been quick to point a finger at him for losing their way, since he was the one who was driving, but she had deliberately included herself in the mix.

Caleb slowly scanned the immediate area behind his vehicle, not just in his rearview mirror but also over both shoulders.

Their tail seemed to have disappeared.

"The important thing is that we've lost the car that was following us," he told his passenger. "But no, we're not lost. I know where we are and I can get us to your home from here." He glanced in her direction. "Better?"

"No," she answered honestly, "but getting there." She leaned back in her seat, doing her best to relax a little. It wasn't easy. "Where did you ever learn to drive like that?" she asked.

"One of the investigators who worked for our firm was an ex–secret service agent." A fond smile curved his mouth as he remembered working with the man. "When I learned that he had been in charge of training the other agents in evasive driving, I asked him to teach me."

That didn't make any sense to her. "You're an attorney, so why would you want to learn how to drive like that?"

"I thought that it might come in handy someday," he told her. "Obviously," he concluded, "it did."

Nadine sat up at attention the moment that the former warehouse that had been turned into a bunch of lofts came into view. "We're almost there," she announced with relief.

"I can see that," Caleb answered. She certainly didn't believe in conventional living quarters, he thought. He spared Nadine a glance. "I think this would be a good time to tell you that there's been a slight change in plans."

The wary look was back in her eyes as she turned them in Caleb's direction. "What kind of change?"

"I'm going to be sleeping on your sofa. If that doesn't work for you, throw a couple of blankets on the floor and that'll do," he said as he drew closer to the converted warehouse's underground parking.

"Why?" she questioned.

"Well, I find that blankets make a hard floor a lot easier to endure."

He knew what she meant, Nadine thought irritably. "I wasn't asking you why you wanted a blanket on the floor. I'm asking you why you would be on my sofa."

"Protecting you," he answered simply. "I want to make sure that the person who was tailing us in that car isn't going to be making a sudden appearance in your loft or however you choose to refer to your living quarters."

So much for being able to relax and reclaim her life, Nadine thought. "It's a loft," she told him, then asked, "You really think that he might turn up here?"

"I think that we would both rather have you be safe than sorry." Threading his way in, he pulled up in the first available space he saw. "So, you didn't answer me. Do I get the sofa or the floor?"

Nadine unbuckled her seat belt, but for the time being, she remained seated. Her entire loft was one large living space, technically divided by curtains and strategically placed furniture.

"I've got what passes for a spare bedroom just off my studio," she volunteered.

He wanted to be as close to her door as possible. "The sofa will be better for my purposes," he told her, explaining, "I want to be close to the front door so I can hear the intruder if anyone has any ideas about breaking in."

Getting out of the vehicle, he quickly came over to her side.

As he opened her door for her, Nadine got the impression that he was on his guard for someone to suddenly jump out of the shadows.

He continued looking around as he quickly brought her into the converted warehouse and escorted her up.

The second she opened the elevator gates, he ushered her in and then closed the door behind them.

Habit had her locking it even though she had her doubts that would actually stop whoever had been pursuing her.

When she turned around, she saw that Caleb was going around, taking in all the windows, pulling the blinds closed to separate them from the rest of the outside world.

She felt really isolated, Nadine thought, looking around her living quarters.

"Is all that really necessary?" she asked Caleb as he pulled the last blinds closed.

"You tell me." He made one more pass around all four corners of the large space. Satisfied, he turned toward the woman whose safety he had undertaken to guard.

"Just how much of a pest did you make yourself to the oil company?" he queried, looking over his shoulder toward Nadine. "From the sound of that call you received in the restaurant, my guess is that they won't be inviting you to any of their Christmas parties anytime soon."

"I'd say that you've guessed correctly," she answered. "Maybe you could call that former secret service agent to come over," she suggested. "Have him look around." No offense intended to Caleb, but she would rather put her life into the hands of a professional, if it came to that.

"I would if I could," Caleb freely admitted. Satisfied that he had seen to all the windows and made sure that they were locked and secured, he came over to the sofa and sat down.

"But?" she asked, waiting for the other part of his sentence.

"Porter died in a plane crash a year ago. It was a tremendous loss to the team. He was a really good man," Caleb couldn't help adding. "Taught me a lot about being able to take care of myself as well as anyone else."

The revelation took her by surprise. "I'm sorry for your loss," she said with genuine sympathy.

"Thank you," he responded. He laughed softly to himself. It was funny how life arranged itself. "You know, losing Porter was harder on me than losing my father. Despite his previous career as a secret service agent, John Porter was exactly what he seemed. There were no deceptions, no pretenses."

His expression hardened a little. "Unlike my father," he told her. "Everyone thought that my father was such an upstanding, principled, charming man. Exactly the way you would envision a judge to be. I was really proud of being his son.

"It was a house of cards," he went on to admit. There was a bitter edge to his voice. "And when it came down, we were all judged to be as guilty as him."

He turned toward Nadine. "Porter was the one who helped me make peace with all that, made me see that my father's 'sins' had nothing to do with me or with anyone else in my family. The sins he was guilty of belonged to my father alone."

She got that, but she also knew what he and the others had been trying to do for the last ten years, thanks to Annie. "But that didn't stop you and your twin sister from trying to make up for what your father did to all those people and their families," she pointed out.

He laughed to himself, remembering everything that had transpired those last few years before the police came for the judge. "My father didn't exactly have a lock on justice—actual justice," Caleb emphasized. "The man wound up meting out a terrible form of 'justice' in order to build up that nest egg he was collecting in order to pay for the lifestyle he felt he needed to give to the family—and himself."

He suddenly paused and looked at Nadine, clearly bewildered. "How did we wind up on this topic?" he wanted to know. It wasn't in his nature to go on and on about himself, certainly not like this.

Nadine smiled. "I have a knack of drawing things out of people," she confessed. And then she laughed quietly. "I think it probably also comes from all that time I spent in holding cells, locked up with lot of other protestors who wound up getting arrested espousing the same causes I believed in and making their voices heard.

"When you're in there," she explained, vividly remembering, "waiting for a loved one—or not so loved one," she amended with a grin, "to post your bail, there's nothing much to do except either pace or talk. Since most of us had done a lot of pacing before we were incarcerated, that left talking."

She looked at Caleb, and for a second, he felt like he was the only one in the whole world besides her.

"You'd be surprised how little coaxing it took to get 'fellow protestors' to suddenly start making a clean break of things, telling me their deepest secrets, things they had no intention of saying just a few minutes ago."

Nadine smiled at him. "I guess that I've just got a face that people like to talk to."

Well, he certainly couldn't argue with that, he thought. Caleb realized that she had a very likable face. That had struck him while they were talking at the restaurant. And now that they were here in her studio loft, it seemed even more evident to him than ever.

"I guess you do," he commented.

For a second, she found herself tempted to draw closer. Catching herself, Nadine changed topics. "I just want you to know that I really appreciate you going out of your way like this," she told Caleb.

He smiled at her. Gratitude always made him feel a little uncomfortable, like he was out of his element.

"Don't mention it. It's just all part of the service."

She nodded her head and, making a decision, she rose to her feet. "Well, if you're going to be spending the night on my sofa, I'd better get you some bedding and some towels."

"Don't go to any trouble," he called after her. "Just a blanket will do."

"No, it won't," she called back, her voice echoing in the barnlike space. Returning in less than a couple of minutes, Nadine had her arms filled with sheets, a pillow, a blanket and several towels.

"If I missed something," she told him, placing everything on the coffee table, "please let me know."

With that, she waved him off the sofa and then proceeded to make it up for him, covering the cushion with a bedsheet, then spreading another matching sheet over it so he could use that as well as the blanket on top of it to cover himself. Finished, Nadine placed a couple of pillows at one end.

"There. Done. I hope you find that comfortable. Like I said, if I left anything out, please let me know," Nadine urged her new protector.

"This looks great," he assured her. "Doesn't look like you left out anything. *And*, to be honest, I don't plan on doing all that much sleeping. Catnaps, maybe, but not out-and-out sleeping."

"Oh? Why?" Cocking her head, she waited for Caleb to continue explaining.

"I have to admit, I've never been a really heavy sleeper, not since—" He stopped himself abruptly. He was doing it again, he thought, and he didn't want to drag her any further into his family's trials and tribulations than he already had. "Well, 'since,'" he merely concluded.

"If I were a heavy sleeper," he told Nadine, veering off into another direction, "there wouldn't be much point in my being here 'guarding' you. Certainly not if I fell asleep on the job."

Nadine wavered. She hesitated to leave him like

this. After all, when she came right down to it, the man was putting himself out for her, and twenty-four hours ago, he had only been vaguely aware of her existence. At that point, she had just been his ex-wife's cousin, nothing more.

"Can I get you anything else?" Nadine asked, at least wanting him to be entirely comfortable before she left him for the night.

"Well," he considered. "Instead of my wandering around at night, making noise, you can point me toward where the kitchen in case I get thirsty—and toward where the bathroom is, in case another need arises. After you do that, I'd like you to go to bed so at least one of us gets a good night's sleep—or what passes for a good night's sleep."

She nodded. Both requests sounded more than reasonable to her.

"That's the kitchen, on the far side of the living room. And the bathroom is that small alcove just down the hall, next to the linen closet. Is there anything else?" she asked.

He shook his head. "Can't think of anything," he told her. "I'll see you in the morning. What time do you get up?" he asked as the afterthought hit him. He assumed that she probably got up around eight, and he didn't want to be guilty of making any noise that might wake her up.

"Six."

That caught him off guard. "Why so early?" he asked.

"I thought I'd try to get some work in," she explained. "Lately, it feels like I've got what's akin to writer's block, except there's jewelry involved," she told him, the corners of her mouth curving in a self-mocking smile.

"Come again?"

"I make jewelry for a living," Nadine reminded him. "Someone tells me what they've envisioned, and I do my best to turn it into reality." She pointed to the other end of the loft. "My tools are over there. I draw the piece of jewelry in question, lay out the necessary pieces, and then when I'm satisfied with what I've envisioned, I forge it until it takes on the required shape." She knew she wasn't being very clear about how she went about the job of creation, but it was the best explanation she could give. What mattered most was that in the end, she always came through with the requested piece or pieces. She had yet to have an unsatisfied customer.

Caleb shook his head in pure wonder. "An activist and a jewelry maker. Quite a combination," he heard himself saying.

Nadine smiled at him. "I never cared very much for the ordinary," she confided.

"Obviously," he agreed. "Well, don't let my being here get in your way. You get started as early as you'd like. Most likely, I'll be up already. Now, good night," Caleb told her. There was finality in his voice this time.

Nadine took that as her cue to leave the immediate area and make her way to what passed as her sleeping quarters.

"Good night," she replied. "And thanks again."

"You're welcome again," Caleb responded good-naturedly.

Chapter Eight

It didn't take long for Caleb to come to the conclusion that Nadine had to have purchased the most uncomfortable sofa he could ever remember lying on. As he sought to find at least a better position, he decided that what he was lying on was more like a torture rack than an actual couch.

Consequently, he wound up getting very little sleep, which actually turned out to be just the way he had wanted it.

Because of the sofa—and his mindset—he found himself waking up every fifteen minutes. Twenty, if he found he was particularly drowsy. It seemed like every noise caught his attention, but in reality, it seemed the way that the loft was constructed was responsible for the creaks and unusual groans that he could hear.

Still, Caleb remained alert, listening to each noise until it faded away and there was no reason to continue listening.

Around six thirty, he began to hear very distinct noises. Not from the loft, which seemed to be in the process of constantly settling, but from the kitchen sounds.

Sitting up against the back of the torture rack that Nadine had referred to as a sofa, Caleb turned toward the noises, wanting to verify that (a) he had actually heard what he thought he had heard and (b) that it wasn't actually someone attempting to break in.

Caleb was fairly certain that he saw a light coming from the far end of the loft. But it was dim, and in truth, it was difficult for him to actually make out anything.

Caleb rose from the sofa and tucked the small firearm he had brought with him into the back of the waistband of his pants. He had a permit to carry, and because of some of the people he had dealt with, he always carried it with him. Last night, he had taken the gun out and left it under the sofa cushion for quick access if he suddenly needed it.

Because of the close-to-sleepless night he had spent, Caleb was having difficulty acclimating his eyes to the darkness as he made his way toward the kitchen.

Halfway across the loft, he let out the breath he had been holding as he relaxed. "I assumed you were kidding, but it looks like you really do get up at six."

Startled, Nadine swung around, stifling the scream that had instantly risen in her throat. She had also dropped the cracked open egg she was about to fry. The egg landed on the floor, the yolk oozing out on the freshly cleaned tile. Swallowing a curse, Nadine grabbed a paper towel, determined to mop up as much of the mess as possible.

Armed with a handkerchief, Caleb evidently had had the same thought. The result was that their heads wound up meeting directly over the yellow pool on the floor, unceremoniously bumping against one another.

Nadine emitted another sharp cry as she tried not to fall backward after their heads hit.

Caleb managed to catch her by her arms, succeeding in steadying her. The egg and the mess that had been created were temporarily forgotten.

Nadine looked at Caleb, annoyed with him and with herself for her reaction. Her nerves were supposed to be steadier than that, she silently upbraided herself.

"Didn't anyone ever teach you not to sneak up on a person in the dark?" she accused, embarrassed.

"Sorry," he apologized. "I did start talking as soon as I realized that it was you."

Calming down, she told him, "Too little, too late." Gesturing toward the small table in the corner, she suggested, "Why don't you just sit down at the table while I finish making breakfast?"

Caleb looked at the remaining mess. "The least I can do is tidy the floor," he said.

"No," Nadine contradicted. "The least you can do is sit at the table. I'll clean up." A smile slipped over her lips as she added, "There's less of a chance of another collision that way." With that, Nadine pulled another paper towel off the roll and wiped away the rest of the yellow liquid.

He didn't like standing around inactive this way. "Is there *anything* I can do?" Caleb asked.

Nadine looked in his direction. "By my reckoning, you were up for most of the night. The way I see it, you've done everything you can do. I don't want you suddenly collapsing on the floor because you didn't get any sleep. This breakfast, by the way," she continued as she worked, "is my small way of thanking you for standing guard over me. No matter what I sound like, I really appreciate your gallantry."

"Couldn't very well go off and leave you, now, could I?" Caleb asked.

She tossed out the paper towels and washed her hands, then got back to making breakfast. "I suspect that someone else might have done just that," she told him.

"I'm not someone else," he answered.

She turned then and looked at him over her shoulder. "No, that you are not," she agreed. "You are uniquely you, and while we're at it, I want to thank you for taking me seriously. People usually don't—except for Annie," she amended. "Other people in the family usually think I'm either exaggerating things or imagining them—or just plain flaky."

"Well, you definitely weren't exaggerating that call you got in the restaurant. I heard it," he reminded her.

To be honest, he was surprised she hadn't freaked out, that she had stayed as together as she had after being on the receiving end of that call. In his opinion, a lot of other people would have gotten really frightened after hearing that unnerving, metallic voice threatening them.

Thinking of how she must have felt hearing that voice, Caleb felt a wave of sympathy washing over him. "Whoever is after you and your dad, we'll get them," he promised.

She smiled up at him. Caleb was a lot nicer than she had first thought he was. "Well, until you do, why don't we have breakfast?" she said.

Nadine placed both plates of bacon, eggs and

toast down on the table. And then she stopped abruptly, raising her eyes to his face as a thought suddenly hit her. "You're not a vegan, are you?"

He met her question with a soft laugh. "Not even remotely. If I were a vegan, I'd have to give up all meat and I'm really not ready to do that," he told her with feeling. "Besides, I had a steak last night," he reminded her.

When had she gotten so scattered? "I'd forgotten about that," she admitted. "And I'm fresh out of cereal," she added, which would be her only other option, normally.

Turning away, Nadine made her way over to the coffee maker that had just finished percolating. She poured them each a cup, then she brought the coffees over and set the cups down next to the milk and sugar.

"Go ahead," she coaxed, nodding toward the plates. "The breakfast isn't going to eat itself."

"This is good," Caleb told her with sincerity after he'd had a chance to swallow that first mouthful.

Her mouth curved with amusement as she sat down over her own plate. "It's a little hard to ruin something as simple as fried eggs and bacon," Nadine pointed out.

A memory of some of his first breakfasts with Annie popped up in his head. Caleb laughed to himself. "You'd think so, wouldn't you? But you would be surprised how many people have managed to do that."

Nadine suspected that he was just trying to make her feel good, but she was not about to argue with him, not over something so minor. She had learned to save arguments for major confrontations, not minor conversations about eggs.

She finished her own quickly enough. "I can make you more if you're still hungry after you finish that," she volunteered, nodding at his plate.

"No, this is just enough." And then Caleb glanced at his watch just before he continued eating.

Nadine picked up on that. "You have to go somewhere after you finish eating, don't you?" she guessed.

He hadn't thought he was being that obvious. "Actually, I do," he admitted. He felt obligated to fill her in. "Arrangements were made before any of this came up," he told her, referring to his having come home with her last night.

Finished eating, he wiped his mouth, put the napkin on his plate and then turned his attention to the coffee.

Nadine noted that he took his coffee black. Unlike her. Her coffee was almost pale in comparison, and there was enough sugar in it to qualify the drink to fill in as a candy substitute.

"Well, by all means, go," she urged. "I wouldn't want to keep you," she told Caleb honestly.

But he shook his head. "I don't like the idea of leaving you alone," he explained to her, not after hearing about the type of person she could be dealing with.

His protest struck her as being extremely sweet, but she didn't want Caleb to feel obligated to hover over her. She felt braver now. Daylight had a way of doing that, and it was definitely getting lighter outside. Despite the drawn curtains, the growing illumination was nudging its way into the loft, making everything feel more positive.

"I was alone before I met you at your office," Nadine reminded him.

Caleb was only half listening to what she was saying. A thought suddenly hit him. Looking at her, he proposed, "Why don't you come with me?"

Nadine all but did a double take, then stared at him. The question had come completely out of the blue, and she really wasn't prepared for it. "Where?"

He realized he hadn't told her where he had to go. "To my mother's."

Nadine felt even more confused than she had a minute ago. Annie had mentioned how caught up her ex was with his family, but she had assumed that involved making amends to the people his father had wronged. She understood—she was still really close with her own dad.

"Excuse me?"

"I promised my mother I'd swing by her place today—before Annie called about you and your 'problem,'" he explained delicately. "I promise this isn't going to take long, and then I can focus my attention on you and whoever is threatening you at the oil company."

The idea of tagging along as he stopped by his mother's was not exactly something that warmed her heart. For one thing, Nadine didn't like butting in where she didn't belong.

"I'm sure your mother isn't going to be all that thrilled that you're bringing your ex-wife's cousin over, especially since I've been arrested and have a rather lengthy 'rap' sheet by some standards," she told him.

In her experience, although her heart was in the right place with every single cause she undertook, being arrested didn't exactly make her someone a man's mother would dream of having her son bring home.

Caleb hadn't expected that he would have to convince Nadine to come with him. "My mother is extremely open-minded." He could see that his words didn't convince her. "Look, if she never condemned my father for all the things he did, you being arrested for standing up for things you believed in is certainly not going to have her looking at you cross-eyed.

"Besides, you'll like my mother," Caleb promised, adding, "Everyone does."

She sighed. "Of course you'd have to say that," Nadine replied, pointing out the obvious. "You're her son."

"Be that as it may," he said, waving away her statement, "everyone likes my mother. I guarantee you, you will, too." He looked at her, waiting for her response. "What do you say?"

He'd been more than kind to her. And, she reminded herself, he was the first one besides Annie who had taken her seriously.

"I'd have to shower and get ready," she told him, thinking that he would probably tell her to never mind, because he had to leave now.

But he surprised her by saying, "Go ahead. I didn't give my mother any specific time that I'd be swinging by, I just said I'd be there in the morning."

Well, she'd painted herself into a corner, she thought.

"Okay," Nadine reluctantly agreed. She looked

toward the sink. "But I have to wash the dishes first. I hate having things piled up," she said.

Caleb waved her away. "Go shower. I'll take care of the dishes," he replied. He saw the look of surprise on her face and grinned. "I know how to clean up after myself. My mom taught us."

Something wasn't making sense. "But didn't you grow up privileged? Or at least thinking you were privileged?" she asked.

"Didn't matter," he assured her. "My mother felt that, rich or not, we always needed to clean up after ourselves. Too bad that lesson was lost on my father," he commented.

Nadine looked back at the dishes doubtfully. She couldn't argue with him about this. It seemed silly. "Well, if you're sure."

Caleb shooed her toward the bathroom. "I'm sure," he told her.

"Okay."

Nadine went by the area she had fashioned into her bedroom and quickly picked up some fresh clothes. Armed, she made her way into the tiny bathroom.

Locking the door, she took what was probably the fastest shower on record. Drying off just as fast, she quickly got dressed, ran a comb through her hair and was out, rejoining Caleb in what served as a kitchen in a little longer than it took her to make breakfast.

He had just put away the last of the dishes when she walked back in. "Done?" he asked.

"I didn't want to keep you waiting," she explained.

"Waiting? Are you even dry?" he questioned, amazed at the speed with which she had gotten ready.

"I'm dry," she assured him, then put out her arm. "See for yourself."

"I believe you," he said, although he had to admit that he was tempted to slide his fingers along her skin, but for an entirely different reason.

He was being punchy, Caleb chided himself even as he felt himself responding to Nadine. That was what he got for not sleeping most of the night.

Still, there had been times when he had managed to push on for two days straight. That shouldn't really be slowing him down, Caleb thought.

"You finished the dishes," she noted, looking at the rack in the sink.

"I said I would," he reminded her. "Well, if you're all set, I guess we can get going," he told her.

"I thought you said you didn't give your mother a specific time."

"I didn't, but she's an early riser like me so there's no point in wasting any time. Got everything you need?"

She nodded. "Just let me get my coat."

He stood back, out of her way, thinking that she really was a rare woman.

And that, along with other things he was learning about her, made Nadine truly special.

Chapter Nine

Nadine was vaguely aware that 201 Richland Avenue, the Colton family home, was in a subdivision of Green Valley and located approximately ten miles west of the city. But since it was so out of the way, she had never had an occasion to drive past the imposing two-story house.

She could hardly take her eyes off it as the building drew closer and closer into view. It brought new meaning to the word *large*.

"That's where you and your brothers and sisters grew up?" she asked incredulously when she finally found her voice.

"Pretty much," Caleb answered casually as he approached what to him was the familiar, rambling wood-and-stone building. He thought it probably appeared somewhat dated to her. "My father had it built for the family a few decades ago, and for the most part, it's been stuck in that era. Although," Caleb continued, "my siblings and I all chipped in to make some renovations. We modernized the kitchen and the connecting family room for Mom for her sixtieth birthday.

"There's an underground parking garage," Caleb said, "but we're not going to be staying here that long, so I'm just going to leave the car out front—unless you'd rather I parked it there," he offered, looking at Nadine for her input.

Nadine had no idea how his mother would react to having her here, so in her opinion, parking the vehicle out front made leaving the premises a little easier.

"No, out front will be just fine," Nadine assured him. "You know," she said as she got out on the passenger side, "it's really none of my business, but you never explained why you were stopping at your mother's."

Was it something important, or something he just routinely did, and did that mean that this handsome attorney was, at bottom, actually a mama's boy? Nadine realized that Annie had left those kinds of details vague when it came to her ex. The only thing she knew for sure was that Annie felt that Caleb was a decent, dedicated man who was always taking off in order to right his father's wrongs, but being one did not necessarily rule out the other.

Caleb paused to think for a moment and realized that she was right. He hadn't told her why they were swinging by. "We all have such busy lives now, I like checking in on her so she doesn't feel quite alone." He didn't mention that he had been by yesterday or that something she had said had prompted this visit on his part.

"Aren't there twelve of you?" Nadine asked. Surely someone in the family had to pop up once in a while, she thought.

Caleb laughed. "I know. It doesn't make much sense, does it? But I'm the oldest and I guess that makes me feel kind of protective of everyone else, especially my mother," he admitted. "Mom still works occasionally," he went on to tell Nadine as he unlocked the rather imposing front door.

His mother worked. She recalled hearing that Isadora Colton was in her seventies. Obviously there were a lot of questions she had neglected to ask Annie, Nadine thought.

"Doing what?" she asked Caleb, curious.

"She's a freelance graphic artist," he answered. Holding open the door for her, Caleb followed Nadine into the house.

Awed, she glanced around the mansion. She couldn't help thinking that it looked to be every bit as huge on the inside as it appeared to be on the outside. Nadine realized that she could have easily fit three of the houses that she had grown up in inside of Caleb's so-called "childhood" home.

"Mom, I'm here," Caleb called out. "Where are you?"

There was no immediate response. "Maybe she went out," Nadine suggested.

But Caleb shook his head. "No, it's too early for her to be out," he told her. He began to investigate the immediate area. "She's around here somewhere. Mom?" he called again.

This time he heard Isa answer from close by.

"I'm looking for my keys. Again," his mother said. She sounded exasperated as she walked into the front room.

Nadine turned toward the woman to get a better look. Caleb's mother was not what she had expected. Looking years younger than her actual age, Isadora Colton was an attractive blonde, with shoulder-length hair, blue eyes and a curvy figure.

But the woman's looks were not the most compelling thing about Caleb's mother. That honor belonged to the baby the woman had tucked in the crook of her arm.

Speechless, Nadine looked at Caleb, a very obvious question in her eyes. She sincerely doubted that Caleb's mother was running a daycare center.

Meanwhile, she was looking at her oldest born for answers to her own questions. When none were immediately forthcoming, Isa switched fronts.

"Hello?" Isa said in greeting, her sky blue eyes

sweeping over the young woman at her son's side. "And you are?"

"Very confused right now," Nadine confessed genially.

Swaying slightly to keep the baby she was holding from beginning to cry, Isa looked back at her son. "Caleb?" she asked. "You're the one with all the answers—except when it comes to the whereabouts of my keys," she qualified, looking around the room again.

"Sorry," Caleb apologized. "Mother, this is Nadine Sutherland." He nodded toward the woman who had become his latest project. "Annie's cousin," he added. "Annie thought I could help her." And then he reversed the introduction. "Nadine, this is my mother, Isadora Colton. And that little person she's holding in her arms is my niece, Iris."

"My *only* grandchild," Isa pointedly emphasized, her eyes meeting Nadine's. "Hard to imagine, isn't it?" she asked.

The next moment, Caleb's mother clarified her point. "All those children and you'd think there would be at least a few more grandchildren, wouldn't you?" Isa deliberately looked at her son. "You would think that the rest of my children would step up and at least give me a few more of these," the woman said, smiling down at the infant she was holding cradled against her hip.

Caleb's mother looked extremely natural that way, Nadine couldn't help thinking.

"One's a good start," she told the woman diplomatically. Coming closer, she looked at the baby, who was waving her hands and gurgling. "How old is she?" Nadine asked.

"This little darling is four months old," Isa answered, looking down into the baby's face. "She belongs to my daughter Rachel."

Things clicked in Nadine's head and she turned toward Caleb. "That wouldn't be Rachel Colton, would it?"

"The County DA." Caleb supplied, nodding his head. "Yes, it would. And Rachel is working, which is why Mother suddenly finds herself in the role of babysitter."

"And loving every moment of it," Isa interjected, smiling broadly at her son.

Caleb had just mentioned that his mother was a graphic artist. Taking care of this infant had to cut into the woman's time. A solution occurred to Nadine.

Turning toward Caleb, she asked, "Why don't you or your sister get a nanny to watch the baby?"

"And hand over Iris to some stranger to take care of?" Isa asked in dismay. "Bite your tongue."

Caleb needlessly told Nadine, "Mother's very maternal."

Isa raised her chin proudly. "After raising

twelve kids, I should hope so," she declared. She looked down at her grandchild. "You don't have any complaints, do you, Iris?" she asked, talking to the infant as if Iris understood every word.

Nadine smiled at the baby. The center of the conversation was cooing and seemed to be completely fascinated with her own fist. Iris was attempting to stuff it into her mouth, but for now, she wasn't getting anywhere with her project.

Nadine came to Caleb's defense by pointing out the pluses of the situation. "Iris is a lucky baby to have her grandmother's attention like this. If you had more grandchildren right now, Mrs. Colton, this little one might miss out and not be the center of your attention the way she most obviously is."

Amused, Caleb laughed. "You don't know my mother. She has a gift of making each and every one of her kids feel as if they are the only one in her universe. I'm sure that she would do the exact same thing with her grandchildren, no matter how many she had."

"I would," Isa answered with conviction. She turned her attention back to her firstborn. "So why don't you get busy, young man, and see about giving me one or two of those grandchildren?" she asked.

This was not an unfamiliar conversation. It was one that his mother circled back to with a fair amount of regularity. Caleb answered her the way he always did.

"When I have the time."

He felt it useless to tell his mother—again—that at this point in his life, he thought of himself as being a confirmed, eternal bachelor. He had taken one dive into the marital pool with a wonderful woman, but that had gone terribly wrong. And, he concluded, if he hadn't been able to make it work with Annie, there was no chance that he was going to make it work with anyone else.

Right now, all that went unspoken, although his mother had given him a long-suffering, knowing look just now.

It did not go unnoticed by the third party in the room, but Nadine didn't think it was her place to comment on it, not in front of the woman who had given Caleb birth and whom he so obviously held in such high esteem.

Changing the subject slightly, Isa turned toward Nadine. "Would like to hold her?" she asked, holding Rachel's daughter up to Nadine.

Caleb knew what his mother was trying to do. She was trying to stir maternal feelings within someone she was hoping was more than just a client to him.

He attempted to put a stop to that as tactfully as he could. "She doesn't want to hold Rachel's baby, Mom."

"Why don't you let her answer for herself, dear?" Isa suggested with a wide smile.

Nadine decided that turning Isa down would be seen as being impolite. "I would, thank you." She carefully took Iris into her arms.

Watching Nadine's every move, Isa beamed. "Look at that, Caleb. She's a natural," she pointed out to her son happily.

It was time to retreat before his mother pulled Nadine in any further, Caleb thought. "If everything's all right, Mother, I think that Nadine and I are going to be going now," he told her.

"Really?" Isa asked in disbelief. "But you just got here," she said.

"To check on how you were doing," Caleb reminded his mother. "And you seem to be doing fine. I've got a lot of other things to see to."

Isa shook her head as she took the baby back from Nadine. "You know, sometimes you need to stop and smell the roses, just to remember what they actually smell like," she reminded her son. "All work and no play is not good for you, dear," she added with concern.

That was not the way he viewed what he was doing. "You were the one who taught me how to juggle all those balls at the same time, remember, Mom?" he asked.

"Yes, but I never juggled more than I knew that I could competently catch," she reminded her son.

"Remember," she said, turning toward Nadine, "never be so busy that you don't leave a sliver of time for yourself." She looked at the baby in her arms. "Uncle Caleb and his friend are leaving, Iris. Say good-bye."

As if on cue, the infant in Isa's arms made a gurgling noise. Her wide eyes seemed to be focused on her uncle and Nadine.

Nothing seemed to escape his mother, Nadine noticed. Isa smiled at her granddaughter's noises. "I think she likes you," she told her son and Nadine.

Caleb humored his mother. "Uh-huh." Looking at Nadine, he began to usher her toward the front door. "Call me if you need anything," he instructed.

"If you could find things for me, that would be lovely," Isa responded, giving the area another cursory look.

That was when Nadine glanced over at the small side table that was standing adjacent to the front door. There, in plain sight, was a set of keys, lying right in the center.

Tugging on Caleb's elbow, Nadine silently pointed.

Caleb grinned at her. "They are on the hall table, Mom," he called out.

Still holding Iris against her hip, Caleb's mother joined them like a shot. She looked down at the keys as if their appearance was akin to the miracle of the loaves and the fishes. "And so they are." She turned toward the infant in her arms. "What do you think of that, Iris?"

"I think you might need glasses, Grandma," Caleb said in a high voice, pretending to be his niece answering his mother.

"Wise guy," his mother stated affectionately.

"Just stating the obvious, Mom," Caleb answered in an equally affectionate voice. Before leaving, he paused to brush a kiss against his mother's cheek. "I'll see you soon, Mom," he promised.

Isa nodded. "I'll hold you to that." And then she looked at Nadine. "Nice meeting you, dear," she told her.

Nadine couldn't help smiling at Caleb's mother. This morning had been an eye-opener for her.

"Same here, Mrs. Colton. It was a real pleasure."

Lifting Iris's hand, Isa waved good-bye to the visitors. Caleb closed the door behind him. "Let's go," he said to Nadine.

They went down the front steps, away from what Nadine could only think of as a mansion. They made their way toward the car that Caleb had left parked out in front.

Nadine turned toward him just as he opened the passenger door, holding it for her. Just before she slipped into her seat, she smiled at him.

"I like her," she told Caleb with genuine feeling.

Caleb smiled and nodded, closing the door for her. Rounding the hood, he got in on the driver's side.

"I thought you would. Everyone does. My mother doesn't have one nasty bone in her whole body," he confided, starting up the vehicle. Although there was nothing around, Caleb looked over his shoulder before backing out. "After everything that my father wound up putting her through, to this day, she still loves the man," he marveled. "She just let me know the other day."

Nadine could easily see that, she thought. "That goodness of hers just seems to radiate out toward everyone who makes even the slightest contact with her."

Caleb's smile grew larger. Nadine couldn't have said anything better if she had tried, he thought, pleased.

Chapter Ten

Settling back in the passenger seat, Nadine was silent for a moment. Caleb had suggested that they get some coffee and was driving them over to a shop in the area.

"You know," she said, turning toward him, "I've got mixed feelings about this whole thing with Rutledge Oil."

"You're going to have to elaborate a little more than that if you want me to understand what you're trying to say," he told her.

Pulling up in front of the coffee shop, they went in. Both of them felt as if they needed a second cup to get them going.

Something else they had in common, he couldn't help thinking as he took their drinks over to a small table by the window.

"Well," Nadine explained, "it's nice to be taken seriously about all this instead of just being viewed as some overly dramatic activist who sees people threatening her behind every shadow and creeping out from under every rock. However, not being taken seriously left me with that small sliver of hope that maybe I *was* overreacting. That the threats that I perceived actually *were* imagined and existed just in my head."

Caleb paused, his hands wrapped around his container of coffee as he thought over the comment she had just voiced.

"In other words, you were hoping that the boogeyman wasn't real," he guessed.

Then, he did understand, Nadine thought happily. "Yes," she exclaimed with feeling.

Much as he hated to burst her bubble, in this case, he had to.

"The only problem here is that this 'boogeyman' *is* real. You weren't the only one who heard him and we both saw the guy following you yesterday," Caleb reminded her.

"Maybe they—he or she," Nadine qualified, although she was more than 80 percent certain the driver following them was a man, "were just doing it to get me to back off or back down," she said. "In the last few weeks, I was pretty much in the oil company's face. With justification, I grant you," she quickly added. "But maybe they still believe I'll back off if they exert enough pressure—and if I do, then they will, too."

He looked at her over the last of his remaining coffee. "Do you plan to back off?" he wanted to know.

Nadine thought for a minute, wanting to be completely honest. And then she sighed. There was only one answer she could give him.

"No. They took away fracking rights under some sort of false pretenses. I can't get him to tell me what those pretenses were, but the fact remains that somehow, Rutledge Oil tricked my father out of his land. They played my father. They *took advantage* of him," she emphasized fiercely, "and I can't just let that happen," she insisted. "I can't just allow him to believe that he allowed fracking rights to family land to just be taken away from him like that."

Impassioned, Nadine leaned over the table to make her point. "There has to be some way I can get them for him." Sitting back in her chair again, she concluded, "That's why I need your help."

Caleb couldn't help thinking that the case certainly didn't look winnable on the surface. The fact was that Nadine's father had signed over fracking rights to fifty acres to Rutledge Oil and it apparently looked as if he had done it of his own free will. Proving otherwise was going to be difficult and tricky, to say the least.

"The best way to do that," Caleb told her, "would be proving that your father wasn't of sound mind when he signed over the rights to his land.

Then you'd have a good chance of taking the oil company to court, saying that they managed to get the rights to that property by taking advantage of a man who was not in a position to be able to do his own negotiating. I'm going to need to see the paperwork he signed as soon as possible."

"I can get that for you. My father said he had it." But Nadine shook her head, stopping him before he could continue. "But saying my father wasn't of sound mind at the time would be tantamount to saying that he wasn't in full command of his faculties," she pointed out, upset for the man.

Caleb raised his shoulders in a half shrug. He would have put the matter more delicately, but that was the unvarnished bottom line. "In a manner of speaking," he agreed.

"I just can't do that to him," Nadine objected. "Even if it's true," she added unhappily. "Can't you see? If I allowed that to go on record and have everyone know, that would just kill my father. There's got to be another way." Her eyes were literally begging Caleb. "Please."

He felt sorry for Nadine and understood where she was coming from, but at the same time, he felt as if his back was up against a wall. Still, he felt he needed to at least try to find a way out of this dilemma for her.

"Offhand, I don't see how it wouldn't come out about your dad," he admitted, "but—" Just then,

Caleb's cell phone rang. "Excuse me for a minute," he said, taking out his phone. He glanced at the number on the screen. "I've got to take this," he told her, getting up from the table. He walked away a few steps.

Perturbed, Nadine took another sip of her coffee. She glanced out the window as she did so. She wasn't really looking at anything in particular, but then she froze.

There was a car cruising down the street at a steady pace. A silver sedan that looked exactly like the one that had been following them yesterday before Caleb had employed those evasive maneuvers he had told her he had learned from a former secret service agent.

Nadine felt her breath backing up in her lungs. The car she had observed drove away from the coffee shop. The pace never picked up.

Was the driver looking for them?

For *her*?

Or was it just some awful coincidence that had a similar-looking vehicle driving in their immediate area?

She didn't really believe in coincidences.

She wasn't safe, Nadine thought. She had just started to relax, to feel safe again, and now she realized that she had just been fooling herself. There was a target on her back and these people weren't the forgiving type.

They certainly weren't going to back off and walk away.

Caleb returned to their table just then, putting his cell phone into the upper pocket of his suit jacket.

"That was one of the firm's investigators," he told her, taking his seat again. "The one I have looking into people who were contesting Rutledge Oil's tactics."

Nadine read between the lines. "I'm not going to like this, am I?"

"No," he said honestly. "I know I don't. It seems that Rutledge Oil is known for harassing anyone who goes up against them."

"Define 'harassing,'" Nadine requested. "Exactly what does that mean in this case?" She could feel her stomach sinking.

"It means that, for one thing, you're not exactly alone in this." He did see that as a good thing. That meant that the oil company was spreading itself thin in trying to fight everyone. It also meant that they were bound to make a mistake.

"There are multiple pending lawsuits against Rutledge Oil. The bad thing," he continued, "is that several of those have just 'gone away' after the person suing the company was involved in an accident or just managed to disappear." Caleb's expression became totally serious. "I don't want that happening to you. I'm not about to have you become another statistic in this war against the oil company."

She was grateful for his display of protective-ness, but that still didn't change the basic situation.

"What do you suggest?" He was probably going to say something about hiring a real bodyguard, but she couldn't afford to do anything like that.

Her mind immediately began searching for something that she *could* do. Nadine wasn't pre-pared to hear Caleb say "I want you to come stay with me."

Nadine was grateful that she wasn't drinking her coffee just then, because she was certain she would have started choking.

She looked at him wide-eyed. "You're kidding, right?"

But the stern look on his face told her that he wasn't.

"Hear me out," Caleb requested before she could turn him down. "The penthouse I live in has supertight, around-the-clock security. There is an underground garage beneath the penthouse that has its own security system. And even more important than that, I implicitly trust everyone who surrounds me. Santa Claus couldn't be safer at the North Pole than you would be in my place," he guaranteed.

Nadine sighed.

Her initial reaction to that sort of a suggestion

would be to say no—or it would have been before she saw that car, which looked as if it had
been circling the area just before Caleb returned
to their table.

The same car, she could have sworn, that had
been following them—or at least her—yesterday
before Caleb wound up spending the night on her
sofa.

She caught her lip between her teeth, conducting an internal argument with herself. Agreeing to
allow Caleb to take her to his penthouse wouldn't
be tantamount to displaying weakness on her part.
If anything, she would be showing good sense.
After all, she wouldn't have come as far as she
had by being just a stubborn fool, she told herself.

Relenting, she surrendered.

"Do you have a spare bedroom?" she asked
Caleb, her voice coming across as being exceedingly cautious.

"I have *two* spare bedrooms," he answered, relieved that he wasn't going to have to argue her
into this. "You can have your pick."

She still wasn't 100 percent won over. "And
how long am I supposed to stay?" Nadine wanted
to know.

He didn't know. He didn't have a pat answer
for her, certainly not one he knew that she wanted
to hear.

"Why don't we take it one day at a time?" Caleb suggested.

Nadine rolled the matter over in her head for a moment, but she knew that she really didn't have a choice here. While it was true that she could get emotionally caught up in her undertakings, she definitely was not reckless.

"All right," she reluctantly agreed. "I'll come and stay at your place. But I'm going to have to stop at my loft first to get a few changes of clothing," she told him, "as well as my jewelry-making tools." She saw the look of surprise pass over his face.

"You want to make jewelry?" he asked, astonished that she could concentrate at a time like this.

She needed something that could take her mind off the immediate circumstances.

"I don't like to waste time." Then she added with a smile, "It's against my religion."

He had no idea if Nadine was kidding or serious. Either way, he already knew the woman didn't like wasting time and he could understand that. He believed in utilizing every second of every day himself.

"Wouldn't want you doing that," he responded. Thinking the situation over, Caleb told her, "I can have someone go by your loft and get your possessions for you."

He thought that it might be safer that way. Caleb

wasn't worried about himself, but he felt that Nadine was already walking around with a bull's-eye firmly attached to her back. He didn't want her out there like that.

"And have some stranger go rifling through my stuff?" she asked, appalled by the thought. "No thank you. I'll pass. I'd rather get my own stuff."

He supposed he could understand why she might feel that way about having an investigator packing up her things. He thought of another solution. "I could have one of my sisters swing by and do it for you."

She shot that down as well. "Right, like they have nothing better to do," Nadine said.

That was all she needed, to have his family think of her as some pampered diva who got herself into trouble and then needed to have her hand held as well as her clothes packed. Well, that certainly wasn't the impression she wanted to create.

Besides, that wasn't the real her, she thought. She hadn't needed hand-holding since she'd been a first grader. Although she liked the idea of the Colton family—and Caleb especially—caring about her.

"That's all right," Nadine assured him, dismissing this suggestion as well. "There's no need to bother anyone or get anyone else involved. It would really be a lot faster if I just went over to the loft and packed everything myself."

"Faster, maybe," Caleb allowed. "But my way would be safer for you."

Nadine sighed. She was not ready to give in. "Tell you what. Let's just agree to disagree," she told Caleb. "In the time that we've just spent disagreeing about this, we could have already gone over to my loft and packed up the necessary things."

The woman was impossible, he thought. Talk about an immovable object.

"Tell me, do you get a kick out of arguing?" he asked.

She didn't answer his question directly. "I like keeping my mind active," she answered. "And we wouldn't even have to be debating this if you had let me get my car from your firm's parking lot," she pointed out. "I could have just driven over to my place myself."

Caleb sighed, shaking his head. "Well, that answers my question."

He had lost her there, Nadine thought. "What question?" she wanted to know, not aware that there was an unanswered question on the table.

"You *do* like to argue," Caleb concluded.

She contradicted him on that point, too. "No, I don't," Nadine insisted. "But I don't back off if I'm right," she stressed. "Now, can we *please* go and get some of my things before the seasons change?"

Caleb surrendered. "Well, if I can't talk you out of it, let's get this over with," he agreed.

ALL IN ALL, Caleb had to admit that he was surprised at how quickly Nadine could move once they pulled up to her loft. True to her word, she quickly grabbed several necessary items and threw them into her suitcase. Because it was a cloth suitcase, and consequently flexible, she was able to stuff a great deal into it.

He noticed that she wasn't one of those fussy people who insisted on neatly folding each item before turning to the next one. Instead, clothing items all but rained into the suitcase, one after another, followed by a number of undergarments and a couple of pairs of shoes as well.

The entire process from entry to zipping up her suitcase took all of approximately twenty minutes.

Her jewelry-making tools went into another, specially made case.

"Okay, I'm done," Nadine announced, one suitcase in her hand. The jewelry-making bag was hanging off her shoulder, balancing out her purse, which was on the other.

Caleb crossed the floor and took her larger suitcase from her. "I have to say I'm impressed."

"I told you," she said with a broad, satisfied smile.

Yes, he thought, gesturing for her to wait and

let him go out of the converted warehouse first, she certainly had.

And, he was beginning to learn, Nadine Sutherland was also a woman of her word.

Chapter Eleven

Caleb's eyes quickly swept over the sidewalk outside the warehouse, making sure there was no one hiding close by, ready to threaten Nadine—or worse.

But everything looked relatively empty. Still, he was not about to take any unnecessary chances. Caleb quickly waved Nadine over to his vehicle, placing himself between her and any possible trigger-happy hitman who might be looking to take her out.

"You really think they might be lurking around, ready to do something in broad daylight?" Nadine asked him once she had gotten inside.

He gunned his car and quickly left the area. "Yes," he confirmed without any emotion, "I do."

Leaving Nadine's loft behind them, Caleb checked his rearview mirror again to make sure they were not being followed.

They weren't.

At least for now.

But that didn't mean that he was planning to relax his guard.

"All right," he announced when he had put a little distance between them and her loft, "you have a choice to make."

"Ah, more choices," Nadine responded cryptically. This couldn't be good. "What is it?"

"Well, I can either take you to my penthouse apartment where you can settle in while I get back to the office to finish up some work..." Caleb began.

Nadine felt as if she had just been completely wound up, only to be disappointed. The thought of going to his place to put her things away and then spending the remainder of the day waiting for him to come back didn't sound all that appealing to her. And she felt too agitated to concentrate on making those earrings for her client. Inspiration didn't just pop up on demand.

But it sounded as if there were two choices. The second one had to be better than the first, she thought. "Or?" she asked, waiting for Caleb to continue.

"Choice number two is a little more complicated," he explained, attempting to ease into it.

Was he going to make her crawl down his throat and pull the words out of him?

"I'm listening," she told him a little less patiently.

Well, here goes nothing, Caleb thought. If he was going to help her, he needed to do this. "I need to talk to your father."

Nadine thought of the last time that she had attempted to communicate with her father. He had not been having one of his better days. Her father had been short-tempered and everything he'd said to her—when he did talk—had bordered on being downright nasty.

At the time, she consoled herself with the realization that this wasn't really the man she knew. Al Sutherland had never exactly been one of a warm kind of men, but he had never been knowingly nasty, either, not to her.

This was the dementia doing this to him, she thought. The disease was responsible for wiping things out of his memory.

Whenever he realized that something was wrong—and that was happening more frequently these days—her father would lash out at the people whose very presence made him realize that there were facts and events that were missing.

Keeping this in mind, Nadine turned toward Caleb. "I really don't think that's a very good idea," she told him.

But Caleb was not about to close the door on that option just yet. If he was going to be of any use in the fight with the oil company, he needed to meet with Nadine's father.

"I'll be the judge of that."

She felt herself growing defensive as well as being protective of her dad.

"You don't have enough facts to be able to judge things when it comes to my father." With effort, she did her best to make him understand. "Caleb, the man is barely hanging on as it is. If you start asking him about things that he finds himself not being able to call up or even vaguely remember, that could wind up pushing him over the brink."

Caleb saw things differently. "Or," he said, "it just might stir up something for him that he had unwittingly buried in his mind. Something he had been coerced into doing that he hadn't wanted to do, so he just let the event fade from his memory to the point that, for him, it no longer existed. That way, your father wouldn't be tortured by it."

She looked at Caleb, impressed at his reasoning, despite herself. "I thought you said that you were an attorney, not a psychiatrist."

Caleb smiled at her observation. "At one point or another, attorneys have to be all things to their clients. I've played a whole variety of roles for the people who my own father had wound up wronging in his last decade on the bench."

She nodded. For a man with his integrity, having to deal with what Ben Colton had done had to have been very hard on Caleb. "I guess you had a lot of wounds that you had to heal."

"To say the least," he agreed. "But what I'm saying is that puts me in a unique position to be able to understand your father—and you when it comes to him," he added. He saw the wary expression on Nadine's face. "Don't worry. I can be very gentle when I have to be," Caleb promised her.

Her eyes met his for a brief moment. She was searching for an unspoken guarantee. She supposed she had known all along that Caleb would have to get his way when it came to this.

"I will hold you to that," Nadine warned.

He smiled as he looked back at the road. "I'd expect nothing less of you," he answered.

Blowing out a breath, she relented just as she knew she had to. "All right, you can talk to my father. But the second he starts to become agitated, I want you to promise me that you'll back off. If you need to, you can come back and try to talk to him again at another time," she told Caleb. "Deal?"

"Deal," he agreed, knowing that he had no real choice in the matter. But he had to admit that this was better than he had hoped for. He had been prepared to go a few verbal rounds with her before this matter was settled between them.

"The oil company told my father that he could remain on his property for now, but once they start the fracking process—which they said would be very soon—he would have to get out. I'm assuming that the oil company thought that would keep my father docile and not have him create any problems."

Nadine smiled to herself. "My father can be quite a handful at times," she confided.

"Yes, I remember," Caleb responded.

"Oh, that's right," she recalled. "You said you had met him back in the day."

"It was just the one time," Caleb stressed. "But even so, he left quite an impression."

She had no doubt about that. "My father was always rather outspoken," she confirmed.

Caleb glanced in Nadine's direction. "I guess that it runs in the family."

Nadine kept her eyes straight ahead. "I'll pretend I didn't hear that."

"But—" Caleb was about to tell her that he hadn't meant that as an insult, but she didn't give him a chance.

"Trust me. It's better that way for you," she told him, then explained, "I need to be in a positive frame of mind when I'm dealing with my father. Trying to talk to him can be a very draining experience. Sometimes, he can be just fine—as fine as he used to be, at any rate." *Cheerful* was not a word that had ever been used to describe Al Sutherland. "And other times," she continued, "he turns into someone who I just don't recognize. And to be honest, I don't think he even recognizes himself."

Caleb nodded. "I hate making you do this," he

confessed. After all, she had enough to deal with as it was, but he honestly thought his talking with her father might be helpful to the situation. "But I did meet him that one time and who knows? Seeing me again just might spark something in his brain," Caleb told her. "The onset of dementia works in very strange ways," he added, recalling what he had learned about the disease.

"Ah, I see that the psychiatrist is back," she quipped.

He was determined not to take offense. "Just giving you the benefit of all the research I've done."

She looked at his profile. "You researched dementia because of my father?" she questioned. Just how thorough was this man?

"No, I researched it because of a family member of one of my father's victims. Long story," he said, not about to get into the particulars at the moment.

But Nadine wasn't about to be put off that easily. "You need to tell it to me someday," she said, then added, "I think I'd really like to hear one story."

Caleb spared her another glance, after first looking into his rearview mirror again, making sure that they were still not being followed.

So far, so good, he noted.

"First, I need to see your father," Caleb told her, getting back to the reason they were out here.

She nodded. "Right. We're almost there. You've

been driving on family land for a few minutes now." At least, she thought, she *hoped* it was still family land. "This was once fifty acres of prime real estate," she recalled nostalgically.

Nadine gestured out the window. "This was all once used for farming. And then my father switched gears, using the land for cattle grazing. Until there were no more cattle to graze.

"After that, the land just sat there, empty and unused—until it was discovered that there was oil running underneath it. That was when my father announced that he was going to explore the idea of doing fracking on the property."

She sighed. Someone should have sat on him or made him understand that he couldn't just tell everyone about fracking.

"I guess he must have mentioned it to the wrong people. In any case, I didn't hear any more from him until—" Nadine paused, taking a breath, as if that would somehow protect her from the unwanted effects that bad memory might create "—until my father said something about the oil company telling him that he was going to have to move once they started fracking.

"You can imagine how I felt hearing that. When I tried asking my father about it, he got really angry and lashed out. That's when I knew they had to have tricked him out of his fracking rights on his land. Rutledge Oil is not exactly known for being upstanding when it comes to conducting business," she told Caleb bitterly.

Just then, she stopped and pointed to what looked as if it had once been a very well built, moderate-sized house, but time and weather had taken their toll on it.

"That's the house," she announced, pointing to it. "Right there."

Caleb blinked. He hadn't expected the building to appear this run-down. But he did his best to hide his reaction.

"You grew up here?" he asked her, drawing close to the two-story building.

"I did," she told him. "When you're a kid, you don't see the flaws and all the work that needs to be done. It's just home. I've tried to get Dad to move in with me. I do have all that room. But he won't hear of it. This is his home. Which is why I'm worried about what the oil company might do to get him off the land," she confessed.

This much he could do for her right off the top, Caleb thought. "You don't have to worry about that. I can arrange to have some protective custody for him. For both of you," he amended, looking at her pointedly.

"Get it for my father. I can take care of myself."

They were back to that again, he thought. The woman had to stop thinking of herself as some superheroine.

But he wasn't about to argue with her about that now. "We'll talk after I speak with your father."

Nadine nodded. Something to look forward to, she thought sarcastically.

"All right, let's get this over with." She paused for a moment to look at him. "Just don't expect too much," she warned.

And then she rang the doorbell to let her father know that there was someone at the door. The next moment, she used her key to enter.

Nadine found her father sitting in the small living room. The wiry man immediately rose to his feet and looked at her sharply.

"What are you doing here?" Al Sutherland demanded. "And who's this?" he wanted to know, glaring at Caleb.

Nadine did the introductions. "Dad, this is Caleb Colton. You've met him before," she told her father gently.

Al Sutherland cocked his head, staring at Caleb. The latter had stepped forward and put out his hand.

Al deliberately ignored it. "No, I haven't," he insisted.

Still keeping his hand out, Caleb smiled at the older man. "It was a few years ago, sir," he said politely. "At the time, I had just married your niece, Annie."

"Annie," Al repeated. It was obvious that he

was attempting to summon an image to go with the name. And then his expression brightened just a little. "Oh, yes. I remember," he said.

Whether it was the meeting or Annie he remembered wasn't clear to Caleb, but he left the matter alone.

Nadine was fairly certain that her father *didn't* remember. But it was one of those things that could very well pop up in his brain at a later moment, so she didn't want to press the matter.

"How is Annie?" Al asked the newcomer.

Nadine caught Caleb's eye, moving her head slightly. Caleb picked up her cue to keep silent and backed away from the topic, simply saying, "She's fine, sir."

"Good," Al pronounced, nodding his head. And then he looked at his daughter and the man she had brought with her, invading his territory. He grew defensive. "So what are you doing here?" he asked again.

"I came to ask you about Rutledge Oil," she told her father, feeling as if she was cautiously picking her way through a minefield.

She and Caleb were both surprised when her father met her response with a self-satisfied smile.

"Yeah, I really put one over on those guys."

Nadine could feel her stomach tightening, but she managed to keep her expression from reflecting how she felt about her father's claim.

In a light voice, she asked, "How did you do that, Dad?"

Al laughed. "I know that everyone thinks I'm just a bumbling fool, but I got those big dumb idiots to pay for all the fracking costs, and they're going to be giving me a percentage of the profits," he all but crowed gleefully. "You know what that means, don't you?" he asked his daughter.

"What does that mean, Dad?" she asked, doing her best not to allow the dread she felt to come out in her voice.

"That means I'll have something to leave you when I die," Al Sutherland answered.

Chapter Twelve

"Mr. Sutherland, did I understand you correctly?" Caleb began cautiously. "You said that you are going to be given a percentage of the profits that the oil company will earn by conducting fracking on your property." Caleb watched the older man's face carefully as he waited for an answer.

Nadine's father looked annoyed as well as impatient. It was clear that he didn't like being questioned.

"Guess there's nothing wrong with your hearing," he said sarcastically. "Yes," he confirmed, "that's what I said."

Caleb continued, trying not to make the man feel as if he was being interrogated. "By any chance, did you sign a contract with them to that effect?"

"Of course I signed a contract," Nadine's father said indignantly, resenting the implication. "I'm not stupid, you know."

Nadine jumped in, running interference. "No one said you were stupid, Dad. We're just trying to get all the facts straight." She knew what Caleb's next question had to be, so she beat him to it and asked her father, "Would you happen to have a copy of that contract?"

Instead of answering her, Al Sutherland jumped to his feet and left the room without saying a word.

Nadine had no idea if her father had just decided to retreat from the conversation or if there was another reason he had departed so abruptly.

After a few minutes had passed and her father hadn't returned, Nadine looked at Caleb. "Maybe I should go after him," she said, at a loss to interpret this latest turn of events.

Before Caleb could answer her or speculate why her father had disappeared like that, Al Sutherland came back. He was carrying a rather large number of what appeared to be bound papers that had been stuffed into a folder.

"Here," he declared dramatically, tossing the folder onto the table. "That's the contract," he added anticlimactically.

The paperwork wound up landing on the floor as well as on the table. Nadine stared at the disorganized storm that went everywhere. Her first reaction was a very strong feeling of being overwhelmed.

Stooping down to pick up the pages that had

landed on the floor, she did what she could to pull them all together. Right now, the contract was in desperate need of being organized, she thought. No easy feat by any means.

She looked from the pile of pages to her father. "Did you read this?" she asked him. She honestly didn't know if he was going to boast that he had and bluff his way through it or if he was just going to wave away her question.

Her father did the latter.

"Too many pages," he informed his daughter, looking at her accusingly. "You know that too much reading gives me a headache," he said, annoyed.

"Why didn't you call me?" she asked, trying her best not to make him think she was accusing him but just gently trying to understand what he had to have been thinking. "I would have gone over the contract for you."

Her father narrowed his eyes. He looked obviously offended that she was even asking such a question.

"I already told you," her father insisted, insulted. "This was supposed to be a surprise."

Nadine looked back at the mass of pages piled up on the table now. She was really afraid that she would discover that her worst fears would turn out to be true.

"It certainly is," she murmured under her breath.

Anger creased her father's features. "I did it for you," her father pointed out, apparently forgetting he had already said as much a few minutes ago.

"I know, Dad. I know," she replied gently. She had not realized that her father actually cared that much about her, and while she was very grateful as well as surprised to be confronted with proof that her father did have such strong feelings about her, she was also devastated and at a loss as to how to get the fracking rights reverted back to him.

"Mr. Sutherland," Caleb interrupted, "would you mind if I took the contract to my law office so I can review it?"

Nadine's father didn't answer right away, as if he was thinking about what Caleb had just proposed. Chewing on his lower lip, he looked from his daughter to this man she had brought with her. His expression was utterly unreadable.

"You'll bring it back, right?" Sutherland finally asked Caleb.

"Absolutely," Caleb promised.

Nadine's father exhaled loudly, as if each word cost him. "Okay, I guess it's all right," he slowly agreed.

The next moment, the older man was scooping up all the loose pages and then unceremoniously thrusting them into Caleb's arms.

"You won't forget?" Sutherland asked, his dark eyes piercing Caleb's.

"No, sir, I definitely won't forget," Caleb promised.

Nadine's father frowned slightly, as if what he was about to say caused him some pain. "All right, take them," he declared, waving for Caleb to leave his home.

It was obvious to both Nadine and the man she had brought with her that their interview with Al Sutherland was officially over.

Rising, Nadine paused as she brushed a quick kiss on her father's wrinkled, pale cheek. "I'll see you soon, Dad," she promised.

Al responded with something that sounded suspiciously like a grunt and then just walked away from both of them.

Caleb left the weathered old house right behind Nadine.

"I'll look this over," Caleb said once they were back in his car and he had placed the contract on the back seat behind the driver. "But offhand, my guess is that there aren't going to be any surprises. I'm pretty sure that your father was tricked into signing away his rights. The promise that his signing the contract would earn him a percentage of the profits from fracking most likely is entirely unsubstantiated. I really doubt that what he believes to be the terms of the contract is reflected anywhere in all those pages." He nodded toward the folder in the back seat.

He wasn't giving voice to anything that hadn't

already crossed her mind and turned her stomach into one giant, painful knot.

"Yes," she admitted with a heavy heart, "that's what I'm thinking, too." Nadine turned in her seat to look at Caleb. "If that turns out to be the case, they just can't be allowed to get away with it," she cried passionately.

"No," Caleb answered without any hesitation, "they can't."

He paused for a moment, choosing his next words carefully before continuing. He knew Nadine was going to be upset. She had already indicated as much. But she had to see that this was the most logical path.

"The best—and fastest—way to get the rights back is to have your father declared mentally incompetent." Caleb saw her stiffening, but he pressed on. "That means stating that he was not in his right mind at the time that he signed the contract. I can have his doctor examine him and then make a statement. Or, if he doesn't have a doctor on record, I could get a court-appointed doctor to examine your father." Caleb was confident that the result would be the same. "He's obviously slipping into dementia. The only question that remains to be asked—and verified—is how far and how fast he had already descended."

Nadine closed her eyes. He could see tears seeping through her eyelashes.

When she opened her eyes again, she told Caleb, "There has to be another way. Now that you've met him, you *know* an admission of that sort would just rip his heart out. If nothing worse, he would be humiliated. And maybe a lot more," she added in a low, morose voice.

Nadine rallied. "There has *got* to be another way. Especially now that he said that his motivation to do what he did was so he could leave me something after he was gone—as if I cared about the money," she concluded dismissively.

Caleb sighed. There didn't seem to be a way out right now. "Your father obviously thinks that you do."

"Well, he got that wrong, too," Nadine informed him. "Caleb, he's slipping further and further away from me, away from the life he's lived. I just can't let this be the last thing that goes down between us."

He nodded. Caleb knew exactly how she had to feel. In his own way, because of his own losses and his dad's misdeeds, he could identify with what Nadine was experiencing.

So he nodded. "All right, I'll go through the contract with a fine-tooth comb and see if there are any options open to us. And I'll see if there's any more information I can gather on the oil company that we can use. Maybe I can find an answer there," he told her.

"I can't thank you enough," Nadine said with feeling.

"No," he agreed, a subdued smile playing on his lips as he thought of what lay ahead of him, "you probably can't."

CALEB'S PENTHOUSE WAS just a ten-minute drive from his office. He took her there, thinking that he could just drop her off and go to work. First, of course, he planned to wait for the investigator, who was also a trained bodyguard, that he had called in to show up. He wouldn't be able to concentrate until he was certain that everything was all right because his man was there, watching over Nadine for the sole purpose of keeping her safe.

But if Caleb was hoping to make a quick escape, it would have to wait.

"This is where you live?" Nadine didn't bother to hide the awe in her voice as she looked around, taking in every overwhelming inch.

Caleb had decided to leave his car out in front of his penthouse instead of parking it in the underground garage the way he usually did. He had every intention of taking off as soon as he dropped off Nadine and the luggage she had brought with her—after his investigator showed up, of course.

The line about the best-laid plans of mice and men going astray insisted on echoing through his mind.

"Yes," Caleb answered. "Why?"

"It's absolutely gorgeous," she told him. "And the view…" Her voice trailed off as she stared out through his window. "That's the waterfront," Nadine marveled.

He tried not to laugh. He found her reaction almost endearing. "Yes, I know."

She turned toward him. "If I were you I would definitely find a way to work out of the house so I could just drink all this in."

He shook his head at her suggestion. "I'm afraid that can't be done. As I'm sure that Annie must have told you, my work takes me all over. Sometimes," he admitted, "I hardly even get a chance to touch home base."

Nadine pressed her lips together. Caleb was being extremely kind to her. He was trying to help her father, not to mention taking her into his house because he wanted to protect her. Dwelling on his failed marriage to Annie didn't seem like the right way to repay the man, she thought. She veered away from the subject that he had brought up.

"Well, this is a beautiful home," she told him with enthusiasm. "Thank you for taking me in, and I promise not to do anything to mess it up in any way."

"I know that," he said.

She turned to look at him, curious. "How? How would you?" she asked.

"Because I saw where you lived," he answered simply. "And how that place was ripe for looking as if a tornado had hit it, and yet everywhere I looked, your loft was incredibly neat."

Still waiting for his man to make an appearance, Caleb smiled as he took her suitcase to the closest bedroom.

"I am confident that I'll be leaving my penthouse in good hands—as soon as Hogan gets here," he qualified, in case Nadine thought he was leaving her alone.

"Hogan?" she questioned. He hadn't mentioned that name to her before.

"Mike Hogan," he told her. "He's one of the firm's investigators. I placed a call to him this morning."

She bristled at the implication that she needed a keeper other than Caleb himself. "Well, my natural inclination is to tell you that you're certainly free to leave right now. You indicated that you regard this penthouse to be a fortress. To me, that means that I'm really safe staying here, even if your investigator was not on his way over.

"But we've already had this conversation and it's gone nowhere, so I'll be quiet," Nadine concluded, resigned.

Caleb looked at her. Just when he thought the topic had finally been put to rest, Nadine added her unique footnote by saying, "But I just want to go on record one last time that you're hanging around here of your own free will and not because of me."

Caleb could only shake his head. "Duly noted." And then humor curved his lips. "Don't worry. I'm not about to tell anyone that you 'made' me stay and hold your hand until the necessary security detail showed up."

"I don't care what anyone else says or thinks," she informed him. "I just wanted the matter to be clear between us."

The smile on his lips turned into a grin. "Oh, it's very clear," he guaranteed.

Before she could say anything further, Caleb heard his doorbell ring. He instantly looked at the closest monitor to see who was standing on his doorstep.

"Hogan's here," he announced for Nadine's benefit.

"Is this where I clap?" she said.

"You can if you want to," he told her cheerfully, striding past her to open the door.

Mike Hogan looked more like a man on his way to a board meeting than someone who was a private investigator. Tall and solemn looking, he was wearing a three-piece suit beneath the tan overcoat he had on to protect him against the biting cold weather.

"This is Nadine Sutherland," Caleb explained to his investigator.

Hogan took off his overcoat and leaned forward to shake her hand.

"A pleasure, ma'am," he stated her in a soft-spoken voice, then added, "You won't even know I'm here."

He had to say that, Nadine thought, but she didn't bother contesting the investigator's assurance.

Instead, she turned toward Caleb and told him, "I guess that's your cue to leave, Caleb. You're free."

He let her remark pass. "If you think of anything, or need anything, you know where to reach me." The words were addressed to both of the people in the room and hung in the air as he walked out of his penthouse.

Leaving Nadine with Hogan, he thought, was going to be very interesting.

Chapter Thirteen

Caleb walked into his private office and deposited his briefcase on his desk. The tan case was stuffed with all the loose pages that, once put together, supposedly comprised the contract that Al Sutherland said he had signed.

If asked, Caleb couldn't very well say that he was looking forward to emptying his briefcase and having the avalanche of papers come tumbling out onto his desk. But he knew that he had to.

Someday, he told himself, he was going to learn to say no. But then, he thought the next moment, if sacrificing his marriage and two long-term relationships hadn't taught him how to hold some of himself back while involved in conducting an investigation, he sincerely doubted that he was ever going to change his ways.

Flipping open the locks on his briefcase, he opened the lid and looked down at the pile waiting for his attention.

A movement going past his open office door caught his attention and he looked up. Rebekah had nearly made it out of his view when Caleb called out her name.

Dutifully, the assistant retraced her steps and stuck her head into Caleb's office. "Is there something that I can do for you?" Rebekah wanted to know.

"Yes, you can send Morgan into my office," Caleb told the assistant.

Rebekah made no attempt to act on his request. "I would if I could, boss man, but I can't."

Caleb's eyes narrowed as he looked at his employee more closely. "And just why is that?" he asked.

"Because Ms. Colton still hasn't come in today," Rebekah answered simply.

Caleb glanced at his watch. It was close to two in the afternoon.

"I know," Rebekah said, noticing the attorney looking at his watch. She guessed at what he had to be thinking. "It must be nice to come and go as you please."

Caleb didn't say anything about his assistant's comment and just went to the heart of the matter. "Did my sister call to tell you where she was or when she would be in?"

It was obvious that Rebekah found the question amusing. "She doesn't check in with me, Mr.

Colton, unless it's to call to find out about something in her schedule. But if I hear anything," the older woman promised him, "I'll be sure to let you know."

Rebekah had just stepped away from his doorway when she suddenly made her way back into his office. He looked at her quizzically.

Never missing a beat, Rebekah announced, "This is me, letting you know that your sister just walked in."

Caleb abandoned his briefcase and the contract he'd been planning to examine. He stepped out into the hallway just in time to practically bump smack into Morgan. The latter was making her way to her own office.

Reflexes had him taking a step back to avoid a collision between them. As he did so, he took a second look at his twin. He was accustomed to Morgan being impeccably groomed. There was never a single hair on her head that was ever out of place.

Until now.

He saw Rebekah looking at him over his twin's head. It was not difficult to read the woman's expression. The assistant was thinking the exact same thing that he was.

There must be something private going on with Morgan, and Caleb was feeling very protective of his twin.

"I'll call you if I need you, Rebekah," he told the assistant, dismissing the woman.

Resigned, Rebekah took her cue and back-tracked out of the office.

Turning back toward his twin, Caleb saw that Morgan had taken the opportunity to go into her office. Caleb was quick to follow her.

"Are you okay?" he asked, crossing her office threshold.

Morgan dropped her purse on the floor and deposited her body into her office chair in like manner. He noticed that she gripped the armrests before answering.

"Just peachy," Morgan responded sarcastically.

Caleb made no bones about his own reaction to her appearance. "Well, you look like hell."

"Thank you," she retorted icily, then backed off a little. "If I knew what hell looks like, I'd probably agree with you. Do we have any coffee left?" she wanted to know. "Or did you and Rebekah drink it all?" Everyone knew that Rebekah claimed to run on caffeine.

"I've had a busy morning and just got in a little while ago myself, so I think it's safe to assume there's still some coffee available for you. If not, I'll have Rebekah make some. Barring that, I can make you coffee myself," he informed his sister. "But first, why don't you tell me why you look like the human equivalent of thirty miles of bad road?"

Morgan didn't answer her brother immediately. Instead, she paused to consider her response before saying anything. "I might have gone to a friend's birthday party at the Corner Pocket," she told him, mentioning a billiard bar that was located downtown. "Toward the end of the evening, the drinks were flowing like water, and I might have gotten a bit too carried away," Morgan admitted, although not too readily.

Without realizing it, she placed her hand to her forehead, as if she was attempting to contain the pain.

"I could swear that my head is throbbing to some sort of rhythmic beat," she murmured, agitated. Blowing out an impatient breath, she signaled the end of the discussion. "That's all I'm going to say about it for now. So, if you were hoping to hear some sort of a tantalizing confession, you're going to be disappointed," she informed her twin.

"You're here in one piece. There's nothing for me to be disappointed about."

About to leave, Caleb paused and opened the bottom left-hand drawer of his twin's desk. Crouching, he extracted a bottle of aspirin and placed it in the center of her desk, then went over to the sink located in her private bathroom, got a glass and filled it with water.

Retracing his steps, Caleb put the glass next to

the bottle of aspirin. "You might want to take a couple of these," he suggested, nodding at the aspirin. "Could help you put a smile on your face," he told her as he turned toward the office door.

Caleb tossed one final thing over his shoulder. "You know where to find me if you want to talk. I should be here for at least another hour."

Resigned, Morgan drew the bottle closer to her. It took her a minute to open the container and then take out two pills. Contemplating them, Morgan took out a third, then swallowed all three.

As she leaned back in her chair, he saw her close her eyes.

Satisfied there wasn't anything further he could do for his sister right now, Caleb withdrew from her office, closing the door quietly behind him.

He and Morgan were usually on the same wavelength, almost eerily so, he thought as he returned to his own office. But there were times when his twin withdrew into herself. While it did arouse his curiosity when that happened, he knew when to leave her alone.

And, he silently argued, when his marriage was beginning to unravel at the seams, he hadn't said anything to Morgan about it for a long time. And then he'd told her only because his divorce looked as if it was going to become a reality. He'd known that his twin would probably feel hurt that he had deliberately shut her out if he didn't tell her about it before it became public news, which was why he'd finally informed her.

That kind of thing was a two-way street. It wasn't traveled often, but when it was, it had to be done very carefully.

Whatever had happened last night to get Morgan to a place where she looked like this the following day, Caleb knew she would eventually tell him. Until then, he would remain supportive from a distance and do his best to keep out of her way.

Heaven knew, he thought, eyeing the stack of papers all but spilling out of his briefcase, he had more than enough to keep him busy. And wading through Nadine's father's contract wasn't nearly the half of it. The firm that he and Morgan ran had expanded since its early days. They didn't just handle cases through the Truth Foundation that involved all those people their father had wrongfully sent to prison.

Caleb settled in to organize the avalanche of papers that comprised the contract between Nadine's father and the oil company. As he did so, he forgot all about the coffee he had meant to get for himself as well as the cup for Morgan.

THREE HOURS WENT BY. In that time, after organizing the profusion of papers and finally getting them all in order, he had managed to read through the contract in its entirety twice. Once to absorb the general gist of it and a second time to make sure that he hadn't managed to miss anything.

He came away with the feeling that whoever had written this document was definitely enamored with the written word, also with finding the most complicated way to state even the simplest of thoughts.

Rutledge Oil, Caleb thought, had tried its best to completely confuse Al Sutherland and, very simply, to put one over on the man. He was convinced that the company had probably told Nadine's father exactly what he wanted to hear, but there was certainly no evidence of that within the actual contract.

What Caleb saw within the contract was that Al Sutherland had sold the fracking rights to his property outright. The monetary compensation for that sale was as small as it could be—for what amounted to a song. And, despite reading the contract twice, he couldn't find any mention of any sort of a percentage being paid on the amount of money that any fracking taking place on the land would yield.

Caleb sighed as he put down the last page. The oil company was definitely cheating Nadine's father. But at the moment, he had no proof to point to other than what an old man with the onset of dementia creeping into his brain said was the bargain he had agreed to.

Caleb closed his eyes and sighed. Frustrated, he could feel a headache threatening to descend.

There had to be a way around this, he thought. There had to be *something* he could do to get the oil company to back off.

He thought about it. Since Nadine absolutely refused to approach this from the angle that the oil company had taken advantage of a man who was losing his mental faculties, Caleb felt he had only one course of behavior open to him.

He had to find something he could use against the oil company. Caleb knew that it wouldn't be easy, but he was fairly certain that the less-than-upstanding-and-honest executives must have done this sort of thing before.

The very fact that there were so many people suing pointed to that. He was going to be banking on the fact that there had to be at least one case that was similar to Al Sutherland's somewhere in all those pending litigations.

All he had to do was just find one case like that. If he did, he felt certain that that could open up a world of possibilities for Nadine's father.

Caleb smiled to himself. At least he had a sliver of hope to offer to Nadine, he thought.

Before returning to his penthouse—and Nadine—Caleb looked in on his sister. Crossing the threshold, he was pleased to see that Morgan looked as if she was in slightly better shape than when she had first walked in.

The color had returned to her face, and while she still looked a little pale, she was no longer an ashen shade of white.

"I'm leaving now."

Morgan didn't look up. "Okay. I'll see you," she said.

Caleb still hesitated. "You'll be all right?"

This time Morgan did look up as she stopped writing. "When *haven't* I been all right?"

"Oh, I can think of a few times," he said loftily.

A hint of a smile touched her lips fleetingly. He was goading her. That was his way of trying to make her come around. "Go, save the world, Caleb. I'll be all right."

He nodded. "All right. But call me if you need anything."

Morgan had already gone back to writing. "I'll call," she murmured.

As he left the office, Caleb still couldn't help wondering what last night, and consequently, the following day had been all about. Morgan was usually a very "together" woman who wasn't fazed by anything.

Well, his sister would tell him in her own time,

he told himself not for the first time. He was well aware that pressing the matter wouldn't get him anywhere. As a matter of fact, he was fairly sure that pressing Morgan would have the exact opposite effect.

Caleb glanced at his phone as he pulled out of his parking space. There didn't appear to be any messages, either text or called in. He hoped that meant that it was "all quiet on the Western front" and that he wouldn't be coming home to any unexpected "surprises."

Even so, he picked up his speed, driving home just under the legal limit. That sort of behavior was ingrained in him. The last thing he wanted was to get a ticket. Not because it would leave a blemish on his perfect driving record, but because being pulled over and waiting for an officer to write him up would eat up more time than he would save by driving fast.

Caleb had learned to be very aware of the consequences that might arise from any sort of action that he undertook. That lesson had been learned by finding out that his father was not the man that everyone had thought him to be for so many years. Caleb had promised himself that, no matter what, he would always lead a good life, so that anyone crossing his path would know that what they saw was what they got.

Anything else, he felt, would just be the height of dishonesty, a blemish that he swore would never touch him.

Chapter Fourteen

Caleb stopped at a nearby restaurant and picked up the dinner he had ordered just before he left his office. Nadine was undoubtedly hungry by now, and in his opinion, the idea of leftovers didn't seem quite the way to go for her first meal at his penthouse.

With the warm, enticing scent of barbecued spareribs wafting through the interior of his car, Caleb drove the short distance home.

Arriving at his place, he parked his vehicle in its regular spot in the underground garage. There were security cameras within the space, but he locked his vehicle anyway and made his way up to his penthouse.

He found Hogan inconspicuously planted near the penthouse's entry. He hadn't expected that the investigator would be outside the living space. When their eyes met, Caleb raised a quizzical eyebrow, silently asking the man why he was out here and not inside.

"I didn't want your lady friend to feel that I was breathing down her neck," Hogan explained. "I felt that she would be more comfortable if she knew I was around, but not necessarily right in her face. Kind of a reversal of that old saying of being seen but not heard. Hope that's all right," Hogan added, looking at his employer.

Caleb had chosen the investigator not just for his expertise but for his sensitivity in various situations as well. He trusted the man's natural intuition. And, of course, there were the security safeguards that had been put in place throughout the penthouse.

"That's fine with me," Caleb assured the other man. "I take it everything has gone smoothly," Caleb said.

"Just like silk," Hogan replied. "If you need anything, I'll be around for the rest of the night. Jacobson will spell me at midnight."

Caleb nodded. That saved him the trouble of calling the other man.

"I appreciate it," he told Hogan. "I'm pretty confident that there's nothing to worry about, but right now, quite honestly, I'd rather err on the side of caution than not."

The investigator looked as if he totally agreed. "Always a good idea," Hogan said. The man was already stepping back into the shadows. "Have a nice evening, sir."

"You, too, Hogan," Caleb replied as he entered his penthouse.

Once inside, he looked around. Everything looked exactly the way he had left it. It didn't even look as if there had been anyone else there, nor did it appear as if anyone was there now. But he knew there had to be. Hogan was far too good at his job for Nadine to have managed to slip out and leave the premises, not that she would have wanted to make good her escape right now.

Besides, he still had the contract that her father had signed in his possession, so even if Nadine had wanted to leave for some reason, she wouldn't have. Not while she needed help in finding a way to make the oil company return the fracking rights to her father.

Still carrying his briefcase and the bag containing their dinner, Caleb made his way into his state-of-the-art kitchen.

She wasn't there, either.

Rather than carry the items around with him through the house, he set them down on the counter.

"Nadine," he called out, "where are you?"

He listened for a response. And that was when he heard it.

Music. It had rather a tinny sound.

It occurred to him that Nadine must have found his old transistor radio. He knew he should have gotten rid of it a long time ago. But he had kept it because it was a holdover from a happier, more innocent childhood. It reminded him of when his father had been his hero and hadn't yet sullied the family name or had been a good man who had time for his wife as well as for all of his children.

Caleb followed the music and it led him into the family room. Nadine was sitting cross-legged on the floor in front of the wide coffee table and she looked to be working. Her jewelry-making tools were all carefully spread out on top of the paper towels she had used to cover the table. She was concentrating on an earring that she was putting the finishing touches on.

Watching her, Caleb crossed into the room. "What are you doing?"

"Well, without anyone to talk to, it got pretty lonely in here," she admitted. She could usually call a friend to talk or go out for a stroll. Neither was possible right now. "I found this cute little radio and I turned it on to keep me company as well as fill up the awful quiet. I didn't think you'd mind," she added as she watched him take the transistor and turn it off. "I guess I thought wrong," she realized. "Sorry."

"Nothing to be sorry about," Caleb responded, then admitted, "I guess I'm a little sentimental about it." He smiled to himself at the memories it brought back and nodded at the radio. "I saw this one day while I was out with my father. I think that I was probably about six at the time. Anyway, being a kid of privilege, I had never seen anything like it and I asked him all sorts of questions about it. He got a kick out of all the things I thought to ask about something that looked so simple to him, so he bought it for me," he told Nadine.

The smile on his face was rather sad, Nadine thought.

"It reminds me of a happier time," Caleb confessed. His eyes met hers. "You probably think that's silly."

"No," she responded in all sincerity. "I think that's sweet. We all need something to hang on to that reminds us of better times," Nadine maintained. "Sometimes, having something to hang on to is all we have to help us move forward."

She said it with such conviction, Caleb knew she had to be thinking of her father. Except that in Al Sutherland's case, there were no better times on the horizon. The best she could hope for was that her father would remain in his present state for a while longer. But they both knew that nothing got better for someone in Sutherland's condition. They just deteriorated.

Caleb's heart went out to her. In an odd sort of way, they shared a kind of darkness that had intruded into their lives and overwhelmed them, even though that darkness had arrived in different ways, he couldn't help thinking.

Their eyes met and he felt this intense desire to comfort her, to find a way to bring a smile back to her face.

He wanted, he realized, to take Nadine into his arms and kiss her.

Wavering, Caleb came very close to doing just that. But at that moment, a rousing song came on the radio and, coupled with the scent of the barbecued spareribs, it proved to be the perfect antidote to the momentary romantic surge that had threatened to wash over him.

Looking into his eyes, Nadine had felt very drawn to Caleb. She had almost gotten carried away.

Nadine took a deep breath, fortifying herself. She clutched at the first thing that presented itself to her.

"What is that amazing smell?" she asked.

Caleb grinned. "I take it you're not referring to my cologne," he told her with a chuckle. "So you're probably talking about the spareribs."

"Spareribs?" she asked.

"In there," he said, pointing toward the large bag he had set down on the counter. "I thought you might be hungry, so I stopped by a restaurant on the way home and picked up some spareribs. I was going with my own tastes," he confessed, then apologized, "I didn't stop to think that you might find eating them to be a kind of messy experience."

This man had to be the poster child for the word *thoughtful*, Nadine couldn't help thinking with a smile.

"'Messy' can always wash off. Unless it's the kind of messy that involves the soul," Nadine qualified as she thought of what the oil company had done to her father.

Caleb looked at her. "Glad you have such a positive attitude," he said, adding, "about dinner."

Nadine smiled at him. Then, walking into the kitchen, she looked around. "You wouldn't by any chance have any paper plates, would you?"

He shook his head. "Sorry, no, I don't." Her question aroused his curiosity. "Why?"

Crossing to the counter, he picked up the bag and brought it over to the kitchen table, placing it in the center. He opened it and took out the large containers with spareribs, then flipped open the tops.

"I just thought if you had paper plates, cleanup would go a lot faster. But don't worry," she quickly assured him, "I'll be happy to wash the dishes."

"I wasn't worried," he said, bringing over three plates, one for each of them and one to place beneath the containers in case they wound up leaking. "And you're not washing anything. That's why dishwashers were created," he added whimsically.

She didn't accept his theory. "Washing dishes is therapeutic," she said.

He had never heard that one before. "Let's eat off those dishes first, then we'll talk about doing something 'therapeutic' with them," he told her. Looking inside the bag, he realized that he had forgotten about the side he had ordered. "How do you feel about potato salad?" he asked her.

Nadine didn't even have to pause to think. "I love potato salad," she freely admitted.

His smile rose all the way up into his eyes. "Good answer, because I picked up some, too." Taking out the large container of potato salad and placing it between the two giant-sized servings of spareribs, Caleb looked at the plates. "Not exactly a meal fit for a king, is it?"

"Well, unless you're hiding him, I didn't see any kings here in your penthouse—unless, of course, you're referring to yourself," Nadine added with a wide smile.

That surprised him. "I wasn't talking about me."

"And you shouldn't be talking like that about the spareribs, either. Because if they taste any-where as good as they smell, I'd say that I'm going to be in for a *real* feast."

Nadine was being extremely upbeat, he thought. So upbeat, Caleb decided, that he was not going to say anything tonight about the contract that her father had signed. There was no immediate hurry.

The discussion could wait until morning. Bad news had a way of keeping, since it wasn't about to go anywhere, certainly not without any sort of constructive help on his part if he was even able to come up with any.

For now, Caleb looked across the table, fascinated as he watched his houseguest eat. She really seemed to enjoy the spareribs, he thought.

Unlike a lot of the women he had known, Nadine wasn't fussy about eating. She dug into her food with gusto, but even so, she somehow managed to make short work of the ribs without getting any of the sauce on herself.

It was a neat trick, he thought.

"I take it that you like them," Caleb concluded, nodding at the quickly disappearing meal.

"Like them?" she echoed. "This is absolutely delicious—and exactly what I need to make me feel like a whole person again." Nadine raised her eyes to his face. "Because," she continued more seriously, "I have a feeling I'm going to need that."

Caleb felt slightly uneasy but told himself that he was probably either just imagining things or reading into her statement, turning it into something she probably didn't intend.

"I don't know what you mean," Caleb responded innocently.

"Oh, I think you do," she said.

There was nothing high-handed in her tone. To

her mind, she was simply stating a fact. She had
been around enough people to become a fairly
good judge of the behavior she witnessed. In Caleb's case, she had found herself becoming a quick
study.

Maybe it had to do with the fact that she felt
they were going to be working closely together,
or perhaps because he had been married to her
cousin. Either way, Nadine felt she had some sort
of special insight into the man, an insight that ex-
ceeded her usual expertise.

Caleb was still hoping that he had jumped to
the wrong conclusion. And she appreciated his caring—more than she'd like to admit.

"Enlighten me," he coaxed.

"You left me in your penthouse under the invisible yet watchful eye of your investigator while
you lugged off that contract that my father signed,
defining his bargain with the oil company. Now
you've been home for a while and you still haven't
said word one about it.

"The only conclusion I can come to is that you
didn't want me to lose my appetite by giving me
any bad news right up front." She paused. "Am I
right?"

Caleb laughed dryly, shaking his head. The
woman was sharp. She had hit the nail right on
the head—as clever as she was attractive.

"You know, if you ever decide you want to

switch careers, I'd be happy to take you on as part of my team, working as an investigator. You've got a natural knack for it."

She knew what he was attempting to do. "Thank you, but you're not going to distract me," she told Caleb. Her eyes pinned him down. "What did you find when you went through that fifty-pound contract?"

Cornered, he had to be honest with her. "Not what any of us wanted to find," he said simply.

Her heart sank. She knew what that meant. "My father really did give those rights over to Rutledge Oil, didn't he?"

He didn't attempt to camouflage his words in any way. "Yes."

She might as well know the whole sordid truth, she thought. "And he won't be getting any sort of a payment from the fracking that's going to be taking place, is he?" she asked.

"No, he's not," Caleb told her. "But I am *not* giving up," he quickly reassured her.

She pulled her shoulders back. "I am not going to have my father humiliated, publicly or privately," she stressed.

"Pending a lawsuit, I'm trying to find another way to get this thrown out of court," he said.

Nadine nodded, relaxing slightly. "All right, as long as we're clear on that point."

He laughed. "I'd have to be a fool not to be clear on that by now."

The comment made her smile. "Well, after knowing you for only a little bit, I can confidently say that you are definitely not a fool," she told him.

With that, Nadine rose, picking up his plate as well as her own and taking both to the sink. "Don't try to stop me," she warned. "I find myself in need of some therapy," she announced.

"I wouldn't dream of stopping you," he said, picking up a dish towel. "I just want to join you."

Smiling, she inclined her head. "By all means," Nadine invited with a wide smile.

Chapter Fifteen

The sound of his ringing cell phone burrowed its way into Caleb's brain, dissolving the remnants of the dream he had been having, instantly driving it from his memory.

Reluctantly opening his eyes, Caleb blinked, focusing on the clock next to his bed. It was almost seven.

Memories played themselves through his head in a backward procession, going from the last thing he recalled to the first. Caleb remembered going to bed after midnight after having stayed up talking to Nadine and going over recent happenings.

He clarified the events for her benefit, although they weren't about anything that concerned her father. What he had told her about were things that had to do with his father and the host of people Ben Colton had wronged in that final decade that he had sat on the bench as a judge.

The throbbing noise continued.

Caleb suddenly realized that he was ignoring his phone.

Sitting up, he picked up his cell phone, opened it and mumbled "Hello?" in a voice that was still thick with the last remnants of sleep.

"Good morning, Sleeping Beauty," the voice in his ear said. "I gather that I just woke you up."

Caleb immediately recognized Morgan's voice. His twin was obviously trying to make up for yesterday, he thought.

Sighing, he dragged his hand through his hair, then passed that hand over his eyes, doing what he could to get them in focus.

"I had a late night," he muttered by way of an excuse for his present condition.

"Oh?"

He could hear barely contained interest in the single word and knew Morgan was dying to shoot questions at him.

He cut her short.

"No 'oh.' It was work. Now, is there any reason you're calling so early?" Morgan never called just to shoot the breeze, Caleb thought.

Morgan's voice became businesslike. "As a matter of fact, Caleb, there is. That man called again."

Longing for a cup of coffee, Caleb kicked off his covers. He told Morgan he'd call her right back, jumped in the shower quickly, and after he got out and finished shaving, reached for the pair of pants he had left hanging off the end of his bed.

"You're going to have to get more specific than that," he told his twin after calling her back. "*What* man?"

"Ronald Spence," she answered impatiently. Spence had been the last man their father had sentenced to prison before his death. "I don't know how he gets to make so many phone calls since he's in prison, but the upshot is he still maintains that Dad railroaded him, sending him to prison, and that he's innocent. He's been saying that for the last six months. He swears that Dad actually hid the papers that would have cleared him of the charges against him."

Holding his phone against his ear by using his shoulder, Caleb finally managed to pull on his pants.

He sighed at what Morgan had just said. "Yeah, there was a lot of that going on."

"Spence wants us to find those papers. He's positive they will exonerate him. He told me that he's got a fairly good idea where they might have been stashed."

"Boy, you certainly have been a busy little bee, haven't you?" Caleb remarked. "And the sun's barely up." Grabbing a fresh shirt, Caleb shrugged into it. "I'm assuming you wrote down the specifics Spence gave you."

His twin replied, "Yes, Caleb, I did."

He pulled on his socks, then stuffed his feet into his shoes. "I'll be there as soon as I can," he promised Morgan.

"Did Annie's cousin stay at your place last night?" his sister suddenly asked him out of the blue.

"Yes, she did—and she still is." He knew that was what Morgan was really asking. "I told you, someone was following her. Why do you ask?" he wanted to know.

"I'm just trying to gauge exactly what you meant by saying 'as soon as I can,'" Morgan answered.

"She's Annie's *cousin*, remember?" Caleb stressed, as if that should be all the answer she needed.

He was not prepared to hear his twin chuckle at his answer. "Yes," Morgan responded, "I am familiar with the family."

This was pointless. He could get ready a lot faster without dealing with Morgan's veiled questions and innuendos.

"Later," he said to his twin firmly just before he terminated their connection.

Caleb frowned to himself. Just because Morgan had gone to a birthday party and come into the office late the following day, looking the worse for wear because of her "adventure," didn't mean that he was going to do anything of the kind just because he had taken Nadine under his wing. He had taken her case pro bono, for heaven's sake. Morgan should know that, he thought.

But then, he'd never seen his sister acting so out of character before, either. Working all these hours, trying to right all those wrongs his father had committed while they were still building up and running a profitable law firm was beginning to take its toll on both of them, he thought. And, just when they felt that they may have finally rid their family of all the shame their father's behavior had brought down on them, Ronald Spence suddenly contacted them.

Caleb took a deep breath, intent on centering himself.

Onward and upward, he silently counseled, tucking in his shirt and grabbing a tie and jacket out of his closet.

It wasn't until he was in the hallway that he thought he detected the smell of something cooking.

Afraid that he had left the stove on for some reason, Caleb quickened his pace. He flew down the stairs and reached the kitchen's threshold in what amounted to record time.

That was when Caleb came to an abrupt halt.

"You're cooking?" he asked, looking at what Nadine was doing.

"I do know how to cook," she told him. "And since you took me out for dinner one day and then brought me takeout last night, I thought that it was only fair that I turned around and returned the favor this morning."

Looking at him over her shoulder, she studied Caleb. He looked like a man who was in a hurry. "Do you have time to sit down and eat or should I just pack this up so you can take it with you?" she asked.

He stared at her. That was a hell of a guess on her part. "How did you—?"

"I heard your cell phone ringing this morning— sound carries. And then you came right down like you were in a hurry—I could hear your feet hitting the ground as you ran," she explained.

Caleb laughed, shaking his head in wonder as he sat down at the table. He figured he could spare a few minutes to eat, since Nadine had obviously gone through all this trouble.

"Like I said," he said to her, not bothering to hide that she had managed to impress him, "that job on my investigative team is open for you anytime you want it."

Nadine placed his breakfast in front of him, then poured a cup of coffee for him before she duplicated the action for herself. Sitting down opposite Caleb, she made herself comfortable.

"So," she asked her host, "where are you off to in such a hurry so early—or am I not supposed to ask." She gestured to the paperwork. "I found a name in your papers—Ronald Spence. Does this have to do with him, by any chance?"

"Well, you can ask," he began to tell her in between bites, then stopped abruptly as what he had just put in his mouth registered. "This is also really good," he declared, nodding at his plate.

"Don't look so surprised," she told him. "Yesterday wasn't an accident. I've been cooking ever since I was a little girl, right after my mother passed away," Nadine confided. "You said I could ask why you're leaving so early, so this is me, asking," Nadine said, waiting for him to give her an answer.

"You have a mind like a homing device, don't you?" he asked, amused.

Nadine saw no reason to dispute that. "I do, and you're stalling," she pointed out. "Are you planning on telling me, or are you going to shut me out after all?"

The fact that it was none of her business didn't really register with her.

"The former," he said, then got to the heart of the matter. "The last man my father sent to prison has been calling the office lately, professing his innocence. He's trying to get us to take on his case." Caleb raised his shoulders in a vague shrug. "I thought I should check it out."

"Doesn't your sister work at the foundation, too?" Nadine asked, fairly certain that the answer was yes.

He knew what Nadine was getting at. His protective nature toward his siblings kicked in. "She does, but she's working on something right now."

"And you thought that you'd take on this Spence person's case because you have so much free time on your hands?" Nadine said with a touch of sarcasm.

The laugh that escaped his lips was dry. "You're beginning to sound like my mother," he told her.

"Well, since I've met your mother, I'm flattered." Noticing that Caleb had finished his breakfast, she cleared away his plate. "Anything I can do to help?" she asked.

The offer sounded genuine to Caleb. He had to admit that this woman really intrigued him.

"You're doing it."

He was referring to making breakfast, she thought. But she wasn't. "I mean, with what you're doing," she said, leaving his dish in the sink for now. She returned to the table and was about to sit down, but Caleb had already begun walking toward the door.

"I'll let you know when I get back," he promised.

A thought hit her. "I could come with you," Nadine offered.

"To prison?" Caleb questioned. "That's where I'm meeting Spence," he told her, thinking he would pick up any information he needed when he swung by his office.

"Well, it's not like it would be my first time," Nadine reminded him. "At this point, I could probably give you a tour of our finer holding establishments."

Caleb was about to turn her down, saying that he would feel better about her staying in his penthouse, knowing that she was safe because Hogan was back and guarding her.

And he almost said it.

But he remembered what it was like, feeling antsy and restless, knocking around four walls and desperately trying to find busywork to occupy his mind, even though it seemed like that had been eons ago now.

His eyes swept over Nadine and he realized that she was already dressed to go out, so he couldn't use that as an excuse to turn her down. He couldn't say that he didn't have time to wait for her to get ready because she already *was* ready.

Who knew? Maybe she would pick up on something that might elude him?

He decided that it wouldn't hurt anything to take her with him.

"Okay," he told her.

"Okay?" she repeated almost numbly, afraid to let herself believe that she had won him over so easily.

There had to be a catch, some condition she had to meet before he actually agreed that she could come along with him.

She waited for the hammer to drop. But all Caleb said was, "Okay, you can come with me to prison. Just let me make a couple of calls to get us around some of the procedures you usually need to go through."

"You make it sound so romantic. You really know how to treat a woman," Nadine told him, trying her best not to laugh.

He was really out of practice in that department, Caleb thought. He couldn't even remember the last time he had taken a woman out when it wasn't directly related to a case he was working.

"You're always free to stay here," he reminded her.

Afraid she had insulted him, she was quick to retrace her steps.

"No thank you, I'm coming with you." And then

she looked at him curiously, asking, "Do you have to set a separate alarm for your sense of humor in the morning? What time does it normally get up?" she wanted to know.

"At the same time I do, wise guy."

"I'll take your word for it," Nadine responded. An afterthought hit her. "I'm going to leave the dishes in the sink for now. That way I won't hold you up. I'll just wash them when we get back," Nadine promised.

"You really don't have to," he reminded her, picking up his briefcase and making his way to the hall closet. "I've still got that dishwasher."

"Well, I wouldn't want to 'hurt' its feelings," she told him, her eyes sparkling. "I'll look into using the dishwasher once we come back again."

Caleb went to make his call. Fifteen minutes later, he was back. "All set," he announced. Glancing at the sink, he saw that it was empty. She didn't waste any time, he thought.

Opening the closet, he took out his overcoat and put it on. The news had promised that today was going to be exceptionally cold and he had found that the weather bureau was rarely wrong when they gleefully predicted frigid conditions.

Leaving the coat unbuttoned, Caleb looked at her. She was still dressed in a tailored suit. "You're going to want to wear something over that," he suggested. "Like a winter coat."

Nadine glanced up the stairs. "It's in the closet in the room you told me to use."

At least she had thought to pack it. "So? Is there any reason why you don't go upstairs and get it?"

Nadine hesitated. There was a reason, all right, but she was afraid if she said it out loud, she would be insulting him. Of course, if she didn't say it out loud, she could very well be left behind.

"Actually, yes," she finally admitted.

"I'm listening," Caleb told her.

Bracing herself, she said, "I'm afraid that if I dash upstairs to get my overcoat, you'll use that as an excuse to leave me behind and go."

He looked at her in surprise. "You actually think I'd do that?" he questioned. What kind of vibrations was he giving off? Caleb wondered.

"Well, you indicated that you would rather that I remained here, busying myself with making jewelry," she reminded him.

"I didn't quite put it that way. And I didn't mean to make it sound as if I didn't want you coming with me. I just didn't think that you would particularly want to come to prison with me."

"I find the nature of your work exciting," she said honestly. "And prison visits are just part of it."

Caleb looked at her thoughtfully. She was one unusual woman, he couldn't help thinking.

"Go get your winter coat," he told her, adding, "You've got five minutes."

Nadine was already racing up the stairs before the last words were out of his mouth.

Chapter Sixteen

Caleb pulled his car into a space within the parking lot that was in front of the private prison where Ronald Spence was currently serving out his several life sentences.

Turning off the ignition, Caleb looked at Nadine. "Last chance to change your mind and wait in the car while I talk to Spence," he offered.

Nadine had been keenly aware of her surroundings for the last five minutes, taking absolutely everything in.

"Right now, I think I'd be safer with you than staying in the car," she told him honestly.

"There are security guards around," Caleb pointed out, thinking that might make her feel more at ease and tip the scales in favor of remaining inside.

"I know," she answered. "But I'd still feel safer with you." She had caught a glimpse of one of the guards as they drove through the gate surrounding the prison. The grim-looking man did *not* look all that happy to be here.

"Okay, then stay close," Caleb said to her.

Nadine's mouth curved. "You don't have to tell me that twice," she responded.

As she continued to take in the atmosphere, Nadine found herself thinking that the facility left a lot to be desired.

Oh, it appeared to be clean enough, she judged, but there was something about the very air around it that left a rather less-than-savory impression of the place.

Walking through the prison's entrance to the desk, Caleb held up his identification for the main guard's benefit. Nadine quickly produced her own ID—her driver's license—and followed Caleb's example.

"We're here to see Ronald Spence," Caleb told the guard whose badge identified him as one D. Adams. "I called ahead to make the arrangements," he added.

The man looked over both of the IDs, lingering over Nadine's before finally nodding his head.

"Visitors have to register in the inmate visitation system prior to having an appointment with the inmate," Adams told them.

When they completed the process and crossed the floor, he waved them over toward a row of haphazardly arranged chairs.

"Wait there," Adams ordered, then disappeared behind another door. Caleb could only presume that the head guard was going to bring back the prisoner.

"What a cheerful place," Nadine couldn't help commenting.

"Compared to some of the other places I've been to, this is positively paradise."

A few minutes went by before the head guard returned. Standing just beyond the doorway's threshold, Adams waved for them to come in. When they did, he ran a search wand over them, looking for any hidden weapons. Satisfied that they were clean, the man ordered, "Come this way." He was looking at Caleb as he said it.

Caleb complied, pausing to glance over his shoulder to make sure that Nadine was following behind him. She was, so he continued walking behind the guard.

They went down a long, winding narrow hallway with several gates, which eventually opened up to what appeared to be a communal visiting area for inmates and their families.

Looking at it, Nadine felt a chill working its way up and down her spine.

"Take a seat," Adams told them gruffly, gesturing toward what appeared to be an abundance of empty tables. There were obviously not too many visitors here today. "I'll bring the prisoner out."

Due to the number of times she had been arrested herself during protest demonstrations that had gotten out of hand, Nadine was used to the way that prisoners and potential inmates were impersonalized by the guards. But she still found it rather disconcerting to hear.

Adams returned quicker this time, bringing with him a man who appeared to be rather unaffected by the living conditions around him.

Ronald Spence looked to be about of average height and medium build. Once he came closer, Nadine realized that he looked like a man who was struggling to hang on to the last vestiges of hope.

"You've got ten minutes," Adams told Caleb before he withdrew to the far end of the large room. Nadine noticed that the dour-faced guard took a post by the door, facing them and watching every move that Caleb, the prisoner and she made.

Even from across the room, Nadine couldn't help thinking Adams gave the impression of a man who didn't trust anyone.

Meanwhile, Spence was busy sizing up the man who had finally come to see him. "You're Ben Colton's son." It wasn't a question; it was a conclusion.

Caleb put his hand out toward the prisoner. "I am."

Spence nodded, more to himself than to Caleb. "You look like him," he said. Belatedly, Spence held out his hand toward Caleb's and shook it. And then his attention turned toward the only unidentified person at the table. He nodded toward Nadine. "Your assistant?" he asked Caleb.

Nadine spoke up before Caleb could answer. "Yes, I am," she said to the man they had come to see, thinking it was a lot simpler that way than telling Spence that Caleb had brought her along to keep her from going stir-crazy, which was what it actually boiled down to.

Spence's attention had already shifted back to Caleb. "I can't believe that you're finally here," the man said, looking at Caleb in disbelief. "I've called your office so many times, I was starting to think that I'd never get anyone to listen to me."

"Well, I'm here now and I'm listening," Caleb told him. "Why don't you tell me what happened in your own words?"

"It's really simple. I know you probably think I sound like every other prisoner who has ever been convicted and incarcerated, but I am innocent," Spence stressed with passion before getting down to the heart of the matter. "I just recently found out that the evidence that would have cleared me of the charges that were leveled against me was deliberately hidden by Judge Colton."

Spence couldn't keep the anger and sense of betrayal out of his voice.

Caught up in the drama, Nadine spoke up.

"Where is this evidence?" she wanted to know, then flashed Caleb an apologetic look for speaking out of turn.

"I don't know where it is," Spence complained, visibly frustrated. "If I knew where, I would have found a way to get my hands on it." He looked at Caleb, remaining, Caleb noted, as calm as he could under the circumstances. "Will you do it? Will you take on my case? The word is that you and your sister are trying to do right by all those people your father unjustly sent away so he could line his pockets and live the high life." Spence looked at Caleb as if his last shred of barely contained hope was seeping from his very being.

"My firm's working several other cases at the moment. But give me all the information you can, including letters in your possession that I might be able to use in your case, and I'll see what I can do."

Spence nodded, then said to the son of the man who had sent him into this prison, "Don't just 'see,'" he told Caleb. *"Do,"* he all but pleaded.

The last man that Ben Colton had sent away to prison went on to tell his visitors where they could find the papers that could at least point them in the right direction. He had placed the documents in a safety-deposit box that was in his ex-wife's name.

Taking all the information down, Caleb promised to do what he could for Spence. This was the last person his father had put away. Despite currently having several other cases to work on, this was a point of honor for Caleb. Maybe even an obsession, he allowed, but he felt he owed it to Spence.

They left the prison shortly after that. Despite the initial restriction that Adams had issued, their visiting time had been mysteriously stretched by an extra five minutes on top of the initial ten.

Adams said nothing when he saw them, he merely pointed toward the exit, indicating that they should leave. Caleb and Nadine gladly complied.

"So, what do you think?" Caleb asked as they made their way back out to the prison's exit.

"You're asking my opinion?" Nadine had to admit that she was surprised by that.

"That's why I decided to bring you," Caleb answered.

She still didn't quite get it. "Why? Because of my numerous arrests?" She couldn't think of any other explanation.

Caleb frowned slightly. "Because of your gut instincts, dealing with people on the other side of the arresting officer, as an activist," he told her.

"All right," Nadine said, accepting his explanation. Taking a deep breath, she added, "My first guess is that Spence is telling the truth—either that," she amended, "or the man's an expert liar."

Caleb laughed as he shook his head. "You're waffling."

Yes, she was, Nadine thought. But then, he had

asked her opinion, and besides, that didn't necessarily mean that he was going to take it once she gave it. One way or the other, Caleb was going to make up his own mind. She sensed that much about him.

"I really think," she told Caleb, "given your father's track record, Spence is being honest."

Caleb nodded. "Well, we're in agreement about that. Let's see if getting our hands on Spence's private papers is as easy as the man seemed to think."

Saying that, Caleb drove to the address that Spence had given him in order to pay a visit to the former Mrs. Spence.

HOLLY SPENCE APPEARED to know that they were coming and was prepared for them. Caleb could only assume that Spence had gotten in contact with her the same way he had initially managed to keep calling his office.

"If you don't mind my asking," Nadine said once they were escorted into the woman's modest apartment. "Since you seem as if you still really care about your ex-husband, why did you divorce him?"

Nadine avoided looking at Caleb, thinking she had probably overstepped her bounds. But when she did finally look his way, he nodded his approval. Hard as it was to believe, he thought, he and Nadine seemed to be on the same wavelength.

And he found that undeniably attractive, no matter how much he tried to keep her at an emotional distance.

Holly brought them into the small living room. She sat down on the lone chair facing her floral sofa.

"That was Ronald's idea," she told Nadine. "When it looked as if he was going to be sent to prison, he didn't want to 'drag me down' with him, as he put it. I didn't want a divorce, but I didn't fight with him about it since he was already dealing with so much. That's why I reluctantly agreed."

Her brown eyes swept from one visitor to the other as passion swelled in her voice. "But I know in my heart that he's innocent," Holly insisted. She rose back to her feet, asking, "Can I get you some coffee?"

It was obviously a foregone conclusion to her that they were going to say yes, so the woman withdrew into her kitchen to get them both some coffee.

And something else.

The brief visit continued over some barely decent coffee and some rather surprisingly bitter chocolate chip cookies. After they had managed to partake of both, Holly Spence then awarded Caleb temporary possession of her safety-deposit-box key.

Caleb knew that wasn't enough. "You're either

going to have to accompany us to your bank, or I'm going to need a copy of your identification as well as a letter written by you allowing me access to the box," Caleb informed the woman.

Holly hesitated, regarding him skeptically. "Are you sure about that?"

"I'm afraid that I'm very sure," Caleb told the woman.

Holly blew out a rather loud breath. "Well, all right. I can't come with you," she said, offering no further explanation. "But I can certainly give you that letter and a picture of my license." Saying that, she switched gears and asked, "How long before you can get Ronald free?"

It was hard to speculate if any of this would even work, and he didn't want to string the woman along, but he needed to tell her something positive. He could see that she desperately needed it.

"The sooner I can get the contents of the safety-deposit box, the sooner I can get to work on investigating his claims," Caleb told her.

That seemed to be enough to satisfy Spence's former spouse. Nodding her head, she quickly went to comply with Caleb's requests.

ARMED WITH THE name and address of Holly Spence's bank, Caleb's next stop was to go there.

Less than ten minutes later, Caleb was parking his vehicle directly in front of the bank's entrance.

Nadine smiled as she got out of Caleb's car. "Your job is certainly more involved than I ever thought," she commented.

Caleb laughed under his breath as he opened the door for her. "You don't know the half of it," he said to Nadine.

As she moved by him, he caught a whiff of her perfume, something light, but at the same time arousing. For a moment, thoughts popped up in his head that had nothing to do with why they were here. He caught himself really wishing that this was a different time and place.

The next moment, he forced himself to focus on their tasks.

Once inside, Caleb approached the first unoccupied teller he saw.

"I need to get into safety-deposit box 3206," he told the young woman. "Do I see you about that?"

The woman offered him a spasmodic smile. "Of course, sir, but I will need to see some identification from you, plus since I'm assuming that your name isn't on the account, I will need to see a letter from the present owner of safety-deposit box number 3206."

Caleb handed the woman a photo of Holly's license, plus Holly's letter stating that she allowed him access to the box.

Another ten minutes went by before Caleb found himself in a tiny space, sequestered with the safety-deposit box as well as with Nadine. The space was so small, there was barely enough room for them to simultaneously take a deep breath. He fought the deep desire to pull her close to him, to protect her and to kiss her more intensely than he'd ever kissed anyone before… Her passion and drive for justice matched his own, he'd found; that was something he'd never expected to discover in a woman. But he had to resist…

Later, he promised himself.

"I'm glad you thought of bringing that letter from Mrs. Spence," Nadine told him. Otherwise, they would have no choice but to go back to Holly and have her write one."

Caleb smiled. "This isn't my first rodeo."

Nadine looked about the tiny, enclosed space. "Good thing because I don't think a rodeo would fit in here."

They barely fit there, she thought. Nadine couldn't help wondering if the room was built with smaller people in mind. It was either that, or it was actually made for only one occupant, she decided. And there was enough room to press herself up against Caleb and do more than just open up that safety-deposit box… They could finally give the sparks that had been flying between them since they first met some oxygen and let them burst into flame.

Caleb opened the elongated safety-deposit box.

He found several folders inside. Not wanting to miss anything and definitely not wanting to remain in the claustrophobic space for the length of time a proper examination took—even if it meant brushing up against Nadine's curves again and again—Caleb opted to bring the entire contents of the box back with him.

Shifting cautiously in the small enclosure, Caleb struggled to put all four folders into his briefcase.

After closing the safety-deposit-box lid, he took it as well as his briefcase with him as he tried to make his way out of the tiny space. Shifting in it caused him to bump against Nadine not once, but twice.

Each contact generated a sharp sliver of electricity that insisted on traveling through his body.

As well as hers, he thought, if that startled look on Nadine's face was any sort of indication that she had felt something.

Caleb debated between apologizing for the accidental contact or just pretending that the whole thing hadn't happened and that he hadn't noticed anything.

He decided to go with the former.

"Sorry," he murmured.

"Me, too," Nadine quickly responded, for once not looking into his eyes.

Caleb was tempted to ask her exactly what *she*

was sorry about but decided that it was more prudent to let the matter go.

At least for now. Until he could get a handle on whatever it was between them, he had to keep his focus on the cases he was handling: Al Sutherland and Ronald Spence. No more, no less.

Chapter Seventeen

Nadine was desperate to move on from the awkwardness that had been created between them. An awkwardness generated within the tiny cubicle at the bank when they brushed up against one another. Or had that been a genuine electricity flaring between them? An electricity like she had never experienced before but desperately wanted to give in to.

She searched for something—anything—noncommittal to say once they finally got back into Caleb's vehicle.

She buckled up. "I can help, you know," she told Caleb as he turned his key in the ignition.

"Help?" he questioned, pulling out of the parking space and onto the main road. "Help with what?"

"With whatever you're looking for in those papers you found at the bank. At the very least, I can sort through them and give you a summary of what each folder contains. That way," Nadine continued, "you're freed up to turn your attention toward something else." *To me, maybe. Or* us, she thought silently.

Rather than jump at the chance, the way she had expected him to, Caleb shook his head. "You don't have to do that."

Nadine had no intentions of being that easily dismissed. Shifting in her seat, she looked at him. "Think of it as my way of paying you back for what you're doing for me." Then, in case he was unclear about what she was referring to, she clarified what she was saying. "Helping me find a way to get the family plot back from Rutledge Oil— not to mention keeping me safe from said oil company," Nadine stressed. And then she got to the heart of the matter. "I'm sure I wouldn't be able to afford you under normal circumstances, but I am *not* a charity case, either." She refused to let him see her as someone to be pitied; she wanted him to see her for the equal that she was.

"I never said you were," he pointed out. Seeing that accepting help without some sort of return on her part didn't sit well with Nadine, he told her, "We'll work something out."

By then, he was pulling into his underground parking space.

"Yes, we will," she agreed very firmly. "You'll take me up on my offer."

This was becoming very familiar to him. "This is another one of those losing arguments I'm having with you, isn't it?" Caleb asked.

For once, he had to admit that he wasn't really that upset about the situation. Right now, he felt he could certainly use some help sorting through things. *Like how I really feel about this woman who barged into my life and has turned it upside down*, he mused silently.

"Depends on how long you're going to continue going around and around about my offer to help you, but yes," she freely admitted, "it is."

"We'll talk later," he promised her. "First, though, I'm going to order some takeout for us." Unbuckling his seat belt, he got out of his vehicle, then waited for her to follow suit. When she did, he locked his car, then asked, "What are you in the mood for?"

"Answers," Nadine told him without a moment's hesitation, then smiled as she added, "and pizza."

"Any particular kind? Pizza, not answers," Caleb clarified, walking toward the underground elevator that would lead them to the penthouse door.

Nadine shrugged. "Anything you like," she responded. "Again, I'm referring to the pizza, not to the answers."

Opening the door to his penthouse, Caleb

walked in and placed a call to his favorite Italian establishment.

No sooner had he ended the call than there was someone at his door, ringing the bell.

Nadine caught his arm as Caleb started for the door. When he looked at her quizzically, she explained her hesitancy.

"I've heard of fast delivery, but that's really going over and above the call of duty," Nadine said. She knew she was being overly suspicious, but she just couldn't help it. "Maybe someone was just waiting for us to get back to the penthouse."

Caleb found her worrying to be rather sweet. "Don't worry. Hogan spelled Jacobson and is back watching the place," he reminded her.

"Are you sure?" Nadine asked, still holding on to his sleeve. He could feel the heat of her through his shirt fabric but did his best to block the sensation. "I didn't see him."

"That's the whole point," Caleb told her. "Hogan knows how to be invisible."

Striding toward the door, he glanced at the monitor on the wall and opened the door. He was pleased to find his sister Aubrey standing right in his doorway.

Two inches taller than Nadine, the curvy thirty-year-old blonde gave her oldest brother an annoyed look through her thick lenses as she strode into the foyer.

"About time you came back. I stopped by earlier, but that somber, dark shadow you have lurking around told me you weren't in." She put her hands on her hips. "Does that man ever smile?" Aubrey asked.

Shutting the door behind his sister, Caleb secured the lock.

"Not to my knowledge," he said glibly, turning back around. And then he paused to make the necessary introductions. "Aubrey, this is Nadine Sutherland. Nadine, this rather outspoken young woman is my sister Aubrey."

"Sutherland," Aubrey repeated, turning the name over in her head. "Is she any relation to your ex-wife?" she asked Caleb.

It was Nadine who answered her. "Annie Sutherland is my cousin. Your brother is helping me with a legal matter," she explained, then to make sure that Caleb's younger sister had all the information, Nadine went on to tell her, "My father is Al Sutherland. He's a rancher."

By now, Aubrey had taken a seat on the sofa in the living room. Her expression grew rather pensive at the revelation Nadine had just made. She looked intrigued.

Trying not to jump to any conclusions, Caleb's sister asked, "Is that the land that's adjacent to the Gemini Ranch?"

Caleb nodded. "It is." The next moment, he

turned toward Nadine, answering her question before she even began to form it.

"Aubrey and her twin, Jasper, are the owners of the Gemini Ranch. We occasionally went trail riding, all of us, in that area when we were kids.

"Needless to say, those were much happier times," he said sadly. "Aubrey and Jasper pooled their money, bought the land and turned it into what quickly became a very successful, all-year-round dude ranch. They've got cattle drives in the summer and horses and cattle grazing there," he told Nadine. Then he added with great pride, "Aubrey and Jasper are doing very well with the ranch."

Aubrey waved her hand dismissively at Caleb's words. At the moment, she was focused on just one thing.

"Do you think that your dad would be willing to lease his land to us so that we could graze our cattle there?" Aubrey was doing her best to keep the mounting excitement out of her voice.

Nadine's mind was going a mile a minute. The very idea of putting her father's property to work this way would solve so many problems for him, she couldn't help thinking. Heaven knew that it would generate an income that he could definitely use. More than that, it would put an end to the idea of his having to do fracking on the land.

There was only one obstacle.

"What you're suggesting would be a godsend," Nadine told Caleb's sister honestly. "There's only one problem getting in the way right now."

Aubrey looked from her oldest brother to Annie's cousin.

"What is it?" she wanted to know, keeping her eye on the prize. "Is there anything I can do to help move things along?"

Caleb shook his head. "I'm afraid not. It seems that Sutherland's strip of land is extremely popular. Rutledge Oil got their hands on the fracking rights in a less-than-scrupulous way."

It was obvious that she wasn't following her brother. "What do you mean?" Aubrey asked.

"Right now, it looks like they tricked Nadine's father into giving up his claim to those rights for next to nothing. But we haven't accepted defeat yet," he was quick to tell his sister. "If we manage to turn this around, I'm confident that you and Jasper can come to terms with Nadine and her father."

He glanced toward Nadine to see if she had any objections to the solution he had just proposed.

Instead of raising objections, Nadine immediately voiced her support. "Oh, absolutely," she assured Caleb's sister. What was it about this Colton family? They all had such kind and earnest attitudes and seemed uncommonly generous with their time—and eager to help her, too. Nadine felt her heart soften a bit at the prospect of her dad working with Caleb's sister; maybe they could see each other, even, after all this was over?

Aubrey rose from the sofa. "Well, you've certainly given me hope. If anyone can get your father's land back," she told Nadine, "it's my big brother. He might speak softly, but trust me, he definitely knows where the jugular vein is located."

"You can put the shovel down now, Aubrey," Caleb said to his sister. "There really is no need to bury her in snow. She has already decided to turn to me for help in the matter."

"But I'm not trying to snow her," Aubrey protested. "If anything, I'm understating the matter." She looked at Nadine. "When my father, to put it politely, was 'removed' from the bench, the scandal that followed was utterly devastating. A lesser man than Caleb would have packed up and moved away, but Caleb dug in and diligently started working on repairing the family's reputation, even though he and Morgan were just teens, going through college and then law school. He and Morgan focused on making it up to all the people—and the families of those people—that our father had wronged in his last ten years as a judge.

"Now, thanks to Caleb and Morgan, the family reputation has been slowly but surely restored. Partially anyway. And some of the people whose lives were irreparably damaged by our father are getting the justice he denied them all those years ago."

"Okay," Caleb announced, getting to his feet, "enough is enough, Aubrey. Off you go. I—we," he amended, glancing toward Nadine, "have work to get to." He felt his face heat despite himself as he contemplated what else he and Nadine could do when they were alone again…

As he said that, the doorbell rang. He took a guess as to who was on the other side of the door. "And that would be our dinner," he told his sister. "I'll call you once we make some headway in getting Mr. Sutherland's rights back," he promised.

Nadine had accompanied the departing woman to the front door as well. "It was really nice meeting you, Aubrey."

"Oh, same here," Nadine responded with enthusiasm.

Aubrey looked at both of them. "Good luck!"

Opening the door, she all but bumped into the delivery boy, a fresh-faced teenager who was still trying to coax a reasonable display of facial hair to grow on his pale complexion. So far, he had just managed to raise a little sparse fuzz.

Startled to see three people on the other side of the door, he needlessly announced in a high voice, "Pizza."

"Just in time," Caleb said, taking out his wallet. He gave the delivery boy the price of the pizza plus an extra ten on top of that. As an afterthought, as the delivery boy was retreating, Caleb looked toward Aubrey. "You're welcome to stay and have some with us," he told her, adding, "I ordered an extra-large pizza with three kinds of cheeses and three kinds of meat toppings."

Once the lid was raised, the scent from the pizza began to fill the air.

Aubrey looked longingly into the pizza box. "You know you're twisting my arm, don't you?"

Caleb grinned at her, bringing the box in. "I figured as much."

Aubrey looked toward Nadine. "I'll stay for a couple of slices," she said, qualifying her choice by adding, "if it's all right with you."

"I don't have any say in this," Nadine pointed out to Caleb's sister. "But sure, stay. Eat your fill," she added.

Aubrey laughed dryly. "That is physically impossible," she confessed. "I never reach that 'full' stage. We'll keep it at a couple of slices."

Moving around the kitchen as if she had been doing it for a long time rather than just for a couple of days, Nadine quickly took three plates from the cupboard and three glasses as well. She took out three cans of soda from the refrigerator, placed them beside the glasses and plates.

"Dinner is served," she announced cheerfully, waiting until Aubrey took a seat before she followed suit. Caleb sat down between them. As much as he wanted to be alone with Nadine, he simultaneously dreaded having to resist the attraction that had arisen between them. So he welcomed Aubrey's presence at their friendly dinner, observing silently how well Nadine connected with his little sister. *Almost as if she was meant to—* He cut off the thought and returned to his meal.

It DIDN'T TAKE long before the extra-large pizza disappeared completely.

"Maybe I should have ordered two," Caleb speculated out loud, looking at the empty box.

Nadine stared at him in disbelief. "Oh, please," she cried, shaking her head. "I can barely move as it is."

Pausing at the door, Aubrey turned toward Nadine and told her in all seriousness, "Remember, my offer still stands. The minute you figure out this situation for your father, I will pay you top dollar for the grazing rights."

Nadine remembered that Aubrey wasn't the sole owner of the dude ranch, though. "Don't you have to ask your partner first?" she asked.

"I was born five minutes before he was," she informed Nadine. "Jasper won't argue," she added confidently. "Besides, he wants to be able to have our cattle graze there as well."

Putting her hand on the doorknob, Aubrey

pushed the door open. "Good luck again," she said, repeating the words she had uttered before they had invited her to stay for dinner. Flashing a smile that instantly warmed up the room, Aubrey added, "And I hope to see you soon," just before she left the penthouse.

Chapter Eighteen

Nadine was eager to keep her promise to Caleb. Early the next morning, she began to slowly and carefully comb through the stack of papers that he had taken out of the former Mrs. Spence's safety-deposit box and brought home. She dove into the task wholeheartedly, realizing as she did so that she was attempting to focus solely on work and not on the way her body and Caleb's had brushed up against one another yesterday...

Initially, Caleb had to admit that he did feel a little guilty about placing this burden on Nadine's shoulders. But right now, he was spread even thinner than normal workwise, and he was well aware that there was no way he could juggle everything that had come under the heading of being "his" responsibility. It was just physically impossible.

So, when Nadine had stepped up and volunteered to go through the files, he gladly took her up on it. She was the perfect partner, he mused. No way would he say that aloud to her—or even so he could hear it.

"HAVE I TOLD you how much I appreciate you doing this?" Caleb asked four days later. He'd just come home for the day—early for a change—and found that Nadine was still working on the papers. She'd been enjoying going through Spence's files and had even asked to take on more work. She was sitting more or less exactly where he had left her early that morning.

Nadine looked up and cocked her head, as if she was thinking his question over, then with a smile creeping over her lips, she shook her head, her dark hair flying about her cheeks.

"No, not today," she answered. "Go ahead, tell me," she coaxed. "I'm listening."

"I have to admit that I had my doubts when I took you on after you volunteered," Caleb confessed. "But happily, I was wrong. I've seen your summary notes," he explained when she raised a quizzical eyebrow. "You really turned out to be an asset." *An irresistible one*, he thought to himself, his hands itching to stroke the brown locks framing her face.

He really didn't need to praise her, Nadine thought. "All I want to do is find something we can use against that awful oil company to knock the pins right out from under them," she told him honestly.

Caleb sat down on the edge of the chair, looking at the way that the papers were spread out. "You've been at this nonstop, haven't you?" he questioned. Most people would have wrapped up by now. But not Nadine. Yet another reason he was beginning to rely on her more than he should.

"I take bathroom breaks," Nadine answered cheerfully.

He glossed over her response. "What about those earrings you were working on when I brought you out here?" he questioned.

"Well, turns out that the woman who commissioned them is currently away on a vacation, so it looks like I have a few weeks to spare before I need to finish them," she told him. "And right now," she said, looking at the papers that were spread out on the table, "this is a lot more important."

Her comment made him smile warmly. "You know, I just realized that you can be just as obsessive about something as I am." *Maybe we'd be a good team in more ways than one*, he couldn't help but think.

Nadine inclined her head as she looked up at Caleb. "I'll take that as a compliment." she said to him.

"Considering the way my single-mindedness has affected my life over the years, I'm not entirely sure that it *can* be taken as a compliment," Caleb admitted. "But the one thing I am definitely sure of is that you need to leave yourself some time to eat."

"Pizza?" Nadine asked, thinking that was where he was going with this.

But Caleb shook his head, vetoing the suggestion.

"No, I think that going to a restaurant would be more in order in this case." He rose to his feet and crossed over to where the coats were hung up. "Get your coat," he told her, leaving no room for an argument. "My guess is that you've been at this all day, and you need to get some fresh air."

Nadine looked down at the pages on the table. Part of her hated leaving the papers like this. In her gut, she felt as if she was getting very close to something.

But Caleb was right, she thought. Besides, the man had more experience than she did in extensive legal matters like this. She felt that she needed to back away for a little while. Doing that would undoubtedly give her the fresh perspective that she needed right now.

"Yes, sir," Nadine responded, giving Caleb a "smart" salute as she got to her feet.

A little more than an hour and a half later, pleasantly full and in a renewed, positive frame of mind, Caleb and Nadine were on their way back from the homey restaurant where they had gone for an early dinner.

"You were right," Nadine said as she looked in Caleb's direction.

"I usually am," he responded glibly. "About anything in particular this time?" Caleb asked good-naturedly.

"About taking a break and eating out," she answered. "I needed that," Nadine admitted. "I feel great." She waited for him to respond. When he didn't, she asked, turning toward him, "What, no comment?"

It was at that point that she picked up on the tension that was suddenly riding in the vehicle with them.

Caleb was not easily spooked.

Instinctively, Nadine looked over her shoulder and then up into the rearview mirror.

She almost missed it.

And then she made out the shape of a silver sedan driving behind them. It looked vaguely familiar.

She had to be wrong, she thought nervously.

"What's up?" she asked. Nadine could feel herself bracing for his response even as the words emerged from her mouth.

He was not about to play games. He wanted her to be prepared. "I think we're being followed," he told her, looking in his rearview mirror again.

Was it his imagination, or was that car speeding up? He pushed down on the gas pedal. "That silver sedan has been shadowing us ever since we left the restaurant."

"It's not a coincidence?" Even as Nadine asked the question, she knew what his answer was going to be.

"I don't think so. That's the same one that was following you when I decided to have you stay at my penthouse," he informed her, turning sharply. "I'm going to try to lose him."

She could feel the breath backing up in her lungs and her fingertips growing icy. Nadine refrained from saying anything. She didn't want to distract Caleb if she could help it.

Caleb picked up speed, trying to outrace the car that was following them, but the latter turned out to have a more powerful engine. Not only did it stay abreast of the vehicle that Caleb was driving, it was also steadily increasing velocity.

Any minute, it would be going neck and neck with him.

"Hang on," Caleb ordered, then employed every evasive maneuver that the former secret service agent had taught him.

It wasn't enough. No matter how fast he drove, the car that was following them drove faster. It looked like he just couldn't lose the other vehicle, which swerved close and almost hit them. Nadine swallowed a scream, digging her fingernails into the armrests.

And then, just like that, it abruptly took off as the sound of an approaching police siren suddenly pierced the air.

The siren grew louder and louder.

Caleb released the breath he realized he had suddenly sucked in. The relief he felt was completely overwhelming.

"Looks like the cavalry's here," he told her. Looking in her direction, Caleb was startled. Although his car had come to an abrupt stop he hadn't been counting on, he hadn't realized that Nadine had been hurt until he saw the gash on her forehead.

She was bleeding from what looked to be a four-inch cut. He realized that she had to have hit her head against the dashboard when the car swerved and he came to an abrupt stop.

So much for thinking he could protect her, Caleb angrily upbraided himself. He shifted toward her as the siren grew louder.

"Nadine," he cried. "You're hurt."

She tried to wave off his concern, moving her hand weakly. "I'm okay," she said to him. Her words didn't exactly carry much conviction.

"No, you are not okay," he insisted. He took his handkerchief out, wiping away the blood that was just above her eye, concern welling up inside him. He tamped it down so Nadine wouldn't panic. "See?" he asked, holding up the handkerchief for her to look at.

Nadine shrugged. "I bleed easily," she said dismissively.

He was still worried, though he admired her tough demeanor despite himself. "How many fingers am I holding up?" he wanted to know, raising his right hand up in front of her. He curled his thumb in front of his fingers.

"All of them," she answered, annoyed. At that moment, a police vehicle with dancing lights pulled up beside Caleb's car.

The gray-haired chief of police stepped out. Theodore Lawson was a tall, well-built man who looked younger than the eighty-one years that was written on his driver's license. He also acted younger. But at the moment, when he recognized both the car and who was driving it, the chief looked close to his age. He also appeared gravely concerned.

Looking into Caleb's car, Lawson motioned for him to lower his window. When Caleb did, the chief immediately asked, "Are you two all right?"

"We're fine," Nadine answered a little too quickly and emphatically. From the way her voice sounded, the chief thought she really seemed to be in pain.

A very skeptical look passed over the chief's

face. "That gash on your forehead says otherwise," he told her. His eyes shifted toward Caleb. "But you're all right?" he asked as he looked Isa's eldest son over.

"I am," Caleb asserted. "But Nadine needs to be taken to the hospital to be checked out."

Nadine frowned at him. "No, I don't," she insisted. "I just need a Band-Aid."

"No," the chief of police contradicted, "you need to go to the hospital to get yourself looked at." And then he looked at Caleb. "You both do. Your mother would never forgive me if anything wound up happening to you as a result of this." As far as Lawson was concerned, that was the end of the argument. "You know who nearly ran you off the road?" he said as he looked from Caleb to the woman whom Caleb had referred to as Nadine.

"I have my suspicions," Caleb said to the chief. "But if you're asking me if I have a name for the individual, I don't."

Lawson nodded. "I'll take down anything you can tell me. And, if I were you, I'd invest in a dashboard camera," he told Caleb. "Hopefully, this is the end of it, but just in case it isn't, and there's a 'next time,' it wouldn't hurt to have one of those cameras recording whatever might happen."

Caleb nodded, thinking that was a good idea. "I'll definitely look into getting one."

The chief nodded. "Wait here. I'm going to radio for an ambulance."

"An ambulance?" Nadine echoed, dismayed. She looked at Caleb. "Can't we just drive there in your car?"

About to place the call, Lawson looked at Isa's oldest son. "Does she argue about everything?" he asked Caleb.

Caleb nodded. "Everything," he replied.

Lawson patted the younger man on his shoulder. "You have my sympathies, my boy," he told Caleb.

The chief added to Caleb, "I'm going to have to tell your mother about this."

Caleb frowned at that. "Is that really necessary? I don't remember hearing that was part of police protocol now," he said.

"No, it's not," Lawson admitted. The breeze had picked up and was ruffling his gray hair, causing it to annoyingly fall into his green eyes. He raked his fingers through it, attempting to push it back into place. "It's part of my attempting to maintain a cordial relationship with your mother," Lawson admitted.

Caleb looked intrigued. "I thought you two had gone past 'cordial' a long time ago," he told the chief.

Lawson laughed under his breath. "We haven't. Not for lack of my trying," he admitted. "Your mother seems to be under the impression that anything beyond a polite exchange of words on her part would be construed as being unfaithful to your father's memory."

It was obvious that the situation did not sit well with the never-married police chief. But Caleb knew Lawson had long been enamored with Isa and felt she was worth waiting for, no matter how long it took for her to come around.

Caleb shook his head. He was well aware of the way his mother felt about his late father. "She really is something else, isn't she?"

"Your mother is a lady," Lawson insisted. The chief evidently felt called upon to come to Isa's defense.

Caleb nodded. There was no disputing that, he thought. "My mother's lucky to have you."

The chief laughed again. "You might try to convince her of that."

Just then, the ambulance the chief had called for arrived. Nadine looked longingly at Caleb's vehicle. Despite the fact that it had been almost run off the road, it really didn't appear the worse for wear to her. She appreciated his concern—more than she really wanted to admit—but surely a small cut on the head wasn't worth all this fuss?

She was also worried about the vehicle being left behind. "What if that animal who followed us comes back and tries to do something to your car?" she asked. "Like maybe rigging it to blow up?"

Caleb looked at her in surprise. He had to admit that hadn't occurred to him. "You're just full of warm thoughts, aren't you?"

"It can happen," Nadine insisted. She wouldn't put anything past the driver she assumed was the oil company's henchman.

"I'll have one of my men drive it over to the hospital for you, so when you're ready to leave, you can," Lawson said, doing his best to reassure Nadine. "And," he continued, "until you are, I'll have the deputy stay with the car and keep an eye on it. Can't have you and one of Blue Larkspur's foremost attorneys meet with an accident as you're driving to his home," he said to Nadine. He smiled as his eyes met hers. "Feel better?" he asked.

"I will once you find whoever did this," Nadine told the chief in no uncertain terms.

"I'm working on it," Lawson promised.

He sounded so serious, Nadine was almost tempted to believe the man. But at bottom, she was a realist and knew that she and Caleb were not his exclusive concern. Crime wasn't exactly rampaging through the town, but the chief surely had more than enough to keep him busy.

The EMTs tried their best to get Nadine to agree to lie down on the gurney—but to no avail.

"I'll sit up, if you don't mind," she informed the attendants firmly. Then, to convince the two men, she said, "If I lie down, my head will start spinning."

"How do you know?" Caleb challenged. "You haven't tried to lie down yet."

Nadine looked directly at Caleb, annoyed that he had raised the point.

"I just know," she said to him.

Caleb heard Lawson chuckle to himself. When he looked back at the chief, Lawson said, "I thought you were kidding before, but she really does argue about everything, doesn't she?"

"That's not something that I would kid about," he informed the police chief seriously. And then Caleb turned his attention toward the attendant who had climbed into the back to stay with Nadine. "I'm going to get in back with her," Caleb told the EMT, "if that's all right with you."

The attendant, whose identification tag proclaimed his name to be Matt, gestured into the ambulance. "Be my guest," he told Caleb.

Still very concerned about Nadine's condition, Caleb climbed into the vehicle and sat down beside her, taking her hand in his.

She didn't pull it away.

Both gestures spoke volumes.

Chapter Nineteen

When Nadine finally walked into the penthouse just ahead of Caleb, she was more than a little relieved.

"I think I've had more tests done tonight than I've had done before in my whole life," she told Caleb.

She and Caleb had just spent the last three hours in the emergency room. She sincerely doubted that there was a part of her that hadn't been poked or prodded or thoroughly checked out from head to foot.

Happy to be in familiar surroundings, Nadine turned around to look at Caleb.

"Why the long face?" she asked. "There was no sign of a concussion, no evidence of internal bleeding or any sort of damage of any kind. Nothing," she declared. "Aside from that ugly cut on my forehead, the doctors couldn't find anything to even be concerned about. And heaven knows that they certainly did try," she stressed. "So I'll ask you again—" Nadine pinned him with a look "—why the long face?"

Caleb thought of just brushing her question off, telling her she was just imagining things, but he decided not to. The time for hiding his feelings was over, now that they'd had a near-death experience and he could have lost her before he'd ever really had her in his life.

"Because all I could think of," Caleb admitted solemnly, attempting to suppress all sorts of thoughts that insisted on crowding in his brain, "is what *could* have happened." When she still looked at him curiously, he stressed, "You could have been killed."

"But I wasn't," Nadine pointed out as she took a seat on the sofa. Even though she wouldn't admit it to him, her legs did feel a little wobbly.

"But you *could* have been," Caleb repeated, doing his best to try to keep his feelings from registering on his face. He took a seat on the sofa beside her.

She looked at him, completely taken aback by what he had just said and by the way that thought made him look so concerned, despite his efforts to the contrary. His brow was furrowed.

"You're really serious, aren't you?" Nadine asked.

Of course he was serious, Caleb thought. To his

way of thinking, he had just found her. He wasn't ready to lose her yet.

Perhaps not ever.

Those words were drumming through his brain in what amounted to a staccato beat, but he still refused to allow them to emerge from his lips.

Experience had taught him not to put himself out there like that.

Nadine drew closer to him. She found herself in the very odd position of trying to comfort Caleb, despite the fact that she had been the one who had received the worst of it. After all, she had been the one who had gotten banged around in the car accident.

Still, her heart went out to him in ways that she knew it shouldn't.

"I'm okay, Caleb," she assured him in a quiet, soothing voice.

When he continued to look distressed, Nadine brushed her lips against his cheek.

And then something clicked.

How that casual contact wound up turning into a full-fledged kiss soon after, she really wasn't able to say. Maybe Caleb had turned his head at the wrong moment—or perhaps the right moment— but Nadine didn't know. What Nadine *did* know for certain was that it happened.

And when it did, happiness leaped up inside

her. Nadine suddenly felt as if there was an entire one-hundred-piece orchestra playing within her.

Moreover, the attraction toward Caleb that she'd kept telling herself she wasn't feeling succeeded in making a liar out of her. Just like that, it suddenly seized possession of her entire being.

Before she knew it, Nadine was leaning into him, turning a simple kiss into something a great deal more as she wrapped her arms around Caleb's neck.

The moment that their lips met, all the restraints Caleb had been trying to convince himself were in place completely evaporated, disappearing like mist into the hot air.

There were no more restraints; there was only desire, desire bursting out and completely covering all of him.

Caleb shifted even closer to Nadine on the sofa, pulling her onto his lap as he continued kissing her over and over.

Each passionate touch only grew in its intensity, feeding the hunger within him rather than managing to satisfy it.

Caleb hardly recognized himself. He did know that he hadn't felt like this in years—perhaps not ever, he amended as he attempted to reevaluate what was happening to him.

The thought made him draw back and look at

Nadine. They had both just gone through a near-death experience.

Maybe he was going too fast, Caleb warned himself. He didn't want his own reaction and the anxiety that had been generated by it to overwhelm her.

With effort, he told Nadine, "If you want me to stop, I will."

She realized that she had felt an attraction sizzling between them almost from the very beginning. Nadine had tried her best to deny it by putting up roadblocks. But she now recognized those self-imposed impediments for what they were: just excuses to keep herself from falling for the handsome attorney wholeheartedly.

But the moment he had kissed her with such feeling, the excuses she was attempting to sell herself completely fell apart, disintegrating like a papier-mâché wall being hit by a hammer. She had nothing to hide behind, nothing to use as a shield except the words he had just uttered.

But she couldn't seek refuge there, either, because they weren't true.

"No," she answered in a sincere whisper. "I don't want you to stop."

It was as if some sort of signal had just gone off. He was no longer the man he had just been, but the man he was on his way to becoming.

A man who was more than eager to make love with her.

Nadine could feel her heart slamming hard against her chest as Caleb embraced her over and over again. Although his very being felt possessed by an eagerness that made him want to divest her of all her clothing in one swift motion, Caleb forced himself to go slowly for two reasons. He didn't want to frighten her, and he wanted to savor every moment.

A more leisurely pace would heighten that delicious sensation.

As he slowly drew her clothing, piece by piece, away from her body, Caleb kissed every new, uncovered area. His overwhelming excitement kept increasing with each passing moment.

Unable to remain a passive recipient any longer, Nadine began to eagerly pull at his clothing, unbuttoning, unzipping and drawing each piece off him. She felt desire and anticipation growing. She was impatient to feel his skin against her own, impatient to experience that heightened sensation as she stripped Caleb's surprisingly sculpted frame bare.

Nadine spread her hands along his body, absorbing the arousing sensation that very act created within her.

And then they found themselves both nude in each other's arms, awaiting the ultimate excitement that waited for them at the end of the road.

Yet they both still wanted the wondrous journey to continue at least a little while longer.

Caleb gently pushed her back onto the sofa, then proceeded to weave a web of warm, openmouthed kisses all along her body. And little by little, he went farther and farther down that same body, causing electricity to shoot all through her.

Nadine thought she knew was what coming, but when it finally did, she discovered that she didn't.

She could barely contain herself.

The explosions that seized her body and shot through it only managed to grow in magnitude and intensity.

Nadine bit her lower lip to keep from crying out. Having Hogan or one of Caleb's other investigators come breaking in to save them from what they could only imagine was some sort of impending danger would be a terrible way to bring this delicious episode to an end.

So she struggled to remain silent. Breathing hard, Nadine bucked and moved, absorbing every wonderful nuance that was being created within her, while still needing more.

Finally exhausted, she fell back on the sofa, trying to pull herself together.

Caleb was just about to bring the dance they were doing to its logical conclusion when she surprised him and suddenly, with renewed energy, reversed their positions.

She managed to flip him over and then straddled him, pinning him down in a sexy, dominant stance.

"What are you up to?" Caleb asked, both amusement and arousal highlighting his face.

"Shh," was all Nadine said.

Her eyes on his, she ran her hand along the most intimate parts of his body, glorying in the look that came over his face as she slowly worked the magic on him that he had so recently performed on her. She deftly used her fingers, and when she had managed to sufficiently prime him, she resorted to using her tongue.

The moan that Caleb emitted told her that she had gone about the task correctly.

He seized Nadine by her shoulders, drawing her to him. With a swift movement, he reversed their positions a second time. And then, his mouth pressed to hers, Caleb slowly entered her, sealing their union.

With slow, deliberate and methodical thrusts, he began to move. With each movement, the intensity of what was happening between them increased until they found themselves racing to that incredible pinnacle at the top of the summit that was waiting for them.

Hearts pounding when they finally reached it, they then plummeted over the edge, savoring the intense sensation seizing them both.

They found themselves wrapped in a wondrous euphoria that took them prisoner, holding them in its grip for what felt like an eternity. But eventually, they found themselves reluctantly slipping back to earth.

Very slowly, Nadine opened her eyes, then turned her head to look at the man who'd slid down to lie beside her. She found that the room was now darker than the inside of midnight. That was when she realized that they had forgotten to turn on the light when they had walked in. Their attention had been so focused on one another that they hadn't even noticed.

As she went to sit up, Nadine felt Caleb's hand on her shoulder, holding her in place.

"Where are you going?" he asked her softly.

"I was just going to turn on the light," Nadine explained.

"Leave it off," he told her. "Just for a moment longer."

Nadine could feel the corner of her eyes crinkle as she smiled. "I take it you're not afraid of the dark?" she teased.

"Some of the nicest things can happen in the dark," Caleb said. And then he turned into her, their nude bodies pressed against one another again. "Would you like to go upstairs?" he asked her.

"Why, Mr. Colton." She was close enough to

Caleb for him to see her batting her eyelashes at him. "Are you trying to lure me into your bed?" she asked, a coquettish lilt to her voice.

Caleb laughed as he pressed a kiss above her cheek. "I might be." And then, in all seriousness, he felt he had to admit this, "You really gave me a hell of a scare today."

"Why?" she asked him innocently. "Was I too rough making love with you?" She was doing her best to sound serious.

To him, though, this was nothing to joke about. "You know what I mean."

"Yes, I know what you mean," she answered seriously. "And the accident wasn't my fault. If you really want to get technical, you were the one who was driving. Very skillfully, I might point out," she said. "Because if you hadn't been, we might have wound up a lot worse off than we did."

Amused, Caleb shook his head. "I'll say one thing about you. You certainly keep me up on my toes."

Her eyebrows drew together as she pretended to study him. "Is that the best thing you can say about me?" she wanted to know.

"Honestly?" he asked. "I'm better when it comes to showing what I mean than talking about it."

"That's a pretty overwhelming admission coming from a lawyer," she informed him, pretending to be surprised.

"Hush," Caleb told her.

Taking her hand, he rose to his feet and drew her up with him.

"Are we going somewhere?" she questioned.

A little moonlight had spread its fingers through the room, enabling Caleb to see the innocent expression on her face.

"Yes," he answered, saying, "I'm taking you upstairs."

"Oh? And what are you planning to do once we get up there?" Nadine asked.

"Well," he continued playfully, "if you haven't guessed, I'm planning on having my way with you again."

Her eyes sparkled. "Okay. As long as I know," she said.

Caleb approached the winding staircase, pausing at the bottom. "Any objections?" he wanted to know.

"Can't think of a single one—as long as you're not too tired," she qualified, laughing.

"I'm not too tired," he said to her, then, a smile still playing on his lips, promised, "I'll let you know when I am."

Opening the door to his room, Caleb surprised her by scooping her up in his arms and then carrying her inside. Once in the room, he gently laid Nadine on the bed.

Doubling back for a moment, Caleb switched on the overhead lamp.

"Now you want the light on?" Nadine asked, pretending to be surprised.

"Yes. I don't want to miss a second of this," he told Nadine as he lay down on the bed beside her.

They proceeded to make love with each other as if this was their first time.

Caleb felt as if he couldn't get enough of her.

All he could think of was that, miraculously, he had been given a second chance to enjoy being with her. For a moment back there, when they had almost been run off the road, he had thought that was the end of it.

But it hadn't been.

He was not about to take that for granted.

Caleb made love with her like a man who had just been reborn.

And when they were finally done, breathing heavily in each other's arms, Caleb gave himself a few minutes—and then repeated the seduction a third time but at a far slower pace.

Like the previous two times, he allowed himself to savor every moment of the experience.

The refrain that kept reminding Caleb that he had almost lost her continued to beat through his head until he reached the point that he was far too exhausted to think of anything at all, even that.

Putting his arms around Nadine, Caleb continued to hold her close to him until they both finally fell asleep that way.

Chapter Twenty

Caleb woke up to find himself alone in his bed.

Not knowing what to think—had he ultimately been too aggressive and driven Nadine away when she'd had a chance to rethink what had happened in the light of day?—Caleb quickly grabbed a pair of pants and pulled them on. Barefoot and holding a shirt in his hands, he was just about to go looking for her when Nadine walked into his bedroom.

She was carrying a tray with breakfast and a cup of coffee on it.

"Good morning, sleepyhead," she said, greeting Caleb with a huge smile that made his stomach do flips. "I thought you might like to have some coffee, toast and scrambled eggs before we get started."

Sitting back down on the bed, Caleb made room for the tray that Nadine set down.

"'Get started'?" he echoed, curious. He noticed that, unlike him, Nadine was fully dressed. And, unless he missed his guess, he could detect the scent of shampoo in her hair. Had she already gotten on with her day because she regretted getting involved with him?

She nodded, sitting on the edge of his bed. "With the investigation," she told him. "I would bet *anything* that the guy who tried to run us off the road last night was someone working for the oil company. That can only mean one thing. That I've—that *we've*—become a thorn in Rutledge Oil's side, trying to get them to admit that they stole my father's land.

"We need to find out what they're trying to hide," she concluded, her voice gaining in volume and momentum. He admired her passion.

"By the way, when I was sifting through the papers that I am going to be reviewing today, I noticed that you're also working on a case that's attempting to free a woman who was wrongfully convicted and imprisoned." Admiration shone in Nadine's eyes as she looked at him. "You really are a crusader, aren't you?"

Caleb shrugged off the compliment although his heart warmed at hearing her speak those words. It wasn't his way to bask in things like that. Praise had never been his end goal. Success was.

"I do my part," he replied modestly.

"Oh, you do more than that," Nadine said. "You put yourself out there when there's no real promise of any sort of actual monetary reward," she stressed. "I happen to think that's extremely noble of you." She grinned at him, hoping her admiration for him genuinely shone through.

About to brush off the compliment that Caleb sensed was coming, he abruptly stopped as her words sank in. "Just how much did you read?" he wanted to know.

"Enough," was all that Nadine said. She looked down at the plate on his tray. "Finish eating," she coaxed as she got off the bed. "I'll be downstairs, working."

Caleb watched her leave, feeling slightly bowled over. Nadine had just let him know that she found the work he did not just interesting, but actually, to use her word, *noble*. None of the women he had interacted with in his life had *ever* said anything that even came close to expressing such an emotion.

For that matter, none of the women outside his family he interacted with personally had ever even expressed an interest in these cases.

Yet Nadine just had.

Who would have ever thought? Caleb found himself musing. But he could have imagined it. Both he and Nadine were big on helping underdogs and getting justice for themselves and others. *Almost like we're the perfect fit...* He shut down that idea before it could even finish developing.

Finished eating, Caleb quickly put on the shirt

he had grabbed earlier, then slipped on a pair of socks and shoes. He hurried down the stairs carrying the tray that Nadine had prepared for him.

He found her working in his office.

Somehow, Caleb thought as he put aside the tray he had just brought down, she looked right at home sitting there, going through the pertinent files. As if she belonged...

Nadine barely glanced up as Caleb took a seat on the other side of his desk. Instead, she slid over a stack of papers and placed them in front of him.

"Take a look at these," she suggested. "I think that some of those pages might help provide the evidence you're looking for."

THEY HAD BEEN working in his office for a while now—Nadine had honestly lost track of time— when the doorbell suddenly rang, shattering the silence. Nadine's attention was instantly focused on whoever must be standing there, waiting for them both.

It occurred to Caleb that she looked not unlike a deer caught in the headlights of an oncoming vehicle. The color had drained from her face.

Why?

"Relax," he said to Nadine warmly. "If that was anyone to worry about, the men working for me would have stopped whoever had driven up to the penthouse and held that person until I had a chance to identify him or her."

Getting up, he crossed the floor and made his way to the front door.

Looking up at the monitor that was mounted on the wall beside, he laughed when he saw who was outside.

"No need to worry," he told Nadine. "It's just Morgan."

The next moment, he was opening the door before Nadine could even respond to what he had just said.

Morgan burst in, her attention entirely riveted on her twin brother. Six inches shorter than Caleb, she still looked formidable as she grabbed both his arms.

"I just heard about what happened," she cried, her blue eyes traveling all over him, visually reassuring herself even as she asked, "Are you all right?"

"I'm fine, Morgan," he assured his sister. "Come on in," Caleb said, although the invitation was really after the fact.

Morgan didn't seem convinced. Nadine admired her obvious concern for her brother; she loved the Colton clan's closeness. "Are you *sure* that you're all right? Why didn't you call me?" she demanded angrily. "I had to find out about the accident from the police chief," his twin complained. "Do you have any idea how that feels?"

"I'm sorry," he apologized. "I didn't call you because it was late and I didn't want you to worry. Nadine received the worst of it," Caleb told her, directing her attention to the other person in the room.

"Nadine?" Morgan questioned. Then, looking farther into the room, she realized who her brother was talking about. "Oh, Nadine. Sorry," she apologized. Her voice was polite but definitely rigid. "I didn't see you."

Her sharp eyes swept over the other woman, taking in every nuance. It was obvious that she had concluded that Nadine didn't look any the worse for wear. And then Morgan noticed the cut on the other woman's forehead.

It looked pretty fresh.

"Is that from…?" Morgan's voice trailed off as she indicated Nadine's forehead.

"Yes," Nadine answered self-consciously. "But it's no big deal."

Morgan slanted a glance toward her brother. "Well, it certainly sounds as if Caleb seems to think it's a big deal," the woman observed.

To Nadine, the other woman's tone sounded rather dismissive. She could tell that Morgan was being protective of her brother and she could also tell that the other woman didn't exactly view her in the most positive light. Nadine felt her stomach flutter; she hadn't realized until now how much the approval of Caleb's family might mean to her.

Morgan turned her attention back to her brother. "Maybe you should just take a vacation, back away from everything for a while," she suggested.

What his sister was saying generated an incredulous response from Caleb. "When have you *ever* known me to back away from anything?" he queried. Especially now that he and Nadine...

"Maybe it's time you thought about doing it," Morgan suggested. She glanced at her watch. "I've got to get back to the office," she told him. "I just wanted to check that you were all right." She paused, looking her brother over from head to foot one final time. "You *are* all right, right?"

"Yes, Morgan," he answered patiently, "I am all right. And so is Nadine," Caleb deliberately added.

"Nadine. Right," Morgan said, nodding her head as her eyes darted over toward the woman she felt had gotten her brother involved in all this to begin with. "I'm glad you're all right," she said to Nadine stiffly.

At the door, she placed her hand on her twin's forearm, securing his attention. "Call me if you need anything," she instructed. Then, as an afterthought, she turned toward Nadine and said, "You, too, Nadine."

Feeling really uncomfortable, Nadine forced herself to smile at Caleb's twin. "Thank you," she said, then added after a beat, just as the woman left, "I'll do my best not to bother you, Ms. Colton."

After he closed the door behind his departing twin, Caleb walked back into the office where he and Nadine had been working.

"Morgan worries too much," he commented.

Nadine was tempted to say something about getting frostbite from the exchange she had just had with his twin, but with effort, she kept her reaction to herself.

She felt that Caleb was probably oblivious to any negative vibes that his twin had given off. Which was why Nadine was taken completely by surprise when, out of the blue, Caleb suddenly said to her, "She can be a bit overprotective of anyone who gets close to her siblings."

Raising her eyes to his, Nadine said, "Excuse me?"

"Morgan," he said, nodding toward the door his twin had gone through when she left. "I know there are times that she can come across as being rather cold, but she doesn't mean anything by it," he assured Nadine. "Give her a little time," he urged.

Nadine shrugged, as if what had happened

hadn't really hurt her feelings and made her defensive. She shouldn't really care what Morgan, a virtual stranger, thought, but she actually did.

"I can give her all the time in the world," she said.

He picked up on Nadine's tone. "She offended you, didn't she?" he asked.

Nadine fell back on a typical explanation, one she would have used to convince herself was the reason for the other woman's cold behavior—if she didn't believe otherwise. "Morgan was just being protective of you," she told Caleb.

"That's right," he agreed. "She was. But once she realizes that you're not a threat or trying to use me for your own 'nefarious' purposes," he added with a grin, "Morgan'll come around. I guarantee it."

Nadine looked at him. Was Caleb just talking hypothetically, or was he thinking of some long-range plan regarding their relationship? She didn't want to get too hopeful—she had been disappointed by men she'd dated in the past. And, quite honestly, it still wasn't clear to her if Morgan did or didn't view her as some sort of an invading threat.

Besides, compared to Caleb's sophisticated twin sister, she felt as if she was the embodiment of a country bumpkin.

"Nadine?" Caleb prodded when she didn't make any response to what he had just said.

Snapping out of the haze that the thoughts that were swirling through her head had created, Nadine nodded.

"Right. I'm sure Morgan will come around once she decides to approve of me."

How had Nadine come to that harsh conclusion, Caleb couldn't help wondering. "That's not what I said," he pointed out. "I meant when she gets to know you," he told her with a grin.

Lowering his eyes, Caleb got back to reviewing the paperwork that was still spread out in front of him.

Nadine pretended to do the same, but her mind was not on reading, or even on finding evidence against the oil company. Right now, what she was dealing with was all far more personal.

Last night had been truly magical, but who was she kidding, Nadine silently demanded. She was never going to blend in or be accepted by his family as anything more than just a friend.

Complicating everything was the fact that Caleb had once been married to her own relative. Annie being Annie, her cousin had always managed to have everyone react positively to her. That meant that his family had to have liked her. Which in turn meant that if she came on the scene in any capacity that remotely resembled being Caleb's girlfriend, she would probably be viewed as an interloper, even though Caleb's marriage to Annie had long been over. Even Isa Colton would probably disapprove of them, she imagined.

Nadine felt herself growing depressed.

She was just asking for trouble, she thought, thinking she had a prayer of her relationship with Caleb ever taking off, or even of getting serious. He was unlike the type of guy she usually fell for—he was made for forever, not a fling, and what they had could never reach that stage.

If she had a brain in her head, Nadine told herself, she would back away before her heart was in danger of being completely trampled on.

Nadine was gun-shy. That sort of thing had happened to her far too many times.

She had a terrible tendency to fall for men who were all wrong for her. Men who, when all the chips were down, simply were not able to commit.

Nadine pressed her lips together, suppressing a sigh.

Eventually, she needed to act like an adult, Nadine knew, not like some lovesick child.

The only thing that was important here, she reminded herself, was finding a way to reclaim what rightfully belonged to her father. Not to fall in love with a man who would likely never feel the same about her.

"Nadine, is everything all right?" Caleb asked,

thinking that perhaps his sister's sudden, unexpected visit had managed to completely throw her off her game.

Nadine took a deep breath, centering herself before she nodded in the affirmative.

"Yes," she answered him, doing her best to cover up her preoccupation, "I was just thinking about how much I'm going to enjoy making the oil company eat crow."

"Did you find anything?" he asked, thinking that perhaps she had, given her optimism.

"No," Nadine answered. "But I will. I feel it in my bones."

He smiled. That sort of positive attitude would help them keep on going until they finally did find something, he thought. He admired her so much—her persistence, her optimism...

Caleb leaned over in his seat to brush a kiss on her lips. He was more than slightly surprised when she pulled back.

"No distractions," she told Caleb. "Not until one of us finds something."

Distractions.

He knew this refrain. It was code for his getting too caught up in his work again. He might as well face it. He was never going to change. It had cost him most of his adult relationships, and he was still at it. There was no reason for him to believe

that he could change just because he was now on
the edge of developing something with Nadine.

If he cared about her at all, Caleb admitted to
himself, he would just back off and spare her the
heartache that was looming over her just down the
line. For both of them.

Chapter Twenty-One

Caleb glanced at Nadine, who was sitting across from him at the kitchen table. Her head was down and she was working.

Damn it, he thought, all he wanted to do was to take her into his arms and make passionate love with her.

Slowly.

What he really needed, Caleb decided, was to get away. To create some space between himself and Nadine so that he could clear his head. Right now, the desire for her he was experiencing was seriously clouding everything up, getting in the way of his thought process.

He couldn't work like this.

"I'm going to go to the office for a while," Caleb told her, getting up from the table.

"All right," Nadine responded. She was afraid to look at him, afraid he would see the desire she felt in her gaze and think of her as some sort of a lovesick puppy. And she did have to admit it to herself—she was falling in love with this man.

"I'm not sure how long I'm going to be," he went on to tell her.

She nodded, forcing herself to continue leafing through the file she had opened in order to avoid meeting his eyes.

It was happening already, she couldn't help thinking. Caleb was putting distance between them. Nadine could feel her heart twisting within her chest.

"I understand," she answered stoically, still not looking up.

"If you need anything, Hogan's here. You just need to buzz him," Caleb informed her. He knew he was lingering; still, he couldn't help himself.

Nadine nodded, but she went on to tell him, "I won't need anything."

"Well, in case you do, he's here," Caleb repeated. Placing a few things he needed into his briefcase, he headed for the door. "I'll see you later."

Nadine nodded, unseeingly shuffling papers just to have something to do with her hands. "Later," she echoed.

She didn't look up until she heard Caleb close the door behind him.

How could everything have just collapsed on itself like this so quickly, she couldn't help wondering. Reliving the last eighteen hours in her head, Nadine couldn't find any actual cause for the sudden change. Everything had been absolutely wonderful—and then it wasn't.

Maybe she had been expecting too much, Nadine told herself. After all, Caleb had all but run out of here. Maybe it had taken his twin coming on the scene to make him realize what a mistake he was making, allowing himself to make love with her. Or maybe—

Just then, her cell phone began to pulsate, intruding into her thoughts. Pulling the phone out of her back pocket, Nadine glanced at the screen. She could feel her disappointment all but consume her. She had really hoped that it was Caleb, calling her under some pretext, maybe even apologizing for having beat such a hasty retreat out of the penthouse.

But the number wasn't Caleb's.

It belonged to her father. He was calling her from his house. Not knowing just what to expect—would he even be lucid? Or would he be that vague human being who was making more and more appearances these days when she talked to him? She didn't know. She did know she had to answer the call.

"Hello?" she said a bit more loudly into the phone than she normally would so that he could hear her.

"Nadine?"

Her father sounded almost fearful as he said her name. At least he knew he was calling her, she thought. That was something.

"Yes, Dad," she answered patiently, "it's me."

"Help me."

Nadine instantly stiffened. There were all sorts of reasons why he had just said what he had. He could be asking her to help him with something as simple as making a meal.

Maybe he was—

Her mind instantly went to a dark place.

Trying not to sound panicky—instinctively feeling that would only make matters worse—she asked her father as cheerfully as she could, "Why do you need help, Dad?"

"There's someone in my house." His voice was barely above a whisper. "What do I do, Nadine? Tell me what to do."

He sounded like a helpless child, she thought, her heart almost breaking. In a very firm voice, she told him, "I want you to call the police, Dad. I'm on my way."

She heard a dial tone in her ear and could only hope her father was doing what she had instructed him to do.

Nadine grabbed her purse, taking out her car keys as she rushed out of the penthouse. She was glad that Caleb had had her car brought over and parked in his underground garage. She had an unnerving feeling that right now, every second counted.

Nadine sprinted to her car, sweaty hands pressing the fob. Pulling the driver's-side door open, she quickly got in.

The moment Nadine was behind the wheel and pulling out of the garage, she placed a call to Caleb.

Her impatience grew as every unanswered ring fed into the next one.

About to give up, Nadine became alert when she heard the phone finally being picked up on the fourth ring.

"Nadine?"

Caleb sounded almost uncertain, as if he couldn't really believe she was on the other end of the call he had just received.

Relief flooded through every part of her. Thank heavens she had managed to reach him.

"Caleb, my father just called. He said that there was someone in the house and he sounded really afraid," she blurted.

"Where are you?" Caleb wanted to know, and the way he asked her, it was obvious that he was worried about her. Her heart warmed despite the fear churning in her belly.

"Where do you *think* I am?" she responded. Not waiting for him to answer, she said, "I'm in the car, driving over to my father's house. I told him to call the police," she added before Caleb could start lecturing her.

"Good. Now I want you to turn around, go back to the penthouse and wait for me there," he instructed. "We'll go over to his place together. You know, he could just be imagining things," he said to her gently.

She knew that was a possibility, but her gut was telling her something else.

"But what if he's not?" she countered. "What if there really is someone in the house?" she challenged. "Caleb, if I turn around and go back to your house and something does happen to my father, I would never be able to forgive myself. *Never*," she emphasized.

"Nadine—" Caleb began, determined to make her listen to reason.

She knew Caleb was going to try to talk her out of this and she was *not* about to listen to him.

"No," Nadine answered in no uncertain terms. "I'm going," she told him just before she ended the call.

Nadine pushed down hard on the accelerator. She was traveling faster than the speed limit, but this was her father, and whatever it took to get to him in time, she felt that her breaking that law was justified. She would explain everything to the police if it wound up coming down to that.

Nadine's heart was all but firmly lodged in her

throat by the time she pulled up in front of her father's house.

Her car had barely come to a full stop when she leaped out of the vehicle. Running up to the front door, she swiftly unlocked it and dashed inside.

"Dad?" Nadine called, her head spinning as she looked from side to side. "Dad, I'm here. Where are you, Dad? Dad, are you here? It's me, Nadine," she called out urgently.

Where was he?

In response, she heard a muffled voice answering her. "I'm down here, Nadine. Down in the basement."

She released a huge sigh. At least he was all right.

"Come back up," she urged.

"No," her father cried defiantly. "I can't. It's not safe."

"Yes, it is," she told him. "Please, Dad. You can come out now. Really."

"No, I can't. Come on down here," her father said to her, then added, "I think I hurt my leg trying to get away."

She closed her eyes, trying to gather strength. That trite old saying was right. When it rained, it really did pour.

Nadine carefully made her way toward the steep stairs that led into the basement.

"I'm coming, Dad," she called to him, then warned, "Don't attempt to come up on your own."

That was all she would need, to have her father injure himself while he was trying to come back upstairs.

Nadine was seriously tempted to just run down the stairs in order to reach him faster, but she was determined not to take any unnecessary chances. So instead, Nadine had her hand hovering over the banister as she made her way down—just in case.

Seeing her, he immediately drew closer to the bottom of the stairs, as if a part of him felt she could protect him. His eyes were wide as he raised them to look overhead—like he could actually see through the ceiling.

"Did you see anybody?" he asked her breathlessly, still whispering. His eyes were darting back and forth across the ceiling.

"No, Dad, I didn't," Nadine told him patiently. She was ready to believe that her father, with his overactive imagination, had just created the whole scenario about a home invasion in his head. Taking his hand in hers, she quietly urged, "Come on, Dad, let's get out of here."

With that, she began to lead her father toward the bottom of the stairs. That was when she heard the basement door being slammed shut.

Startled, Nadine could feel the sound reverberating in her chest. She knew that sound. Someone had just locked them in.

"See?" he cried, vindicated. "I wasn't just imagining things! There *is* someone in the house!"

Her mind began racing. There definitely *was* someone in the house.

Nadine led her father back toward the side of the basement where he had been crouching. She was hoping to find a way out.

But there were no windows to break or crawl through. This area of the basement hadn't changed in years. There was no way to get out. The wall looked completely solid.

Her father looked at her, breathing louder and louder as his fear continued to mount. "We're trapped down here, aren't we?" he cried.

"No, we're not," Nadine insisted, doing her best to calm him, despite her own growing anxiety. "The police are on their way." When he just stared at her, she asked, "You did call them, didn't you?"

Sutherland looked at his daughter, wide-eyed and befuddled. "I don't know," he cried. "Maybe I did."

Just then Nadine heard an odd noise directly above them. The noise was followed by a crackling.

Within moments, the smell of smoke began to work its way through the cracks and openings in the basement, permeating the air.

The house was on fire.

DRIVING AS FAST as his car was capable of going, Caleb could make out the flames shooting up into the sky before he was able to even draw close to the Sutherland house.

His heart froze.

When he reached the home, he could see a ring of police cars and fire trucks surrounding the all-but-crumbled building that was being eaten up by flames.

Nadine was in there!

He just knew it!

As if to underscore his suspicions, Caleb saw Nadine's car parked just short of the ring of fire.

His heart plummeted down to the pit of his stomach.

Nadine *was* inside the burning house.

Why hadn't she listened to him? Why couldn't she have been reasonable and waited for him to get there?

The question echoed in his brain over and over again, taunting him. What was wrong with her anyway? his mind demanded. Did she think she was some sort of a superhero, able to do things mere mortals couldn't?

Damn it, why had he left her? He loved her!

Feeling physically sick, Caleb drove his car as close to the burning building as he could. Then, abandoning the vehicle, he wove his way toward what was left of the burning building, even as it was being totally consumed by the flames.

Damn it, he had finally found the woman he had been looking for all of his life, someone who felt as passionately about her work as he did, and he was about to lose her because all sorts of logical thoughts had gotten in his way, immobilizing him and making him behave like some sort of programmed robot. He should have gone after her, after someone who had made him happier in an incredibly short time than he could recall being in a very long, long time.

"Hey, you can't go in there!" a burly firefighter yelled out, grabbing Caleb firmly by the shoulders.

Caleb managed to shrug off the other man. "The hell I can't! The woman I love is in there. Don't you understand? I have to rescue her!" he shouted.

"That's our job, son, not yours," an older fire chief told him. "Why don't you just let us do our job? We don't want to have to rescue you, too."

Caleb managed to shrug that man off as well. Pulling away, he looked at the fire chief defiantly.

"You don't understand," he argued. "I have to go get her. I *have* to," Caleb insisted, ready to run into the burning inferno right now, no matter what.

"Caleb?"

He froze when he heard Nadine's voice calling out to him.

Chapter Twenty-Two

Turning toward the sound of the voice he could only pray that he had heard, Caleb couldn't believe his eyes. For a split second, he was convinced that he was actually hallucinating.

But then Nadine, tears shimmering in her eyes because of what had very nearly happened, threw herself into his arms, and Caleb knew that this was no hallucination. She was real.

Nadine was real. His feelings for her were real.

Holding her, Caleb ran his hands up and down her back, pressing her close to him as if that very act somehow reinforced her presence for him.

"I thought—I thought—" Unable to finish, he just held her, absorbing the feel of her and finding infinite comfort in the fact that she was alive. "I really thought that I had lost you," he finally managed to say. "How did you manage to get away?" Her escape from the burning building had been nothing short of a miracle to him.

Even from the corner of his eye, he could see that the entire house was a total loss. The very sound of the building collapsing into itself was still reverberating through the air.

"It was Dad," Nadine told him, a bit of wonder still evident in her voice. She looked back at the man who was even now being placed onto the gurney. "For some reason, he suddenly remembered that there was an old root cellar put in beneath the basement and that it led out a distance beyond the house."

Caleb became aware of the smell of smoke embedded in her hair, but he didn't care. He was just happy that she was alive and here. He held Nadine close to him, kissing her face and raining kisses on her hair.

Caleb felt simply overwhelmed that she was all right, and he was doing his best to deal with the very unnerving thought of what could have been if her father hadn't put in that root cellar or remembered its existence.

With one arm around Nadine's shoulder, Caleb guided her over to the ambulance. There was nothing but gratitude in his voice as he asked her father, "How are you doing, sir?"

From his head to his toes, Nadine's father looked as if he had gone one-on-one with a fire-breathing dragon and had somehow, just barely, managed to emerge the victor. His clothes were a sooty mess and they reeked of smoke, but the man was very much alive.

"I'll be a lot better once I get my hands on those guys from the freaking oil company who burned down my house," Al Sutherland proclaimed angrily. His usual vacant appearance was nowhere to be seen. He was utterly furious and indignant.

The EMT politely interrupted the two men. "We're going to have to take you to the hospital to be checked out, sir," the attendant told Sutherland.

Sutherland scowled. "I don't need no one fussing over me," he insisted, only to suddenly have a coughing fit. It was obvious that Nadine's father had managed to swallow more than his share of smoke as they made their way through the root cellar.

"You do need to get checked out, Dad," Nadine said. As he stopped coughing, she saw that her father was about to start arguing again, so she made the request personal, saying, "Do it for me." Her eyes met his. "I almost lost you today."

Al sighed rather dramatically, like a man who knew he didn't have a leg to stand on. "Okay, okay. For you. But you gotta come, too," he told his daughter.

"I'm all right, Dad," Nadine tried to assure her father. She had had her fill of hospitals after nearly being run off the road the other day. But this time, it was Caleb who spoke up.

"I think your father and I would feel a lot better if you went to the hospital, as well, and got checked out." He knew that he certainly would. "And, if you're okay," he went on, "they won't keep you."

She saw her going to the ER in a different light.

"I don't want to waste any more time," Nadine insisted. "We have to go after those people who set fire to the house before they do any more damage. They almost killed Dad and me. Who knows what they might wind up doing next time?" she cried. She was positive that the men who did this weren't going to accept that their targets were still alive and walking around.

"And we will, I promise," Caleb told her. "But right now, your dad needs to be checked out—and so do you."

She had already explained to him that she was all right. "But—" Nadine protested.

"You know I'm right," Caleb countered. "I'll follow the ambulance—I'll have one of my people come to take your car to the penthouse," he promised, then got back to the immediate subject. "Once the ER doctor gives you the high sign, we'll focus all our attention on making the oil company pay for what they did. Deal?" he asked.

Nadine sighed, knowing she had no choice. Especially if it meant getting her father to go to the hospital, since he wasn't too keen on it. And she knew Caleb was right, too—and his care warmed her heart.

"Deal," she murmured.

Turning, she climbed into the back of the ambulance, taking a seat next to her father's gurney.

Caleb closed and secured the doors behind her. Once again, he felt infinitely relieved that she had managed to escape injury and was alive.

THE ER PHYSICIAN on duty—R. Rosenthal, according to his name tag—checked Nadine out very carefully after she gave her insurance and personal information upon arrival. He told her in no uncertain terms how lucky she had been to survive the fire and then he let her know that she could go.

"Your Dad, though," Rosenthal told her, "needs to be kept under observation for the next twelve hours or so, but I'm optimistic about his prognosis. However, because of his age, we just want to be supercautious."

Nadine nodded, clearly relieved in both instances.

"That's wonderful," she said to the doctor. "Can I see my father? I'd like to say good-bye before I go. I don't want him to think that I'm abandoning him," she explained.

"He's asleep right now," the ER physician stated. "Besides the smoke inhalation, he was somewhat agitated, so we gave him a sedative because he did need to rest. Most likely, he'll probably be out until morning."

Nadine nodded. "All right. Then that's when I'll be back," she replied.

Waiting off to the side, Caleb was about to say something to Nadine about taking her home when he heard his cell phone ringing. Pulling it out, he automatically checked the screen to see who was calling.

"I've got to take this," he told Nadine, putting a little distance between himself and her as well as the ER physician.

Caleb answered his phone, instructing the person on the other end, "Talk to me."

Nadine watched as Caleb moved just out of range so she was unable to hear his end of the conversation. She had no absolutely idea why, but something made her realize that this call was not just important, but directly related to what had just happened to her father and the house he was no longer able to live in.

As far as that went, Nadine thought, her father could stay with her in the loft for now. She was prepared to take things one step at a time.

Nadine continued watching Caleb's back, trying to second-guess what was going on just by observing the tension in his back. She wasn't getting very far, despite her feelings for him.

Caleb ended the call and slipped the phone back

in his pocket as he walked back over to Nadine. Dr. Rosenthal had left, but Nadine's attention was entirely riveted on Caleb.

"Who was just on the phone?" she asked. She knew Caleb was an important man in the community, but even so, Nadine thought that getting late-evening phone calls had to mean something out of the ordinary was going on.

Caleb didn't give her a direct answer immediately. Instead, what he did tell her was, "You won't have to worry about Rutledge Oil anymore."

That immediately set off her radar. She was shocked.

"Why?" Nadine asked. "Did something happen to them?" She knew she shouldn't let herself get carried away like this, but she couldn't help it. Glee and confusion flowed through her in equal measure as she barely kept herself from hugging Caleb.

"Let's get you checked out of here first so we can talk about the call I just got without being interrupted," Caleb told her.

The look on his face promised her that this was all going to be well worth it, so she kept her questions and her curiosity under wraps as a nurse wheeled her out and Caleb walked beside her.

Because of the late hour, the process of checking out went quickly. There was no one else ahead of her.

Once they were in the parking lot, Nadine got

up and into Caleb's car. Settling in, she buckled up, turned toward Caleb and proceeded to repeat her initial question.

"Who was that calling you on your phone?"

He started up his car and pulled out of the near-empty parking lot. "That was one of my other investigators," he told her. "Brady O'Neill. O'Neill is a tech whiz," he added. "Once I realized that Rutledge's henchmen might not be content just trying to harass you, I instructed him to install a number of hidden monitors around your dad's place, like I have installed around the penthouse. Turns out that paid off," he informed her. He glanced at her face as he drove home, "We have our proof."

"Go on," she urged impatiently when Caleb paused for a moment to allow his words to sink in.

"It seems that these guys aren't overly bright. They were caught on camera setting fire to your father's house." He saw a whole collection of emotions and thoughts pass over her face. This was the mother lode, what they had been hoping to find, and he felt a warm sense of vindication for Nadine and Al. "I can only guess that they were doing it to put an end to the threat that your father—and you—posed by poking around into their dealings.

"Apparently, they were trying to eliminate you once and for all." The very idea of that had his complexion turning a very bright shade of red as his anger flared. "But now it looks like they're the ones who are going to be eliminated—once and for all."

Nadine immediately jumped to the only conclusion she could.

"Does this mean that Dad can get his rights back?" she wanted to know, hopefully crossing her fingers.

He had been dealing with human tragedies for close to two decades now. Caleb really enjoyed being the bearer of good news for a change—and he especially enjoyed delivering it to Nadine. "It does indeed."

Because they were stopped at a red light, Nadine took the opportunity to throw her arms around his neck and kiss him soundly. "It's finally over!"

"Yes, it is," he answered.

She hugged him even harder, then released him as the light turned green. "I don't know how to thank you."

Slanting a quick glance in her direction, he laughed. "Well, that was a good start," he told her.

She grinned up at him. "To be continued once we get to your penthouse," she promised. In response, she saw an unexpected sad look suddenly come over his face. "We don't have to continue once we get to your place," she admitted to him, having no idea how to read his expression. Even though she wanted nothing more than to admit to him how she felt and have him return those emotions...

"It's not that. I'd like nothing better than to continue this once we're behind closed doors, it's just that I want you to know how very sorry I am about you losing your family home." He knew seeing it burn down to the ground had to have been extremely painful for her. After all, this was the place where she had grown up.

"I'm sorry, too, but at least because of you, we'll be able to get those horrible guys who did this—and their boss," she stressed. "And then no one else opposing Rutledge Oil will *ever* have to go through this kind of awful pain again," she pointed out.

Leave it to Nadine to see things in the best possible light, Caleb thought. She didn't belabor what she had gone through; she just saw the good that came out of the whole thing. And that was the kind of person he knew he wanted to spend the rest of his life with. Hopefully, she felt the same way.

"What do you think about building something brand-new on that spot where your old house stood?" he asked her.

She thought for a moment. "I think that it's a wonderful idea," she told him honestly. "A house that's up-to-date and that my father won't look so lost in. He'll love it," she concluded.

Caleb drove his car into the underground garage. After parking it, he went around to the passenger side and, opening the door, he helped her out. *What a gentleman*, she mused.

"I'm fine," she informed him, not wanting any special treatment. She didn't know whether he wanted a future with her, so she refused to let him treat her like she wasn't an independent woman.

He brought his face down next to her ear. "Humor me. I almost lost you twice now," he reminded her. "Let me savor the fact that you're here."

Nadine laughed, her heart pounding. "Far be it from me not to allow you to savor," she teased. "But shouldn't we file a report with the chief and have him go after those two arsonists just to be on the safe side?" she asked.

He smiled at her. "Already done," he told her. "I instructed O'Neill to give the chief a copy of the video capturing those two would-be killers in the act. They are being picked up and arrested even as we speak," he said as he escorted her into his penthouse.

She looked at him in amazement. "No grass grows on you, does it?" she asked.

"Hasn't been known to yet," he answered Nadine, feeling his heart swell with affection.

Once they were inside the penthouse, Caleb locked the door behind him, then turned to take her into his arms.

"You have no idea how relieved I am to be able to do this, that you're really all right," he told her. "That you're alive," he added, working his way past the lump in his throat.

"And here I thought that maybe you were getting tired of me," she replied.

He looked at her and realized that she was serious. "Are you kidding?"

"No," Nadine answered honestly, "I'm not."

"Why would you ever think that?" he asked her, stunned.

"Well, after Morgan left, I felt you thought that maybe you had just gotten carried away last night and realized that you needed to rethink the situation. A situation that you actually regretted," she added.

"The only thing I *needed* to do," he emphasized, "was to rethink my priorities. I'll keep investigating Ronald Spence's claims that he was innocent tomorrow—I won't forget them, but you come first. That was when I realized that nothing is more important to me than you." He stopped himself before he wound up overwhelming her. "Don't worry, I'm not rushing you. We're going to take this one day at a time," he promised. "And then, who knows?" he said with a hopeful lilt in his voice, letting it trail off.

Her mouth curved. "Who knows?" Nadine echoed, confident now that she knew exactly what would follow. She knew they'd win over Morgan and the rest of the family, that they'd be able to smooth over any awkwardness that resulted from her being Annie's cousin. They were just that good together—and they both knew it.

"Tell you what," Caleb said after kissing Nadine long and hard, just as he'd been longing to since he had found her standing outside her destroyed childhood home. "Let's go upstairs so that we can continue this conversation in more comfortable surroundings."

"Let's." Nadine's eyes were shining as she agreed.

Standing on the step just above the one Caleb was currently on so that she was closer to his height, she placed her hands on his face, tilted it and brought her lips to his.

Eventually, they finally made it upstairs, where they continued their "discussion" at a far more gratifying pace—and whispers of "I love you" and plans for their future together permeated the bedroom.

* * * * *

COMING SOON!

We really hope you enjoyed reading this book.
If you're looking for more romance, be sure to
head to the shops when new books are
available on

Thursday 3rd February

To see which titles are coming soon, please visit
millsandboon.co.uk/nextmonth

MILLS & BOON

THE HEART OF ROMANCE

A ROMANCE FOR EVERY READER

MODERN

Prepare to be swept off your feet by sophisticated, sexy and seductive heroes, in some of the world's most glamourous and romantic locations, where power and passion collide.

HISTORICAL

Escape with historical heroes from time gone by. Whether your passion i for wicked Regency Rakes, muscled Vikings or rugged Highlanders, awa the romance of the past.

MEDICAL

Set your pulse racing with dedicated, delectable doctors in the high-pres sure world of medicine, where emotions run high and passion, comfort a love are the best medicine.

True Love

Celebrate true love with tender stories of heartfelt romance, from the rush of falling in love to the joy a new baby can bring, and a focus on th emotional heart of a relationship.

Desire

Indulge in secrets and scandal, intense drama and plenty of sizzling hot action with powerful and passionate heroes who have it all: wealth, statu good looks…everything but the right woman.

HEROES

Experience all the excitement of a gripping thriller, with an intense romance at its heart. Resourceful, true-to-life women and strong, fearless face danger and desire - a killer combination!

To see which titles are coming soon, please visit

millsandboon.co.uk/nextmonth

LET'S TALK

Romance

For exclusive extracts, competitions
and special offers, find us online:

- **f** facebook.com/millsandboon
- **🐦** @MillsandBoon
- **📷** @MillsandBoonUK

Get in touch on 01413 063232

For all the latest titles coming soon, visit
millsandboon.co.uk/nextmonth

might just be true love...

MILLS & BOON

Desire

Indulge in secrets and scandal, intense drama and plenty of sizzling hot action with powerful and passionate heroes who have it all: wealth, status, good looks…everything but the right woman.

Four Desire stories published every month, find them all at:

millsandboon.co.uk

MILLS & BOON
MEDICAL
Pulse-Racing Passion

Set your pulse racing with dedicated, delectable doctors in the high-pressure world of medicine, where emotions run high and passion, comfort and love are the best medicine.